The Red Scrolls
of Magic

ALSO BY CASSANDRA CLARE

THE MORTAL INSTRUMENTS
City of Bones
City of Ashes
City of Glass
City of Fallen Angels
City of Lost Souls
City of Heavenly Fire

THE INFERNAL DEVICES
Clockwork Angel
Clockwork Prince
Clockwork Princess

THE DARK ARTIFICES
Lady Midnight
Lord of Shadows
Queen of Air and Darkness

The Shadowhunter's Codex
With Joshua Lewis

The Bane Chronicles
With Sarah Rees Brennan and Maureen Johnson

Tales from the Shadowhunter Academy
With Sarah Rees Brennan, Maureen Johnson,
and Robin Wasserman

THE ELDEST CURSES ∗ BOOK ONE

The Red Scrolls of Magic

CASSANDRA CLARE
and WESLEY CHU

Margaret K. McElderry Books

NEW YORK LONDON TORONTO SYDNEY NEW DELHI

MARGARET K. McELDERRY BOOKS
An imprint of Simon & Schuster Children's Publishing Division
1230 Avenue of the Americas, New York, New York 10020
MARGARET K. McELDERRY BOOKS is a trademark of Simon & Schuster, Inc.
For information about special discounts for bulk purchases, please contact
Simon & Schuster Special Sales at 1-866-506-1949 or business@simonandschuster.com.
The Simon & Schuster Speakers Bureau can bring authors to your live event.
For more information or to book an event, contact the Simon & Schuster Speakers Bureau
at 1-866-248-3049 or visit our website at www.simonspeakers.com.
Interior design by Mike Rosamilia
Jacket design by Russell Gordon
The text for this book was set in ITC Galliard Std.
Manufactured in the United States of America
First Edition
2 4 6 8 10 9 7 5 3 1
Library of Congress Cataloging-in-Publication Data
Names: Clare, Cassandra, author. | Chu, Wesley, author.
Title: The red scrolls of magic / Cassandra Clare and Wesley Chu.
Description: First edition. | New York : Margaret K. McElderry Books, 2019. |
Series: The eldest curses ; book 1 | Summary: High Warlock Magnus Bane learns
that a demon-worshipping cult, the Crimson Hand, is wreaking havoc across Europe,
threatening more than just his romantic getaway with new boyfriend, Alec Lightwood.
Identifiers: LCCN 2018030577 (print) | LCCN 2018037578 (eBook) |
ISBN 9781481495080 (hardback) | ISBN 9781481495103 (eBook)
Subjects: | CYAC: Warlocks—Fiction. | Magic—Fiction. | Cults—Fiction. |
Demonology—Fiction. | Gays—Fiction. | Love—Fiction. | Europe—Fiction.
Classification: LCC PZ7.C5265 (eBook) | LCC PZ7.C5265 Red 2019 (print) |
DDC [Fic]—dc23
LC record available at https://lccn.loc.gov/2018030577

Because everyone deserves
a great love story
—C. C.

To love, the grandest adventure
—W. C.

To desire immortality is to desire the
eternal perpetuation of a great mistake.
—Arthur Schopenhauer

Now I see the mystery of your loneliness.
—William Shakespeare

PART I
City of Love

† † †

You can't escape the past in Paris.
—Allen Ginsberg

CHAPTER ONE

Collision in Paris

FROM THE OBSERVATION DECK OF THE EIFFEL TOWER, the city was spread at Magnus Bane and Alec Lightwood's feet like a gift. The stars twinkled as if they knew they had competition, the cobbled streets were narrow gold, and the Seine was a silver ribbon twined around a filigree box of bonbons. Paris, city of boulevards and bohemians, of lovers and the Louvre.

Paris had also been the setting for many of Magnus's most embarrassing mishaps and ill-conceived plots, and several romantic catastrophes, but the past did not matter now.

This time Magnus intended to get Paris right. In his four hundred years of wandering the world, he had learned that wherever you traveled, it was the company that mattered. He looked across the small table at Alec Lightwood, who was ignoring the glitter and glamour of Paris in order to write postcards to his family back home, and smiled.

Each time he finished a postcard, Alec wrote *Wish you were here* at the end. And each time, Magnus snatched the card and wrote, with a flourish, *Except not really.*

Alec's broad shoulders were hunched over their table as he wrote. Runes flowed along the muscled strength of his arms, one rune already fading against his throat, just under the clean line of his jaw. A lock of his always-disheveled black hair was falling into his eyes. Magnus had the fleeting impulse to reach over and push his hair back, but he repressed the urge. Alec was sometimes self-conscious about public displays of affection. There might be no Shadowhunters here, but it was not as if all ordinary humans were totally accepting of such gestures either. Magnus wished they were.

"Thinking deep thoughts?" Alec asked.

Magnus scoffed. "I try not to."

Enjoying life was essential, but sometimes it was an effort. Planning the perfect trip to Europe had not been easy. Magnus had been forced to invent several brilliant schemes single-handed. He could only imagine trying to describe his somewhat unique requirements to a travel agent.

"Going somewhere?" she might ask when he called.

"First holiday with my new boyfriend," Magnus might reply, since being able to tell the world he was dating Alec was a recent development, and Magnus liked to brag. "Very new. So new we still have that new-car smell."

So new that each was still learning the rhythms of the other, every glance or touch a move in a territory both wonderful and strange. Sometimes he caught himself looking at Alec, or found Alec looking at him, with luminous shock. It was as though each of them had discovered something unexpected but infinitely desirable. They were not yet sure of each other, but they wanted to be.

Or at least, that was what Magnus wanted.

"It's a classic love story. I hit on him at a party, he asked me out, then we fought an epic magical battle between good and evil side by side, and now we need a vacation. The thing is, he's a Shadowhunter," he would say.

"Sorry, what?" his imaginary travel agent would ask.

"Oh, you know how it is. Back in the day, the world was being overrun with demons. Think Black Friday, with more rivers of blood and slightly fewer howls of desperation. As happens in times of despair for the noble and true—so, never for me—an angel came. The Angel gave to his chosen warriors and all their descendants the power of angels to defend mankind. He also gave them their own secret country. The Angel Raziel was a big gift giver. The Shadowhunters continue their fight to this day, invisible protectors, shining and virtuous, the actual non-ironic definition of 'holier than thou.' It is incredibly annoying. They literally are holier than thou! Certainly holier than me, as I am demonspawn."

Even Magnus could not think of what his travel agent would say to that. Probably she'd just whimper in confusion.

"Did I forget to mention?" Magnus would go on. "There are beings very different from Shadowhunters: there are Downworlders, too. Alec is a child of the Angel, and the son of one of the oldest families in Idris, the Nephilim home country. I'm sure his parents would not have been thrilled to see him squiring a faerie or a vampire or a werewolf about New York. I'm also certain they would have preferred that to a warlock. My kind are considered the most dangerous and suspect in Downworld. We are the children of demons, and I am the immortal child of a certain infamous Greater Demon, though I may have forgotten to mention that fact to my boyfriend. Respectable Shadowhunters are not supposed to bring my sort home to meet Mom and Dad. I have a past. I have several pasts. Besides, good Shadowhunter boys aren't meant to bring home boyfriends at all."

Only Alec had. He'd stood in the hall of his ancestors and kissed Magnus full on the mouth under the eyes of all the Nephilim assembled there. It had been the most profound and lovely surprise of Magnus's long life.

"We recently fought in a great war that averted disaster to all humankind, not that humankind is grateful, since they don't know. We received neither glory nor adequate financial compensation, and suffered losses I cannot describe. Alec lost his brother, and I lost my friend, and both of us could really use a break. I fear the closest thing to treating himself Alec has ever experienced is buying a shiny new knife. I want to do something nice for him, and with him. I want to take a step away from the mess that is our lives, and see if we can work out a way to be really together. Do you have a recommended itinerary?"

Even in his head, the travel agent hung up on him.

No, Magnus had been forced to plan out an elaborately romantic European getaway by himself. But he was Magnus Bane, glamorous and enigmatic. He could accomplish a trip of this kind in style. A warrior chosen by angels and a well-dressed demon's child, in love and intent on adventure through Europe. What could go wrong?

Considering the issue of style, Magnus adjusted his crimson beret to a rakish angle. Alec looked up at the movement, then kept looking.

"Do you want to wear a beret after all?" Magnus asked. "Say the word. I happen to have several berets concealed on my person. In a variety of colors. I'm a beret cornucopia."

"I'm going to pass on the beret," said Alec. "Again. But thanks." The corners of his mouth curved upward, the smile uncertain but real.

Magnus propped his chin on his hand. He wanted to savor this moment of Alec, starlight, and possibility in Paris, and keep it to look at, years in the future. He hoped the memory would not hurt later.

"What are you thinking about?" Alec asked. "Seriously."

"Seriously," said Magnus. "You."

Alec looked startled at the idea that Magnus might be thinking of him. He was both very easy and very difficult to surprise—

Shadowhunter vision and reflexes were no joke. Whether it was coming around a corner or in the bed they shared—only to sleep, for now, until or if Alec wanted anything else—Alec always anticipated him. Yet he could be caught off guard by something as small as knowing that he was in Magnus's thoughts.

Right now, Magnus thought it was well past time for Alec to have a proper surprise. He just so happened to have one ready.

Paris was the first stop on their trip. Perhaps it was a cliché to begin a romantic European vacation in the City of Love, but Magnus believed classics were classics for a reason. They had been here almost a week, and Magnus felt it was time to put his own particular spin on things.

Alec finished his last postcard, and Magnus reached for it, then let his hand drop. He read what Alec had written and smiled, charmed and surprised.

On the postcard to his sister, Alec had added, *Wish you were here. Except not really* himself. He shot Magnus a tiny grin.

"Ready for the next adventure?" Magnus asked.

Alec looked intrigued, but he said, "You mean the cabaret? Our tickets are for nine o'clock. We should check how long it'll take us to get there from here."

It was very clear Alec had not been on a proper vacation before. He kept trying to plan the holiday as if they were going into battle.

Magnus waved his hand lazily, as if shooing a fly. "There's always time for the late show at the Moulin Rouge. Turn around."

He pointed over the Shadowhunter's shoulder. Alec turned.

Drifting toward the Eiffel Tower, bobbing unsteadily against the crosswind, was a brightly striped purple-and-blue hot-air balloon. In place of a basket, a table and two chairs rested on a wooden platform hanging below the balloon by four ropes. The table was set for two, and a rose sat in a thin vase at its center. A three-pronged candelabra completed the setting, although the winds swirling around the Eiffel Tower kept blowing out the candles. Annoyed, Magnus snapped his fingers, and all three candles lit up again.

"Uh," said Alec. "Can you fly a hot-air balloon?"

"Of course!" Magnus declared. "Did I ever tell you about the time I stole a hot-air balloon to rescue the queen of France?"

Alec grinned as if Magnus was making a joke. Magnus smiled back. Marie Antoinette had actually been quite a handful.

"It's just," Alec said thoughtfully, "I've never even seen you drive a car."

He stood to admire the balloon, which was glamoured to be invisible. As far as the mundanes around them were concerned, Alec solemnly gazed at the open air.

"I can drive. I can also fly, and pilot, and otherwise direct any vehicle you like. I'm hardly going to crash the balloon into a chimney," Magnus protested.

"Uh-huh," said Alec, frowning.

"You seem lost in thought," Magnus remarked. "Are you considering how glamorous and romantic your boyfriend is?"

"I'm considering," said Alec, "how to protect you if we crash the balloon into a chimney."

As he moved past Magnus, Alec stopped and pushed a wayward lock of hair off Magnus's brow. His touch was light, tender but casual, as if he did not even really realize he was doing it. Magnus had not even realized his own hair was in his eyes.

Magnus ducked his head and smiled. Being taken care of was strange to him, but he thought perhaps he could get used to it.

Magnus glamoured the attention of mundane eyes away from him, and then he used his chair as a step and climbed onto the swaying platform. The moment he planted both feet on the floor, it felt as if he were standing on solid ground. He offered his hand. "Trust me."

Alec hesitated, then accepted Magnus's hand. His grip was strong, and his smile sweet. "I do."

He followed Magnus, vaulting lightly over the railing onto the platform. They sat down at the table, and the balloon, ascending bumpily like a rowboat on a choppy ocean, drifted away unseen from the Eiffel Tower. Seconds later they were floating high above the skyline as the sprawl of Paris expanded in every direction around them.

Magnus watched Alec take in the city from a thousand feet in the air. Magnus had been in love before, and it had gone wrong before. He'd been hurt and learned how to recover from the pain. Many times.

Other lovers had told Magnus that he was impossible to take seriously, that he was terrifying, that he was too much, that he was not enough. Magnus might disappoint Alec. He probably would.

If Alec's feelings did not last, Magnus at least wanted this trip to be a good memory. He hoped this would be a foundation for something more, but if this was all they ever had, Magnus would make it count.

The crystalline glow of the Eiffel Tower receded. People had not expected it to last, either. Yet there it stood, the blazon of the city.

There was a sudden strong gust of wind; the platform tilted and the balloon plummeted fifty feet. They spun against the crosswind for several rotations before Magnus made an emphatic gesture and the balloon righted itself.

Alec glanced over with a small frown, clutching the arms of his chair. "So, how do you work the controls on this thing?"

"No idea!" Magnus called back cheerfully. "I was just going to use magic!"

The hot-air balloon passed over L'Arc de Triomphe with inches to spare and made a sharp turn to head toward the Louvre, dipping low over the tops of buildings.

Magnus did not feel as carefree as he wished to appear. It was an awfully windy day. Keeping the balloon upright, steady, headed in the right direction, and invisible was a greater strain than he cared to admit. And he still had dinner to serve. And he had to keep relighting the candles.

Romance was a lot of work.

Below, dark leaves hung heavy on the red-brick walls along the riverbank, and streetlights shone pink and orange and blue amid the white-painted buildings and narrow cobbled streets. On the other side of the balloon lay the Jardin des Tuileries, its round pond staring up at them like an eye, and the glass pyramid of the Louvre, a beam of red light cutting through its center. Magnus thought suddenly of how the Paris Commune had set the Tuileries on fire, remembered ash rising in the air and the blood on the guillotine. This was a city bearing the stains of long history and old sorrows; through Alec's clear eyes, Magnus hoped it would be washed clean.

He snapped his fingers, and a bottle chilling in an ice bucket materialized next to the table. "Champagne?"

Alec shot out of his chair. "Magnus, you see that plume of smoke down there? Is that a fire?"

"So that's a no to champagne?"

The Shadowhunter pointed at an avenue running parallel to the Seine. "There's something weird about that smoke. It's drifting *against* the wind."

Magnus waved his champagne flute. "Nothing the *pompiers* can't handle."

"Now the smoke is jumping across the rooftops. It just made a right turn. Now it's hiding behind a chimney."

Magnus paused. "I'm sorry?"

"Okay, the smoke has just leaped over Rue des Pyramides." Alec squinted.

"You recognize the Rue des Pyramides from up here?"

Alec looked at Magnus, surprised. "I studied the maps of the city very closely before we left," said Alec. "To prepare."

Magnus was reminded again of the fact that Alec prepared for a vacation like he was preparing for a Shadowhunter mission because this was his first-ever vacation. He eyed the thick black plume drifting into the evening sky, hoping Alec was wrong and they could return to his planned evening of romance. But Alec was, unfortunately, not wrong: the cloud was too black and too compact; its plumes extended like solid tentacles fluttering in the air, blatantly ignoring the wind that should have dispersed them. Under the trails of smoke, he saw a sudden gleam.

Alec was at the edge of the platform, leaning alarmingly far over the side. "There are two people chasing the smoke . . . thing. I think those are seraph blades. They're Shadowhunters."

"Hooray, Shadowhunters," said Magnus. "Present company excepted from my sarcastic hooray, of course."

He stood, and with a decisive gesture brought the balloon rapidly lower in altitude, recognizing with some disappointment the need to get a closer look. His vision was not as keen as Alec's rune-enhanced sight, but beneath the smoke he could soon make out two dark shapes, running along the Paris rooftops in hot pursuit.

Magnus discerned a woman's face, uplifted to the sky and shining pale as a pearl. A long plait trailed behind her as she ran, like a snake of silver and gold. The two Shadowhunters were going desperately fast.

The smoke eddied down a block of commercial buildings and over a narrow road, and spilled onto an apartment complex, dodging skylights and piping and ventilation shafts. All the while the Shadowhunters pursued, slicing at any black tentacles that whipped too close. Inside the dark maelstrom of smoke, a crowd of yellow lights like fireflies swarmed in pairs.

"Iblis demons," muttered Alec, seizing his bow and nocking an arrow. Magnus had groaned when he realized Alec was taking his bow with him to their dinner. "How could you possibly need to shoot anything with a bow and arrow at the Eiffel Tower?" he'd said, and Alec had just smiled gently and, with a small shrug, strapped the weapon in place.

Magnus knew better than to suggest they let the Paris Shadowhunters take care of whatever irritating demonic disaster was unfolding. Alec was congenitally incapable of turning away from a good cause. It was one of his most appealing qualities.

They were closer to the rooftops now. The platform swayed dangerously as Magnus skirted around chimneys, cable wires, and roof stairwells.

The wind was dangerously strong. Magnus felt as if he were fighting the whole sky. The balloon wobbled, swinging side to side, and the ice bucket tumbled over. Magnus managed to just avoid crashing into a tall chimney stack as he watched the champagne bottle roll off the edge. It exploded in a spray of glass and foam as it impacted the roof below.

He opened his mouth to make a remark about the sad waste of champagne.

"Sorry about the champagne," said Alec. "I hope it wasn't one of your most-prized bottles or anything."

Magnus laughed. Alec anticipating him, yet again.

"I only bring the medium-prized bottles to drink on a dangling platform a thousand feet in the air."

He overcompensated for the wind a bit too much and the platform swung dangerously in the other direction like a pendulum, nearly putting a hole in a giant billboard. He righted the balloon hastily and checked on the situation below.

The swarm of Iblis demons had split in two, encircling the Shadowhunters on the roof below. The unlucky pair were trapped, though they continued fighting valiantly. The fair-haired woman moved like cornered lightning. The first Iblis demon that leaped at them was cut down by a slice of her seraph blade, as were the second and third. But there were too many. As Magnus watched, a fourth demon launched itself toward the Shadowhunter woman, its glowing eyes streaking through the darkness.

Magnus glanced at Alec, and Alec nodded at him. Magnus used a great deal of his magic to hold the hot-air balloon perfectly still, for just a moment. Alec let his first arrow fly.

The Iblis demon never reached the woman. The glow from its eyes dimmed as its smoky body dissipated, leaving behind nothing but an arrow embedded into the ground. Three more demons suffered a similar fate.

Alec's hands were a blur, raining arrow after arrow at the swarm below. Any time a pair of glowing eyes moved toward the Shadowhunters, a streaking arrow would meet it before it could reach them.

It was a pity Magnus had to devote his attention to controlling the elements rather than admiring his boyfriend.

The rear guard of the Iblis demons turned toward the new threat in the sky. Three broke off their attack on the Shadowhunters and launched themselves toward the balloon. Two were dropped by arrows before they could make it onto the platform, but Alec was too late to draw on the third. The demon, gaping maw exposing a row of sharp black teeth, struck at Alec.

But Alec had already dropped the bow and drawn a seraph blade. *"Puriel,"* said Alec, and the blade lit up with angelic power. The runes on his body shimmered as he thrust the blade through the Iblis demon and sliced, separating head from body. The demon crumbled away into black ash.

Another group of demons reached the platform, and quickly met a similar fate. This was what Shadowhunters did, what Alec was born to do. His body was a weapon, graceful and swift, an instrument honed to slay demons and shield his loved ones. Alec was very good at both.

Magnus's skills were more in the areas of magic and fashion

sense. He ensnared one demon in a web of electricity and held off another with an invisible barrier made of wind. Alec shot the demon Magnus was holding off, then shot the last demon lingering below. At this point, the fair-haired Shadowhunter woman and her male companion had nothing left to do. They were standing in a whirl of smoky ash and destruction and appeared somewhat at a loss.

"You're welcome!" Magnus called down to them, waving. "No charge!"

"Magnus," said Alec. "Magnus!"

The note of real alarm in Alec's voice was what made Magnus aware that the wind had slipped out of his grasp, even before he felt the lurch of the balloon platform beneath their feet. Magnus made a last frantic, futile gesture, and Alec rushed at him, curling his body around Magnus's.

"Brace for—" Alec shouted in his ear, as the balloon careened down toward earth and, more specifically, a theater marquee with CARMEN spelled across the front in brilliant yellow bulbs.

Magnus Bane did his best, in life, to always be spectacular.

This crash was.

CHAPTER TWO

Stars Spell Your Name

JUST AS THE PLATFORM WAS ABOUT TO PLOW INTO the letter *R*, Alec clutched a fistful of Magnus's sleeve, yanked him into a rough embrace, and launched them both over the side of the platform. The glittering sky and glittering city changed places as the world spun. He lost track of up and down, until down got his full attention by hitting hard. An instant of dark followed, then he found himself lying on the grass, cradled in Alec's arms.

Magnus blinked stars out of his eyes just in time to see the balloon smash into the marquee, causing an impressive explosion of sparks and splinters. The gas flame that had been keeping it aloft lurched, and the balloon rapidly deflated as it and the marquee caught fire.

People were already massing across the street to gawk. The distinctive *beep-boop* of Parisian police sirens became audible and quickly grew louder. Some things couldn't be glamoured away.

Strong hands pulled Magnus to his feet. "Are you all right?"

Surprisingly, he was. Falling safely from absurd heights was apparently one of the Shadowhunters' many skills. Magnus was more shaken by Alec's look of concern than he was by the crash. Magnus found himself wanting to glance over his shoulder to find who the look was really directed at, not altogether able to believe it was for him.

Magnus had been dodging death for centuries. He was not used to anyone worrying this much about his near misses.

"Can't complain," said Magnus, adjusting his cuffs. "If I did, I would only be doing so for attention from a handsome gentleman."

Fortunately, *Carmen* was not being performed tonight, so there appeared to be no injuries. The two got to their feet and stared at the wreckage. They were thankfully invisible to the gathering crowd, who would soon be mystified at the balloon's apparent lack of passengers. The air became quiet, and then the marquee dipped and squealed as the fire finished eating through the remaining supports and sent the entire thing crashing to the ground, sending a fresh plume of smoke and sparks into the air. Several in the crowd moved back cautiously, but continued to take photos.

"I admit," said Magnus, tugging at a torn piece of shirt fluttering in the wind, "this evening isn't going exactly to plan."

Alec looked glum. "Sorry about ruining our night."

"Nothing is ruined. The night is young, and reservations are available," said Magnus. "The theater will receive a generous donation from an unknown patron to effect the repairs necessary after this freak accident. We are about to enjoy a nighttime stroll through the most romantic city on earth. Seems an excellent night to me. Evil has been defeated, which is nice too."

Alec frowned. "Seeing that many Iblis demons gathered together is unusual."

"We have to leave some evil for the Paris Institute to amuse themselves with. It would be gauche for us to hog all the evil to fight. Besides, we are on vacation. Carpe diem. Seize the day, not the demons."

Alec conceded the issue with a shrug and a small smile.

"Also, you are just great with that bow, and it is very, very attractive," Magnus added. In his opinion, Alec needed to be complimented more. Alec looked taken aback, but not displeased. "All right. Now. New clothes. If one of the Paris fey sees me looking like this, my reputation will be toast for a century."

"I don't know," Alec said shyly. "I like how you look."

Magnus beamed but remained determined. A hot-air balloon crash was not how he had pictured his clothing getting torn on this trip. To Rue Saint-Honoré, then, for a quick wardrobe refresh.

They breezed through several stores that were open late, or that could be persuaded to open for a longtime valued customer. Magnus selected a red velvet paisley blazer over a rust-red ruffled shirt, while Alec could not be talked into anything more elaborate than a dark striped hoodie under a loose-fitting leather jacket with a few too many zippers.

This accomplished, Magnus made a few calls and was pleased to tell Alec that they would be dining at the chef's table in A Midsummer Night's Dining, the hottest faerie restaurant in the city.

From outside, it looked ordinary, with a quaint brickwork-and-plaster facade. Inside, it resembled a faerie grotto. Luxuriant emerald-green moss carpeted the ground, and the walls and roof were irregular stone like that of a cavern. Vines emerged like snakes from the trees and drifted among the tables, and several of the customers were chasing their food, as their meals had levitated from their plates and were making a break for freedom.

"It always feels weird to order faerie restaurant food," Alec mused once they ordered their salads. "I mean, I do in New York all the time, but I know those places. *The Shadowhunter's Codex* says never to eat any faerie foods, under any circumstances."

"This place is perfectly safe," Magnus said, munching on one of the leaves as it tried to crawl out of his mouth. "Perfectly mostly safe. As long as we are paying for the meal, it is not considered an offering but a purchase. The financial transaction makes all the difference. It's a fine line, but isn't that always the case when it comes to the Fair Folk? Don't let your salad get away!"

Alec laughed and stabbed at his faerie caprese. Those Shadowhunter reflexes yet again, Magnus noted.

Magnus had always been careful, with mundane lovers, to minimize their interaction with Downworld. For their safety and their peace of mind. He'd always assumed that Shadowhunters would want to minimize their interaction with Downworld too. They held themselves apart, declaring themselves not mundane but not of Downworld either—a third thing, rather, separate and maybe even a little bit better. But Alec seemed glad to be here, not taken aback by any of Paris or Magnus's world. It was possible, maybe, that Alec might be as happy as Magnus was, just to be together.

He linked elbows with Alec as they left the restaurant, feeling the hard muscle of the Shadowhunter's arm against his. Alec would be ready to fight again in an instant, but in this moment, he was simply relaxed. Magnus leaned in.

They turned onto the Quai de Valmy and encountered a strong headwind. Alec threw on his hood, zipped up his jacket, and pulled Magnus closer. Magnus led him along as they walked through the Canal Saint-Martin neighborhood, following the waterway as it bent around the corner. Couples strolled along the shore, and small clusters of people chatted on picnic blankets at the water's edge. A merman in a fedora had joined one group of picnickers. Magnus and Alec walked underneath a blue iron footbridge. On the other side of the canal, violin music accompanied by percussion filled the air. The mundanes of Paris would be able to hear the mortal drummer, but only people like Magnus and Alec could see and hear the faerie violinist spinning around him, with flowers in her hair sparkling like gems.

Magnus guided Alec away from the busy canal and down a quieter street. The moon painted a row of squat gray houses sand-wiched side by side with a pale glow that split into a kaleidoscope of silver among the wavering trees. They turned at random inter-sections, letting chance be their guide. Magnus could feel his blood coursing through his veins. He felt alive, he felt awake. He hoped Alec was as electrified as he was.

Cool wind stroked the back of Magnus's neck, prickling his skin. For a moment, he felt something strange. An itch, a nagging sensation, a presence. He stopped in his tracks and looked back the way they'd come.

Magnus watched the crowds move past. He still felt it: eyes watching, ears listening, or possibly thoughts focused on him float-ing in the air.

"Something wrong?" asked Alec.

Magnus realized he had pulled away from Alec, ready to face a threat alone. He shook off his unease.

"What could be wrong?" he asked. "I'm with you."

He reached for Alec and laced their fingers together, Alec's cal-loused palm pressed tight against his own. Alec held himself more at ease in the night than during the day. Possibly he felt more com-fortable hidden from the view of even those with the Sight. Perhaps all Shadowhunters felt more at home in the shadows.

They stopped just inside the entrance of the Parc des Buttes-Chaumont. The glow from the city lights gave the horizon a soft brown hue as it merged with the blackness of the night sky, punc-tuated only by the moon. Magnus pointed at a faint cluster of stars sparkling to his right. "There's Boötes, the bear watcher, and Corona and Hercules next to it."

"Why is it supposed to be romantic to point out stars?" Alec said, but with a smile on his face. "Look, that one is . . . Dave . . . the Hunter . . . and that one is the . . . Frog, and . . . the Helicopter. I don't know constellations, sorry."

"It's romantic because it's sharing knowledge about the world," said Magnus. "The one who knows about stars teaches the one who doesn't know. That's romantic."

Alec said, "I don't think there's anything I can teach you." He was still smiling, but Magnus felt a pang.

"Sure there is," said Magnus. "What's that on the back of your hand?"

Alec lifted his hand and examined it as if it were new to him. "It's a rune. You've seen them before."

"I know the basic idea. You draw the runes on your skin, you get powers," said Magnus. "I'm not all that clear on the details. Humor me. The Mark on your hand is the first one you get, right?"

"Yes," Alec said slowly. "Voyance. That's the rune they usually put first on Shadowhunter children, the rune to verify that they can bear runes at all. And it lets you see through glamour. Which is always useful."

Magnus looked at the shadowy curve of an eye against Alec's pale skin. Glamours protected Downworlders. Shadowhunters needed to see through glamours because Downworlders were potential threats.

Did Alec not think the same thought when he looked at the Mark on his hand? Or was he simply kind enough not to speak it? To protect Magnus, as he had protected him in the fall from the balloon. *Strange,* thought Magnus. *But sweet.*

"What about this one?" he said, and found himself trailing an index finger down the curve of Alec's bicep, watching Alec shiver at the unexpected intimacy of the gesture.

Alec looked Magnus in the eyes. "Accuracy," he said.

"So I have this one to thank for your skills with the bow?" He used his hold on Alec's hand to draw him in, so they met in the middle of the path under the soft shine of the moon. He leaned over to plant a small kiss on Alec's arm.

"Thanks," he whispered. "And this one?"

Now he grazed his fingers along the side of Alec's throat. Alec's shuddering breath broke the soft stillness of the night. His arm snaked around Magnus's waist, pressing their bodies tighter together, and Magnus felt Alec's heart pounding through his shirt.

"Equilibrium," Alec said breathlessly. "Keeps me steady on my feet."

Magnus bowed his head and laid his lips gently on the rune, faded to silvery almost-invisibility against the smooth skin of Alec's neck. Alec inhaled sharply.

Magnus slid his mouth along warm skin until he reached Alec's ear and purred, "I don't think it's working."

"I don't want it to," Alec murmured.

He turned his face into Magnus's and caught Magnus's mouth with his own. Alec kissed as he did all things, so dedicated and wholehearted he swept Magnus away. Magnus curled his hand in the soft leather of Alec's jacket and saw through his eyelashes new skin being bared to the moonlight. Another rune, filigreed like a musical note, was inscribed below the dip of Alec's collarbone.

Magnus said, in a low voice, "And what's that one?"

Alec answered, "Stamina."

Magnus stared. "Are you serious?"

Alec began to grin. "Yeah."

"Really, though," Magnus said. "I want to be clear on this. You're not just saying that to be sexy?"

"No," Alec answered, his voice husky, and swallowed. "But I'm glad if it is."

Magnus laid his rings against the space beneath Alec's collarbone and saw Alec shiver at the cool touch of metal. He traced up the back of Alec's neck and palmed the back of his head to pull him close again.

As he did, Magnus whispered, "God, I love Shadowhunters."

Alec said again, "I'm glad."

His mouth was soft and warm, a contradiction with his strong hands until it was not, until the kiss became both encircling comfort and burning urgency. Magnus pulled back eventually, gasping for breath, because the other choice was pulling Alec down into the grass and the dark.

He couldn't do that. Alec had never done anything like this before. On their first night in Paris, Magnus had woken in the early hours to find Alec still awake and pacing the floor. He knew that Alec must worry sometimes about what he'd gotten himself into. The decision about whether to take things further had to be entirely Alec's.

Alec asked in a strained voice: "Do you think we could skip the cabaret?"

"What cabaret?" said Magnus.

They took off, out of the park and toward the general direction of Magnus's apartment, stopping twice because they got turned around by the narrow streets of the city and twice more to make out in dimly lit alleys. They would have become a great deal more lost if not for Alec's keen sense of direction. Shadowhunters were so useful when traveling. Magnus planned to never again leave home without one.

He had been a revolutionary and a bad painter in this apartment, had been robbed of his life's savings here in the eighteenth century. It was the first time he had been rich and had lost everything. Magnus had lost everything a few more times since then.

These days he was based in Brooklyn, and the Paris apartment stood empty save for the memories. He kept it for sentimental reasons, and because trying to find a hotel during Paris Fashion Week was its own special bonus level of Hell.

Not bothering with keys, Magnus flicked a finger at the front door and used what little magic reserves he had left to swing it open. He and Alec entered the building still kissing, fetching up against the walls and stumbling up four flights of stairs. His apartment door slammed open with a loud bang and they spilled inside.

The velvet blazer didn't even make it inside his apartment, since Alec tore it off and dropped it in the hallway just short of the front door. As they crossed the threshold, he was ripping Magnus's shirt open. Cuff links and buttons chimed distantly against the floorboards. Magnus was savagely unzipping the leather jacket as he pressed Alec against the arm of the sofa and tipped him over onto the cushions. Alec fell with easy grace onto his back, pulling Magnus down on top of him.

Magnus kissed the Equilibrium rune, then the Stamina rune. Alec's body arched beneath him, and his hands tightened on Magnus's shoulders.

Alec's voice was insistent as he said *something something* "Magnus" *something something*.

"Alexander," Magnus murmured back, and felt Alec's body surge underneath his in response. Alec's hands locked on his shoulders. Magnus studied him with sudden concern.

Alec, wide-eyed, was staring off to the side. "Magnus. Over there."

Magnus followed Alec's gaze and realized they had company. There was a figure sitting on the purple love seat opposite them. In the shimmer of city lights through the window, Magnus saw a woman with a cloud of brown hair, startled gray eyes, and the beginnings of a familiar wry smile.

Magnus said, *"Tessa?"*

CHAPTER THREE

The Crimson Hand

THE THREE OF THEM SAT IN THE LIVING ROOM IN uncomfortable silence. Alec was sitting on the other end of the sofa, far from Magnus. Nothing was going according to plan tonight.

"Tessa!" Magnus said again, marveling. "Aren't you unexpected. And uninvited."

Tessa sat and sipped her tea, looking perfectly composed. Since she was one of Magnus's dearest and oldest friends, he felt it would be nice if she looked even slightly apologetic. She did not.

"You told me once that you would not forgive me if I didn't drop by whenever I found myself in the same city as you."

"I would have forgiven you," Magnus said with conviction. "I would have thanked you."

Tessa glanced Alec's way. Alec was blushing. The ends of Tessa's lips curled up, but she was kind and hid her smile behind her teacup.

"Call it even," said Tessa. "You once walked in on me in an embarrassing situation with a gentleman in a mountain fortress, after all."

Her half-concealed smile flickered. She looked again at Alec, who had inherited his coloring from Shadowhunters long gone. Shadowhunters Tessa had loved.

"You should let that go," Magnus advised.

Tessa was a warlock like Magnus, and like Magnus, she was used to overcoming the memory of what had been loved and lost. They were in the longtime habit of comforting each other. She took another sip of tea, her smile restored as if it had never been gone.

"I certainly have let it go," she replied. "Now."

Alec, who was watching this back-and-forth as if sitting center court in a tennis match, raised a hand. "I'm sorry, but did you two used to date?"

That stopped the conversation dead in its tracks. Both Tessa and Magnus turned to him with identical looks of shock.

"You seem more horrified than I do," Magnus told Tessa, "and somehow I am deeply wounded."

Tessa gave Magnus a tiny smile, then turned to Alec. "Magnus and I have been friends for more than a hundred years."

"Okay," said Alec. "So this is a friendly visit?"

There was an edge to his voice that made Magnus raise an eyebrow. Alec was sometimes uncomfortable around new people. Magnus supposed that explained his tone. Magnus was so obviously, embarrassingly infatuated. There was no way Alec could possibly be jealous.

Tessa sighed. The light of amusement in her gray eyes died away. "I wish this was a friendly visit," she said softly. "It's not."

She shifted in her seat, moving a little stiffly. Magnus's eyes narrowed.

"Tessa," he said. "Are you hurt?"

"Nothing that won't heal," she said.

"Are you in trouble?"

She gave him a long, unreadable look.

"No," said Tessa. "You are."

"What do you mean?" Alec asked, his voice suddenly urgent.

Tessa bit her lip. "Magnus," she said, "can I talk to you alone?"

"You can talk to us both," said Magnus. "I trust Alec."

Very quietly, Tessa asked, "Do you trust him with your life?"

With someone else, Magnus would have thought they were being overdramatic. Tessa wasn't like that. What she said, she usually meant.

"Yes," Magnus said. "With my life."

Many Downworlders would never have told secrets to a Shadowhunter, no matter what Magnus said, but Tessa was different. She grabbed a worn leather satchel by her feet, brought out a wax-sealed scroll, and unrolled it. "The Spiral Council have issued a formal demand that you, Magnus Bane, High Warlock of Brooklyn, neutralize the human cult of demon worshippers known as the Crimson Hand. Immediately."

"I understand that the Spiral Council want the best," Magnus said modestly. "I can't say I care for their tone. I've heard of the Crimson Hand. They're a joke. They're a bunch of humans who like to party wearing demon masks. They're more interested in doing body shots than demon worship. I'm on vacation, and I won't be bothered with this nonsense. Tell the Spiral Council I will be giving my cat, Chairman Meow, a bath."

The Spiral Council was the closest thing warlocks had to a governing body, but it was secretive and not entirely official. In general, warlocks had issues with authority. Magnus had more than most.

A shadow touched Tessa's face. "Magnus, I had to beg the Council to let me come to you. Yes, the Crimson Hand has always been a joke. But it appears they have a new leader, someone who has whipped them into shape. They've gotten powerful, have deep pockets, and have been recruiting heavily. There have been several deaths and far more disappearances. A dead faerie was found in Venice, next to a pentagram painted with her blood."

Magnus started, and forced himself to be still. Tessa didn't have to spell it out for him: they both knew faerie blood could be used to summon Greater Demons, who had once been among the highest of angels, and who had fallen so far.

Unspoken between Tessa and Magnus was their knowledge that they were each the child of a different Greater Demon. Magnus felt a certain kinship with Tessa as a result. There were very few children of Greater Demons around.

Magnus hadn't told Alec that his father was a Prince of Hell. It seemed bound to put a crimp in any new relationship.

"Is that so?" Magnus asked, trying to keep his voice neutral. "If this cult is mixed up with trying to raise a Greater Demon, that is very bad news. For the cult, and potentially for many other inno-cents."

Tessa nodded, leaning forward. "The Crimson Hand is clearly poised to cause chaos in the Shadow World, so the Spiral Council sent me to deal with them. I was impersonating one of their aco-lytes at their headquarters in Venice, trying to find out what they were up to and who their leader might be. But then, during one of their rituals, I was exposed to a potion that made me lose control of my shape-shifting abilities. I barely escaped with my life. When I returned a few days later, the cult had abandoned the place. You need to find them."

"As I so often say," Magnus remarked, "why me?"

Tessa was not smiling now. "I don't give it a lot of credence, but the rumor in Downworld is that the Crimson Hand's new leader isn't actually new. People are saying their original founder has returned."

"And who, may I ask, is their founder?"

Tessa took out a photo and slapped it down on the table. The photo was of a painting drawn on a wall. The painting was crude, amateurishly drawn, almost as if by a child. It depicted several images of a man with dark hair lounging on a throne. Next to him were two people fanning him with palm leaves, while a third knelt in front of him. No, not bowing, but giving him what appeared to be a foot rub.

Even roughly painted, they could all recognize the cult founder's jet-black hair, etched cheekbones, and yellow catlike eyes.

"They call their founder 'the Great Poison,'" Tessa said. "Look familiar? Magnus, people are saying that *you* are the original founder and the new leader of the Crimson Hand."

A chill passed through Magnus. Then indignation took over.

"Tessa, I most certainly did not found a cult!" he protested. "I don't even like demon worshippers. They're boring idiots who worship boring demons." He paused. "It's the kind of thing I would joke about, really." He paused again. "Not that I would. Even as a prank. I would never . . ." He trailed off.

"You would joke about starting a cult that worshipped demons?" Alec asked.

Magnus gestured helplessly. "I would joke about anything."

Mundanes had a phrase for when they didn't remember something: "doesn't ring a bell." This was the opposite of that. A cult called the Crimson Hand . . . a joke long ago. It rang through him, almost exactly like a bell.

He remembered telling a joke, centuries ago. Ragnor Fell had been there, he was almost sure. He remembered a hot day and a very long night. He remembered nothing else.

Magnus drew in a deep breath and forced himself to remain calm. His old friend Ragnor was dead now, a casualty of the recent war. Magnus had been trying not to think about that too much. Now there was a gap in his own memories. Keeping centuries of life clear in your mind was difficult, but Magnus could tell the difference between memory that was clouded and memory that had been scythed away. He had cast spells to cloud and remove memories before. Warlocks did it for each other sometimes, to help their friends get through the trials presented by immortality.

Why would he have had memories of a demon-worshipping cult that were removed? Who would have removed them? He did not dare look in Alec's direction.

"Tessa," he said carefully, "are you sure you haven't become confused by the Great Poison's handsome face and dashing demeanor?"

"There's a painting on the wall," said Alec, his voice calm and factual. "You're wearing the same jacket in both pictures."

Rather than look at Alec, Magnus looked at the painting, which was of himself and his fellow warlocks Ragnor Fell and Catarina Loss. A werewolf acquaintance of an artistic persuasion had painted the picture, so none of their warlock marks were masked with glamour. Catarina was in a low-cut dress, showing a good deal of beautiful blue skin, and Ragnor's horns curved in a forest of pomaded curls, his green face a contrast with his white cravat like spring leaves against snow. The corners of Magnus's glowing cat eyes were crinkled as he smiled. Magnus had always treasured this painting.

And he *was* wearing the same jacket in both pictures.

He considered but rejected the possibility that the Great Poison had coincidentally owned the same jacket. It had been custom-made for him, as a thank-you, by the Russian tsar's personal tailor. It seemed unlikely Dmitri would have made a second one for some random cult leader.

"I can't remember anything about the Crimson Hand," Magnus said. "But memories can be tampered with. I think mine might have been."

"Magnus," said Tessa, "*I* know you are not the leader of a demon-worshipping cult, but not everyone in the Spiral Labyrinth knows you like I do. They think you might be the one doing this. They wanted to go to the Shadowhunters. I persuaded the Spiral Labyrinth to give you the chance to stop the cult and prove your innocence, before they get any of the Institutes involved. I wish I could do more, but I can't."

"That's all right," Magnus said. He didn't want to worry Tessa, so he forced his voice into breeziness, though he felt more like a storm. "I can handle this on my own."

He hadn't looked at Alec in some time. He wondered if he would ever have the courage to look at Alec again. According to all the laws of the Accords, the Shadowhunters should have been told about the demonic cult, and the murders, and the warlock suspect immediately.

Tessa was the one who looked at Alec.

"Magnus didn't do it," she assured him.

Alec said, "I don't need you to tell me that."

Tension eased out of Tessa's shoulders. She placed her cup on the side table and stood up. Her gaze lingered on Alec and her smile spread, warm and sweet, and Magnus understood that she was seeing within him not just Will but Cecily and Anna and Christopher, generations of beloved faces now gone. "It was a pleasure meeting you, Alexander."

"Alec," said Alec. He was studying Tessa closely in return.

"Alec," said Tessa. "I wish I could stay and help, but I must return to the Labyrinth as quickly as possible. They're opening a Portal for me. Please take care of Magnus."

"Excuse me?" asked Magnus, startled.

"Of course I will," said Alec. "Tessa, before you go. You look . . . familiar. Have we met before?"

Tessa stood looking down at him. Her face was serious and kind.

"No," she said. "But I hope we meet again."

She turned toward the back wall, where a Portal was opening, illuminating the furniture and the lamps and the windows with an uncanny light. Through the curving doorway of light cut out of the air, Magnus could see the infamously uncomfortable chairs of the Spiral Labyrinth's receiving room.

"Whoever the cult's new leader is," Tessa said, pausing before the Portal, "be careful. I think it must be a warlock. I did not learn much, but even as an acolyte of the cult I encountered powerful wards and saw spells turned aside as if they were nothing. They have a sacred book they spoke of, called the Red Scrolls of Magic. I was not able to get a copy."

"I'll ask around at the Paris Shadow Market," said Magnus.

"They are watching for magic, so avoid traveling by Portal whenever possible," Tessa said.

"You're using a Portal right now," said Magnus, amused. "Always 'do as I say and not as I do,' I see. Will *you* be safe?"

Tessa was more than a century old, but she was so much younger than Magnus, and he had known her almost her whole life. He had never stopped feeling protective of her.

"I'm headed for the Spiral Labyrinth and staying there. It's always safe there. You, on the other hand, will probably be headed to more dangerous places. Good luck. Also—sorry about your vacation."

"You shouldn't apologize," said Magnus. Tessa blew him a kiss as she stepped through the Portal, and both she and its bright glow vanished from Magnus's living room.

Magnus and Alec didn't move for several beats. Magnus still could not bring himself to look directly at Alec. He was too afraid of what he would see on Alec's face. He stood in the middle of his Paris apartment with the man he loved, and felt very alone.

Magnus had harbored such high hopes for this getaway. It was only the start of their vacation, and now Magnus had an awful secret he was conspiring with a Downworlder friend to keep from Shadowhunters. Worse than that, he could not swear to Alec that he was entirely innocent. He could not remember.

Magnus couldn't blame Alec if he was reconsidering the entire relationship. *Date me, Alec Lightwood. Your parents hate me, I don't fit into your world and you won't like mine, and we won't be able to go on a romantic vacation without my dark past casting a shadow over our whole future.*

Magnus wanted them to get to know each other better. Magnus had a hard-won high opinion of himself, and he had an even higher opinion of Alec. He had thought he had unearthed every dark secret, wrestled every demon, accepted every personal flaw. The possibility that there might be secrets about himself even he did not know was a troubling one.

"Tessa didn't have to apologize," he said eventually. "I should. I'm sorry for ruining our vacation."

"Nothing's ruined," said Alec.

It was the echo of what Magnus had said earlier that made him look at Alec at last. When he did, he found Alec smiling at him faintly.

Truth came tumbling helplessly from Magnus's lips, as it sometimes did around Alec. "I don't understand what's happening."

Alec said, "We'll figure it out."

Magnus knew there had been times in his long life when he was furious and lost. He might not recall the Crimson Hand, but he remembered the first man he had ever killed, when he was a child with another name in a land that would become Indonesia. Magnus had been a person he now regretted being, but he could not wipe away the red stains of his past.

He didn't want Alec to see those stains, or be touched by them. He did not want Alec to think of him the way he knew other Shadowhunters thought of him.

There had been other loves in Magnus's life who would have run screaming long before now, and Alec was a Shadowhunter. He had his high duty, more sacred to the Nephilim than love.

"If you felt you had to tell the Clave," Magnus said slowly, "I would understand."

"Are you joking?" Alec demanded. "I'm not going to repeat

any of these stupid lies to the Clave. I'm not going to tell anyone. Magnus, I promise I won't."

Alec's expression was appalled. Magnus was shaken by the intensity of his own relief, by how much it mattered that Alec had not believed the worst.

"I swear, I truly don't remember anything."

"I believe you. We can handle this. We just need to find and stop whoever's actually in charge of the Crimson Hand." Alec shrugged. "Okay. Let's do that then."

Magnus wondered if he would ever get used to being surprised by Alec Lightwood. He hoped not.

"Also, we'll find out why you can't remember this. We'll figure out who did it, and why. I'm not worried."

Magnus was worried. Tessa believed in him, because she was kind. Astonishingly, Alec believed in him. Even dazzled and dizzy with relief over Alec, Magnus could not entirely banish his own creeping unease. He couldn't remember, and so it was possible— not likely, but possible—he might have done something then that he would be ashamed of now. Magnus wished he could be sure he deserved Alec's faith. He wished he could swear to Alec that he had never committed any unforgivable sins.

But he could not.

CHAPTER FOUR

Much Abides

ON THEIR FIRST NIGHT IN PARIS, ALEC HADN'T BEEN ABLE to sleep. He'd risen from bed and paced the floor. He kept looking at Magnus asleep in their bed—the bed they slept in together. Nothing else had happened in that bed yet, and Alec was torn between hope and fear when he thought about what might happen there soon. Magnus's silky black hair was spread on the white pillow, his skin was rich brown against the sheets. Magnus's strong, lean arm was flung out into the space where Alec had been, a slender gold bracelet glittering on his wrist. Alec couldn't entirely believe this was happening to him. He didn't want to mess it up.

A week later, he felt exactly the same. He didn't care if they were fighting a cult or in a hot-air balloon, or, for that matter, fighting a cult from the platform of a hot-air balloon, which was starting to feel like a plausible future development in his life. He was just happy to be with Magnus. He'd never imagined that a romantic vacation, with someone he really wanted to be with, was something he could actually have, or even something it was okay to want.

That said, he didn't particularly want his father to hear about his new boyfriend's possible status as founder of a demon-worshipping cult, and he went cold all over at the idea of the Clave hearing these whispers about Magnus. Eventually they would probably hear about it through other channels, no matter how closely Alec and Magnus guarded the information.

The Law is hard, but it is the Law, his people said, and Alec knew how hard it could be. He had seen how the Clave treated Shadow-hunters under suspicion of wrongdoing. It would be far worse for a Downworlder. Alec had seen Clary's Downworlder friend Simon thrown in prison, when Simon had done nothing at all. The thought of Magnus, such a bright presence, being put away in the dark made Alec physically flinch.

Last night, they had both gone to bed shortly after Tessa had left, but Magnus had tossed and turned restlessly. At one point Alec had awoken briefly and discovered Magnus, sitting bolt upright in bed, staring into the darkness. When Alec had left this morning, Magnus had been asleep, but splayed awkwardly on the bed, as though his body had given up in exhaustion, mid-thrash. His mouth hung open. He was not the picture of grace he normally presented.

Alec was used to feeling a combination of affection and annoyance toward the people he loved. Typically, he'd start the relationship with a feeling of total annoyance and minimal affection, and then as time passed, the annoyance diminished and the affection grew. This described the arc of his relationship with Jace, his *parabatai* and closest friend, and more recently described how he'd felt about Clary Fairchild when she'd come into their lives. Clary had had her own lost memories, and the return of those memories had helped win a war. In that case, Magnus had done the memory charms himself. And now it seemed someone had messed around with Magnus's memories, years and years before.

Alec had never found Magnus annoying at all. He wasn't sure what to make of that. Chaos swirled and orbited around Magnus like a cloud of glitter, and Alec's own tolerance of that chaos never ceased to astonish him.

Now he made his way back to Magnus's apartment, returning from his morning workout. It was a cool morning, and a layer of dew blanketed much of Paris. The sun was beginning to peek over the tops of the buildings on the horizon.

Magnus's apartment was intimidatingly nice, but there were no training rooms and nobody to train with, so Alec had to improvise. He had discovered a swimming pool next to the river. For some reason the people of Paris had built a place to swim next to a place they could swim. Mundanes were strange.

Alec had ended up swimming laps in the pool. His hair and clothes were still damp. A woman in very large sunglasses she could not possibly need whistled at him and called out *"Beau gosse!"* as she went by.

Now Alec high-stepped up the front stairs of Magnus's building and bounded up the four flights to the apartment, taking three steps at a time. He opened the front door of the apartment, calling, "Magnus?" He paused. "What the hell!"

Magnus was in the middle of the living room, floating knee-height off the ground, orbited by dozens of books and photographs. Three large walnut bookcases summoned from his Brooklyn loft, with most of their contents spilled on the floor, took up the right half of the room. One of the shelves was tilted on one corner and looked as if it was about to tip over and smash into the window. Plates of half-eaten pastries littered the table and chairs.

The entire room seemed to be immersed in black-and-white static, which blanketed it with an eerie, ghostly sheen. An occasional white flash would wash out the room. It seemed, Alec thought, hugely, obviously demonic in nature.

"Magnus, what's going on?"

The warlock's head swiveled around until his eyes settled on

Alec. They were glassy. He blinked and then brightened. "Alexander, you're back. How was your cardio?"

"It was fine," said Alec slowly. "Is everything all right?"

"Just doing some research. I was trying to figure out how and where and when I could possibly have a missing memory, especially one that covers the amount of time it would take to establish a demon-worshipping cult, so I decided to go through all the events in my life chronologically."

"That sounds like it might take a while," said Alec.

Magnus was talking rapidly, reveling in his investigation. Or maybe he had drunk too much coffee. Alec noticed three French presses and half a dozen coffee mugs floating among the debris.

Magnus had told him not to worry, but it appeared that Magnus himself was worrying a lot.

"You see," continued Magnus, "memories rarely stand alone. They are interconnected, created from other memories that give meaning to them. Each specific memory will help in producing even more, giving those new ones their meanings. It's like a giant spiderweb. If you make one specific memory disappear, you leave the other strands dangling."

Alec thought this over. "So all you have to do is find a piece of memory that leads to nothing."

"Exactly."

"But what if you just forgot something? You can't possibly remember every moment that's happened in your life."

"That's why I got help." He gestured at the objects in the air surrounding him. "I summoned my photo albums from Brooklyn. I've been going through any moments that could lead to the creation of the Crimson Hand, and then I've been magically imprinting the memories onto paper so I can properly catalog them."

Alec furrowed his brow. "So you're scrapbooking?"

Magnus made a face. "To the lay observer, what I'm doing might look similar, yes."

Alec looked at the photos as they floated by. One appeared to be of Magnus on a flying carpet over a desert. The next was of Magnus at a ball in Victorian clothes, waltzing with a coldly beautiful blond woman. Another showed Magnus with his arms around a handsome older man's shoulders. Alec leaned forward, squinting at it. He thought he could make out tears on Magnus's face.

Before his fingers could grasp the photo, it flittered away as if it were a leaf, somersaulting in the air.

"That one is sort of a private memory," Magnus said hastily.

Alec didn't press the issue. This wasn't the first time in their fledgling relationship that he'd bumped up against Magnus's past and his boyfriend had closed the door on him. Alec hated it, but he was trying to be understanding. They didn't know each other all that well yet, but they would. Everyone had secrets. Alec had kept secrets from those closest to him before. There were a lot of reasons Magnus might be holding back.

Alec wanted Magnus to be able to tell him everything. At the same time, he didn't know if he could handle what "everything" might be. He remembered the sick, scared feeling in his stomach when he'd asked whether Magnus and the beautiful brown-haired woman he was looking at so fondly used to be a couple. He'd been so relieved when Magnus and Tessa said they were just friends.

Maybe Alec would never have to meet any of Magnus's exes. Maybe he would never have to think about them. Ever. There might not be any in New York. They might all be dead, Alec told himself encouragingly, and then felt bad about that.

"Did you find what you were looking for?" he asked, doing his best to smooth over the momentary awkwardness.

"Not yet," said Magnus. "I'm just getting started."

Alec opened his mouth to volunteer to help, and then shut it again before he spoke. It was one thing to want Magnus to open up to him, but another to try to enter the swirl and ferment of centuries of memories, covering however many hundreds of people, dozens of homes, thousands of events.

"This will be a long, messy process," said Magnus gently. "Seize this opportunity to see a few of the Parisian sights, Alexander. Some of the minor churches. Or one of the smaller art museums."

"Okay," said Alec. "I'll be back in a little while to check in."

"Great!" said Magnus, and gave Alec a slight, sideways smile, as if to thank him for understanding.

So Alec spent most of the day taking in some of the more famous sights of the city. He knew Paris was known for its churches, so he decided to make a survey of some of the most famous. He started amid the throngs at Notre Dame and went on to the stunning stained glass of Sainte-Chapelle, the famously massive pipe organ at Saint-Eustache, the peaceful, shadowed hush of Saint-Sulpice. In the Église de la Madeleine, he gazed at its statue of Joan of Arc for much longer than he expected to. Joan stood prepared for battle, both hands on her sword, which she brandished upright, prepared to strike. Her face was tilted up at a sharp angle, as though whatever she faced down was much taller than her. It was a very Shadowhunter pose, though as far as he knew she hadn't been one. The determination and grit in her expression as she beheld some unseen monster, towering over her, was inspiring nonetheless. For all the beauty of rose windows and Corinthian columns he'd beheld that day, it was the expression on Joan's face that stayed with him for hours after.

In each church, he couldn't help but wonder where the stash of Nephilim weapons was hidden. In almost every church in the world, a Shadowhunter rune pointed the way to a cache of arms, available for their use in case of emergency. He could have asked any of the Shadowhunters of the Paris Enclave, of course, but he was keeping his and Magnus's presence in the city quiet. In Notre Dame he spent a few minutes examining the stone floors, looking for a rune he recognized, but he was beginning to attract looks—most visitors to Notre Dame spent their time there looking up, not down at the floor. He gave up; the place was massive, and the weapons cache could be anywhere.

Mostly he attracted no attention, but he had a terrible moment when among a crowd crossing the Pont des Arts he spotted two figures with familiar marks on their bare arms. He turned abruptly and walked the other way, taking the first turn into a narrow alley that he could. When he emerged after a few minutes, the unknown Shadowhunters were gone.

He stood on the crowded street for a moment, then, feeling very alone. He wasn't used to hiding from other Shadowhunters; they were his colleagues and allies, after all. It was an unusual, uncomfortable sensation. But with this cult business to sort out, he didn't want to cross paths with them. It wasn't that he didn't trust Magnus—he didn't believe for a second that Magnus was involved with the Crimson Hand right now. But might Magnus have been involved with them as a joke, a couple hundred years ago on a drunken night? That was closer to the realm of possibility. He wanted to call Magnus, but he didn't want to bother him in the middle of his research.

Walking on, he took out his phone and called home. A few seconds later he heard his sister's familiar voice. "Hey! How's Paris?"

A grin curved Alec's mouth. "Hi, Isabelle."

In the background, he heard a terrible crash and another voice. "Is that Alec? Give the phone to me!"

"What was that noise?" Alec asked, mildly alarmed.

"Oh, it's just Jace," Isabelle said dismissively. "Hands off, Jace! He called *me*."

"No, the sound like a thousand trash-can lids falling out of the sky."

"Oh, Jace was swinging a big ax on a chain when you called," Isabelle said. "Jace! Your ax is stuck in the wall. It's not important, Alec. Tell me about your trip! How is Magnus? And I don't mean his well-being."

Alec coughed.

"I mean, how are his skills, and I'm not talking about the magical ones," Isabelle clarified.

"Yes, I picked up on your meaning," said Alec dryly.

He did not exactly have an answer for Isabelle on that topic. When he and Magnus had been dating in New York, there had been several times when Alec really wanted to take things further, but he was scared off by the immensity of his feelings. They had kissed, they had fooled around a little. That was it, so far, and Magnus had never pushed. Then the war came, and after the war, Magnus asked him to go on vacation to Europe, and he said yes. Alec had presumed they both understood that meant he was ready to go anywhere and do anything with Magnus. He was over eighteen; he was an adult. He could make his own decisions.

Only Magnus had not made a move. Magnus was always so careful with Alec. Alec wished he was a little less careful, because Alec was not very good at conversations, especially awkward conversations about feelings—that is, all conversations about feelings—and he could not work out how to bring up the topic of going further. Alec had never even kissed anyone before Magnus. He knew Magnus must have a lot of experience. That made Alec even more nervous, but at the same time, kissing Magnus was the most fantastic feeling in the world. When they kissed, Alec's body moved naturally toward Magnus, getting as close as he could, in the instinctive way his body only otherwise moved when he was fighting. He hadn't known that it was possible for anything to feel so right or mean so much, and now they were in Paris together, alone, and anything could happen. It was exhilarating as well as terrifying.

Surely Magnus wanted to go further too. Didn't he?

Alec had thought something might happen on the night of the hot-air balloon, but Magnus had become understandably distracted by the demonic cult.

"Alec!" Isabelle shouted into the phone. "Are you still there?"

"Oh—right, sorry. Yes."

Her voice softened. "Is it awkward? I know the first vacation is the make-or-break time for a couple."

"What do you mean 'make-or-break time'? You've never gone on vacation with anyone!"

"I know, but Clary loaned me some mundane magazines," Isabelle said, her voice brightening. Clary and Isabelle's friendship had been hard-won, but Isabelle seemed to value it all the more for that. "The magazines say that the first trip is a crucial test for a couple's compatibility. It's when you truly get to know each other, and how you work together, and decide whether the relationship will work long-term."

Alec felt something drop in his stomach and quickly changed the subject. "How is Simon?"

It was a sign of Alec's desperation that he brought up Simon, since he did not much like the idea of his sister dating a vampire. Though for a vampire, he seemed like a good enough guy. Alec didn't know him that well. Simon talked a lot, mostly about things from the mundane world Alec had never heard of.

Isabelle laughed, a little too loudly. "Fine. I mean, I don't know. I see him occasionally, and he seems fine, but I don't care. You know how I am with boys; he's like a little toy. A little fanged toy."

Isabelle had dated plenty of people, but she never got defensive like this. Maybe that was what made Alec feel uneasy about Simon.

"Just so long as *you* don't become *his* chew toy," said Alec. "Listen, I need a favor."

Isabelle's tone went sharp. "Why are you using the voice?"

"What voice?"

"The 'I'm a Shadowhunter on official business' voice. Alec, you're on vacation. You're supposed to be having fun."

"I am having fun."

"I don't believe you."

"Are you going to help me or not?"

Isabelle laughed. "Of course I am. What are you and Magnus getting into?"

Alec had promised Magnus he wouldn't tell anyone, but surely Isabelle didn't count.

He turned away from the crowd and covered the phone with his free hand. "I need you to keep this quiet. Mom and Dad don't need to find out. I don't want Jace to know either."

There was a rustling on the phone. "Alec, are you in trouble? I can be in Alicante in half an hour and Paris in three."

"No, no, it's not like that."

Alec abruptly realized he had neglected to glamour himself undetectable, so that mundanes wouldn't overhear his conversation, but just as in New York, the crowds of Paris streamed by without paying the slightest attention to him. Cell phone conversations, no matter how public, were to be ignored; apparently this was a universal law. "Can you search through the Institute archives for a cult called the Crimson Hand?"

"Of course. Can you tell me why?"

"Nope."

"I'll see what I can do."

She didn't press him further. Isabelle never had pushed, not about any of Alec's secrets. That was one of the many reasons Alec trusted his sister.

On the other end of the line came the sounds of a scuffle. "Shove off, Jace!" Isabelle hissed.

"Actually," Alec said, "could I talk to Jace for a second?"

There was something he wanted to ask, and he did not feel comfortable talking about this stuff with his sister.

"Oh, fine," said Isabelle. "Here he is."

There was another rustle, and then Jace cleared his throat and said casually, as if he had not been fighting Isabelle for the phone a minute ago, "Hey."

Alec smiled. "Hey."

He could visualize Jace, who had asked Alec to be his *parabatai* and then always pretended as if he did not need one. Alec was not fooled.

Jace had lived in the New York Institute with them since Alec was eleven. Alec had always loved Jace, found him so familiar and so dear that for a while he'd been confused about what kind of love it was. Thinking of Jace now, he realized whom the warlock woman Tessa had reminded him of.

Her expression, serious but with a quiet light behind it, was exactly Jace's when he was playing the piano.

Alec shook off the strange thought.

"How's Paris?" asked Jace idly. "If you're not having fun, you could come back early."

"Paris is nice," said Alec. "How are things?"

"Well, my business is looking great and fighting demons, and business is good," said Jace.

"Cool. Um, Jace, can I ask you something? If you want something to happen, and you feel like it could but maybe the other person is waiting for you to give a signal that you're ready—that you're maybe ready—no, that you're definitely ready, maybe, what should you do? In this hypothetical scenario."

There was a pause.

"Hmm," said Jace. "Good question. I'm glad you came to me with this. I think you should go ahead and give a signal."

"Great," said Alec. "Yes, that's what I was wondering. Thanks, Jace."

"Hard to work out signals on the phone," Jace said thoughtfully. "I'll think about various signals and show you when you get home. Like, one signal is for 'there is a demon creeping up behind you and you should stab it,' right? But there should be a different signal for if a demon is creeping up behind you, but I have it in my sights. That just makes sense."

There was another silence.

"Put Isabelle back on the phone," said Alec.

"Wait, wait," said Jace. "When are you coming home?"

"Isabelle!" said Alec.

There were sounds of another scuffle as Isabelle repossessed her phone.

"Sure you don't want me to come help out? Or do you and Magnus prefer to be *alone*?"

"We prefer to be alone," he said firmly. "And actually, I should get back. Love you, Isabelle."

"Love you," said Isabelle. "Wait! Jace says he needs the phone back. He says he thinks he may have misunderstood your question."

MAGNUS WAS IN THE SAME POSITION HE'D BEEN IN WHEN Alec left. It seemed he hadn't moved at all, but the cyclone of paper, photos, and books that surrounded him was about twice as large and twice as messy. "Alec!" he said brightly, his mood seemingly much improved. "How is Paris?"

"If I were a Shadowhunter based in Paris," Alec said, "I would have to train twice as hard to make up for all the times I stopped for a coffee and a little something to eat."

"Paris," Magnus declared, "is the single greatest city on earth in which to stop for a coffee and a little something to eat."

"I brought you some *pain au chocolat*," Alec said, holding up a now slightly wilted white paper bag.

Magnus parted the wall of books and papers like a curtain and gestured Alec within. "I've found something," he said. "Come in." Alec went to put down the bag and Magnus shook his head. "Bring the *pain au chocolat* with you."

Alec took a hesitant step inside and stood next to Magnus. The warlock fished a pastry out of Alec's bag with one hand and beckoned at one of the frozen images with the other, drawing it down in front of them. It was an image of a glum, green-skinned, white-haired warlock wearing a potato sack, sitting at a wooden table filled with tin mugs.

That was Ragnor Fell, Alec thought. Magnus had his picture on the wall. Magnus had mentioned casually, several days after Ragnor's death, that he and the dead warlock had been friends. It was becoming very clear that they had been close. Alec wondered why Magnus had not said so when Ragnor died, but they had been in the middle of a war. Alec and Magnus had still been working out what they were to each other.

Magnus had not kept it from him, exactly.

Across the table from Ragnor Fell was a shirtless Magnus, who had both of his hands open, palms out. He seemed to be trying to enchant a bottle.

Magnus flipped his fingers and the photo wavered and then grew in size. He swallowed.

"I remember this night in detail. We were playing a drinking game. We had previously literally lost our shirts to several cheese-mongers who turned out to be gifted amateur cardsharps. Somewhere between the fourth and ninth pitcher of glögg, we got into a deep discussion about the meaning of life, or more specifically how much easier life would be if there was a way we could openly use our powers without mundanes always soiling themselves and trying to burn us at the stake every time they saw a little sparkle of magic."

"You and Ragnor thought creating a demon-worshipping cult would make your lives easier?" Alec asked in disbelief.

"The world is sometimes unkind to warlocks. Sometimes we feel a temptation to be unkind back."

There was a silence. Eventually, Magnus sighed.

"We weren't talking about summoning demons," he said. "We were talking about how hilarious it would be to impersonate a demon and get gullible mundanes to do stuff."

"What sort of stuff?"

"Whatever it was we wanted. Massage our feet, run naked through the village square, throw rotten eggs at members of the clergy. You know, normal things joke cults do."

"Sure," said Alec. "Normal things."

"I don't remember actually following through with it. One would think founding a cult would be memorable. In fact, I don't remember much of anything after that night. The next memory I have is almost three years later, heading to a vacation in South America. That was awfully strong glögg, but three years of amnesia seems excessive."

Magnus looked grim.

"The conversation plus the three years of memory loss does not look good for me. The conversation is very suspicious, and the memory loss is very convenient. I have to find the Crimson Hand immediately."

Alec nodded resolutely. "Where do we start?"

There was a long silence, as if Magnus was carefully considering his next words. He eyed Alec, almost as if he was wary of him. Did Magnus think Alec wouldn't be able to help?

"I'm going to start by reaching out to some sources in Downworld for information on the cult."

"What can I do? I can help you," Alec insisted.

"You always do," said Magnus. He cleared his throat and added, "I was thinking, it seems a shame to interrupt your first time in Paris with silly problems from my past and a bunch of delusional mundanes. You had a good time today, right? You should enjoy yourself. This shouldn't take long. I'll be back before you even get the chance to miss me."

"How could I possibly enjoy myself," Alec said, "if you were in trouble without me?"

Magnus was still giving him that strange, careful look. Alec did not understand anything that was happening.

"There's always the cabaret," Magnus murmured.

He smiled, but Alec did not smile back. This was not a joke. He thought of all the bright pictures flittering through the air and crossed his arms.

Alec had three close friends in the world: Isabelle, Jace, and their childhood friend Aline, who was actually more Isabelle's friend than his. He had known them all, and fought with them all, for years. He was used to being part of a team.

He wasn't used to liking someone so much but not knowing them inside out. He'd assumed that when Magnus fought by his side, it meant they were a team now. Alec didn't know what to do if Magnus didn't want to be a team, but he knew one thing.

"Magnus, I'm a Shadowhunter. Shutting down demons and their worshippers is part of the job. It's *most* of the job. More importantly, someone has to watch your back. You're not leaving me behind."

Alec suddenly felt very alone. He'd come on this trip to get to know Magnus better, but maybe it was impossible for him to know Magnus. Maybe Magnus didn't want to be known. Maybe he saw Alec as just a future one of those flying pictures, the fleeting moments that Magnus now had to struggle to recall.

Because Magnus wanted to keep this whole demon cult business *private*, and neither of them was sure, Alec suddenly realized, that *private* included Alec. What if Magnus really had done something terrible, hundreds of years ago? What if in the lost memories, Alec would find Magnus being foolish, or callous, or cruel?

Magnus leaned forward, serious for once. "If you come with me, you may not like what we find out. *I* may not like what we find out."

Alec relaxed a fraction. He couldn't imagine Magnus ever being cruel. "I'm willing to take the chance. So what's our move?"

"I want some names, a meeting place, and/or a copy of the Red Scrolls of Magic," said Magnus. "So I know exactly where to go. It's almost sundown—we'll make it to the Paris Shadow Market just about when it opens."

"I've never been to a Shadow Market," Alec remarked. "Is the Paris one especially glamorous and elegant?"

Magnus laughed. "Oh, no! It's a total dump."

CHAPTER FIVE

Shadow Market

"WELCOME," SAID MAGNUS, "TO THE ARÈNES DE LUTÈCE. It was a gladiatorial arena in classical Rome. It was a cemetery. It's Paris's sixty-eighth-most-popular tourist stop. And tonight, it's where your faerie aunt Martha comes to buy her monthly supply of illegal newt eyeballs."

They stood at the entrance to the Market, a narrow alley passing between ancient stone bleachers. To those without Sight, the alley spilled into a large depressed circle of sand, still very clearly denoting a gladiator's pit, empty but for a few stragglers. But for the denizens of the Market, it was a labyrinth of stalls crowded with Downworlders, a chaos of shouts and smells.

Even before they made their entrance they were under scrutiny. Alec knew it, and was jumpy and alert. A selkie sneaked an anxious side-eye at them as he passed, then not-so-subtly veered away.

Alec wore his leather jacket on top of his hoodie pulled low over his head, shielding his face. Soft leather gloves masked the runes on his hands. He wasn't fooling anyone. Alec would never pass as anything but a child of the Angel. It was obvious from his bearing, his grace, the look in his eyes.

Nephilim weren't prohibited from attending the Market, but neither were they welcome. Magnus was glad to have Alec beside him, but it did complicate things.

In the crush of people passing through the narrow alley to get into the Market proper, they had a moment of brief but intense claustrophobia. There was a smell like wet animals and stagnant water, and everyone was uncomfortably close. And then a burst of blinding light greeted their emergence into what the Market denizens called La Place des Ombres. The smells were of woodsmoke and spice, of incense, and of herbs drying in the sun. It was pleasantly familiar to Magnus, a constant through decades, centuries, of change.

"The Paris Shadow Market isn't like most other Shadow Markets. It's the oldest in the world and its history is political and bloody. Nearly every major conflict the Downworlders had with mundanes, Nephilim, or each other before the nineteenth century started right here." Magnus weighed his next words. "What I'm saying is, watch out."

As they began to pass down the first row of stalls, Magnus noticed that they created a bubble of tension around them as they moved. Downworlders were leaning together, whispering. Some shot them accusatory glares, and a few of the vendors actually pulled their curtains down or closed their windows as they approached.

Alec's brow was furrowed, his bearing stiff. Magnus stopped, made a show of reaching for Alec's hand, and clasped it tightly. A werewolf slammed his stall's window shut with a growl as they went by.

"Didn't want to shop there anyway," said Alec.

"Obviously not," said Magnus. "Nobody wants to eat at a place called Wolfsburger. Way to come across like a cannibal, guy."

Alec smiled, but Magnus suspected it was only for his own bene-fit. Alec's eyes continued to scan his surroundings, his vigilance a reflex trained into him his whole life. Magnus let his hand slip out of Alec's and let Alec drift a little away and back as they walked; he knew Alec was placing himself so as to have the best vantage point for situational awareness.

Magnus's first stop was a large red tent standing prominently in one of the main streets. The tent was long, tall, and narrow, divided into a front foyer area and a large main room in the back. To the left of the entrance was a sign of a wine bottle filled with red liquid, bearing the legend THE BLOOD IS THE LIFE. LIVE WELL.

Magnus pushed the red drapes to the side and poked his head into the back room, where he saw the world's first (and proba-bly only) blood sommelier sitting behind a curved mahogany desk. Peng Fang had the appearance of a young man in his midtwenties, his face broad and pleasant, with a mercurial air and twinkling eyes. A tuft of his black hair was dyed violent yellow, which made him resemble a friendly bee. His feet were up on the desk and he was humming a jaunty tune.

Magnus had known Peng Fang casually since the early 1700s, when blood transfusions started to be all the rage. Magnus admired an entrepreneur, and Peng Fang was that above all else. He'd spot-ted a gap in the market—also the Market—and he'd filled it.

"Why, the High Warlock of Brooklyn," said Peng Fang, a slow, delighted smile spreading across his face. "Just dropping in for a chat? Usually I'm intent on business, but with you, business would be a pleasure."

Peng Fang was flirty with everyone. He was so consistent that Magnus had occasionally wondered if his interest was genuine. Now, of course, it did not matter.

"Business, I'm afraid," Magnus said, with a shrug and a smile.

Peng Fang mirrored the shrug. He was already smiling, and

continued to do so. "I never turn down a chance at a profit. Looking for potion ingredients? I have a vial of Dragon demons' blood. One hundred percent fireproof."

"Sure, I constantly worry about whether my blood is going to catch on fire," said Magnus. "No blood today, actually. I need some information about the Crimson Hand."

"I've been hearing a lot about them lately," said Peng Fang, then looked over Magnus's shoulder and stopped talking. Magnus turned his head and saw Alec emerging uncertainly through the curtain. Peng Fang rose from his desk and regarded Alec coldly. "My apologies, Shadowhunter. As you can see, I am with a client. Perhaps if you return at a later time, I can be of service."

"He's with me," said Magnus. "Alexander Lightwood, this is Peng Fang."

Peng Fang narrowed his eyes. "Do not make comments about my name. Obviously, my parents did not expect their little boy to become a vampire when he grew up. I do not find comments about my name humorous."

Magnus decided not to mention at that moment that Peng Fang was known as Fang Fang among his friends. Peng Fang was clearly not interested in making friends with Alec. His gaze was fixed on Alec as though Alec might attack him at any moment. To be fair to Peng Fang, Alec's hand was resting casually on the hilt of the seraph blade at his side.

"Hi," said Alec. "I'm here with Magnus. I'm here *for* Magnus. No other Shadowhunters know I'm here. We just want to know about the Crimson Hand." After a brief silence he added, "It's important."

"What could I possibly know about them?" asked Peng Fang. "Let me assure you, Shadowhunter, I do not do business with cults. I am strictly aboveboard. A simple blood merchant, selling the finest legal and licensed blood to law-abiding Downworlders. If you are interested in purchasing blood, High Warlock, I will gladly advise you in your selection. Otherwise, I am afraid I can't help you."

"We hear they have a new leader," asked Alec.

"Don't know anything about him," said Peng Fang firmly.

"Him?" said Magnus. "Well, that's something." Peng Fang scowled. "You seemed willing to help a few moments ago."

The three stood at an impasse for several moments before Peng Fang sat back down at his desk and began shuffling papers.

"Yes, well, I can't have people saying I leaked information to Shadowhunters."

"We've known each other a long time," Magnus said. "If you trust me, you can trust him."

Peng Fang glanced up from his papers.

"I trust you. But that doesn't mean I'm going to trust Shadowhunters. Nobody trusts Shadowhunters."

After a moment, Alec said in a tight voice, "Come on, Magnus. Let's go."

Magnus tried to catch Peng Fang's eye as they exited. Peng Fang industriously studied his papers and ignored them. They regrouped back outside. Alec's arms were folded tightly over his chest and he restlessly watched the crowd pass. It looked like he was Peng Fang's bouncer.

"I apologize for that," Magnus said.

Magnus could not blame any Downworlder for being suspicious of a Shadowhunter. Nor could he blame Alec for feeling insulted.

"Look," Alec said. "This isn't going to work. Why don't you go on ahead. I'll keep out of sight and we can meet up once you've gotten some information."

Magnus nodded. "If you want to head back to the apartment—"

"That's not what I meant. I meant, you go ahead, and I'll keep out of sight and shadow you while you go through the Market. I won't step in unless you're in danger." Alec hesitated. "Or if you want me to go . . ."

"No," said Magnus. "I want you nearby."

Alec glanced around a little self-consciously, then pulled Magnus to him. The clatter and bustle of the Shadow Market faded to a faint, low-key mumble. The tight knot of frustration in Magnus's chest eased somewhat. His eyes shut. Everything was quiet, and still, and sweet.

"Get away from my stall!" yelled Peng Fang suddenly, and Magnus and Alec leaped away from one another. Magnus turned to see Peng Fang glaring through the flap of the tent. "Stop hugging Shadowhunters in front of my place of business! No one is going to buy blood from someone who has a Shadowhunter hugging booth in front of his stall! Go away!"

Alec began to melt into the crowd passing by. He extended his hand and trailed it along Magnus's arm as he disappeared. "I'll be close," he said, just loud enough for Magnus to hear. "I have your back."

He let go, and the outside world returned to Magnus in a rush. Alec was abruptly gone, blended into the background.

Magnus rolled up his bottle-green silk sleeves.

He tried to banish the uneasy feeling that had crept over him when Alec said, *This isn't going to work.*

For the next half hour, Magnus wandered among the warlocks and faeries of the Shadow Market, trying to buy information. Now that Alec wasn't around, he was able to blend in seamlessly. He tried to seem normal and carefree, and not under a cloud of suspicion or on a clock. He dropped by Les Changelings en Cage (a stall with anti-faerie charms run by a disgruntled warlock) and Le Tombeau des Loups (the Tomb of the Wolves, a stall selling anti-werewolf magics, obviously run by vampires). He petted various illicit and strange-looking creatures who he suspected would soon be potion ingredients.

He stopped several times to watch various magical demonstrations given by warlocks from faraway places, out of professional curiosity. He purchased rare spell ingredients that were available only in the Shadow Markets of Europe. He was going to be able to make a pack of werewolves in Mexico very happy by providing them with a potion that would restore their leader's lost sense of smell.

He even acquired some new business, for when this pesky cult matter was wrapped up, of course. A fishing fleet in Amsterdam was having trouble with a school of mermaids luring their sailors overboard. He would be in touch.

He did not, however, learn anything about the Crimson Hand.

Magnus occasionally glanced behind him, searching for Alec. He never spotted him.

It was during one of these occasional glances back that the feeling crept over Magnus, as it had on the walk after their balloon crash, that he was being watched by unfriendly eyes. There was a cold sense of threat, like bad weather coming.

He murmured a spell to alert him if undue attention was being paid to him and brushed his ears with his hands. He immediately felt a tickling sensation in his left lobe, light, as if brushed with a feather. Passing glances, nothing out of the ordinary. Maybe it was only Alec watching.

Magnus was passing a stall full of cloaks when he felt a stronger touch on his ear, two distinct flicks that nearly made him jump.

"Real selkie fur," said the stall owner hopefully. "Ethically sourced. Or how about this one? Fur from werewolves who wanted to be shaved for that sleek aerodynamic feeling."

"Lovely," said Magnus, passing on.

He turned down a side alley leading away from the main body of the market, and then again to a dead end. The flicking of his ear was still there, this time followed by a tug.

His hands lit with magic, and he spoke to the empty air. "I'm flattered, but perhaps it's best we drop the coyness and talk face-to-face."

No one answered.

Magnus waited a few beats before letting the flames die in his hands. He walked back to the entrance of the alley. No sooner had he stepped back into civilization than he felt a hard yank on his ear. Someone was staring at him very intently.

"Magnus Bane! I thought it was you."

Magnus turned toward the voice. "Johnny Rook! What are you doing in Paris?"

Johnny Rook was one of the rare mundanes who had the ability to see the Shadow World. He was usually based at the Los Angeles Shadow Market.

Magnus surveyed Johnny unenthusiastically. He wore a black trench coat and sunglasses (though it was night), with short Caesar-cut dirty blond hair and five o'clock scruff. There was something slightly off about his face: Magnus had heard a rumor that Johnny had hired faeries to permanently magically enhance his features, but if it was true, Magnus felt Johnny had wasted his money. The man was also known as Rook the Crook, and he was committed to his aesthetic.

"About to ask the same of you," said Johnny, avidly curious.

"Vacation," Magnus said noncommittally. "How is your son? Cat, is it?"

"Kit. He's a good boy. Growing like a sprout. Quick hands, very useful in my line of work."

"You have your child picking pockets?"

"Some of that. Some passing on trifles like keys. Some sleight of hand. All sorts. He's multitalented."

"Isn't he about ten years old?" Magnus asked.

Johnny shrugged. "He's very advanced."

"Clearly."

"Looking for anything special at the Market? Perhaps I can be of service."

Magnus closed his eyes and counted to five slowly. Against his better judgment he said casually, "What do you know about the Crimson Hand?"

Johnny rolled his eyes. "Culties. Worship Asmodeus."

Magnus's heart gave a hard, spiky thump. *"Asmodeus?"*

Johnny glanced at him sharply.

"Not a name you hear every day," Magnus added, hoping that was enough explanation.

It was a name Magnus had heard oftener than he liked. In what Magnus hoped was total coincidence, Asmodeus was the Prince of Hell who had fathered Magnus himself.

Would he really have set up a cult in the name of his father? They were not exactly close. He couldn't imagine having done so, even as a joke.

Would he have to tell Alec that Asmodeus was his father? Alec had never asked who Magnus's demon parent was and Magnus had no desire to tell him. Most warlocks were fathered or mothered by ordinary demons. It was Magnus's bad luck that his father was one of Hell's Nine Princes.

"Asmodeus?" he said again to Johnny. "Are you sure?"

Johnny shrugged. "I didn't think it was some big secret. That's just what I heard somewhere."

So it might not be true. There was no point telling Alec, Magnus thought, if it might not be true. Tessa hadn't mentioned it, and she certainly would have if she'd thought the cult worshiped Magnus's father.

Magnus breathed a little more freely. Alas, Johnny had a sly look on his face that Magnus knew all too well.

"I might know more," Johnny said casually.

Magnus snapped his fingers. A small yellow bubble shimmered up from his fingertips and expanded until it enveloped them. The background noise of the Shadow Market died, leaving the two of them in a sphere of complete silence.

Magnus sighed heavily. He'd been here before. "What's your price?"

"The information is yours for the low, low price of a small favor, owed by you, to me, to be determined in the future."

Johnny gave him a big, encouraging grin. Magnus regarded him with what he hoped was a patrician air.

"We all know where an unspecified favor ends," he said. "I made a vague promise to help someone once and spent seven months under an enchantment, living in a dryad's aquarium. I don't want to talk about it," he added quickly as Johnny started to speak. "No nonspecific favors owed!"

"Okay," said Johnny, "how about a specific favor, delivered now? You know of anything that would, say, divert the attention of the Nephilim away from something? Or someone?"

"You doing something the Nephilim wouldn't approve of?"

"Obviously yes," said Johnny, "but maybe more now than before."

"I can get you some ointment," said Magnus. "It discourages attention away from the person coated in it."

"Ointment?" said Johnny.

"It's an ointment, yes," said Magnus, a little impatient.

"You don't maybe have anything you can drink, or eat?"

"No," said Magnus. "It's an ointment. That's how it comes."

"I just hate being all greasy."

"Well, that's the price you pay, I guess," said Magnus, "for your constant criminal activities."

Johnny shrugged. "How much can I get?"

"I guess that depends on how much you know," said Magnus.

Magnus was surprised Johnny hadn't made a specific request; he usually tried to be in control of negotiations. For whatever reason, Johnny was desperate to get his hands on this stuff. It was not Magnus's business why. It wasn't a crime to avoid Shadowhunters.

Magnus had met many Shadowhunters he'd prefer to avoid. They weren't all as charming as Alec.

"My information says the Crimson Hand recently left their headquarters in Venice," said Magnus. "Any idea where they went?"

"No," said Johnny. "I do know that the Crimson Hand had a secret sanctum in the Venice headquarters where they kept their holy book. It's called the Chamber." Johnny's smile got wider and toothier. "There's a secret password to get inside. I'll give it to you for ten bottles of the potion."

"It's an ointment."

"Ten bottles of the ointment."

"One."

"Three."

"Done." They shook hands. That was how you did business.

"Okay. You find the stone head of the goat, and speak the word 'Asmodeus.'"

One of Magnus's eyebrows rose. "The password to get into the lair of the Asmodeus-worshipping cult is 'Asmodeus'?"

"I don't know if you've noticed this," Johnny said thoughtfully, "but cultists aren't usually the brightest the mundane world has to offer."

"I have noticed that," said Magnus. "I also need to know—who's your source?"

"I never said I would tell you that!" said Johnny.

"But you will," said Magnus, "because you want three jars of ointment, and because you are compulsively disloyal."

Johnny hesitated, but only for a moment. "Warlock called Mori Shu. He's a former member of the Crimson Hand."

"What's a warlock doing in a mundane cult? He should know better."

"Who knows? Word is, he offended the new leader and he's on the run, looking for protection. He'd know more about the Crimson Hand than anyone who isn't still in it. He was in Paris not long ago, but I hear he's headed to Venice now. He'd tell you anything, if you helped him out."

Just when the Crimson Hand was leaving Venice, Mori Shu was headed there.

"Thanks, Johnny. I'll have the ointment sent to you in L.A. right when I get back from vacation."

The yellow bubble began to dissolve into gold flakes that drifted glitteringly into the breeze. As it went, Johnny grabbed hold of Magnus's sleeve and hissed with unexpected intensity: "There have been a lot of faerie disappearances in Shadow Markets lately. Everybody's on edge. People are saying the Crimson Hand is responsible. I hate the idea of people hunting down faeries. Stop them." There was a look on Johnny's face Magnus couldn't remember seeing before, a mix of anger and fear.

Then the cacophony of the Paris Shadow Market returned in a rush.

"Now," Magnus murmured. "Where is Alec?"

"That your Shadowhunter?" Johnny said, grinning wickedly, all hint of his previous expression gone. "You do know how to make a stir in a public place, my friend."

"We're not friends, Johnny," said Magnus absently, scanning the crowd. Johnny barked a laugh.

Alec appeared like a rabbit from a hat, out from behind the corner of a nearby stall. He looked as though he had been rolling in the mud.

"Your Shadowhunter is filthy," observed Johnny.

"Well, he cleans up nice," said Magnus.

"I'm sure he's a real special dreamboat, but by a total coincidence, I have an urgent appointment elsewhere. Until next time, High Warlock."

Johnny threw him a casual salute and vanished into the crowd.

Magnus let him go. He was more concerned with the state of his boyfriend. He looked Alec up and down, taking in the mud caked over his clothes and liberally sprinkled in his black hair. Alec was carrying his bow close to his body, and his chest was rising and falling hard.

"Hey, honey," said Magnus. "What's new?"

CHAPTER SIX

Clash by Night

FIVE MINUTES AFTER LEAVING MAGNUS'S SIDE, ALEC watched Magnus put his hand into a cage of sharp-clawed, poisonous, demonic monkeys. Alec gripped his seraph blade lightly but held back.

He was in the Shadow Market. The rules were different here. He knew that.

Fortunately, Magnus only patted one snarling creature with a careless ringed hand, then backed away from that stall and toward another that was being picketed by disgruntled werewolves.

"Stop the oppression of werewolves by the undead!" said one werewolf woman, waving a DOWNWORLDER UNITY sign. Magnus took a pamphlet and gave the werewolf a smile, leaving her dazzled. Magnus had that effect on people. Alec recalled how the vampire blood merchant had looked at Magnus earlier. Before Alec met Magnus he used to sneak nervous glances at guys sometimes: at Jace, or Shadowhunters visiting the Institute, or mundanes in the busy New York streets. Now when Magnus was in a room, it was difficult for Alec to notice anybody but him. Did Magnus still notice men were handsome, or think women were beautiful? Alec felt a sharp prickle of nerves at the thought of how many people might be delighted if Alec did fail this relationship test.

Alec pulled his hoodie a little lower and followed at a distance.

Magnus then turned into an apothecary and began to shop for herbs. After that, he stopped and talked to a violet-haired faerie asking for gold to feed his pet basilisk. Next he went to the opposite stall and spent what felt like an hour haggling for what looked suspiciously like human hair.

Alec trusted that Magnus knew what he was doing. Magnus exuded confidence with such little effort. He seemed always in control of every situation, even when he wasn't. It was one of the things Alec admired most about him.

Alec crept down the adjacent street when Magnus went on the move again. He was far enough back not to arouse suspicion, but only five bounding steps away. He watched not only his boyfriend but everyone around him, from the group of dryads trying to lure Magnus to their tent to the scrawny young pickpocket with a crown of thorns on her head, not-so-innocently trailing Magnus.

When the girl made her move, Alec did as well, catching her sticky fingers just before they slid into Magnus's pocket. Alec swooped in and yanked her in between two stalls so quickly no one noticed.

The faerie girl twisted away from him so violently that one of his gloves slipped off, and she saw his runes. The pale green flush drained out of her skin, leaving her gray.

"Je suis désolée," she whispered, and on Alec's look of incomprehension: "I'm sorry. Please don't hurt me. I promise I won't do it again."

The girl was so thin Alec could encircle her wrist with his thumb and forefinger. Faeries were seldom the age they appeared, but she looked as young as his brother, Max, who had been killed in the war. *Shadowhunters are warriors,* his father said. *We lose, and we fight on.*

Max had been too young to fight. He would never learn now.

Alec always worried about his sister and his *parabatai*, who were both reckless and fearless. He had always been so desperate to protect them. It had never occurred to him that he had to be on guard to shield Max. He had failed his little brother.

Max had been almost as skinny. He used to stare up at him, just as this girl was doing, his eyes big behind his glasses.

Alec struggled to breathe for an instant and looked away. The girl did not try to seize this opportunity to slip from his slackened grasp. When he glanced back at her, she was still staring at him.

"Um, Shadowhunter?" she asked. "Are you all right?"

Alec shook himself out of the daze. *Shadowhunters fight on,* his father's voice said in his head.

"I'm fine," he told the girl, his own voice a little hoarse. "What's your name?"

"Rose," she said.

"Are you hungry, Rose?"

The girl's lip trembled. She tried to run away, but he grabbed her shirt. She slapped his arm and seemed to be about to bite him when she saw the fistful of euros in his hand.

Alec handed them to her. "Go buy some food." No sooner had he opened his palm than the euros disappeared. She did not thank him, only nodded and scampered away. "And stop stealing," he called after her.

Now he was out of the money he'd brought with him. As he'd left the New York Institute, duffel bag slung over his shoulder, to begin this trip, his mother had chased him out and pressed money into his hands, even though he'd tried to refuse it.

"Go be happy," she had said.

Alec wondered whether he'd been scammed by the faerie girl. She might be hundreds of years old, and faeries were well-known for their love of scamming mortals. But he decided to believe that she was what she seemed—a scared, hungry kid—and it made him feel happy to have helped. So the money was well spent.

His father had not liked it when Alec announced he was leaving the Institute to go on a trip with Magnus.

"What has he told you about us?" Robert Lightwood had asked, pacing Alec's room like a distressed cat.

His parents had once been followers of Valentine, the evil Shadowhunter who had started the recent war. Alec imagined Magnus could tell him some stories about them if he wanted.

"Nothing," Alec had replied angrily. "He's not like that."

"And what has he told you about himself?" Robert asked. When Alec was silent, Robert added, "Nothing as well, I imagine."

Alec did not know what expression he wore in that moment, how afraid he might have looked, but his father's face softened.

"Look, son, you can't think there's any future in this," he said. "Not with a Downworlder, or a man. I—I understand you feel like you have to be true to yourself, but sometimes it's best to be wise and take a different path even if you feel—feel tempted. I don't want your life to be more difficult than it has to be. You're so young, and you don't know what the world is really like. I don't want you to be unhappy."

Alec stared at him.

"What about lying is supposed to make me so happy? I wasn't happy before. I'm happy now."

"How can you be?"

"Telling the truth makes me happy," Alec said. "Magnus makes me happy. I don't care if it's difficult."

There had been so much sorrow and worry on his father's face. Alec had been scared his whole life of putting that expression on his face. He'd tried so hard to avoid it.

"Alec," his father had whispered. "I don't want you to go."

"Dad," Alec had said. "I'm going."

A reflex response interrupted his time within his memories, as his eyes caught Magnus's red velvet blazer flash by in the distance. Alec returned to himself and hurried in the direction he'd seen the jacket go.

When he caught up, he saw Magnus turning into a dark alley behind a row of stalls, and then a figure in a cloak appeared from a hiding place and carefully followed Magnus down the alley.

Alec did not have time to slowly follow; he'd already lost sight of Magnus and would soon lose sight of the cloaked figure as well. He broke into a run, squeezing in between a vampire and a peri locked in an embrace and pushing aside a group of werewolves rolling sticks. He reached the entrance of the alley and pressed his back against the wall. He peered around the corner and saw the figure halfway down the alley, headed for Magnus's unprotected back.

He nocked an arrow onto his bow and swung inside the alley.

He spoke, just loud enough for his voice to carry.

"Don't move. Turn around slowly."

The cloaked figure froze, its hands slowly reaching outward as if to comply with his orders. Alec inched closer, moving to his left to get a better view of the person's face. He just caught a glimpse of a narrow chin—human, a woman, by the looks of it, with a sandy complexion—when she whirled toward him, her fingers outstretched. Alec staggered backward as a bright flash slammed into him, obscuring his vision with white static, save for the woman's shadow, a dark stamp superimposed on the dazzling light. He loosed the arrow blind, trusting his training to keep his aim steady. The arrow leaped from his bow and was about to hit its mark when she somehow blurred out of its path. "Blurring" was the only way to describe it. One moment his arrow was flying toward her, the next her silhouette had twisted and stretched and she was standing at the opposite wall of the alley.

The woman blurred again, appearing right next to him. Alec leaped away, barely avoiding the slashing blade of a sword. He blocked another attack with his bow. *Adamas*-treated wood clattered against metal and Alec, still half-blind, swung his bow low and hooked his assailant's ankles, sweeping her off her feet. He raised his bow high in the air and was about to bring it down on her head when she blurred away again, this time reappearing at the entrance to the alley.

A gust howled past behind her and whipped her cloak sideways. Part of her hood flapped back, revealing the left half of her face under the light of the lamppost. A woman with deep brown eyes and thin lips. Straight shoulder-length black hair fell down the side of her face and curved around her chin. The blade she carried was a Korean *samgakdo*, three-sided, the kind designed to inflict irreparable damage on human flesh.

Alec squinted. Her face looked completely human, but there was something peculiar about it. It was her expression; there was a strange blankness to it, as if she were always gazing off into a faraway place.

A screech of metal grinding against brick pierced the air behind him. Alec's attention flickered for an instant.

The mystery woman took advantage of this slight distraction. She twirled her sword over her head while calling out words in a language Alec didn't understand, and then pointed it at him. Orange spiraling light shot from its tip, and then the ground at his feet erupted, nearly knocking him over. Alec dove away, pulled another arrow out of his quiver, and nocked it. He brought his aim up to where she had last stood, but she was gone.

Alec swept the bow across the entrance of the alley and then caught sight of his target crouching on the lip of a building ledge. He loosed the arrow and was on the move, bursting out of the alleyway almost as fast as the arrow could fly. The woman blurred and reappeared on a higher ledge of the same building. The arrow clanged against the stone. The cloaked woman jumped, rolling gracefully across the roof of a stall, and she came up running. She began to bound across the tops of the stalls.

Alec gave chase, sprinting down the path behind those stalls, jumping over garbage bags and bins of goods, ropes and stakes and crates. The woman was fast, but Alec's speed drew from the power of angels. He was gaining.

The woman reached a dead end at the edge of the Market and blurred to the ground. She began to call out more demonic language, and the air before her shimmered and tore. The outlines of a rough Portal began to emerge.

Alec drew an arrow and held it between his fingers. He lunged at her and she turned toward him, expecting an attack. Instead the sharp edge of the arrow pierced her cloak, pinning her to the side of a Market stall.

"Got you." Alec drew his bow fast, another arrow pointing dead center at her.

The woman shook her head. "I don't think you do."

He kept his eyes trained on her weapon. This was his mistake. Light blasted from her other hand and Alec felt himself flying, flailing, falling. He saw the wall barreling straight at him and twisted his body so his feet struck first. He flipped forward, landing in a crouch in the mud.

He shot up, his bow miraculously not broken, and he reflexively moved to bring it back into position. The woman—the *warlock*— had disappeared. All that was left were the remnants of the Portal as it closed and blinked out of existence. Alec kept his bow drawn as he pivoted in a full circle. It was only after he was sure she was gone that he let his guard down.

This woman was a warlock, but also a trained fighter. She was a serious threat.

"Magnus," Alec breathed. It suddenly occurred to him that there was no guarantee the warlock was working alone. What if she had been trying to lure him away from Magnus? He backtracked to the alley, barreling through the narrow path, not bothering to hurdle any of the things in his way as he uprooted stakes and collapsed tents. Outraged shouts from the people of the Shadow Market followed him as he went.

Thank the Angel, Magnus looked perfectly safe, having emerged at the other end of the alley without noticing anything, and having made his way to an unobtrusive corner nearby, where he stood talking to a disreputable-looking mundane wearing a trench coat and sunglasses. As soon as the man caught sight of Alec, he startled and bolted away. Alec understood that Downworlders and Shadowhunters didn't always get along, but he was beginning to take the Shadow Market's attitude personally.

Magnus beamed at Alec and waved him over. Alec felt his own stern expression soften. He worried too much. But there always seemed a lot to worry about. Demon attacks. Trying to protect the people he loved from demon attacks. Strangers trying to make conversation with him. Sometimes all the thoughts seemed to press down on his shoulders, an invisible burden that Alec could hardly bear, one that couldn't be laid down.

Magnus stood with his hand reached out to Alec. His jeweled rings gleamed, and he looked for a moment wild and strange, but then he smiled tenderly. Alec's affection, and feeling of sheer luck that he'd earned Magnus's affection back, overwhelmed him.

"Hey, honey," said Magnus, and it was a little marvelous that he meant Alec. "What's new?"

"Well," said Alec, "someone was following you. I chased her off. She was a warlock. A warlock pretty ready for a fight, too."

Magnus asked, "Someone from the Crimson Hand?"

"I'm not sure," said Alec. "Wouldn't they send more than one person, if they have a whole cult?"

Magnus paused. "Usually, yes."

"Did you find what you were looking for?"

"Sort of." Magnus linked elbows with Alec, careless of the mud on Alec's clothes, and pulled him along. "I'll tell you every detail when we get home, but the main thing is we're off to Venice."

"I was kind of hoping," said Alec, "that we could rest. And go to Venice tomorrow."

"Yes, yes," said Magnus. "We'll sleep in, and then it will take me ages to pack, so we'll leave tomorrow evening and be there by the morning."

"Magnus." Alec laughed. "Is this a dangerous mission or are we still on vacation?"

"Well, I'm hoping a little bit of both," Magnus said. "Venice is especially beautiful this time of year. What am I saying? Venice is especially beautiful any time of year."

"*Magnus,*" Alec said again. "We're leaving in the evening and getting there in the morning? Aren't we taking a Portal?"

"We are not," said Magnus. "The Crimson Hand is tracking Portal use, according to Tessa. We will have to rough it like mundanes do, and take the fanciest, most luxurious train available on a romantic overnight through the Alps. You see the sacrifices I am willing to make for the sake of safety."

"Shadowhunters would just use the permanent Portals in Idris to transfer through," Alec pointed out.

"Shadowhunters have to worry about justifying their expenses to the Clave. I do not. Get ready. No mission is so dangerous it isn't worth doing in *style.*"

CHAPTER SEVEN

The Orient Express

THEY SLEPT IN, AND THEN IT TOOK MOST OF THE DAY for Magnus to pack.

Magnus summoned some extra clothes for Alec from one of his favorite boutiques "for unforeseen emergencies." Alec protested that he didn't want anything too fancy, but Magnus couldn't be stopped from summoning him several beautiful sweaters without any holes in them, as well as a tuxedo he promised Alec was absolutely necessary. Breakfast came from the bakery down the street; lunch came from the *traiteur* the other way on the same street.

Finally, they took an unromantic but practical taxi to the Gare de l'Est, where he had the enjoyable experience of seeing Alec's eyes widen as the luxurious blue-and-white train cars of the Orient Express pulled up, coming to a stop with a long, pronounced hiss. Several liveried men and women spilled out and began to assist the waiting passengers with their luggage.

Alec fiddled with the retractable handle of the rolling garment bag Magnus had made him organize his things into. He'd watched Alec stuff a shapeless duffel bag with wadded-up laundry until he had been seized by a great madness, had summoned several very nice pieces of luggage from his own matched purple set, and had stood watchful while Alec packed them carefully with his nicest and most appropriate outfits.

Now Alec set his own bag down and came over to Magnus. He squared his shoulders and prepared to heft Magnus's largest suitcase up onto the steps of the train.

"No, no," said Magnus. He kept the tip of his hand gently on the top of the lead bag and looked around with an expression of polite befuddlement. Soon, one of the handsomely dressed porters appeared, held out his hand for Magnus to provide him with their tickets, and took control of the entire luggage situation. Magnus felt mildly guilty when the young man grunted in surprise, straining to carry the bags up the steps, but generous tipping would make up for a lot.

They were escorted down the length of a richly detailed sleeper car. The plush carpeting, mahogany-accented walls, and ornate bass railings and fixtures reminded Magnus of the years he had spent with Camille Belcourt, his vampire paramour.

Camille. When their relationship ended, the Orient Express train hadn't even started running yet. Now it was a tourist's throwback—still luxe, still comfortable, but hearkening back self-consciously to an era that for almost everyone alive today was the almost unimaginably olden days.

Magnus returned himself to the present moment. For Alec, the Orient Express wasn't a nostalgic throwback or a distant fond memory, but an adventure in the present moment, an adventure of grand meals taken among a forest of snowcapped mountains, an adventure of sleeping in a comfortable bed while still feeling the rhythmic, regular thump of the train over the track.

They reached their assigned cabin in the corner near the end of the sleeper car. True to his word, Magnus had sprung for the fanciest option available, a large suite with a sitting room in front and a bedroom behind. In between the two rooms was a small bathroom with a shower surrounded by glass walls. Lacquered rosewood walls and Turkish accents gave the whole suite a decadent feel. Magnus deeply approved.

"Our grand suites are all decorated in the style of cities along our route," the porter said, still struggling to carry Magnus's luggage inside. "This one is Istanbul."

Magnus gave him the generous tip he deserved for his efforts, then closed the door behind him and spun to face Alec, just as the train jolted into movement around them. "What do you think?"

Alec smiled. "Why Istanbul?"

"The Paris suite and the Venice suite seemed silly. We've had a lot of Paris and we're just about to have a lot of Venice. So, Istanbul."

They sat on the couch in the sitting room and watched the scenery go by. The train was picking up speed. Within minutes, it was out of the station and slipping out of Paris. The cityscape gave way to residential neighborhoods until finally they were speeding through rolling green hills and soft fields of dying lavender in the French countryside.

"This is . . ." Alec gestured at their surroundings. "This is . . ." He blinked, unable to find words.

"Isn't it great? So let's get dressed and go get dinner. We can explore the rest of the train too."

"Yes," said Alec, still struck mostly dumb. "Dinner. Yes. Good. What do you wear to dinner on this kind of train?" He leaned over the garment bag as Magnus began unfolding it. "Can I get away with just a nice jacket and jeans?"

"Alec," Magnus admonished him. "This is the Orient Express. You wear a tuxedo."

Where tuxedos were concerned, Magnus had learned over decades to be a purist. Trends came and went. And he loved bright colors and showiness, it was true. But the dinner jackets he had brought for himself and Alec were black, with grosgrain peak lapels and a two-button front.

The bow ties were black. Alec had no idea how to tie one. "Where would I have ever needed to wear a bow tie before in my life?" said Alec. Magnus conceded the point and tied Alec's for him, without the teasing that they both understood at some level that Alec deserved.

The secret of the tuxedo, Magnus knew from many decades of experience, was that every man looked good in a tuxedo. If you were already a very attractive man, like Alec, you would look very, very good in a tuxedo. Magnus briefly allowed himself a moment of reverie to simply take in the sight of Alec in black tie, fiddling with the studs in his shirt. Alec caught his eye and a slow, shy smile emerged as he realized Magnus had been looking.

Alec owned no cuff links, of course. Magnus had so many ideas for cuff links to buy Alec in the future, but on short notice he'd found a pair of his own with a bow-and-arrow motif, and now provided them to Alec with a flourish.

"What about you?" said Alec, doing up his cuffs.

Magnus went back into the garment bag and withdrew two enormous square-cut amethysts, set in gold. Alec laughed.

They left their cabin and were about to join the throng of like-minded mundanes heading toward the restaurant car, when a giddy nymph rushed past them toward the rear of the train. A moment later, a small group of visibly drunk sprites pushed their way past Alec, heading in the same direction.

Alec tapped Magnus on the shoulder. "Where do you think all the Downworlders are going?"

Magnus looked over just in time to see two werewolves enter the next car. When they opened the door, loud singing streamed out. Magnus was hungry, but distractible. "Sounds like a party. Let us follow the siren song."

They followed the Downworlders and poked their heads into the back bar, in the last car of the train, which indeed seemed to be hosting a party in full swing. The decor reminded Magnus of the speakeasy he'd owned during Prohibition. A full-size bar counter hugged the right side, and plush purple sectional sofas occupied the other. In the center of the car, a grand piano was being played by a dapper-looking man with a beard and goat legs. A siren wearing a dress made from swirling water lounged on top of it, entertaining the audience.

A group of brownies huddled in the corner, one of them strumming a twisted instrument that looked like a lute carved out of a branch. Two phoukas were smoking pipes near the window, admiring the landscape. A purple-skinned warlock was playing dice with some goblins. Above the bar was a sign reading NO BITING. NO FIGHTING. NO MAGIC.

The mood in the car was festive, relaxed. Despite the sheer number of Downworlders, they all seemed to know each other.

"Where are you headed?" Magnus asked a goblin.

"To Venice!" said the goblin. A bunch of other goblins in various parts of the car yelled, "To Venice!" back. He hoisted his mug, which hissed and foamed alarmingly. "To the party!"

"What party?" asked Magnus as the goblin clocked Alec behind him.

"No, no," the goblin said. "No party. I'm seven hundred years old. I get confused."

Alec had clocked the goblin right back. "Maybe," he said quietly into Magnus's ear, "we should go to the restaurant."

Magnus was relieved and embarrassed and annoyed and grateful, all at once. "I think that's an excellent idea."

Once the door was safely closed between them and the bar car, Alec said, "Are there always this many Downworlders on trains?"

"Not usually," Magnus said. "Not unless they're going to some big Downworlder party in Venice that no one thought to tell me about. Which they are, in this case."

Alec didn't say anything. Neither of them mentioned that without Alec, Magnus would be on his way to that party right now. Magnus wanted to tell Alec that he didn't care about a party, that he was happier to have dinner with Alec, because Alec mattered and some party didn't, really.

They passed two more lounge cars—a champagne car and a viewing car—before reaching the restaurant car. A host met them at the entrance and escorted them to an elegantly draped booth in the corner. A small brass chandelier above them bathed the table in a warm yellow glow, and the table was set with an intimidating number of different forks, spoons, and knives at various orientations to the plates.

Magnus ordered a bottle of Barolo and swished the drink as they admired the scenery rolling by outside their window. Dinner was Noirmoutier lobster, oven-baked with a drizzle of butter and lemon juice. There was a plate of caviar-laden potatoes served on the side.

Alec was dubious of the caviar. Then he looked embarrassed about being dubious of the caviar. "I just always assumed people ate it because it was expensive."

"No," said Magnus, "they eat it because it's expensive and delicious. But it's complicated. You have to eat it slowly, really experience the subtlety and the complexity." He took a piece of potato, topped it with sour cream and a healthy dollop of caviar, and popped it into his mouth. He chewed slowly and deliberately, eyes closed.

When he opened his eyes again, Alec was gazing intently at him, nodding thoughtfully. Then his expression broke into laughter.

"It's not funny," said Magnus. "Here, I'll make you one." He assembled another potato and fed it to Alec from his fork.

Alec copied Magnus's performance, chewing with great exaggerated movements and rolling his eyes back in his head in mock ecstasy. Magnus waited.

Finally, Alec swallowed and opened his eyes. "It really is good, actually."

"See?"

"Do I have to do the eye-rolling every time?"

"It's better with the eye-rolling. Wait—look."

Alec gave a gratifying, wondering, "Oh," as the train emerged around a bend into the heart of the French countryside. Dense, dark green forest framed mirrored lakes, and in the distance, white snowcapped mountains watched over the landscape. Closer, a rocky promontory rose like the prow of a ship from the distinctive tidy grid of bright vineyards below.

Magnus watched the landscape, then Alec's face, then the landscape again. Seeing this with him was like seeing the world made new. Magnus had been through the Parc du Morvan before, but for the first time in a long while, he felt wonder too.

"At some point," said Alec, "we'll cross the Idris wards, and the whole train will jump from the near border to the far border in an instant. I wonder if we'll be able to tell."

There was a yearning note to his voice, though Alec had not lived in Idris since he was small. The Nephilim always had some-place they could return to, no matter what, a country of enchanted forests and rolling fields, and in its center, a city of shining glass towers. Given by the Angel. Magnus was a man with no homeland, and had been for longer than he could remember. Odd, to see the compass of Alec's soul swing around surely and point home. The compass of Magnus's soul spun freely within him, and he'd long been used to that.

Their hands lingered together, Magnus's fingers curling around Alec's as they looked out at heavy clouds rolling in from the east.

Magnus pointed at one of the clusters of storm clouds. "That long one looks like a serpent that tied itself into a knot. That looks like the croissant I had this morning. That one . . . a llama, I guess? Or possibly my dad? Bye, Dad! Hope not to see you soon!" He blew a sarcastic kiss.

"Is this like the thing with the stars?" said Alec. "It's romantic to name the stuff you see in the sky?"

Magnus was silent.

"You can talk about him if you want," said Alec.

"My father the demon, or my stepfather who tried to kill me?" Magnus asked.

"Either."

"I don't want to put us off our lobster," said Magnus. "I try not to think about either of them." He seldom mentioned his father, but after Johnny Rook's information, Magnus couldn't get him off his mind. He kept considering what it might mean for his father to be the demon worshipped by the Crimson Hand.

"I was thinking about my dad yesterday," Alec offered hesitantly. "He told me I should stay in New York and pretend I was straight. That's what he meant, anyway."

Magnus remembered one long, cold night, in which he had to stand between a family of terrified werewolves and a group of Shadowhunters, Alec's father and mother among them. There was so much hate and fear in the world, even among those chosen by the Angel. He looked into Alec's face and saw the doubt and fear Alec's father had put there.

"You don't talk about your parents much," said Magnus.

Alec hesitated. "I don't want you to think badly of my dad. I know he's done things in the past . . . that he was involved in stuff he's not proud of."

"I've done things I'm not proud of myself," Magnus murmured, not trusting himself to say more. In truth, Magnus did not like Robert Lightwood, and never had. In any other universe, he would have thought it was impossible to start.

But in this universe, they both loved Alec. Sometimes, love worked, past any hope of change, when no other force in this world could. Without love, the miracle never came.

Magnus lifted Alec's hand to his mouth and kissed it.

Robert couldn't be a complete monster. He'd raised this man as his son, after all.

They finished their dinner in companionable silence, pausing to watch the sun set the mountains in the distance on fire as it dipped below their peaks. The first of the stars began to pierce the darkening sky.

The server came and asked if they wanted dessert, or perhaps a digestif.

Magnus was about to ask about the options available when Alec, a small gleam in his eye, gave the man a bright smile.

"Actually," he said, "I think we're going to have some of the champagne waiting in our stateroom. Shall we, Magnus?"

Magnus had actually frozen with his mouth hanging a little open. He was used to two very distinct Alecs: the confident Shadowhunter, and the shy, uncertain boyfriend. He wasn't sure about the Alec with the gleam in his eye.

Alec stood and held out his hand to draw Magnus out of his chair. He gave Magnus a little peck on the cheek and kept his hand.

The server gave a sideways polite nod and a small understanding smile. "Indeed. I bid you both *bonne nuit*, then."

As soon as they reached their cabin, Alec shucked off his jacket and headed for the bed. Magnus felt a flutter deep in his chest—there wasn't much sexier than a man in a tuxedo shirt, and Alec filled his out exceptionally well.

Silently thanking the Angel Raziel for all the cardio Shadowhunters had to do, Magnus conjured up a chilled bottle of Pol Roger and placed it on the counter. He raised two glasses and smiled as they filled on their own, leaving the cork intact in the bottle even as the level of champagne lowered. He joined Alec on the bed, offering him a glass. Alec accepted.

"To being together," said Magnus. "Anywhere we want."

"I like being together," said Alec. "Anywhere we want."

"Santé," said Magnus. They clinked and sipped, Alec looking at Magnus over the rim of the glass with that gleam in his eye. Magnus could no more resist Alec with that look than he could resist mischief, adventure, or a beautifully cut coat. He leaned forward, pressing his lips to Alec's, which were full and soft. A deep shiver went through Magnus. He could taste the crisp, tart wine in Alec's mouth as he swept his tongue over Alec's lower lip. Alec gasped and opened his mouth to Magnus's exploration. He looped his arm around Magnus's neck, his hand still gripping the champagne glass, arching his body up so the stiff pleats of their tuxedo shirts scratched together.

Blue fire sparked, and the champagne glasses were suddenly on the nightstand next to the bed. "Oh, thank the Angel," said Alec, and pulled Magnus down on top of him.

It was bliss. Alec's lean arms were around Magnus, his kisses firm and deep and bone-melting. Alec's strong body held Magnus's weight with no effort at all.

Magnus relaxed, sinking deeper into the long, slow kisses, into the feel of Alec's hands in his hair. They were still kissing as the train's smooth glide hitched, and the carriage jerked, hard. Magnus tumbled aside and found himself on his back. The champagne flutes had flown off the nightstand onto the bed, spilling sparkling wine over both of them. He glanced over and found Alec blinking champagne out of his eyelashes.

"Be careful," said Alec, grasping Magnus's arms and hauling him out of bed.

The sheet was soaked, and Magnus had fallen onto a glass, crushing it. Magnus realized that Alec had been concerned Magnus might be cut. He hesitated, caught more off guard by the concern than by broken glass.

"I should call to have the sheets changed," said Magnus. "We could go to the viewing car to wait . . . ?"

"I don't care," Alec said, uncharacteristically sharp. After a moment he calmed. "I mean—yes. That would be fine. Nice."

Magnus reviewed the situation, and decided that as often happened, the solution was magic. He waved his fingers and the bed changed itself, sheets fluttering in the air amid a shower of blue sparks, then settling down so the bed was again a smooth stretch of snowy white.

Alec was taken aback by the sheets and pillows suddenly becoming a disarray of linen flying around in the air, and Magnus took the opportunity to shrug out of his jacket completely and undo his bow tie. He stepped toward Alec and whispered, "I think we can do better than fine."

They kissed, and instead of guiding him toward the bed, Magnus pulled his boyfriend toward the shower by the loops of his trousers. Surprise touched Alec's face, but he followed easily.

"Your shirt's covered in champagne," Magnus explained.

Alec's eyes flickered down to Magnus's shirt, which had gone translucent. Alec flushed slightly as he murmured, "So's yours."

Magnus smiled, pressing the curve of his mouth against Alec's. "Excellent point."

He made a small gesture and hot water began to spray from the shower, drenching them both. Magnus could see the faint dark curves of runes beneath the thin, soaked material of Alec's shirt. Silver points of light and water glittered in the tiny space between them. Magnus put his hands on Alec, peeling Alec's shirt and undershirt off his body and over his head. Streams of water sparkled on the surface of Alec's bare chest, tracing along the grooves of his muscles.

Magnus drew Alec closer to him and kissed him as he undid the studs of his own shirt with his free hand. He felt Alec's strong hands on his back, the thin and thoroughly wet shirt almost no barrier at all, and yet far too much of a barrier. Magnus dipped his head and ran his mouth down the wet line of Alec's neck to his bare shoulder.

Alec shuddered and pinned Magnus up against the glass wall. Magnus was having real trouble getting his shirt undone.

Alec caught his mouth, swallowing Magnus's moan. The kiss was deep and urgent, their mouths sliding together, as hungry as their wet hands. As Magnus tried to concentrate on fine motor control, he noticed a strange shimmer in the air outside the shower, near the ceiling.

He felt Alec freeze when he noticed the new, different tension in Magnus's body. Alec followed Magnus's line of sight. A pair of sinister, glowing eyes blinked at them through the steam.

"Not now," Alec whispered against Magnus's mouth. "You *have* to be kidding me."

Magnus murmured a spell against Alec's lips. Steam fountained out of the top of the shower and gathered around the shimmer. Through the haze emerged the outline of a giant centipede-shaped creature. The Drevak demon lunged.

Magnus snapped several more sharp words, these in demonic Cthonian. The shower walls immediately frosted and hardened just as the Drevak demon let loose a jet of corrosive acid in their direction.

Alec pulled Magnus to the ground and dove out of the shower, sliding along the wet floor and slamming into the wooden closet doors on the other side of the wall. Awkwardly, he grabbed at the bottom of one of the doors and wrenched it open.

Magnus had no idea why until he saw Alec rise to his feet, seraph blade in hand. *"Muriel."*

Before the Drevak could attack again, Alec launched himself toward the ceiling and executed a long forward slice. The two pieces of the demon dropped to the floor behind him and vanished.

"It's so weird that there's an angel Muriel," Magnus commented. "Muriel sounds like a disapproving piano teacher." He held up an imaginary seraph blade and intoned at it. *"My great-aunt Muriel."*

Alec turned back to Magnus, shirtless in wet trousers, lit by starshine and the glow of his seraph blade, and Magnus was briefly rendered speechless by pure physical attraction. Alec said, "The Drevak won't be alone."

"Demons," Magnus said bitterly. "They do know how to kill the mood."

The window to their cabin exploded inward, showering glass and debris into the room. Magnus momentarily lost sight of Alec in a cloud of dust. He took a step forward and was met by a creature with a long black body, spindly legs, and a domed head extending to an elongated snout. It landed in front of him and hissed, exposing rows of sharp serrated teeth.

Magnus gestured, and a pool of water on the floor surged up to engulf the demon in a large translucent bubble. The demon became disoriented as the sphere rotated upside down. Then Magnus made a batting motion and flung the ball of water out the window.

Instantly another demon took its place. This insect tried to ambush him from the side, nearly taking a chunk of his leg off with its snapping jaws. Magnus stumbled back toward the bed, flicking his fingers as he retreated, causing the closet doors to swing open and smash into the giant bug as it advanced.

The distraction barely slowed the demon down. It hissed and, with a crushing bite, broke the wooden doors into pieces. Just as it was about to leap, the harsh white glow of Alec's seraph blade cut down between its two clusters of eyes, splitting its domed head in half.

Alec drew his blade from the body and said, "We need to move."

He scooped up his bow, signaling for Magnus to follow, and they escaped out of the wreckage of their cabin and into an otherwise undisturbed sleeper car. After the mayhem of a moment ago, the hallway's peaceful quietude was strange. All was still, save for the rhythmic clicking of the tracks and the soft classical music playing through hidden speakers in the ceiling. Soft yellow lights swayed the shadows gently in a waltz measured to the train's rhythm.

Alec pivoted back and forth, bow at the ready, waiting for the next attack. The eerie quiet held for several more seconds until they heard it. A faint tapping, nearly imperceptible at first, like light rain on a roof. It was soon followed by more of its kind, rattling and thumps growing in frequency and number.

Alec aimed his bow upward as the noise grew louder and louder, a hundred clicks of nails or claws on metal, as if the train were passing under a thunderstorm. "They're all around us. Get to the next car. Hurry." Magnus headed to the near door, but Alec called out sharply, "That's the way toward the other sleeper cars. There are mundanes there."

Magnus changed directions and ran toward the far door, with Alec close on his heels. They moved along the corridor leading to the end car, with the bar full of Downworlders. A young werewolf in a beaded dress was making her way down the corridor. She stopped short at the sight of them.

Five hulking Raum demons barreled through the windows on either side, and she screamed. Alec threw himself onto her, shielding her with his own body and stabbing the demon trying to crush them. Another demon's tentacles wrapped around them both, and Alec rolled with the werewolf girl in his arms, scything away the tentacles with his seraph blade.

One of the remaining Raums lumbered toward the sounds emanating from the bar. Magnus sent a blast of scorching light in its direction.

"Is that a demon?" he heard someone yell. "Who invited them?"

Someone else said, "Read the sign, demon!"

"Is everyone all right?" called Magnus, and a demon seized this split second of distraction and went for him.

A nightmare of tentacles and teeth loomed before Magnus; then the demon exploded into nothing, an arrow in its back. Magnus looked through the haze and the flash to Alec, crouched on the floor with his bow in his hands.

The werewolf girl was regarding Alec with some awe. The dark dust of slain demons and a faint sheen of sweat gleamed on Alec's rune-marked bare skin.

"I had Shadowhunters all wrong. From now on, you can ask me to do anything for your fight against demons," the werewolf girl announced with conviction. "And I will do it."

Alec turned his head to look at her. "Anything?"

"Gladly," said the girl.

"What's your name?" Alec asked.

"Juliette."

"Are you from Paris?" asked Alec. "Do you go to the Paris Shadow Market? Do you know a faerie child called Rose?"

"I am," said the werewolf girl. "I do. Is she really a child? I thought it was just faerie trickiness."

"Next time you see her," said Alec, "can you feed her?"

The werewolf girl blinked, her expression softening. "Yes," she said. "I can do that."

"What's going on out there?" asked the goblin they'd spoken to earlier, barging out of the party and into the corridor. His eyes widened. "There's demon gunk all over the place and a lot of Shadowhunter skin out here!" he called over his shoulder.

Alec rose to his feet and went to Magnus, who snapped his fingers and made Alec's still-wet undershirt appear in his hand. Alec grabbed for it with obvious relief. Magnus and the werewolf girl watched a little sadly as he put it on.

Once his shirt was on, Alec took Magnus's hand. "Stay close to—"

Magnus didn't hear the rest. Before he could utter a cry, something looped around his waist, wrenched him off his feet, and tore him out of Alec's grasp. A bone-jarring pain stunned him, forcing the breath from his body. He heard the sound of shattering glass and felt hundreds of tiny shards cutting into his skin.

The world blinked, and consciousness returned a moment later to the sound of wind howling in his ears and freezing air slapping him in the face. Dazed and disoriented, Magnus looked up and saw the full white moon hovering above the jagged mountaintops. Beneath him, the train was speeding along a bridge.

Magnus was dangling in the air above a ravine. All that prevented him from falling to his death was the black tentacle wrapped around his waist.

The tentacle was not a huge comfort.

CHAPTER EIGHT
Speed of Fire

ALEC LOOKED, HIS HAND STILL EXTENDED, HIS HEART forgetting to beat, at the empty space where Magnus had been standing just seconds ago.

One moment he had been holding Magnus's hand. Now he stood, his hand outstretched toward a window that had become ten thousand tiny jagged shards littering the plush wine-colored carpet.

A shudder passed through Alec: he couldn't suppress the thought of all he had lost in the battle at Alicante. He could not lose Magnus, too. He was meant to be a warrior and soldier, a steady light against the darkness. But the terror that went through him now was visceral and deep, stronger than any fear he'd ever felt in battle.

Alec heard a cry, barely perceptible over the sound of the howling wind. He rushed to the broken window.

There was Magnus, suspended in the air next to the train. He was in the grip of a creature, squatting on top of the train, that looked like a tree made of smoke. Magnus was caught in its black branches, his hands pinned by dark tentacles. Below them was a plummeting fall of hundreds of feet.

The demon's smoky surface bubbled and rippled in the air. Alec was tempted to put a few arrows into it, but he didn't want to provoke it, not with Magnus in its grasp. Nor could Magnus use magic without his hands free. Alec looked down at the ravine; it was too dark to see the bottom.

"Magnus!" he shouted. "I'm coming!"

"Wonderful!" Magnus yelled back. "I'll just hang around until then!"

Alec climbed out onto the window frame and steadied himself as the train shook from side to side, silently thanking his Dexterity rune for maintaining his balance. He reached up and grabbed the *T* and *E* at the beginning of the word INTERNATIONALE that was blazoned in brass letters affixed to the train car, above the windows. All he had to do was pull himself up and swing his legs over onto the roof.

It should have worked. Alec had completed similar feats hundreds of times in his training. But the letter *T* was less well-attached than he'd thought, and with a groan it pulled halfway out of the train, its screws stripped and bent. He managed to get only one leg onto the roof before it broke off completely. He scrambled for purchase, his arms and legs splayed against the curved edge of the train car.

"Are you all right?" Magnus shouted.

"All according to plan!" Alec began to slide off, one slow inch at a time.

Sheer urgency ran hot through his veins. Desperation tightened his hands to claws. With a force borne only of his will to save Magnus, he managed to find some leverage beneath one foot, and with this he frantically scrambled his way up onto the roof.

Before he could uncurl himself and stand up, something large and heavy barreled into him from behind. Tentacles closed around his legs and waist and squeezed. Dozens of small red suction cups pinched through the wet fabric of his shirt, burning his skin.

Alec stared into the large buggy eyes and gaping maw of a Raum demon. It made a wet clicking sound as it snapped at him. Unable to use his bow or reach his seraph blade, Alec used the only weapon he had available. He raised his fist and punched the Raum demon in the face.

His fist connected with a buggy eye. His elbow smashed into its snout. Alec battered the demon's face until its tentacles loosened just enough for him to kick out and escape. He fell onto his back and somersaulted into a kneeling position. His bow was out, an arrow nocked, and he shot just as the Raum demon came at him.

It blocked the first arrow with a tentacle, but stumbled when the second sank into its knee. It finally stopped its charge when, at near-point-blank range, the third punched into its chest. The demon chittered in agony, staggered, lost its balance, and toppled over the side of the train.

The bow clattered to the ground. Alec exhaled and put a hand on the train's roof to steady himself. His body burned from dozens of tiny poisonous wounds left by the demon's tentacles. He fumbled for his stele and pressed it to his heart, drawing the *iratze* rune. Immediately the tightness in his chest lifted and the numbness subsided.

He drew in a harsh breath. Demon poison wasn't easily remedied. This relief was only temporary.

He had to make the next few minutes count.

He willed himself to his feet and focused on Magnus, still in the grasp of some dark octopus-like monster. It was unlike any demon he had ever seen before, and definitely not something he'd read about in the *Codex*. It didn't matter. It had Magnus, and it was getting away.

Alec picked up his bow and gave chase, speeding down the length of the train and hurdling over the gaps between the cars. He kept his eyes on Magnus, intent on not letting him out of sight again. His terror drove him forward with reckless abandon. He barely stayed on the train as it curved around a sharp turn.

Several Ravener demons appeared, blocking his path with hissing jaws and poisonous scorpion tails. It was unusual, said an analytic voice in the back of his mind, to have so many different demon types attacking together. They tended to stay in packs of their own kind.

This meant, almost certainly, that they had been summoned. That there was malicious purpose beyond this attack, directed at them in particular.

Alec didn't have time to pursue this insight at the moment, and didn't have time to suffer Ravener demons, either. Every second lost meant Magnus got one second farther away. He fired arrows while running at full speed, sacrificing some accuracy to keep up. One arrow caught a Ravener in mid-leap, and Alec battered two more off the train with his bow. Another Raum demon got an arrow to the throat. His seraph blade seared through flesh as if it were night air.

Alec stood wreathed in ichor and blood, and realized he had cut through the whole pack.

His body ached in a hundred places, and the *iratze* rune was starting to wear off. He wasn't done. He set his teeth and staggered forward. The smoke demon was just at the end of the train car. It had stopped moving. Two of its tentacles were still wrapped around Magnus, four were holding on to the sides of the train near the tracks, and the last two were dragging along the air as if testing the wind. No, the ends of the tentacles were glowing in a light that became more complex as the tentacles moved, remaining in place next to the demon even as the train rushed on.

Alec squinted and realized the light was the red glow of a pentagram, emerging into the air beside the train. He nocked an arrow, aimed at a space in between the monster's two eyes, and loosed it.

The arrow bounced harmlessly off the demon's roiling skin. He drew another and struck it again; same result. By now the pentagram had opened and the demon was moving Magnus into it. It could drop him into another dimension or some bottomless abyss.

Alec drew yet another arrow. This time he aimed at one of the tentacles holding Magnus. He whispered a prayer to the Angel and fired.

The arrow sank into the tentacle a few feet away from Magnus's body. The monster reared and relaxed its grip just a bit. Magnus didn't waste any time and, as soon as he had a hand free, began weaving it through the air rapidly. A web of blue electricity flared onto the remaining tentacle holding him. The smoke demon screamed and its tentacles jerked back, releasing Magnus. The warlock hit the roof of the train with a heavy thud and rolled, beginning to slip over the side.

Alec dove forward, sliding along the cold metal, perilously close to the edge. He brushed Magnus's fingertips and grasped only air as Magnus tumbled off the train.

Alec lunged off the side of the train and grasped a handful of wet material. He grabbed hold of Magnus's shirt in both hands and strained to pull him up, using all the strength he had left.

His vision blurred with the effort, but then Magnus was in his arms, blinking his still-stunned golden eyes.

"Thank you, Alexander," Magnus said. "Alas, the octopus monster is attacking again."

Alec rolled them both to the side. A black tentacle slammed into the place they had just been. The tentacle rose to strike again. Magnus shot into a sitting position and threw up his hands, a beam of blue fire slicing across one of the whipping tentacles. Black ichor sprayed as the demon jerked the injured tentacle back.

Magnus rose to his feet. Alec started to get up, but a wave of dizziness struck him. The effects of the *iratze* rune were almost entirely gone, and the Raum poison was again a corroding agent within his veins.

"Alec!" Magnus shouted. His hair was wild in the wind whipping across the train's roof. He hauled Alec to his feet even as the smoke demon moved toward them once again. "Alec, what's wrong?"

Alec felt for his stele, but his vision was fading. He could hear Magnus calling his name, hear the approach of the demon. There was no way Magnus could both help Alec and fend off the demon at the same time.

Magnus, he thought. *Run. Protect yourself.*

The smoke monster lunged, just as a dark shape threw itself between the demon and Alec and Magnus.

A woman, her dark cloak and dark hair whipping in the wind. In one hand she gripped a three-sided sword. It gleamed under the moonlight.

"Stay back!" she shouted. "I'll take care of this."

She waved a hand and the smoky demon gave a long crackling squeal, like the sound of wood breaking as it was burned.

"I've seen her before," Alec said, wondering. "It's the woman I fought at the Shadow Market in Paris. Magnus . . ."

Another bolt of sick, poisonous pain coursed through him. His vision dimmed. He felt as though he was being beaten, struck in the stomach, his legs cut out from under him.

"Magnus," he said again.

The sky began to fail, the stars blinking out one by one, but then Magnus was there, catching him. "Alec," he was saying, over and over, and his voice wasn't at all like Magnus's voice, which was cool and dismissive and charming. It was ragged and desperate. "Alec, please."

There was a heavy weight on Alec's eyelids. Everything in the world wanted him to shut them. Alec forced them open, to catch one final glimpse: Magnus hovering above him, his strange lovely eyes the last light Alec had left.

Alec wanted to tell him that it was all right. Magnus was safe. Alec had everything he wanted.

He tried to lift a hand and touch Magnus's cheek. He could not.

The world was so dark. Magnus's face faded and, like everything else, was swallowed by the now starless night sky.

CHAPTER NINE

Shinyun

DEMONIC ACID HAD DESTROYED HALF THEIR COMPART-ment. In fact, the entire train had suffered a great deal of damage, which had been concealed from the mundane staff and passengers with a clever combination of glamours and dropped words about partying European royalty.

Magnus was regrowing the wood frame, and incidentally doing a little redecorating, when he heard Alec stir. It was only a tiny movement beneath the covers, but Magnus had been waiting for it all night.

He turned in time to see Alec stir again. He hastened over to sit on the side of the bed.

"Hey, gorgeous, how are you feeling?" he murmured.

Alec reached out his hand, his eyes still closed. It was a mute but trusting gesture—the gesture of a boy who could always count on loving hands and loving voices when he was sick or injured. Magnus remembered when he himself had turned up at the Institute, summoned there to heal Alec from demon injuries. Isabelle had been in a panic, Jace pacing the halls, white-faced.

It had reminded Magnus of times long ago, the memory of Nephilim he had cared for once, and how very much they had cared for each other. Knowing the way Will and Jem loved each other had changed his feelings for Nephilim, and seeing Jace—calm, superior Jace—in pieces over Alec had made him like the boy much more.

Now Alec's hand was outstretched to him, and Magnus took it like the offer of trust it was. Alec's skin was cool. Magnus pressed his cheek to their joined hands, closing his eyes for just a moment, letting his relief that Alec was all right wash over him. Alec's skin had been hot with fever for a while there, but Magnus was very experienced in treating the Nephilim.

Since Shadowhunters, however loving, were all reckless lunatics.

Of course, Alec had been a reckless lunatic in the cause of saving Magnus's life. He thought of Alec balancing atop the train car as it hurtled around twisting mountain passes, his clothes wet, his skin smeared with blood and dust. It was heartbreaking and hot, all at once.

"I've been better." Alec's bedsheets were damp from sweat, but color was returning to his face. He sat up and the blanket slid down to his bare waist. "I've been worse, too. Thanks for healing me."

Magnus sat up and hovered his free hand over Alec's chest. A faint blue glow expanded from his palm and shimmered before disappearing through Alec's skin. "Your heartbeat is stronger. You should've asked me to take care of that poison immediately."

Alec shook his head. "If you recall, an octopus demon was carrying you away."

"Yes," Magnus said. "About that. I deeply appreciate you saving my life. I'm very attached to my life. However, if it comes to a choice between your life and mine, Alec, remember I have already lived a very long time."

It was strange to say. Immortality was a difficult thing to talk about. Magnus barely remembered being young, but he had never been old, either. He had been with mortals of varying ages, and he had never been able to comprehend how time felt for them. Nor had they ever been able to understand him.

Yet cutting himself off from mortals would mean severing his ties with the world. Life would become a long wait, without warmth or connection, until his heart died. After a century of loneliness, anyone would go mad.

Alec risking himself for Magnus's sake—that felt like madness as well.

Alec's eyes were narrowed. "What are you saying?"

Magnus linked his fingers with Alec's. Their hands lay on the bedsheet, Alec's pale and rune-marked, Magnus's brown and gleaming with rings.

"You should keep yourself safe—first. Your safety, it's more important, it means more than mine."

Alec said, "I would say the same thing to you."

"But you'd be wrong."

"That's a matter of opinion. What was that demon?" Magnus had to admire the brazenness with which Alec changed the subject. "Why did it attack you?"

Magnus had been wondering that himself.

"Attacking is what demons usually do," said Magnus. "If it was after me specifically, I assume it was jealous of my style and charm."

Alec wasn't distracted. Magnus hadn't really believed he would be.

"Have you ever seen anything like it? We need to figure out the best way to fight another one if it comes. If I could get to the New York library, check the bestiaries . . . Maybe I could get Isabelle to do it. . . ."

"Oh, you relentless Nephilim," said Magnus, letting Alec's hand go before Alec could let him go first. "Can't you get your bursts of energy from caffeine like everybody else?"

"The demon was a Raum brood mother," said a woman's voice

from behind them. "It takes powerful magic to coax one out of its lair."

Alec snatched the blanket up with one hand to cover himself, while grabbing his seraph blade with the other.

"Also," said Magnus without raising his voice, "may I introduce our new friend, Shinyun Jung? She dissolved the demon attacking us into vapor. It made an excellent first impression."

Alec and Shinyun both regarded Magnus with disbelief.

"My first impression of her," Alec pointed out with some sharpness, "was her attacking me at the Shadow Market."

"My first impression of *you*," Shinyun returned, "was *you* attacking *me*. All I wanted to do was talk to Magnus, but you drew a weapon on me."

"We should probably have a little chat to clear things up," Magnus agreed.

He'd been too worried about Alec to think it through before. Shinyun had dropped to her knees and started helping him heal Alec's wounds. At the time, that was all he had needed to know.

"Yes," Shinyun agreed. "Why don't we continue this conversation outside, with all of us dressed?"

"I'd appreciate that," said Alec.

"I suggest the bar car."

Magnus brightened. "I'd appreciate *that*."

THEY REGROUPED IN THE DOWNWORLDER BAR. THE room was still packed, but the crowd was noticeably more subdued after the demon attack. Three spots in a row at the main bar were suddenly vacant, and as they sat down on the stools, a free bottle of champagne and three glasses appeared without them having ordered it. When Alec looked suspiciously around, a vampire shot him a wink and finger guns.

Magnus might not have to worry so much about all Downworlders hating Alec. Not on this train, anyway.

"I didn't think Shadowhunters were this popular among Downworlders," said Shinyun.

"Only my Shadowhunter," Magnus said, pouring.

The bar was lit from above with hanging brass pendants. Their warm light fell full on Shinyun's countenance. Her lips and eyes moved when she spoke, but the rest of her round face, unblinking eyelids, and smooth cheeks did not. Her voice was dry and seemed to float from her mouth without cadence.

That was her warlock mark, the affectless face. All warlocks were uniquely marked, the markings usually appearing in early childhood, often resulting in tragedy. Magnus's mark was his golden cat eyes. Magnus's stepfather had called them windows into Hell.

Magnus could not stop remembering kneeling on top of the train car, frantic with fear, Alec losing consciousness in his arms. Magnus had seen the demon dissipate into smoke around Shinyun as she threw her hood back and looked down at him. He'd recognized her immediately—not who she was, but that she was like him. A warlock.

It had been quite an entrance.

"Let's chat," said Alec. "Why were you following us? Specifically, why were you following Magnus through the Shadow Market in Paris?"

"I'm after the Crimson Hand," Shinyun answered. "I heard Magnus Bane was their leader."

"I'm not."

"He's not," Alec said sharply.

"I know," Shinyun said. Magnus saw a tiny relaxation of tension in Alec's shoulders. Her dark eyes returned to Magnus and held his gaze. "I'd already heard of you, of course. Magnus Bane, the High Warlock of Brooklyn. Everyone has something to say about you."

"That makes sense," said Magnus. "I'm well-known for my taste in fashion and the hospitality of my parties."

"It's true that everybody seems to trust you," Shinyun continued. "It's not like I wanted to believe you were running some cult, but recently I've been hearing it over and over. 'Magnus Bane is the Crimson Hand's founder.' The one they call the Great Poison."

Magnus hesitated. "Maybe. But I don't remember it. My memories of that time period have been—altered. I wish I did know."

Alec gave him a look that, though Magnus was unable to read minds, very clearly communicated the idea that he was shocked Magnus was trusting this total stranger with an important and dangerous secret.

Magnus, on the other hand, felt oddly relieved that he'd admitted out loud that he might have founded the Crimson Hand, even to a peculiar stranger. After all, he had made the joke to Ragnor. He'd seen Tessa's picture. He knew he was missing years of memory. Which was likelier, that those were all coincidences or that he'd actually done it?

He wished he could travel back in time and kick himself in the head.

"You're missing memories? You think the Crimson Hand took them?" Shinyun said.

"Possibly," said Magnus. "Look, I don't want a cult," he added. He felt strongly he should make his position on cults well understood. "I am not out to take over the cult. I am out to shut down the cult, and try to pay back whatever fault I bear for the bad stuff they've done. I want the memories back, and I want to know why they're gone, but that's more out of personal curiosity. The important thing is, no more demonic cults that feel any kinship with Magnus Bane. Also, they have ruined a romantic vacation that was getting off, I thought, to a very good start."

He drained his drink. After almost getting thrown off a train, he deserved one. He deserved more than one.

"It was getting off to a very good start," Alec muttered, looking at Shinyun in a manner that suggested that though she'd saved his life, her presence was no longer required.

Magnus considered saying something about how now no one was getting off at all, but decided it was not the time.

"You can understand why I might have been suspicious—" began Shinyun.

"You can understand why *we* might be more suspicious!" countered Alec.

Shinyun glared. "Until I saw that Raum brood mother attacking you," she said. "I know the Crimson Hand well enough to know the way they operate. The current leader must be trying to kill you, Bane. Which means that whatever happened in the past, now they consider you their enemy. I may have stopped them last night, but they will likely try again."

"How do you know so much about them?" said Alec. "And what do you want?"

Shinyun lifted her glass to her lips and took a slow, careful sip. Magnus admired, not for the first time, her intuitive sense of dramatic timing.

"My goal is the same as yours. I intend to destroy the Crimson Hand."

Magnus felt uncomfortable at the presumption of her declaring his goal for him. He wanted to quibble with it, but the more he thought about it, the more he realized she was right. In the end, it probably would come to that.

"Why?" Alec asked, focusing on the more important thing. "What did the Crimson Hand do to *you*?"

Shinyun looked out the window, at the pale reflected globes of lamplight against the night. "They hurt me very badly," she said, and Magnus felt a sinking feeling at the pit of his stomach. Whatever the Crimson Hand had done, if he had founded them, he was at least somewhat responsible.

Shinyun's hands began to tremble and she pressed them together to hide it. "The details are not important. The Crimson Hand is amassing sacrifices—human sacrifices, of course—toward raising a Greater Demon. They've been killing faeries. Mundanes. Even warlocks." She looked back at Magnus, unblinking. "They think that is their path to ultimate power."

"A Greater Demon?" exclaimed Alec.

The horror and loathing in his voice was entirely understandable. He had nearly been killed by a Greater Demon. It still made Magnus's stomach twist. He finished his second drink and poured himself another.

"So the most banal, typical thing for an evil cult to want. Power. Power through some demon. Why do they always think they'll be spared? Demons aren't known for their sense of fair play." Magnus sighed. "Wouldn't you think a cult I founded might have a more creative spirit? Also, I would have assumed a cult I founded wouldn't be evil; that part remains a surprise to me."

"People I loved are dead because of the Crimson Hand," Shinyun went on.

"Maybe the details do matter," said Alec.

Shinyun gripped her glass so tightly that her knuckles went white. "I still would prefer not to speak of it."

Alec looked dubious.

"If you want me to trust you, you'll have to trust me," said Shinyun plainly. "For now, all you need know is that I wish for revenge against the Crimson Hand for the crimes they have committed against me and against my loved ones. That is all. If you're against them, we're on the same side."

"Everyone has their secrets, Alec," said Magnus softly, feeling awash in his own. "If the Crimson Hand is trying to kill me for some reason, we can use all the help we can get."

Magnus could be forgiving of Shinyun choosing not to disclose her past. After all, apparently he couldn't even remember his own. He wanted to believe that talking about things made them better, but in his experience, sometimes talking made everything worse.

A silence fell between them. Shinyun sipped her drink and remained silent herself. Magnus was terrified, and not for his own life. He kept thinking about the moment Alec had collapsed on the roof of the train, when he had believed with cold horror that Alec was dying for him. He was afraid for Alec, and afraid of what he himself might have done that he could not now remember.

He couldn't tell what Alec was thinking, but as he watched, Alec smiled, just a little, and reached out across the bar. His strong, scarred fingers curled around Magnus's, their hands joined in the tiny pool of light cast by the candle.

Magnus wanted to grab Alec and kiss him breathless, but he suspected Shinyun would not appreciate the show.

"You're right," Alec said. "I guess the enemy of my enemy is my friend, or at least a friendly acquaintance. Better if we team up." He lowered his voice. "But she's not sleeping in our hotel rooms."

"All reconciled?" asked Shinyun. "Because, sorry to be rude, but this is incredibly awkward to sit through. I'm not here to witness your relationship growth. I just want to defeat the evil cult."

Magnus had made up his mind. Whatever else was going on—whether he owed Shinyun for saving their lives, or for how the Crimson Hand had harmed her—she knew a great deal. It would be foolishness not to keep her close by.

"Let's all enjoy our refreshments and assume for now that we're all on the same side. Can you tell us about your more recent past, at least?"

Shinyun considered for a moment and then seemed to come to some decision within herself.

"I've been hunting the Crimson Hand for some time. I received updates from an informant in their ranks called Mori Shu. I was closing in on them, and then they found another spy in their ranks, abandoned their mansion, and went into hiding. I ran out of leads, but then I heard from a reliable source that the Spiral Labyrinth had given you a chance to go after the cult."

"If she learned that, maybe someone else did," Alec said. "Maybe that's why the Hand wants you dead, Magnus."

"Maybe," Magnus said. It was a solid theory, but there was still too much he didn't remember. He had the sinking feeling there was plenty he could have done to turn the Hand against him.

Shinyun didn't seem interested. "I tracked you around Paris, watching your movements, and I decided to approach you at the Shadow Market when the Shadowhunter attacked me."

"I was protecting Magnus," Alec said.

"I understand that," said Shinyun. "You fight well."

There was a tiny pause.

"So do you," Alec said.

The leader of the Crimson Hand, whoever he might be, knew they were coming. Magnus wanted to be safe. He wanted Alec to be safe. He wanted this to be over.

"Let's get another bottle," he said, gesturing with one hand toward the bartender, "and toast to our new partnership."

The fresh bottle arrived at the table, and their glasses refilled. Magnus raised his in a toast. "Well," he said with a small smile, "on to Venice." They toasted and drank. Magnus thought of more pleasant things than demonic cults. He considered the city of liquid glass and moving waters, the city of canals and dreamers. He watched Alec, whole and well, his blue eyes clear and his voice an anchor in a wild sea.

Magnus realized he'd been wrong to think Paris was the city

to get their relationship off to a good start. Even before the demon-worshipping cult, Alec hadn't been that impressed with the Eiffel Tower or the hot-air balloon, not the way Magnus wanted him to be. Paris was a city of love, but it could also be a city of surfaces, of bright lights that slid away and were quickly lost. Magnus did not want to lose this one. He would set a better scene. He would get things right this time.

Venice was the place for Alec. Venice had depth.

PART II
City of Masks

† † †

. . . Venice once was dear,
The pleasant place of all festivity,
The revel of the earth, the masque of Italy!
—Lord Byron

CHAPTER TEN

Labyrinth of Water

MAGNUS THREW THE CURTAINS OPEN AND STEPPED onto the balcony of the hotel room. "Ah, Venice. There is no city in the world like you."

Alec trailed him outside and leaned over the railing. His gaze followed a gondola snaking along the canal and disappearing around a corner.

"It's a bit smelly."

"That's the ambiance."

Alec grinned. "Well, the ambiance is pretty strong."

The only good thing about the previous night's demon attack was that between the dozen or so glamour spells in place on the part of all the participants and a number of the bystanders, the mundanes responsible for the actual running of the train hadn't noticed the enormous ruckus or the giant hole in one of their passenger cars. They pulled into Venice at ten in the morning, almost on time.

One water taxi ride later, they had arrived at the Belmond Hotel Cipriani, just a few blocks from the Crimson Hand's former headquarters.

Magnus wandered back into their suite and pointed at his suit-cases. They each split open and began to unload themselves. Blazers and coats flew into the waiting closet, undergarments folded themselves into the drawers, shoes walked into a neat row by the door, and valuables locked themselves into the safe.

He spun back to Alec, who was watching the movement of the sun through the cloudless sky with a slight frown.

"I know what you're thinking," said Magnus. "Breakfast."

"We don't have time," said Shinyun, barging into their suite without knocking. "We should go search the abandoned headquarters at once."

She, of course, had already changed into a kind of Italian-cut power suit that shone iridescent with enchantments and protections.

Magnus gave her a disapproving look. "We have not worked together very long, Shinyun Jung, but one thing you should learn about me quickly is that I am very serious about my meals."

Shinyun looked at Alec, who nodded.

"I may, at any moment, organize an entire step in our mission around visiting a particular restaurant or bar. If I do so, it will be worth your while."

"If it's so important—" Shinyun began.

"We will be eating three meals a day. Breakfast will be one of those meals. In fact, breakfast will be the most important of those meals, because breakfast is the most important meal of the day."

Shinyun looked at Alec, who said in a deadpan voice, "Many a mission to end a great evil has failed because of low blood sugar."

"You *do* listen when I talk!" exclaimed Magnus. Alec gave Shinyun an apologetic smile that she did not return.

"Fine," said Shinyun. "So where does *your* agenda begin today?"

Magnus's agenda, luckily, began downstairs at the hotel's own Oro Restaurant. They sat alfresco on the deck, watching a small parade of boats float by along the lagoon. Alec wolfed down two crepes and considered ordering a third. Magnus enjoyed an espresso, the menu's most complicated-sounding egg dish, and the gleaming turquoise canal.

"I was thinking that you might enjoy Venice more than Paris," he told Alec.

"I liked Paris," said Alec. "This is nice too." He braced himself with a visible effort, turned to Shinyun, and tried to make conversation. "This is my first time traveling for fun. I've always stayed close to home before. Where's home for you?"

Magnus had to turn his face away to watch the boats for a moment. Sometimes the tenderness he felt for Alec actually hurt.

Shinyun hesitated. "Korea was home, when I had a home. The Korea of the Joseon Dynasty."

There was a pause. "Was it a hard place to be a warlock?"

Shinyun looked at Magnus and said, "Every place is a hard place to be a warlock child."

"That's true," Magnus said.

"Originally I am from a small village near Mount Kuwol. My warlock marks manifested late. I was fourteen and betrothed to Yoosung, a handsome boy from a good family in my village. When my face froze over, everyone believed I had turned into a Hannya demon or had been possessed by a *gwisin*. My betrothed said he did not care." Her voice trembled, very slightly. "He would still have married me, but he was killed by a demon. I've devoted my life to hunting demons in his honor. I've made a detailed study of demons over centuries. I know their ways. I know their *names*. And I have never, and will never, summon a demon."

Magnus sat back and took a sip of coffee. "Alec, remember last night, when our new acquaintance told us that she couldn't tell us anything about her past?"

Shinyun laughed. "That's ancient history. I had many years

between then and now to have a *past* in, after all of that was behind me."

"Well," said Magnus, "I understand why you've made your choice, but for the record, *I* summon demons all the time. Well, not literally all the time. But when I'm paid to do so, within the bounds of my code of ethics, obviously."

Shinyun thought this over. "But you don't . . . *like* demons. You don't mind killing them."

"They're violent, mindless despoilers of our world, so, no," said Magnus. "I don't mind killing them. My boyfriend is a Shadow-hunter, for heaven's sake. Literally, for heaven's sake."

"I'd noticed," said Shinyun dryly.

There was a brief, awkward silence, broken by Shinyun gesturing into the air a miniature floating image of the octopus monster they'd fought the night before.

"I'm going to have another espresso," said Magnus, gesturing to the waiter with his empty cup.

"This Raum brood mother, for example. It has no bones and can regrow its flesh. You can cut it or pierce it as much as you like, but it will regenerate its organs and limbs too quickly to end it that way. You must instead tear it apart from the inside. That is why I used a sonic spell."

"You've fought them before?" said Alec.

"I hunted one in the Himalayas a hundred years ago, when it terrorized a local village."

The discussion veered into demon hunting, which was deeply boring to Magnus, but intensely exciting to Alec. So he sat back, sipped his espresso, and watched as the minutes passed, until there was a pause in the conversation and he cleared his throat and said quietly, "If we're all done with breakfast, we could go check out that Crimson Hand headquarters we've all heard so much about."

Shinyun had the grace to look a little embarrassed as they went back from the restaurant to the lobby. Magnus arranged for the hotel to call a water taxi for them. By the time it arrived to pick them up, Shinyun and Alec were back to swapping demon murder tips.

The secret of Venice is that its streets are an unknowable maze, but its canals make a strange kind of sense. Rather than navigating the alleys of a city with no posted street signs of any kind, their water taxi was able to let them off within sight of the palazzo that was their destination.

That palazzo's golden walls were festooned with white marble pillars and arches, decorated in scarlet stucco. The windows of what was referred to elsewhere as the ground floor, and in Venice was called the "water floor," were unusually large, risking flooding for beauty. The glass reflected the canal waters, turning moody turquoise into shining jade.

Magnus could not imagine setting up a cult, but if he were going to, he could easily envision himself choosing this building for it.

"It's your kind of place," said Alec.

"It's amazing," said Magnus.

"What I mostly notice about it, though," said Alec, "is all the people going in and out of it. Didn't your friend Tessa say it was abandoned?"

Venice was always crowded with people, turning the streets into as much living motion as the canals, but Alec was right. There was a steady stream of people passing through the double front doors of the palazzo.

"What if the Crimson Hand is still operating here?" Alec asked.

Shinyun's voice was eager. "Then that makes our job easier."

"These are obviously not cultists," said Magnus. "Look how bored they are."

Indeed, the men and women going in and out of the palazzo seemed like they were just going about their jobs. They carried piles of cloth, or cardboard boxes, or stacks of chairs. Someone in chef's whites came through with a stack of chafing dishes covered in aluminum foil. No robes, no masks, no vials of blood, no live animals for sacrifice. Some of them were Downworlders, Magnus could see.

He headed for the most Downworldly he could find, a green-skinned dryad standing just next to the front doors, talking intensely to a satyr who was holding a clipboard.

As he approached, the dryad started. "Wow—are you *Magnus Bane?*"

"Do I know you?" said Magnus.

"No, but you definitely could," the dryad said, blowing Magnus a kiss.

Alec coughed loudly from behind Magnus.

"I'm flattered, but as you can hear, I'm spoken for. Well, coughed for."

"Pity," said the dryad. He tapped the satyr on the chest. "This is Magnus Bane!"

Without looking up from the clipboard, the satyr said, "Magnus Bane isn't invited to the party. Because he's dating a Shadowhunter, I heard."

The dryad gave them an apologetic look. "Ix-nay on the Adowhunter-shay," he stage-whispered to the satyr. "The Adowhunter-shay is right there and he can ear-hay ou-yay!"

"Yeah, I've also cracked your secret code language," Alec said dryly.

Magnus looked hurt and turned to his companions. "I can't believe I'm not invited to the party. I'm Magnus Bane! Even these guys know it."

"What party?" said Shinyun.

"I'm sorry," Magnus went on, "let me get a hold of myself. A party where Alec isn't welcome isn't a party I'd want to attend."

"Magnus, *what party?*" said Shinyun.

"I think Shinyun finds it unusual," said Alec very slowly to Magnus, "that there's a party, with Downworlders, being thrown in the Crimson Hand's former headquarters."

"You," said Shinyun to the dryad, in a commanding tone. "What did he say about a party?"

The dryad looked puzzled, but he answered readily enough. "The masked ball tonight, to celebrate Valentine Morgenstern's defeat in the Mortal War. This huge place just turned up on the market, and a warlock rented it out for a big bash. People from all over the Shadow World are attending. A whole bunch of us came down by train from Paris." He puffed his chest out, cheeks emerald with pride. "You know, if the Downworlders hadn't banded together to defeat him, the whole world would have been endangered."

"The Shadowhunters *were* involved," said Alec.

The dryad flapped a hand, leaves fluttering at his wrist. "I heard they helped."

"So a lot of people are coming to this fete?" Magnus asked. "I was hoping to meet up with a warlock friend of mine. His name is Mori Shu. Is he on the list?"

Behind him, Magnus heard Shinyun draw in a quick breath.

The satyr flipped through his papers. "Yes, here he is. Someone told me he might not make it, though, something about him laying low recently. Some demon thing."

"You are, of course, completely invited," said the dryad to Magnus. "You and your companions. It was an oversight that you weren't on the guest list already."

The satyr took this in and dutifully flipped to the end of his list to write in Magnus's name.

"I am very offended to have been excluded from the invitations, and therefore I, and my companions, will definitely be attending," said Magnus loftily.

The dryad took a moment to comprehend, then nodded. "Doors will open at eight."

"We'll be there much, much later than that," said Magnus, "because of our already very packed social calendar."

"Of course," said the dryad.

They headed down the steps and reconnoitered there.

"This is perfect," said Alec. "We go to the party, we sneak away, we find the Chamber. Easy enough."

Shinyun nodded agreement.

"You two think you're going to a party?" Magnus asked. "Dressed like that?"

Alec and Shinyun looked at each other. Shinyun was wearing her power suit, which was expensive, but the opposite of party wear. Her *samgakdo* was at her belt. Alec was wearing a faded T-shirt and jeans that somehow had paint on them. Magnus had already added to Alec's wardrobe in Paris, but they definitely didn't have carnival masks or elaborate costumes, which as far as Magnus was concerned made for an excellent opportunity for one of his favorite things.

"Come, demon hunters," he said grandly. "We're going shopping."

CHAPTER ELEVEN

Masks

"I DON'T SAY THIS LIGHTLY," SAID MAGNUS. "BUT—TA-DA!"

Magnus had taken them to Le Mercerie for what he promised would be a shopping extravaganza. Alec had gone shopping with Magnus before, so he was pretty familiar with the process. He waited at each store with half a dozen bags as the warlock tried on nearly everything, from traditional suits to matador *traje de luces* to something that looked suspiciously like a mariachi costume. Every style and color seemed to work with his dark hair and green-gold cat eyes, so Alec wasn't sure what Magnus was searching for. Whatever he chose, Alec was sure it would look good.

This outfit was no exception. Magnus was wearing black leather trousers, the material sleeking along his long legs as if the lean muscle had been dipped in ink. His belt was a metal snake, the links scales and the buckle a cobra's head with sapphire eyes. His cowl-neck shirt was a waterfall of midnight-blue and indigo sequins, dipping low in front to show not only collarbones but a long stretch of skin.

Magnus spun, then regarded himself consideringly in the mirror, his back to Alec. The view made Alec's mouth go dry.

Alec said, "I think you look—nice."

"Any concerns?"

"Well," Alec said. "Those pants would make it difficult to maneuver in a fight, but you won't need to fight. I can fight for you, if it comes up."

Magnus looked taken aback, and Alec was not sure if he'd said something wrong, until Magnus's expression softened. "I appreciate your offer. Now," he added, "I'm just going to try on one more thing." He disappeared back into the dressing room.

Next he appeared in a collarless suit with a matching uneven short-cloak hanging carelessly from his shoulders. Shinyun appeared in what seemed to be a combination of armor and a wedding dress.

Five minutes into their first store, Alec had picked out what Magnus described as a frock coat, long and black with medium-length tails. It was flexible enough to move and fight in, and loose enough in the right places to store his stele and seraph blades. Magnus had wanted him to try on something with a little more color, but Alec had said no and Magnus had not pushed the issue. The shirt beneath it was silk and deep blue, the color of Alec's eyes.

After trying on a few rather quiet dresses, Shinyun had seen Magnus parade out of the changing room wearing a gold suit based loosely on an Egyptian pharaoh's burial chamber, and came out next in an elaborate peach-colored *hanbok*. Magnus offered several compliments, and the race was on.

Shinyun was competitive with Magnus. Maybe all warlocks were competitive with each other. Alec hadn't met many, and wouldn't know.

He was trying not to worry too much about Shinyun. Magnus clearly liked her, but Alec was awkward with strangers, and he desperately didn't want to be any more awkward on their romantic trip. How were he and Magnus meant to get to know each other better with a third wheel always around?

Maybe not worrying was a lost cause. Alec was trying not to show he was worried, at least.

Alec nudged the wide-eyed sales attendant next to him. "Where did you get these costumes?"

The young woman shook her head, speaking in careful English. "I have no idea. I have never seen any of these clothes before."

"Huh," Alec said. "Weird."

In the end, Magnus was sporting a shimmering white suit decorated with what looked like iridescent dragon scales, wreathing him in opalescent light. He wore an ivory cloak that hung to his knees, and the collar of his shirt was undone, pearly material curling against the brown of his skin.

Shinyun had decided to go big with an ornate black dress with massive ribbons looping around her hips. Intricate silver vines hung from her neck to the floor, and a fountain of flowers rose from behind her head.

They asked Alec to help them with their final mask choices. For Magnus, it was between a gold mask with a plume of orange feathers fanning out in a half circle, and a reflective silver domino mask that was almost too bright to look at. Shinyun's two choices were either a plain full-face marble mask or a thin, naked wired mask that hardly covered anything, both ironic choices. Alec went with the silver one for Magnus and the wired one for Shinyun. She fixed it over her impassive face with a faint air of satisfaction.

"You look good," Magnus told her. His eyes slid to Alec, and he handed Alec a silk half-mask, the deep blue color of twilight. Alec accepted it, and Magnus smiled. "And you look perfect. Let's go."

DUSK CURTAINED THE CITY. THE PALAZZO WAS DECO-rated with torches that dotted the tops of the walls. A white fog had settled over the streets around the palazzo, curling around pillars and blanketing canals, lending the scene an eerie glow. Alec could not tell if it was magic or naturally occurring.

Over the marble facade of the building were faerie lights that sparkled and shifted, moving every other minute to spell out the words ANY DAY BUT VALENTINE'S DAY.

Alec was not a fan of parties, but he could at least appreciate the reason behind this one.

He had fought to stop Valentine Morgenstern. He would have given his life to do it. He hadn't given much thought to how Downworlders overall regarded Valentine, who thought they were unclean and planned to wipe the stain of their existence from the earth. Now he saw how scared they must have been.

The Shadowhunters had many celebrated warriors. Alec hadn't realized how it would be for Downworlders to have a Downworlder victory and war heroes of their own—not just of one clan or one family or one pack, but that belonged to all of Downworld together.

He would have been even more sympathetic if the werewolf security team had not insisted on patting him down. Twice. The security didn't seem all that strict, until they spotted Alec's runes.

"This is ridiculous," he snapped. "I fought in the war whose victory you're celebrating. On the winning side," he added quickly.

The head of security, the largest of the werewolves—Alec figured that made sense—had been summoned. He said to Alec in a low voice, "We just don't want any trouble."

"I wasn't planning to be any trouble. I am only," Alec said clearly, "here to party."

"And I thought there were going to be two of you," the werewolf muttered.

"What?" said Alec. "Two Shadowhunters?"

The werewolf shrugged his burly shoulders. "Lord, I hope not."

Magnus said, "Are you finished with my dance partner yet? I

understand it's difficult to keep your hands off him, but I really must insist."

The security head shrugged and waved a hand. "Fine, go."

"Thanks," said Alec in a low voice, and reached for Magnus's hand. The security guards had confiscated his bow and arrow, but he wasn't too bothered since they'd missed the six seraph blades and four daggers he also had concealed about his person. "These people are impossible."

Magnus moved back a fraction, so Alec missed catching his hand.

"Some of these people are my friends," said Magnus. But then he shrugged and smiled. "Some of my friends are impossible."

Alec was not entirely convinced. He was unsettled by the space between their hands. They went into the glittering mansion with that small, cold distance between them.

CHAPTER TWELVE

Tread Softly

JOHANN STRAUSS'S "EMPEROR WALTZ" WAS PLAYING IN the grand ballroom. Magnus saw hundreds of masked people in elaborate costumes dancing in unison, and around them was music that could be seen as well as heard. As if ripped from a black-and-white sheet of paper and turned into bright, living shapes, the notes floated in the air, drifting along currents of musical lines and wrapping around the glittering masks and elaborate hair of the dancers.

Along the ceiling, the constellations were moving; no, they were the orchestra. Stars moved to suggest the shapes of people and instruments. Libra was first chair, playing the violin, Ursa Major next to him his second. Aquila played the viola while Scorpio was on the bass. Orion played the cello, Hercules was on percussion. The stars played, while the masked couples danced, and the musical notes floated in between.

Magnus moved down the Carrara marble stairs from the foyer into the ballroom with Alec and Shinyun shadowing him like bodyguards.

"Prince Adaon," he called, recognizing a friend.

Prince Adaon, his swan mask a gorgeous contrast to his dark skin, sent Magnus a grin over the heads of his courtiers.

"You're on speaking terms with a prince?" Alec asked.

"I wouldn't speak to most of the Unseelie Court princes," said Magnus. "You wouldn't believe the kind of things they get up to. They should only be thankful there are no faerie tabloids. Adaon's the best of the bunch."

As they came to the foot of the staircase, they met a man in a lavender tuxedo and a full-face mask of El Muerto, his white hair slicked back. Magnus grinned.

"Our host, I believe."

"What makes you think that?" asked the man in a low English accent.

"Who else could have thrown this party? I commend you on going all out. No sense in going half out." Magnus reached over and shook his hand. "Malcolm Fade. It's been a long time."

"Just before the millennium turned. I remember you were going through a particularly grungy period last I saw you."

"Yes. It was called grunge. I was surprised to hear you moved to Los Angeles, and they made you High Warlock."

Malcolm raised his mask, and Magnus saw him smile, the expression always sweet and more than a little sad.

"I know. Those fools."

"Belated congratulations," said Magnus. "How's it going? You've been working on something, and clearly it was not your tan."

"Oh, I dabble in many things, party planning among them." Malcolm waved a hand toward the spectacle of the grand ballroom. He pulled off his absentminded routine beautifully, but Magnus had known him a long time. "Glad you are enjoying my little soiree."

Two people came up behind Malcolm, one a blue-skinned faerie with lavender hair and webbed hands, and one a familiar face. Johnny Rook's sunglasses were pushed down his nose, which was reasonable if you thought wearing sunglasses indoors at night was reasonable in the first place. Over his sunglasses, Magnus saw his eyes widen in recognition, and he averted his gaze from Magnus's.

"Oh, do you know each other? You must know each other," said Malcolm dreamily. "This is Hyacinth, who is my indispensable party planner. And Johnny Rook. I'm sure he's indispensable to somebody."

Magnus gestured. "These are Alexander Lightwood, Shadow-hunter, New York Institute, and Shinyun Jung, mysterious warrior with a mysterious past."

"How mysterious," began Malcolm, and then his attention was diverted by the arrival of several pallets of raw meat. He looked around helplessly. "Does anyone know what's to be done with all this raw meat?"

"That's for the werewolves." Hyacinth waved the deliveryman over. "I'll take care of it. However, your personal attention may be required in the drawing room."

She put her hand to a glittering seashell fixed in her ear and whispered something to Malcolm. The blood drained from the High Warlock of Los Angeles's already pale face.

"Oh dear. You'll excuse me. Our sirens have taken up residence next to the champagne fountain and are trying to drown guests in it." He hurried off.

"You were in the Shadow Market," Alec said to Johnny Rook, recognition dawning.

"You've never seen me before," said Johnny. "You're not even seeing me right now." He sprinted out of the ballroom.

Alec was watching the whole room with a closed-off, suspicious look on his face. Many people in the crowd were returning his look with interest.

Magnus had brought a cop to the party. He understood that. He couldn't blame Alec for being wary. Almost all Downworlders had pasts stained red. Vampires did suck blood, faerie and warlock magic went wrong, werewolves lost control and other people lost limbs. At the same time, Magnus could not blame his fellow Downworlders for being guarded either. Not so long ago, Shadowhunters had decorated their walls with Downworlder heads.

"Hey, Magnus!" called out a warlock wearing a plain green dress and a white plague doctor's mask, deep blue skin showing beneath.

Magnus was delighted by her appearance.

"Hello, darling," he said, and swept her into a hug. After spinning her off her feet, he presented her proudly to his companions. "Alec, Shinyun, this is Catarina Loss. She's one of my oldest friends."

"Oh," said Catarina. "I've heard a lot about you, Alexander Lightwood."

Alec looked alarmed.

Magnus wanted them to like each other. He watched them watching each other. Well, these things took time.

"May I speak to you a moment, Magnus?" Catarina asked. "In private?"

"I'll go search for our stone goat," said Shinyun, heading off.

Catarina looked puzzled. "Just one of her more colorful figures of speech," Magnus said. "She has a mysterious past, you see."

"I should go too," said Alec. He jogged to catch up with Shinyun and conferred with her—it looked to Magnus like they were deciding who would search where.

"I'll see you back here in the foyer!" Magnus called. Alec gave a thumbs-up without turning around.

Catarina hooked her hand around Magnus's elbow and hauled him away, like a schoolteacher with a misbehaving student. They entered a narrow alcove around the corner, where the music and noise of the party was muffled. She rounded on him.

"I recently treated Tessa for wounds she said were inflicted on her by members of a demon-worshipping cult," Catarina said. "She told me you were, and I quote, 'handling' the cult. What's going on? Explain."

Magnus made a face. "I may have had a hand in founding it."

"How much of a hand?"

"Well, both."

Catarina bristled. "I specifically told you not to do that!"

"You did?" Magnus said. A bubble of hope grew within him. "You remember what happened?"

She gave him a look of distress. "You don't?"

"Someone took all my memories around the subject of this cult," said Magnus. "I don't know who, or why."

He sounded more desperate than he would've liked, more desperate than he wanted to be. His old friend's face was full of sympathy.

"I don't know anything about it," she said. "I met up with you and Ragnor for a brief vacation. You seemed troubled, but you were trying to laugh it off, the way you always do. You and Ragnor said you had a brilliant idea to start a joke cult. I told you not to do it. That's it."

He, Catarina, and Ragnor had taken many trips together, over the centuries. One memorable trip had gotten Magnus banished from Peru. He had always enjoyed those adventures more than any others. Being with his friends almost felt like having a home.

He did not know if there would ever be another trip. Ragnor was dead, and Magnus might have done something terrible.

"Why didn't you stop me?" he asked. "You usually stop me!"

"I had to take an orphan child across an ocean to save his life."

"Right," said Magnus. "That's a good reason."

Catarina shook her head. "I took my eyes off you for one second."

She had worked in mundane hospitals in New York for decades. She saved orphans. She healed the sick. She'd always been the voice of reason in the trio that was Ragnor, Catarina, and Magnus.

"So I planned with Ragnor to start a joke cult, and I guess I did it. Now the joke cult is a real cult, and they have a new leader. It sounds like they're mixed up with a Greater Demon."

Even to Catarina, he wouldn't say the name of his father.

"Sounds like the joke has gotten a little out of hand," Catarina said dryly.

"Sounds like I'm the punch line. There are all these rumors the new leader is me. I have to find these guys. Do you know a man called Mori Shu?"

Catarina shook her head. "You know I don't know anyone."

A group of drunken faeries stumbled past. The celebration was noticeably ratcheting up in decibels and wildness. Catarina waited until they were alone again to continue.

"You're in this mess and you still have a Shadowhunter with you?" she demanded. "Magnus, I knew you were seeing him, but this is a long way past having fun. It's his *duty* to tell the Clave about you founding this cult. They'll hear the rumor you're leading it eventually, whether your Lightwood tells them or not. The Nephilim won't look any further for a culprit. The Nephilim do not admit weakness. There is no room in their hearts for pity or mercy. I have seen the children of the Angel murder their own for breaking their precious Law. Magnus, we're talking about your life."

"Catarina," said Magnus, "I love him."

She stared at him. Her eyes were the color of the ocean, swept by storms and with treasure sunk below the waves. She had worn a plague mask during real plagues. She had seen so many tragedies, and they both knew the worst tragedies were born of love.

"Are you sure?" she said quietly. "You always hope for the best, but this time hope is too dangerous. This one could hurt you worse than the others. This one could get you killed."

"I'm sure," said Magnus. "Am I sure it will work out?" He thought of the small coldness between him and Alec before they had entered the party. He thought of all the secrets he was still keeping. "No. But I'm sure I love him."

Catarina's eyes were sad. "But does he love you?"

"For now," Magnus said. "And if you'll excuse me, I need to go search out the stone goat, if you understand my meaning."

"I don't," said Catarina, "but good luck, I guess."

For the next hour, Magnus dedicated himself to his task of finding the stupid goat. He decided to cover the main floor, since Shinyun and Alec had both gone elsewhere, and commenced a careful study of the rooms one by one, first the sitting and then the music and then the game room, subtly using his magic to detect hidden latches or levers or buttons that opened up to secret passageways. Unfortunately, the entire mansion was so steeped in magic from the celebration that all his discovery spells came back distorted and inconclusive.

Magnus kept at it, taking his time to feel through the rooms as he navigated around the crowds, brushing his hand along all the usual suspects: twisting candelabras, pulling books, pushing against statues. He tugged a bellpull that turned out to be seaweed, revealing a mostly underwater room where a group of mermaids were frolicking with a lone vampire.

The vampire, a lunatic of Magnus's acquaintance named Elliott, waved at him until the water foamed.

"Don't mind me," Magnus called. "Carry on splashing."

Nothing was out of the ordinary.

He reached the smoking room at the end of the west wing. A large mantel on the side wall served as the centerpiece of this richly furnished room, filled with curved and heavily plush Victorian furniture. Each of the pieces was monstrously out of proportion. A gigantic button-tucked red settee the size of a car was arranged next to a pair of blue high-backed chairs that looked as if they were meant for children. Along each wall were moving wallpapers and brass sconces alternating with gramophones piping jazz.

A dryad, not the one he'd met earlier, was sitting on a swing dangling from a chandelier in the center of the room. A taupe day-bed hung vertically against the far wall and was currently being enjoyed by a vampire lounging as if she were right side up. Magnus hadn't known that Malcolm dabbled in antigravity magic, but he appreciated the High Warlock of the City of Angels' flair.

"You look like you could use a smoke, Magnus Bane," said a woman from somewhere off to the side.

He followed the sound of the voice and saw a mahogany-skinned woman wearing a chic metal dress that matched her bronze hair perfectly. Her mask was a cascade of golden stars that ran from the top of her head down past her chin. They matched her pupils, which were star-shaped too.

"Hypatia," said Magnus. "Thanks, but I quit a hundred years ago. I was going through a rebellious phase."

Hypatia Vex was a London-based warlock with an affinity for business and property ownership. Their paths had crossed a few times over the years, and they had been rather close at one point, but that was long ago. Over a century.

He took a seat opposite Hypatia, in the slightly too-small high-backed chairs. Hypatia crossed her legs and leaned forward, taking a long drag. "I heard a rather nasty rumor about you."

Magnus also crossed his legs but leaned back. "Do tell. I love a good nasty rumor."

"Leading a cult called the Crimson Hand to glory and destruction?" Hypatia asked. "You naughty boy."

Magnus supposed he shouldn't be surprised that Hypatia knew about the cult. Unlike small-time Johnny Rook, Hypatia was the big leagues. She'd run a Downworld salon in the early 1900s, the center for every scandal in London. Magnus remembered all the secrets she'd known then, and she was a collector: he could only imagine she had a great many more by now.

"I cannot deny being a naughty boy in the more general sense," Magnus admitted. "Glory and destruction, however, is not my style. The rumor's totally unfounded."

Hypatia gave a graceful shrug. "It did seem far-fetched, but it appears to be spreading like wildfire these last few days. You might want to consider how it looks—running a whole cult *and* carrying on with a Shadowhunter? Not just a Shadowhunter, but the son of two members of Valentine's Circle?"

"That's not a rumor."

"Glad to hear it," Hypatia said. "He sounds like a disaster."

"It's a fact," said Magnus. "And he is a delight."

The expression on Hypatia's face was a picture. In all the years he'd known her, Magnus had never actually seen her look shocked before.

"You would do well to remember that you are one of the most prominent warlocks in the world," said Hypatia when she'd recovered herself. "There are Downworlders who look to you as an example. There are eyes on you."

"Usually," said Magnus. "It's my dashing good looks."

"Don't be dismissive," Hypatia said sharply.

"Hypatia," said Magnus. "Have you ever known me to care how things look?"

Gold earrings swung against her dark brown skin as she shook her head. "No. But you do care about others, and I am sure you care about this Alec Lightwood. I know who your father is, if you recall, Magnus. You and I used to be quite close."

Magnus did recall. "I don't see what that has to do with Alec."

"Have you told him about your father?" she demanded.

After a long pause, Magnus said, "No."

Hypatia relaxed slightly. "Good. I hope you're not thinking of doing so."

"I don't see that it's any of your business what I tell my boyfriend."

"I'm sure you regard Alec Lightwood as being of the highest moral caliber, Magnus," Hypatia said, choosing her words with care. "And you might not be wrong. But imagine the position you would be putting him in if he knew that the Council's warlock representative is also the son of the demon worshipped by the Crimson Hand, a cult that is wreaking havoc right now. If he truly cares for you, he'd conceal that knowledge, and if it ever got out, both of you would be implicated by your shared secrecy. History has shown that the Nephilim are capable of cruelty to their own as well as to Downworlders. Especially those among them who do not fall into the status quo."

"We all have demon parents, Hypatia. It isn't like that's a surprise," Magnus said.

"You know as well as I do that not all demons are created equal. Not all of them would be regarded with the same hate and fear your father is. But since you bring it up, this *does* impact all of us. Warlocks have walked a fine line with the Nephilim for centuries. We are tolerated because our talents are useful. Many of us have professional relationships with the Clave. You're one of the most famous warlocks in the world, and like it or not, the way you are perceived reflects upon all of us. Please don't do anything that could jeopardize the safety we've fought for. You know it has been hard-won."

Magnus wanted to be angry. He wanted to tell Hypatia to stay out of his business, his love life.

But he could tell she was speaking earnestly. The edge to her voice was real. She was afraid.

He cleared his throat. "I'll take it under advisement. Hypatia, since you seem to be so well-informed, do you know someone called Mori Shu?"

"I do," said Hypatia, sitting back in her chair. She seemed a bit embarrassed by the passion of her outburst. "Isn't he part of your cult?"

"It's not *my* cult," Magnus said doggedly.

"He's here tonight," Hypatia said. "I saw him earlier. Maybe you two should have a chat, get all this cult business cleared up."

"Well, maybe we will."

"If you'll take my advice," said Hypatia, "I'd get the Shadow-hunter business cleared up too."

Magnus gave her a ferociously bright smile. "Unasked-for advice is criticism, my dear."

"Well, your funeral," said Hypatia. "Wait. Do the Nephilim give you a funeral, after they execute you?"

"Nice seeing you, Hypatia," said Magnus, and left.

He felt in need of a drink. He wended his way through the crowd until he found a bar. He took a seat at it, and ordered a Dark and Stormy to match his mood. Catarina's worry and Hypatia's horror had left a dent in his usually hopeful heart.

The bar was set up against a window. Through the bottles, Magnus could see another dance party in full swing in the court-yard below, and hear faint music filtering out from the glowing green bubble that surrounded the dancers. He had pictured danc-ing with Alec, in beautiful places around Europe, but they weren't. Because of something from Magnus's past.

Magnus snapped his fingers and a crystal glass fell into his hand, filling with amber liquid as the bottle on the shelf began to drain.

"Hello there," said Shinyun, wandering up to him with a glass of red wine in hand.

Magnus touched glasses with her. "Any luck?"

"No. I tried some detection spells, but they've been unclear."

"I've had the same problem," he said. Magnus sipped his drink and studied Shinyun's immobile face. "The cult is personal to you," he continued. It was not a question. "You talk about demon-hunting, but you won't talk about the cult. They didn't just kill people you loved. You feel guilty about something connected to the Crimson Hand. What is it?"

They both looked out into the courtyard full of dancers. Several moments passed.

"Can you keep a secret?" Shinyun asked.

"It depends on the secret," said Magnus.

"I will trust you with this one. You can do with it whatever you please." She turned to face him. "I—I used to be a part of it. The Crimson Hand is mostly a human cult, but they recruit warlock children." Shinyun's voice turned wry. "There was a time when I used to worship you, the Great Poison, holy founder and prophet of the Crimson Hand, the worshippers of Asmodeus."

"Asmodeus?" Magnus repeated softly, as any hope he'd had that Johnny Rook had been wrong trickled away like blood from a wound.

He remembered, hundreds of years ago, wanting to find out who his father was. That was how he'd found out that you could use faerie blood to summon a Greater Demon.

Magnus hadn't harmed a Downworlder to call his father to him. He'd found another way. He'd looked his father in the face, and spoken to him, then turned away, sick at heart.

"Nobody ever tried to summon Asmodeus, in those days, of course," said Shinyun. "That's a new wrinkle. But we talked about him all the time. Every orphaned warlock child was his child, the cult said. I thought of myself as his daughter. Everything I did was in his service."

Warlock children. He remembered how he had felt as a warlock child, desperate and alone. Anyone could have taken advantage of his desperation.

He felt overwhelmed by horror. He had heard the name of the Crimson Hand over the years—they were a joke, as he had said to Tessa, and Tessa had agreed. Was it only their new leader who was a problem, or had they been a problem for much longer than anyone realized and somehow kept their true nature quiet?

"You worshipped me?" Magnus asked, and could not suppress the despairing edge to his voice. "I'm glad you've been cured of that nonsense. How long were you in this cult?"

"Many decades," she said bitterly. "A lifetime's worth. I used to—I used to kill for them. I thought I was killing for you, in your name." She paused. "Please don't tell the Shadowhunter—Alec— that I killed for them. You can tell him I was in the cult, if you must."

"No," Magnus whispered, but he didn't know if he was saying it for Shinyun's sake or for his own. Shinyun said she'd thought of herself as Asmodeus's child. He could only imagine her horror if she knew Magnus actually was Asmodeus's child. He thought of Hypatia, her warning that he must not reveal his father's identity to Alec. *Imagine the position you would be putting him in. History has shown that the Nephilim are capable of cruelty to their own as well as to Downworlders.*

"It has been many more lifetimes since I broke free from their clutches. I've been trying to bring them down ever since, but I wasn't strong enough to do it on my own, and then this mysterious new leader came. I didn't have anyone to turn to. I felt so helpless."

"How did you happen to join them?"

Shinyun bowed her head. "I've already told you more than I ever intended to."

Magnus didn't press further. He didn't talk about his childhood either.

"You are brave to come back and face your past," he said quietly. "I'd say 'face your demons,' but that seems too on the nose."

Shinyun snorted.

"I don't suppose you know where the Crimson Hand's Chamber is?" Shinyun was already shaking her head as Magnus added, without much hope: "Or these Red Scrolls of Magic?"

"Mori would know," Shinyun told him. "The members of the Crimson Hand trusted him more than me. We used to be close, but I had to leave him behind when I fled. It's been years—but I would know him if I saw him, and he would trust me."

"He's here," said Magnus, "supposedly." Magnus clicked his fingers, and his glass disappeared in a crystal-bright wink. Then he reached for a bottle of champagne from a nearby chiller. This was an impressive party, but Magnus was having a terrible time. He had turned up no secret lairs, and found no sign of this annoying mystery man. He wanted to dance, and he wanted to forget that there was so much he didn't remember.

"I'll ask around about him," said Shinyun.

"You do that," Magnus said, rising from the bar. "I have someone to attend to."

He loved Alec, and he wanted to lay his past and his truths in front of Alec, like bolts of shining silk at his feet. He wanted to tell Alec who his father was, and hope it would not matter. But how could he confess to Alec what he didn't remember? And how could he tell Alec secrets that had the potential to make him a target of the Clave, like Hypatia had said?

He trusted Alec. He trusted him implicitly. But trust did not guarantee Alec's safety. Besides, Magnus had trusted and been wrong before. As he headed out in search of Alec, he could not silence the echo of his old friend's voice in his ears.

But does he love you?

CHAPTER THIRTEEN

Dance Me to Your Beauty

ALEC WATCHED AS MAGNUS'S FRIEND CATARINA LOSS LED him away. A moment later Shinyun exited through the large double doors, presumably to check the estate grounds, leaving Alec standing alone in the midst of a ball.

Alec was very glad he was wearing a mask. He felt abandoned in hostile territory. Actually, he would much rather have been abandoned in hostile territory than left to stand around at a party.

Magnus had said some of these people were his friends.

During their adventures in New York, Magnus had always seemed so independent and self-sufficient. Alec was the one with the ties: to his fellow Shadowhunters, and above all to his sister and his *parabatai*. It had never occurred to Alec that Magnus had multiple loyalties as well. Magnus was not getting invited to parties, was being cut out of his own world, because he was with Alec.

If Alec wanted to be with Magnus, he had to be able to get along with Magnus's friends. Magnus always made the effort to help out Alec's friends. Alec had to find some way to do this, though he could not imagine how.

He remembered with deep relief that he had a mission.

He twisted his way through the crowded hallways into what must be the servants' quarters, which were only slightly less crowded than the main rooms. Here, a small army of staff—mostly djinns, kelpies, and sprites—flitted about, making sure the music and lights stayed on, the alcohol remained flowing, and the mansion was kept clean. There was a sitting room for a dozen or so warlocks, who were constantly rotating shifts to maintain the magic. An entire pack of werewolves handled security.

He made one quick pass down the servants' hall behind the dining room and entered the kitchen, only to get thrown out by the head chef, a very angry goblin.

He left the kitchen hastily. The goblin, waving a cleaver and a spatula, could not keep up.

There was no sign anywhere of a stone goat. Alec tried to find his way back to the party, where he could ask if anyone had seen this Mori Shu guy, though the idea of interrupting strangers to interrogate them wasn't the most attractive.

He heard faint music coming from behind one door. He opened the door and walked into a room painted with murals of forest scenes, feathery vines, and deep pools. Against the mural, two women were making out. One woman was tiny and wearing bright purple that shone in the romantic gloom. The taller one, a woman with long, silvery-blond hair pulled back from the curve of her faerie ears, raised her eyebrow at Alec over her companion's shoulder. Her companion giggled and slid her hand up the blond faerie woman's black-clad thigh.

Alec walked backward out of the room.

He closed the door.

He wondered where Magnus was.

He wandered through the mansion. The next room he passed contained a group of Downworlders playing cards. He poked his head in and realized what sort of game it was when someone said something about fish, and then a brownie wearing a bird mask, who had apparently lost the hand, stood up and began to unbutton his shirt.

"Oh, wow, excuse me," said Alec, fleeing.

A pixie grabbed his hand. "You can stay, Shadowhunter. Show us some of your runes."

"Let go, please," said Alec.

Her eyes sparkled mischievously at him.

"I asked politely," said Alec. "I won't again."

She let go. Alec continued his weary quest for Mori Shu, any signs of cult activity, or at the very least someone who wouldn't make a pass at him.

In one hallway, the floor gleaming parquet and the ceiling festooned with golden cherubs, there was a boy in a grumpy cat mask and biker boots, not involved in any sexual activity, legs crossed and leaning against the wall. As a bevy of faeries passed the boy, giggling and groping, the boy scooted away.

Alec remembered being younger, and how overwhelming large groups of people had seemed. He came over and leaned against the wall beside the boy. He saw the boy texting, PARTIES WERE INVENTED TO ANNOY ME. THEY FEATURE MY LEAST FAVORITE THING: PEOPLE, ALL INTENT ON MY LEAST FAVORITE ACTIVITY: SOCIAL INTERACTION.

"I don't really like parties either," Alec said sympathetically.

"No hablo italiano," the boy mumbled without looking up.

"Er," said Alec. "This conversation is happening in English."

"No hablo ingles," he said without missing a beat.

"Oh, come on. Really?"

"Worth a shot," said the boy.

Alec considered going away. The boy wrote another text to a contact he had saved as *RF*. Alec could not help but notice that the conversation was entirely one-sided, the boy sending text after text with no response. The last text read VENICE SMELLS LIKE A TOILET. AS A NEW YORKER, I DO NOT SAY THIS LIGHTLY.

The weird coincidence emboldened Alec to try again.

"I get shy when there are strangers too," Alec told the kid.

"I'm not shy," the boy sneered. "I just hate everyone around me and everything that is happening."

"Well." Alec shrugged. "Those feel like similar things sometimes."

The boy lifted his curly head, pushing the grumpy cat mask off his face, and froze. Alec froze too, at the twin shock of fangs and familiarity. This was a vampire, and Alec knew him.

"Raphael?" he asked. "Raphael Santiago?"

He wondered what the second-in-command of the New York clan was doing here. Downworlders might be flooding in from all over the world, but Raphael had never struck Alec as a party animal.

Of course, he was not exactly coming off as a party animal now.

"Oh no, it's you," said Raphael. "The twelve-year-old idiot."

Alec was not keen on vampires. They were, after all, people who had died. Alec had seen too much death to want reminders of it.

He understood that they were immortal, but there was no need to show off about it.

"We just fought a war together. I was with you in the graveyard when Simon came back as a vampire. You've seen me *multiple* times since I was twelve."

"The thought of you at twelve haunts me," Raphael said darkly.

"Okay," Alec said, humoring him. "So have you seen a guy called Mori Shu anywhere around here?"

"I am trying not to make eye contact with anyone here," said Raphael. "And I'm not a snitch for Shadowhunters. Or a fan of talking to people, of any kind, in any place."

Alec rolled his eyes. At this point, a faerie woman came twirling through. She had leaves in her updo and was swathed in ribbons and ivy and not much else. She tripped on a trailing line of ivy and Alec caught her.

"Good reflexes!" she said brightly. "Also great arms. Would you be interested in a night of tumultuous forbidden passion, with an option to extend to seven years?"

"Um, I am gay," Alec said.

He was not used to saying that casually, to any random person. It was strange to say it, and feel both relief and a shadow of his old fear, twined together.

Of course, the declaration might not mean much to faeries. The faerie woman accepted it with a shrug, then looked over at Raphael and lit up. Something about the leather jacket or the scowl seemed to appeal to her strongly.

"How about you, Vampire Without a Cause?"

"I'm not gay," said Raphael. "I'm not straight. I'm not interested."

"Your sexuality is 'not interested'?" Alec asked curiously.

Raphael said, "That's right."

The faerie thought for a moment, then ventured, "I can also assume the appearance of a tree!"

"I didn't say, 'not interested unless you're a tree.'"

"Wait," said the faerie suddenly. "I recognize you. You're Raphael Santiago! I've heard of you."

Raphael made a gesture of dismissal. "Have you heard I like it when people go away?"

"You were one of the heroes in the Downworlder victory over Valentine."

"He was one of the heroes of the Downworlder and Shadowhunter alliance, which led to the victory," Alec said.

Raphael stopped looking annoyed and began to look nastily amused.

"Oh, did the Shadowhunters help a little?" he asked.

"You were there!" said Alec.

"Can I have your autograph, Raphael?" asked the faerie lady.

She produced a large, shiny green leaf and a quill. Raphael wrote *LEAVE ME ALONE* on the leaf.

"I'll cherish it," said the faerie. She ran away, clutching the leaf to her bosom.

"Don't," Raphael yelled after her.

A blast of music echoing down the corridors was his only reply. Alec and Raphael both winced. Raphael glanced up at him.

"This is the worst party I've ever been to," he said. "And I hate parties. People keep asking me whether I have extra superpowers, and I tell them they are thinking of Simon, whom I dislike."

"That's a little harsh," said Alec.

"You have to be harsh with fledglings or they do not learn," said Raphael sternly. "Besides, his jokes are stupid."

"They're not all gold," Alec admitted.

"How do you know him?" Raphael snapped his fingers. "Wait, I remember. He's friends with your annoying blond *parabatai*, right?"

He was, though Simon would probably be surprised to hear it. Alec was very familiar with how Jace behaved when he wanted to be your friend. He didn't act friendly, which would have been too easy. Instead he just spent a lot of time in your presence until you got used to him being there, which he was clearly now doing with regard to Simon. When Jace and Alec were little, Jace had done a lot of hostile hanging around him, hoping to be noticed and loved. Alec honestly preferred it to awkward getting-to-know-you conversations.

"Right. Plus, Simon is sort of dating my sister, Isabelle," said Alec.

"That can't be," said Raphael. "Isabelle can do better."

"Er, do you know my sister?" Alec asked.

"She threatened me with a candelabra once, but we don't really chat," said Raphael. "Which means we have my ideal relationship." He gave Alec a cold glare. "It's the relationship I wish I had with all Shadowhunters."

Alec was about to give up and walk away, when a pretty vampire woman in a cheongsam came flying down the hallway, ribbons waving from her purple-streaked hair like a silken flag. Her face was familiar. Alec had seen her at Taki's, and around the city more generally, usually with Raphael.

"Save us, oh fearless leader," said Raphael's lady friend. "Elliott's in a huge aquarium puking blue and green. He tried to drink mermaid blood. He tried to drink selkie blood. He tried to—"

"*Ahem,*" said Raphael, with a savage jerk of his head in Alec's direction.

Alec waved. "Shadowhunter," he said. "Right here. Hi."

"He tried to keep to the Accords and obey all the known Laws!" the woman declared. "Because that's the New York clan's idea of a truly festive good time."

Alec remembered Magnus and tried not to look like he was here to ruin the Downworlder party. There was one thing he and this woman had in common. He recognized the bright purple she was wearing.

"I think I saw you earlier," said Alec hesitantly. "You were—making out with a faerie girl?"

"Yeah, you're gonna have to be more specific than that," said the vampire woman. "This is a party. I've made out with six faerie girls, four faerie boys, and a talking toadstool whose gender I'm unsure about. Pretty sexy for a toadstool, though."

Raphael covered his face briefly with his non-texting hand.

"Why, you want to make something of it?" The woman bristled. "How happy I am to see the Nephilim constantly crashing our parties. Were you even invited?"

"I'm a plus-one," said Alec.

The vampire girl relaxed slightly. "Oh, right, you're Magnus's latest disaster," she said. "That's what Raphael calls you. I'm Lily."

She lifted a hand in a halfhearted wave. Alec glanced at Raphael, who arched his eyebrow at Alec in an unfriendly way.

"Didn't realize Raphael and I were on pet name terms," said Alec. He continued to study Raphael. "Do you know Magnus well?"

"Hardly at all," said Raphael. "Barely acquainted. I don't think much of his personality. Or his dress sense. Or the company he keeps. Come away, Lily. Alexander, I hope I never see you again."

"I've decided I detest you," Lily told Alec.

"It's mutual," Alec said dryly.

Unexpectedly, that made the vampire woman smile, before Raphael dragged her away.

Alec was almost sorry to see them go. They were a piece of New York, even if they were vampires and, for some reason, incredibly hostile toward him in particular. Alec had never met anyone worse at parties than he was before.

He could not give up his search yet. He made his way downward, searching for the basement, and found a bowling alley that had been turned into an impromptu dueling venue. Next to it was a theater that he could only describe as a Roman toga orgy room. At the far end was a swimming pool that had been changed into a massive bubble-bath party. It was all very overwhelming and uncomfortable. There were still no stone goats in sight.

He entered a side door and found himself alone in a lighted passageway leading to what looked like a cellar. The noise from the party was dampened by the thick stone walls. Alec proceeded down the corridor and descended a set of stairs, noting the thick layer of dust on just about everything that conveniently betrayed footprints on the steps. Someone had been here recently.

The lower level opened to a roughly cut stone cellar filled with racks of wooden barrels on one side, and stacks of food stores on the other. This place would make the perfect entrance to a secret lair if there ever were one. He began to probe the caskets, checking for a false bottom or a hidden latch or anything out of the ordinary. He was halfway along the wall when he heard it: distant voices and the sound of scraping. Alec went still. He cocked his head to the side and listened with his rune-enhanced hearing.

"These used to be the Crimson Hand's headquarters," said a man's French-accented voice. "But I've seen no sign of cult activity and every sign of a seriously amazing party. I even heard Magnus Bane was here."

"And yet, we still have to search the whole building," said a woman in return. "Imagine that."

Alec drew a seraph blade as he crept toward the voices, though he didn't activate it. At the end of the wall, a short hallway extended that opened to a wine cellar. On the walls were floor-to-ceiling shelves filled with bottles. There was a blinding white light emanating from a point on one of the shelves, illuminating the room. Standing in front of it were two silhouettes studying what appeared to be a small statue of Bacchus. Alec could make out a woman's side profile, and the curve of one faerie ear.

He couldn't get a good view of their faces in the harsh light, so he continued creeping forward, one soft step at a time. No Downworlder could hear a Shadowhunter coming, if the Shadowhunter didn't want them to.

A dagger flew through the air, just missing the sleeve of Alec's black coat.

Maybe some Downworlders *could* hear a Shadowhunter coming.

"*Atheed!*" the woman shouted, and her seraph blade caught fire in her hand. The man beside her drew his bow.

"Wait!" said Alec, and pulled his silk mask down with his free hand. "I'm a Shadowhunter! I'm Alec Lightwood; I'm from the New York Institute!"

"Oh," said the man, and lowered his bow. "Hi there."

The Shadowhunter woman who had drawn first did not put her seraph blade away but stepped closer, studying him. Alec studied her in turn, and recognized her, pale as a pearl, with streaming fair hair, delicately pointed ears, and striking blue-green eyes. Her pretty face was set in grim lines now.

She was the faerie woman who had been kissing the vampire girl, in the first room Alec had stumbled into at this ball.

She was the Shadowhunter woman Alec had seen from the vantage of a hot-air balloon, chasing a demon in Paris.

There was only one Shadowhunter woman with faerie heritage Alec knew of.

"And you're Helen Blackthorn," he said slowly, "from Los Angeles. What are you doing here?"

"I'm on my travel year," said Helen. "I was in the Paris Institute, intending to go on to the Institute in Rome, when we heard rumors about a warlock commanding demons and leading a cult called the Crimson Hand."

"What rumors?" asked Alec. "What have you heard, and where from?"

Helen ignored the questions. "I've been chasing the demons and the warlock ever since. Malcolm Fade, High Warlock of Los Angeles, gave me an invitation to this party, and I came hoping to find answers. What are you doing here?"

Alec blinked. "Oh. Um. I'm on vacation."

He realized how stupid that sounded. It was as close to the truth as he could admit, though, without exposing Magnus and leading to a situation where he was standing in front of the Clave explaining, *My warlock boyfriend accidentally founded a demon cult.*

When Alec was in trouble, he was used to being able to turn to his fellow Shadowhunters for help. If it hadn't been for Magnus, he would've told these two about Mori Shu and the stone goat. They could all have gone searching together. But Alec couldn't do that now. These Shadowhunters and he might not be on the same side.

He looked at the Shadowhunters, and instead of relief that they were here, he felt only anxiety about the lies he had to tell them.

"I'm just here to have a good time," Alec added weakly.

Disbelief flashed across Helen's face. "In the subbasement of a former cult headquarters, during a Downworlder party full of miscreants, armed with a seraph blade?"

"That isn't your idea of a good time?" Alec asked.

"I've heard of you," said Helen. "You were in the war. You were the one with Magnus Bane."

"He's my boyfriend," Alec said flatly.

He deliberately did not look at the face of the Shadowhunter man, who had hung back silently. Given what Alec had seen earlier, Helen might be okay with same-sex relationships, but Shadowhunters often were not.

She didn't look shocked, though. She looked worried. "Malcolm Fade told me there's a rumor Magnus Bane is the warlock leading the Crimson Hand," said Helen.

So now Shadowhunters had heard the rumor. Alec told himself to be calm. Malcolm was the High Warlock of Los Angeles. Helen lived in the Los Angeles Institute. They knew each other. That didn't mean the story had spread to the rest of the Clave.

"It's not true," said Alec, with all the conviction he could muster.

"Malcolm did say he didn't believe it," Helen admitted.

"Right," Alec said. "I can see you've got the situation handled. I'll just head back upstairs to the party."

Helen casually walked past him to look up the steps to see if anyone else was there. It wasn't lost on Alec that she still held the seraph blade in her hand, nor that she had just cut off his escape route. She turned to him and said, "I think you should come with us to the Rome Institute to answer some questions."

Alec kept his face neutral, but a chill swept through his body. If it came to it, the Clave could put the Mortal Sword in his hands and he would be forced to tell the truth. He'd have to say that Magnus thought he had founded the cult.

"I think we're blowing this way out of proportion," he said.

"I agree," said the Shadowhunter man unexpectedly, and caught Alec's attention for the first time. He was short and good-looking, with a dramatic sweep of dark red hair and a French accent. "Excuse me, Monsieur Lightwood, have you been to Paris lately?"

"Yes, right before I arrived in Venice."

"And were you by chance on a hot-air balloon?"

He almost said no, but realized he was caught. "Yeah, I was."

"I knew it!" The Shadowhunter rushed forward and grabbed his hand, pumping it enthusiastically. "I want to thank you, Monsieur Lightwood. Can I call you Alec? I am Leon Verlac, of the Paris Institute. The *ravissante* Helen and I were the Shadowhunters you aided on the rooftop. We cannot thank you enough."

Helen's expression suggested that she could probably thank Alec enough. Or possibly not thank him at all. Alec withdrew his hand from Leon's with difficulty. Leon seemed inclined to hang on to it.

"So you were in Paris as well?" Helen said casually. "What an astonishing coincidence."

"Visiting Paris on a European vacation is a coincidence?" said Alec.

"It would be a crime not to visit Paris!" Leon agreed. "You should have stopped by the Paris Institute while you were there, Alec. I would have shown you the sights as I did for our charming Helen, whom I would follow anywhere. Even to this terrible party."

Alec glanced between Helen and Leon, trying to work out if they were together. Helen had been kissing that vampire woman, so he assumed not, but he was naive about these things. Perhaps they would have a couple's squabble and let him go.

"Go fetch the car, Leon," said Helen. "You can ask Alec anything you like on the ride down to Rome."

"Now hold on," said Leon. "Alec saved our lives on the rooftop. He wouldn't do that if he had a hand in this. I, for one, believe him. He was just investigating suspicious activity in the basement, specifically us, like any Shadowhunter would. Even though he is on vacation."

He gave Alec an appreciative nod.

"It was no problem," said Alec carefully.

"Besides, look at him!" said Leon. "He is clearly here to party. He looks fantastic. I told you we should have masks. Let the poor man get back to his vacation, Helen, while we find some real leads."

Helen regarded Alec for another long moment, then slowly lowered her seraph blade.

"All right," she said grudgingly.

Alec did not ask them about Mori Shu, or anything else. He headed for the stairs without delay.

"Wait!" said Helen.

Alec turned around, trying to conceal his dread. "What?"

"Thanks," said Helen. "For the rescue in Paris."

That surprised a smile from Alec. "You're welcome."

Helen smiled back. She was pretty when she smiled.

Still, Alec felt shaken as he reached the upper floors, wading upstream against the throng of partygoers heading to the dance floor.

He wondered if the cold apprehension he'd felt talking to Helen was how Downworlders always felt when they were being questioned by Shadowhunters. Not that he blamed Helen for being suspicious. Alec would be too, in her shoes. Alec knew too well that anyone could be a traitor—like his tutor, Hodge Starkweather, who had betrayed them to Valentine during the Mortal War. Helen's suspicions were warranted—after all, he had lied, or at least omitted important information. Lying to fellow Shadowhunters, who should have been on his side, felt awful. He felt like a traitor.

But he'd feel worse if he failed to protect Magnus. The Clave should be set up to protect people like Magnus, not pose another threat to him. Alec had always believed in the Law, but if the Law didn't shield Magnus, the Law should be changed.

Alec trusted maybe six people in the world without question, but one of them was Magnus. He just hadn't expected trusting someone to be so complicated.

If only he could *find* Magnus. He wouldn't have thought it was possible, but the mansion was busier now than when they had arrived just a short time ago.

Alec kept heading upstairs, until he came to a long stone balcony running along the walls of the grand ballroom. It was a useful vantage point from which to oversee the whole party. He only had to walk the perimeter once before he caught sight of Magnus dancing in the crowd of Downworlders and mundanes below. The sight of him made Alec's whole body relax. Before he met Magnus, Alec was not sure he'd ever really believed he could be entirely himself, and entirely happy. Then there was Magnus, and what had seemed impossible became possible. Seeing him was always a small shock, his face a glimpse of hope that everything might be all right.

Two of the ballroom walls were lined with enormous arches open to the night, making the room a golden orb rising between black waters and black sky. The ballroom floor was a wide expanse of blue, the blue of a lake in summertime. The ceiling was crowded with an orchestra of stars, the chandelier a cascade of falling stars that faeries were using as a swing. As Alec watched, one faerie pushed another off the chandelier. Alec tensed, but then gauzy turquoise wings unfolded from the faerie's back and he landed safely among the dancers.

There were winged faeries flying, werewolves tumbling like

acrobats through the crowd, vampires' fangs glittering as they laughed, and warlocks wrapped in light. Masks were lifted and dropped, torches trailed fire like burning ribbons, and the silver shadows of moonlit water danced on the walls. Alec had seen beauty before in the shining towers of Alicante, in the fluid fighting of his sister and his *parabatai*, in many familiar beloved things. He had not seen beauty in Downworld, until Magnus. Yet here it was, simply waiting to be found.

Alec began to feel bad about his indignation that Downworlders were claiming the victory against Valentine as their own. He knew what had happened. He had been there, fighting side by side with Downworlders, and the war had made this golden freedom possible. This was their victory as much as his.

Alec remembered he and Magnus lending each other strength through the Alliance rune, magic only reinforcing the connection between them, and thought, *This victory is ours.*

He and Magnus would work through this puzzle too. They would find someone to help them in this maze of gold columns and dark rivers. They had overcome worse. Alec's heart lifted at the thought, and at that moment, he saw his warlock in the crowd.

Magnus's head was tipped back, his shimmering white suit rumpled like bedsheets in the morning, his white cloak swaying after him like a moonbeam. His mirrorlike mask was askew, his black hair wild, his slim body arching with the dance, and wrapped around his fingers like ten shimmering rings was the light of his magic, casting a spotlight on one dancer, then another.

The faerie Hyacinth caught one radiant stream of magic and whirled, holding on to it as if the light were a ribbon on a maypole. The vampire woman in the violet cheongsam, Lily, was dancing with another vampire who Alec presumed was Elliott, given the blue and green stains around his mouth and all down his shirtfront. Malcolm Fade joined in the dance with Hyacinth, though he appeared to be doing a jig and she seemed very puzzled. The blue warlock who Magnus had called Catarina was waltzing with a tall horned faerie. The dark-skinned faerie whom Magnus had addressed as a prince was surrounded by others whom Alec presumed were courtiers, dancing in a circle around him.

Magnus laughed as he saw Hyacinth using his magic like a ribbon, and sent shimmering streamers of blue light in several directions. Catarina batted away Magnus's magic, her own hand glowing faintly white. The two vampires Lily and Elliott both let a magic ribbon wrap around one of their wrists. They did not seem like trusting types, but they instantly leaned into Magnus with perfect faith, Lily pretending to be a captive and Elliott shimmying enthusiastically as Magnus laughed and pulled them toward him in the dance. Music and starshine filled the room, and Magnus shone brightest in all that bright company.

As Alec made for the stairs, he brushed past Raphael Santiago, who was leaning against the balcony rail and looking down at the dancing crowd, his dark eyes lingering on Lily and Elliott and Magnus. There was a tiny smile on the vampire's face. When Raphael noticed Alec, the scowl snapped immediately back on.

"I find such wanton expressions of joy disgusting," he declaimed.

"If you say so," said Alec. "I like it myself."

He reached the foot of the stairs and was crossing the gleaming ballroom floor when a voice boomed out from above.

"This is DJ Bat, greatest werewolf DJ in the world, or at least in the top five, coming to you live from Venice because warlocks make irresponsible financial decisions, and this one is for the lovers! Or people with friends who will dance with them. Some of us are lonely jerks, and we'll be doing shots at the bar."

A slow, sweet song with a shivery beat began. Alec would not have thought the dance floor could become more crowded, but it happened. Dozens of masked Downworlders in formal wear who had been standing near the walls converged on the floor. Alec found himself standing awkwardly alone in the center of the room as couples twirled around him. Crowns of thorns and towering multi-colored feathers blocked his vision. He looked around in alarm for an escape route.

"May I have this dance, sir?"

Instead he saw Magnus, all in white and silver.

"I was coming to find you," said Alec.

"I saw you coming." Magnus pushed his mask halfway up his face. "We found each other."

He moved in close to Alec, one hand settling on his lower back, laced their fingers together with the other, and kissed him. The glancing touch of his mouth was like a ray of light on water, illuminating and transforming. Alec moved instinctively closer, longing to be illuminated and transformed again, then remembered, reluctantly, than they should remain on task.

"I met a Shadowhunter here called Helen Blackthorn," he murmured against Magnus's mouth. "She said—"

Magnus kissed him again.

"Something fascinating, I'm sure," he said. "You haven't answered my question."

"What question?"

"May I have this dance?"

"Of course," said Alec. "I mean—I would love this dance. It's only . . . we should work this out."

Magnus drew in a breath and nodded. "We will. Tell me."

He had been smiling before, but the smile had faded. Instead there was a certain burdened set to his shoulders. Magnus felt guilty, Alec realized for the first time, for spoiling their vacation. Alec thought that was silly—he'd have had no vacation at all without Magnus, no shine of magic and no shocks of joy, no lights and no music.

Alec reached up and touched Magnus's mask. He could see his own face reflected in it like a mirror, his eyes wide and blue against the glittering carnival around them. He almost did not recognize himself, he looked so happy.

Then he pushed the mask up and he could see Magnus's face clearly. That was better.

"Let's dance first," he said.

He wrapped his arm around Magnus's back, felt unsure about that, fumbled, and tried repositioning his hands on Magnus's shoulders.

Magnus was smiling again. "Allow me."

Alec had never given much thought to dancing before, aside from a few awkward childhood attempts with his sister or their friend Aline. Magnus slid his arm around Alec's waist and began to dance. Alec was no dancer, but he was a fighter, and he found he intuitively understood how to respond to Magnus's movements and how to move with them. They were suddenly synchronized, gliding across the floor as gracefully as any other couple in the room, and all at once Alec knew how it was to really dance with someone—a thing Alec had never even known to want. He'd always assumed that storybook moments like these were meant for Jace, Isabelle, anyone but him. Yet here he was.

The chandelier seemed to shine directly on them. A faerie on the balcony tossed down a handful of glittering stars. Tiny shimmering points of light settled in Magnus's black hair and floated in the tiny space between their faces. Alec leaned forward, so their foreheads touched, and their lips met again. Magnus's mouth was curved against Alec's. Their smiles fitted against each other perfectly. Alec closed his eyes, but he could still see light.

Maybe his life could be amazing. Maybe it always could have, and he'd needed Magnus to open the door and let him see all the wonders he held inside himself. All the capacity for joy.

Magnus's mouth slid against his. He looped his arms around Alec's neck, drawing him in tighter and closer. Magnus's body moved sinuously against his, and light became heat. Magnus drew a hand down the lapel of Alec's jacket, slipping it inside and resting his palm against Alec's shirt, over his frantically beating heart. Alec lifted his hand from the lean line of Magnus's waist, catching on the metal scales of Magnus's elaborate belt before he took Magnus's hand again, and interlaced their fingers together, there against his chest. Alec could feel a flush creeping up the back of his neck and flooding his face, leaving him light-headed and embarrassed and wishing for more. Every feeling was new—he kept being caught off guard by the combination of the sharp, cutting ache of desire and the tenderness, incongruous and yet impossible to untangle. He had never expected anything like this, but now that he had it, he did not know how he would ever do without it. He hoped he never had to find out.

"Alexander, do you—" Magnus began, his murmur faint under the song and the shrieks of laughter. His voice was low and warm and the only important sound in the world.

"Yes," Alec whispered before Magnus could finish. All he wanted was to say yes to anything Magnus asked. His mouth clashed against Magnus's, hungry and hot, their bodies locking together. They were kissing wildly, as if starved for it, and Alec didn't care about any of the people looking. He had kissed Magnus in the Accords Hall partly to show the world what he felt. In this moment, he didn't care about the world. He cared about what he and Magnus were making between them: the heat and the friction that made him want to die, to drop to his knees and pull Magnus down with him.

Then there was a crash of sound and a blaze of fire, as if a meteor was landing in the center of the ballroom, and both Alec and Magnus froze, tense and uncertain. A new warlock had appeared at the foot of the stairs, his eyes locked with Malcolm Fade's, and though

Alec didn't recognize him, he certainly recognized the frisson of alarm and distress that rippled across the crowd.

Alec used his hold on Magnus's hand to swing Magnus behind him, keeping their fingers locked. With his free hand, he drew a seraph blade and murmured an angel's name. Across the room, Bat the DJ and Raphael put their shot glasses down on the bar. Raphael began to elbow his way through the crowd toward his vampires. Lily and Elliott were heading toward Raphael as well. Alec lifted his voice so it rang through the marble room, in the same way the light of his seraph blade blazed.

"Anyone who wants a Shadowhunter's protection," Alec shouted, "come to me!"

CHAPTER FOURTEEN

High Water

ALEC HAD ONE HAND IN MAGNUS'S, AND HIS OTHER hand on the hilt of his seraph blade. Several of the party guests were cautiously creeping toward him and his offered protection. Magnus scanned the room, waiting to see who made the first move.

The werewolf head of security was storming down the stairs. The warlock at the foot of the stairs made a small gesture and the head of security flew over the crowd on the dance floor, hit the marble floor, and skidded all the way into the wall. Catarina ran to his side immediately, helping him up as he hunched over and clutched his ribs.

The warlock did not look to see what had happened to the werewolf. He was a short man with a beard, snakelike eyes, and white-scaled skin. He scanned the crowd as he made his way onto the floor.

"Malcolm Fade." The look on the warlock's face was thunderous as he pointed a finger at the High Warlock of Los Angeles. A light vapor seemed to drift from the tip of his finger. "You stole my party and my mansion."

"Hello, Barnabas," said Malcolm. "Did you lose a mansion? That's so sad. I hope you find it."

"I bought this mansion last week! The moment it went up for sale!" Barnabas bellowed. "We are standing right now in the mansion you stole from me!"

"Oh, hooray! Consider it found then," Malcolm said.

Alec nudged Magnus. "Who is that?"

Magnus leaned in. "Barnabas Hale. He runs the Shadow Market in Los Angeles. I believe he was a contender for High Warlock before Malcolm got it. Bit of a rivalry there."

"Oh," Alec said. "Great."

Barnabas swept a menacing finger across the room. "I was going to be the one who celebrated our amazing Downworlder victory! I purchased this venue for my Barnabas Bash. Or I might have called it my Barnabash. I hadn't decided yet! Now we'll never know."

"Well, someone has definitely had a few drinks tonight," Magnus muttered. "Barnabash? Really?"

Barnabas's rant was not over.

"You swoop in like the thief you are and undermine me, just like you stole my rightful position as High Warlock of L.A. Well, this party is canceled! You've made me look a fool." Barnabas's hands began to hiss and smoke.

The crowd melted back, giving them more space in the middle of the dance floor. More and more people were collecting behind Alec.

"You really don't need my help for that, Barnabas," Malcolm observed. His hands began to glow, and two glasses of champagne appeared at the tips of his fingers. He sipped from one and floated the other to Barnabas. "Relax. Enjoy the party."

"This is what I think of your party." Barnabas flipped his hand, and the glass tumbled back toward Malcolm, spilling on Malcolm's lavender jacket.

A gasp passed through the crowd, but Malcolm didn't miss a beat. He looked down at his ruined outfit, pulled out a handkerchief, and began dabbing his face with it.

There was a feverish glitter in Malcolm's eyes, as if he was enjoying himself. Once, Magnus knew, Malcolm had wanted a calm, quiet life. That had been a long time ago.

"I did you a favor," Malcolm declared. "We all know your party-throwing abilities are *subpar*. I saved you the embarrassment of throwing a party and having nobody come."

"How dare you?" It seemed as if vapor was rising from Barnabas's head. The warlock knelt and slammed his palm to the floor, sending a white line of jagged ice racing toward Malcolm.

Alec stepped forward, as if to intervene, but Magnus gripped his elbow tightly and shook his head.

Malcolm waved dismissively and melted the ice into a hiss of steam. Then the constellation Orion leaped down from the grand ballroom's ceiling and took a position next to him. The other constellations, forming vaguely human outlines, drifted down from the ceiling to join the fight on Malcolm's side. Malcolm pointed lazily at Barnabas, and Orion loosed a roar and charged the short warlock, waving his musical instrument like a club. Barnabas froze the constellation before it reached him, then shattered it into a cloud of stardust.

"That was my first cello!" snapped Malcolm. "Do you know how hard they are to replace?" The constellations flanking Malcolm, their bodies transparent with hundreds of blinking specks of stardust and veins of light, charged Barnabas. They were halfway across the floor when the giant chandelier in the middle of the room came alive and began to use its many arms like an octopus, grabbing at any of the constellations within reach. The marble floor crumbled away near Malcolm, allowing metal pipes to emerge from the dust, snaking toward Malcolm. Before they could reach him, the ceiling exploded.

Most of the crowd scattered through the open arches of the room out into the night, terrified. Others, either braver or more stupid, remained frozen, unable to look away. The two warlocks flung ice, fire, lightning, and green globs of goo at each other. The mansion groaned as windows shattered, bolts of ice punched holes into walls, and jets of flame sprayed across the floor.

An ice bolt struck the wall a few feet away, raining a hail of debris on a group of nymphs. Alec leaped for them, grabbing up a shard of piano and lifting it over their heads as a shield.

"We should do something!" he shouted to Magnus.

"Or," said Magnus, "we could recognize this has nothing to do with us, and get out of here."

"They're going to bring down the entire mansion. Someone is going to get hurt!"

Magnus threw his hands out and blocks of marble ripped loose from the floor, forming a short wall shielding the nymphs from a second ice bolt. "Someone is definitely going to get hurt, very probably us." But Alec was in hero mode, and there wasn't much Magnus could do to stop him. "And yet, I'll try to mitigate the damage," he added.

The room moaned and shook, and one of the walls buckled. Raphael pushed Elliott out of the way of falling masonry, then brushed white marble dust impatiently out of the other vampire's dreadlocks.

"I am *not* feeling well," said Elliott. "Is the building falling down or did I drink way too much?"

"Both," said Lily.

"I am feeling fairly sick myself," Raphael contributed, "of you being an idiot, Elliott."

"Hello, Raphael," said Magnus. "Maybe you'd like to follow Alec outside?"

He pointed to the place where Alec had been. He did not see

Alec there. Instead he saw the railing on the balcony break loose. It tumbled in pieces toward Catarina's oblivious head as she ministered to several injured werewolves.

Magnus watched as Alec—who had retrieved his confiscated bow and arrows, now slung across his back—ran into the crossfire, swerving around two metal pipes clutching at him, barely avoiding getting his head taken off by a swipe of the chandelier octopus. He dove just in time to tackle Catarina out of the way, and landed on his knees with her safe in his arms.

"Following Alec seems unwise," said Raphael from behind Magnus. "Since he seems to be running directly toward danger."

"Shadowhunters always do," said Magnus.

Raphael examined his fingernails. "It might be nice," he said, "to have a partner you knew was always going to choose *you*, not duty or saving the world."

Magnus did not respond. His attention was caught by Catarina and Alec. Catarina had been blinking up at Alec, looking mildly surprised. Suddenly she began to struggle, crying out a warning.

Alec glanced up, but it was already too late. Another chunk of the ceiling had come free; it was dangling, about to fall and crush them. It was too late to escape, and Magnus knew Catarina was always dangerously low on magic. She healed whoever came to her and never saved enough to protect herself.

Magnus watched in horror as Alec flung his body over hers, bracing himself for the cave-in that would bury them both alive.

Blue fire sparked. Magnus raised his hands, glowing like lamps in the shadows. "Alexander!" he shouted. "Move aside!"

Alec looked up, surprised not to be crushed to death. He glanced across the ruin of the ballroom at Magnus, blue eyes wide. Magnus kept both hands steady, straining to keep the large chunk of concrete hovering just above their heads.

Alec and Catarina scrambled to their feet, fleeing across the treacherous ballroom toward Magnus. More living pipes blocked their path, trying to wrap their metal tentacles around Alec's ankles. He dodged and jumped to avoid them. One managed to curl around his ankle, causing him to stumble. He pushed Catarina out in front, and Magnus caught her hand and pulled her to him and safety.

Magnus heard Alec say, *"Cael,"* and saw the blaze of the seraph blade.

One slash of it cut away the tentacle at his feet. Alec reached Magnus just as Barnabas set the entire floor of the ballroom ablaze. Malcolm responded with a tidal wave of canal water crashing in from the kitchen. The water swirled around Malcolm, knocking him off his feet, and then took out Barnabas. Both warlocks were carried out of the palazzo, Malcolm whooping with delight as if he were on a water ride at an amusement park.

Everyone, aside from the vampires, took a deep breath. The palazzo continued to fall to ruin around them.

"I've changed my mind," Catarina announced. She put her arm around Alec's neck and gave him a kiss on the cheek. "I like you."

"Oh," said Alec, looking baffled. "Thanks."

"Please take care of Magnus," Catarina added.

"I try," said Alec.

Catarina gave Magnus a delighted look over Alec's shoulder. "At last," she murmured. "A keeper."

"Can we get out of the collapsing building now?" said Magnus crossly, though he was secretly pleased.

She and Hyacinth made for the doors, guiding a few ragged and wounded Downworlders. The vampires, the werewolf Juliette from the train, and many others hovered by Alec.

Alec looked around. "The stairway to the upper floor collapsed. There are people trapped upstairs."

Magnus cursed, then nodded. He reached out and tapped the half-empty quiver at Alec's shoulder with two fingers. A faint blue light shimmered, and the quiver was suddenly full of arrows.

"I'll go after Barnabas and Malcolm and try to contain them," Magnus said. "You do what you do best and get everyone to safety."

He waved his hands in a broad gesture, and the metallic vines that had been the palazzo's plumbing straightened and gathered themselves into a bridge over the torrent of canal water, leading out of the palazzo to where the warlocks had disappeared. Magnus turned to look at Alec, who had moved to intervene in a fight that had broken out between werewolves and pixies. Then Magnus turned back, flung himself in the direction of the smoke and sparks, and was gone.

CHAPTER FIFTEEN

Mori Shu

WITH A BUILDING FALLING DOWN AROUND THEIR EARS, some of the werewolves had panicked. Alec found this understandable, but unfortunate. When werewolves panicked, fur tended to fly. Also blood, teeth, and intestines.

Three werewolves in a snarling knot were closing in on a huddle of terrified pixies. Alec ran to put his body between the two groups, as the masonry dust fell like rain all around, blinding and choking them. Alec just barely ducked underneath the swipe of a clawed paw and then threw himself to the side as one of the werewolves barreled into him.

Then the others reached him and it was all he could do to avoid being disemboweled. Muscle memory and years of training took over as he danced through the slashes coming from all sides.

Five long claws just missed raking him across the face, and then the tip of one managed to slice his arm. A set of fangs reached his shoulder and were just about to clamp down when he grabbed a handful of chin fur and rolled, executing a throw that sent the werewolf hurtling onto his back, sliding until he hit rubble.

The last werewolf tripped over Raphael Santiago's foot. Alec hastily hit him in the back of the head with the hilt of his seraph blade, and the werewolf stayed down.

"That was an accident," said Raphael, with Lily and Elliott sticking close behind him. "He got in my way as I was trying to leave."

"Okay," Alec panted.

He wiped dust and sweat out of his eyes. Bat the DJ staggered toward them, claws out, and Alec flipped his seraph blade so he was holding the hilt again.

"Someone dropped a piece of roof on me," Bat told him, blinking in a way that was more owlish than wolfish. "Inconsiderate."

Alec realized Bat was not so much on a murderous out-of-control rampage as mildly concussed.

"Easy there," he said, as Bat tumbled against his chest.

He looked around for the most trustworthy person, for someone to be on his team. He took a gamble and dumped Bat into Lily's arms.

"Watch him for me, will you?" he asked. "Make sure he gets out all right."

"Put that werewolf down immediately, Lily," Raphael ordered.

"It really hurts that you would say that," Bat muttered, and shut his eyes.

Lily considered Bat's head, pillowed on her lavender bosom. "I don't want to put him down," she announced. "The Shadowhunter gave this DJ to me."

Bat opened one eye. "Do you like music?"

"I do," said Lily. "I like jazz."

"Cool," said Bat.

Raphael threw up his hands. "This is ridiculous! Fine," he snapped. "Fine. Let's just vacate the collapsing mansion, shall we? Can we all agree on that one fun, non-suicidal activity?"

Alec ushered his group of unruly Downworlders to the nearest exit, collecting stray faeries with broken wings and a couple of dazed or drunk warlocks as they went. He made sure most of them were out, flooding the streets of Venice in a bright rush that made the canals look still, before he turned back to the vampires. Lily had entrusted Bat to Catarina, and they were all looking at him expectantly.

"Could you give me a boost up to the second floor?"

"I will not," Raphael said icily.

"Sure, any friend of Magnus's," said Elliott, and then, off Raphael's glare, added, "is someone we don't like, definitely, not even a little bit, at all."

The steps had caved in near the top of the staircase, and there was now only a jagged cliff off the top of the landing. Lily and Elliott launched Alec above their heads, his leap given velocity by their strength. He waved to them before he turned away, and Lily and Elliott waved back. Raphael had his arms crossed.

The mansion was quieter upstairs, save for the occasional crack of wood splintering and groan of the mansion's weakening foundations. Alec began a room-by-room search. Most were empty, of course.

There was a crying werewolf girl in one room, huddled in a nest of bedclothes. Alec helped her out the window and saw her jump into the canal and dog-paddle away.

He discovered a pair of peris hiding in a bedroom closet. At least, he thought they were hiding, but he realized they had been making out the entire time and had no idea the party was over. He also freed a mermaid who had accidentally locked herself in one of the bathrooms.

Alec had just about covered the entire floor when he ventured into the library and came upon a group of Sighted mundanes overpowered by vines. A jungle of floorboards and pipes and other assorted home construction items had come to life and wrapped them up like mummies. The library was above the grand ballroom, and some of the magic from the battle had clearly seeped in.

Alec hacked his way to them with his seraph blade, cutting through the floorboards like a sickle across rows of wheat. He wrenched a strangling lamp from around a woman's neck.

The living furniture seemed to be turning its attention toward Alec as the threat. That meant he was able to get the mundanes free as floorboards, pipes, and murderous footstools concentrated on him. He guided the terrified little group to the window and shouted for help.

Elliott appeared and caught the mundanes one by one as Alec threw them down.

"Pretty sure I know the answer to this," Elliott called up to Alec, "but your position on me biting these people is . . ."

"No!" Alec shouted.

"Just checking, just checking," Elliott said hastily. "No need to get worked up about it." Alec felt wary about throwing down the last mundane, but then Catarina appeared, wielding bandages. The mundanes would be safe with her.

Alec's own situation had become slightly worrying. For every pipe he cut, another took its place. The wooden boards curled around his ankles and wrapped around his wrists. The more Alec struggled, the more he became entangled.

Far too fast, his legs were tightly circled by copper piping, his waist by floorboards, and his arms by two wooden planks that had burst from the walls. A wooden vine wrapped around his wrist and squeezed so tight Alec's blade dropped from his hand.

At this opportune moment, Shinyun prowled into the room.

"Alec?" she demanded. "What on earth is going on? Why is the palazzo falling down?"

Alec stared at her. "Where have you *been*?"

"Do you need help?" she said. Her unblinking, unmoving face was turned in his direction for several moments more, during which

Alec did not know if she was amused, thoughtful, or marveling at what an idiot he was.

"I could burn you free," she offered. Her hand began to glow, turning from orange to a hot, red, searing light. Alec could feel the heat through the vines, which were melting away quickly.

Alec was deeply relieved to see Magnus stroll into view, Malcolm at his side, dripping canal water. "Please don't risk my boyfriend's life or limbs," said Magnus. "I am attached to both. Malcolm, please call off your . . . plants and things."

The light died in Shinyun's hands. Malcolm appraised the nest and then clapped his hands several times, taking turns alternating which hand was on top. With each clap, the vines receded.

"Where's Barnabas?" Alec asked, shaking off the scraps and rubble as he stepped free of the mess.

"I encouraged him to leave," said Magnus. "Subtly."

"How?" asked Alec.

Magnus considered. "Maybe not all that subtly."

Malcolm's face was even more pallid than usual. "This is terrible," he announced. "I think I may have lost my security deposit."

"You don't have a security deposit," Alec reminded him. "You stole that Barnabas guy's house."

"Oh yes," said Malcolm, cheering up.

Alec held Magnus's hand as they made their way out of the ruins of the palazzo. It was a relief to have that link between them, the warm, strong clasp of Magnus's hand a solid promise he was safe.

"So, as Alec was saying," said Magnus as they passed through the remains of the foyer, "where *have* you been?"

"Out in the courtyard, when the building started to fall down," Shinyun said. "I had no idea what was going on. I tried to make my way back in to you, but there were people who needed help."

"That was occupying us, too," said Alec, as they walked down the front steps.

A huge chunk of fallen marble blocked the bottom of the staircase. Malcolm was looking weary, but he and Magnus made a simultaneous gesture, and the marble began to slowly slide away.

The fading night painted the marble violet. There were still a few stragglers from the party waiting in the cobbled street outside the palazzo. Juliette gave a small cheer when she saw Alec and the others emerge. Raphael did not cheer.

"The important thing," said Magnus, "is that I don't think there were any casualties."

The marble slid away, and they all saw the man lying beneath, facedown on the marble steps to the ruined mansion. He was dark-haired and middle-aged, his skin blue-tinged from the blood loss that had soaked and stiffened his clothes.

A phoenix mask was still clutched in his hand, an incongruous reminder of past festivity.

"Spoke too soon," Malcolm said softly.

Magnus knelt down and gently turned the broken body over, though the man was long past caring. He closed the man's open eyes.

Shinyun's breath hissed in between her teeth.

"That's him," she said. "That's Mori Shu."

Horror washed over Alec as well. They would never get any answers from Mori Shu, lying still and silent forever in the cobbled streets.

"And he wasn't killed by the building falling on him," Shinyun continued, the horror in her voice turning to fury as she spoke. "He was murdered by vampires."

They could all see the holes in his throat, the blood glimmering darkly in the moonlight. The New York vampires took several steps back.

"It wasn't us," said Lily, after a moment. "Let me look at the body."

"*No, Lily.*" Raphael flung his hand out to arrest her step. "This has nothing to do with us. We're leaving now."

"They were with me," said Alec.

"The whole night?" asked Shinyun. "Looks like he's been dead a while."

Alec was silent. There was blood on Elliott's shirt, though it was not the color of human blood. The idea of a vampire feeding on someone helpless made him feel sick.

"We don't feed on warlocks," Lily said.

"*Shut up,*" Raphael snarled at her. "Don't run your mouth in front of Nephilim!"

"Vampires don't feed on warlocks," said Magnus. "Nobody killed Mori Shu out of hunger. Someone killed him to silence him. Raphael and his people don't have any reason to do that."

"We don't even know him," Elliott said.

"This is literally the first time I've ever seen him," said Lily.

"There were a lot of vampires on my guest list," Malcolm remarked, "who have already left. And a lot of party crashers. Including the offensive one who sent the party crashing about our ears. I'm going to have to find a whole new palazzo for tomorrow night."

"Tomorrow night?" Alec demanded.

"Of course," said Malcolm. "You thought this was a *one night* victory party? The show must go on!"

Alec shook his head. He couldn't imagine anyone wanting to keep partying at this point.

Shinyun was kneeling over Mori Shu's body, searching for clues. Mori Shu had been a warlock—immortal. But no warlock was invulnerable. Any warlock could be hurt or killed.

Magnus, his silver mask pushed back into his hair, intercepted the New York vampires before they could fully depart. Alec heard Magnus pitch his voice low.

Alec felt guilty for listening in, but he couldn't just turn off his Shadowhunter instincts.

"How are you, Raphael?" asked Magnus.

"Annoyed," said Raphael. "As usual."

"I'm familiar with the emotion," said Magnus. "I experience it whenever we speak. What I meant was, I know that you and Ragnor were often in contact."

There was a beat, in which Magnus studied Raphael with an expression of concern, and Raphael regarded Magnus with obvious scorn.

"Oh, you're asking if I am prostrate with grief over the warlock that the Shadowhunters killed?"

Alec opened his mouth to point out the *evil* Shadowhunter Sebastian Morgenstern had killed the warlock Ragnor Fell in the recent war, as he had killed Alec's own brother.

Then he remembered Raphael sitting alone and texting a number saved as *RF*, and never getting any texts back.

Ragnor Fell.

Alec felt a sudden and unexpected pang of sympathy for Raphael, recognizing his loneliness. He was at a party surrounded by hundreds of people, and there he sat texting a dead man over and over, knowing he'd never get a message back.

There must have been very few people in Raphael's life he'd ever counted as friends.

"I do not like it," said Raphael, "when Shadowhunters murder my colleagues, but it's not as if that hasn't happened before. It happens all the time. It's their hobby. Thank you for asking. Of course one wishes to break down on a heart-shaped sofa and weep into one's lace handkerchief, but I am somehow managing to hold it together. After all, I still have a warlock contact."

Magnus inclined his head with a slight smile.

"Tessa Gray," said Raphael. "Very dignified lady. Very well-read. I think you know her?"

Magnus made a face at him. "It's not being a sass-monkey that I object to. That I like. It's the joyless attitude. One of the chief pleasures of life is mocking others, so occasionally show some glee about doing it. Have some joie de vivre."

"I'm undead," said Raphael.

"What about joie de unvivre?"

Raphael eyed him coldly. Magnus gestured his own question aside, his rings and trails of leftover magic leaving a sweep of sparks in the night air, and sighed.

"Tessa," Magnus said with a long exhale. "She is a harbinger of ill news and I will be annoyed with her for dumping this problem in my lap for weeks. At least."

"What problem? Are you in trouble?" asked Raphael.

"Nothing I can't handle," said Magnus.

"Pity," said Raphael. "I was planning to point and laugh. Well, time to go. I'd say good luck with your dead-body bad-news thing, but . . . I don't care."

"Take care of yourself, Raphael," said Magnus.

Raphael waved a dismissive hand over his shoulder. "I always do."

The vampires made their way down the dark street, the canal a line of silver beside them. Malcolm wandered over to Hyacinth and began to discuss alternate party venues with a good deal more interest than he had shown in the dead body.

Alec stared after the vampires. "He wanted to help you."

Magnus gave him a startled glance. "Raphael? I don't think so. He's not really the warlock's little helper type."

He turned to aid Shinyun in poring over the body. Alec let him, trusting Magnus to find anything relevant, and jogged after the vampires.

"Wait," he said.

The vampires walked on, ignoring him entirely.

"Hold on."

"Don't speak to the Shadowhunter," Raphael instructed the others. "Don't even look at him."

"Okay. Sorry to bother you. I forgot you have no interest in Magnus. I'll just go back and help him myself," said Alec.

Raphael stopped walking.

"Talk," he said, not turning. When Alec hesitated, trying to think of how to phrase the problem, Raphael held up fingers. "Three. Two. One—"

"You basically run the vampire clan, don't you?" Alec asked. "So you must know a lot about what is going on with Downworlders."

"More than you ever will, Shadowhunter."

Alec rolled his eyes. "Do you know anything about the Crimson Hand? They're a cult."

"I've heard of them," said Raphael. "There's a rumor Magnus founded it."

Alec was silent.

"I don't believe it," said Raphael. "I'll tell anyone who asks."

"Great," said Alec. "Thanks."

"And I'll ask around," Raphael conceded.

"Okay," said Alec. "Give me your phone."

"I don't have a phone."

"Raphael, you obviously have a phone, you were texting on it when I first saw you at the party."

Raphael finally turned and studied Alec warily. Elliott and Lily hung back, exchanging glances with each other. After a pause, Raphael closed the distance between them, slid his phone out of his pocket, and laid it in Alec's waiting hand. Alec sent himself a text from Raphael's phone. He tried to think of a pithy and cutting message to send, but he wound up just writing, HI.

Jace would have thought of something pithy. Oh well. Everyone had their skills.

"This is a historic occasion," Lily said. "The first time in fifty years Raphael has given someone his phone number at a party."

Elliott lifted his drooping head. "This calls for another drink!"

Raphael and Alec both ignored them. Alec gave Raphael back his phone. Raphael accepted it. They nodded at each other.

"About Bane. Don't hurt him," Raphael said abruptly.

Alec hesitated. "No," he said, his voice softer. "I would never—"

Raphael held up a peremptory hand. "Stop being disgusting, please," he said. "I don't care if you wound his, as the kids say, 'wittle fee-fees.' Dump him like a ton of magic bricks. I wish you would. I just meant, don't kill him."

"I'm not going to *kill him*," Alec said, appalled.

His blood ran cold at the idea, and colder as he looked down into Raphael's face. The vampire was serious.

"Aren't you?" Raphael asked. "Shadowhunter."

He said the word the same way as the Downworlders of the Shadow Market had, but it sounded different in service of protecting someone Alec would gladly give his life to shield from harm.

It made Alec wonder if the people of the Market were all looking at him and seeing a threat to someone they cared for.

"Stop it, Raphael," said Lily. She gave Alec a brief, surprisingly sympathetic look. "Kid's obviously in love."

"Ugh," said Raphael. "Terrible business. Let's get out of here."

Elliott cheered. "Can we go to the after-party?"

"No," Raphael said with distaste. He left Alec and walked away without a look back. After a quick last glance, Lily and then Elliott turned to follow.

Alec stood alone in the street for a moment, and then returned to Magnus, who had given up on finding clues and was on his phone making arrangements for the quiet disposal of Mori Shu's body. Alec approached him with caution. Magnus's cloak was hanging from shoulders that were a little more hunched than usual. His face, beneath his shock of glitter-strewn black hair, was a little tired.

Alec didn't know what to say. "How did you meet Raphael? You two seem to know each other pretty well."

"I helped him out a little once, I suppose," said Magnus. "It was nothing."

Magnus had come and healed Alec, the second time they had ever met. Alec remembered waking from delirium and agony to Magnus's strange bright eyes, his careful, gentle hands. *It hurts,* Alec had whispered. *I know,* Magnus had said. *I'm going to help with that.*

And Alec, believing him, had let go of some of the pain.

That memory had stayed with him until he followed it to Magnus's doorstep. Magnus did not think of himself that way, but he was kind. He was so kind that he could dismiss healing or helping as just another day.

Whatever Magnus had done for Raphael, clearly Raphael did not think it was nothing.

Magnus's life was crowded with strange incidents and stranger people. Alec did not know a lot about it yet, but he could learn, and he knew one thing. His sister had said that a trip was how you got to truly know each other, and Alec was now absolutely sure that in the bright chaos of his long, strange life, Magnus had stayed kind.

While Alec had been talking to Raphael, two identical brownies had arrived in what looked like a huge green melon on large rickety wheels but which Alec figured was some kind of faerie ambulance, to take Mori Shu's body away. Shinyun gave them some money, spoke with them briefly in Italian, and came to join Magnus and Alec. She gazed upon the ruins of the palazzo, drawing Alec's attention there too.

"If there was ever a stone goat," she said, "it's buried under a few tons of rubble."

"We'd better get going," said Magnus, sounding uncharacteristically tired. "I guess we're done here."

"Wait," said Alec. "The Chamber. We never found it. And I don't think it can have been in the part of the palazzo that was destroyed."

"That is," said Shinyun slowly, "the part of the palazzo aboveground. Or we would be looking at it in pieces in front of us."

"There are stairs outside, behind the building," Magnus said. "They go down into the palazzo basement, I assume. But maybe they go elsewhere after that."

Alec looked out at the canal nearby. "How far underground can you even build here? Would you be underwater?"

"Without magic? Not very far," said Magnus. "With magic?" He shrugged, a smile creeping back on his face. "Who wants to go explore a creepy dungeon?"

There was a long pause and then Shinyun, very slowly, raised her hand.

"Me too," said Alec.

CHAPTER SIXTEEN

The Red Scrolls of Magic

MAGNUS'S MEMORY WAS CORRECT. A STONE STAIRCASE descended into darkness in the alley behind the ruined palazzo. Alec kindled a witchlight runestone as they reached the heavy wooden door at the bottom of the steps. Shinyun caused a beam of light to shine from her index finger, which she pointed around like a flashlight.

Inside the door (unlocked by Alec with an Open rune), damp packed-earth walls held empty barrels and ancient rags, nothing more exciting. They turned a corner, then another and another, and then came upon a much nicer door, smooth and polished, with an image of a winged lion carved into it.

Once through the door, Magnus and Shinyun exclaimed in excitement, but Alec sighed in disappointment. "I've been here," he said. "I remember this little statue of Bacchus."

Magnus regarded it. "For the god of wine and revelry," he said, "I always thought Bacchus was dressed much too plainly in his statues."

Shinyun was poking at the walls of the chamber, looking for a secret panel or catch. Magnus was drawn to the statue on its plinth.

"I always thought," he continued slowly, "that if it had been up to me, the statues of the gods would dress a little more . . . fun."

As he finished the sentence, he reached out to touch the statue of Bacchus. Blue sparks flew from his fingers, and color and texture began to appear along the toga's folds, his magic sifting away the plain white stone as though the marble had been dust that now fell away to reveal the more vivid, decorated statue underneath.

With a grinding noise, the section of wall beside the statue slid open to reveal a narrow staircase.

"A colorful solution," said Shinyun. "Good work." She sounded amused. Alec, however, was giving Magnus a strange, thoughtful look.

Magnus started down the stairs, Alec following just behind. Magnus almost wished that he was not there. He could not conquer his dread of what they might find, and what Alec might think of him when they did. The Bacchus statue had been a joke—one that no longer struck him as in the least bit funny.

The staircase leveled out into a long stone corridor that ended in darkness. "How is this all not underwater?" said Alec. "We're in Venice."

"One of the cult's warlocks must have put up barriers against water coming in," Magnus said. "Like Mori Shu." *Or me,* he did not add.

At the end the corridor suddenly opened up to a large, high-ceilinged chamber that had been built for storage or cellaring food. Alec waved his witchlight around, revealing rows of unlit candles all over the room.

"Well, that's easy enough," said Magnus, and with a snap of his fingers all the candles kindled, bringing bright warm light into the room.

This was definitely a former cellar. On the far end was a shoddy, rickety altar that cavemen might have erected to worship a fire god. Two wooden columns flanked a large stone block cut into a perfect cube on a raised platform.

On the left wall was a table that looked like cheap plastic lawn furniture covered with incense and prayer beads and other generic-looking knickknacks that someone could buy at a yoga studio.

"Oh my God, my cult is so low-rent," moaned Magnus. "I am deeply shamed. I am disowning my followers for being evil and having no panache."

"But it's not your cult," Alec said distractedly. He walked over to the side table and ran his finger along its surface. "There's a lot of dust. This place hasn't been used in a while."

"I'm joking," said Magnus. "Whistling in the dark." He glanced at the empty corner of the room, where a tree root had pushed its way inside from between two stones. He walked up to the vine and yanked it. Nothing happened. He cast some detection magic over the corner. Still nothing.

"There has to be more," said Shinyun. "Where are the signs of terrible rituals being done? Where is the blood on the walls?"

Alec picked up a small statuette and shook his head.

"There's a manufacturer's sticker here. Someone bought this in a souvenir shop. If this thing is magical, then I'm the Angel Raziel."

"The Shadowhunters *really* wouldn't approve of me dating the Angel Raziel," said Magnus.

"But they'd have to be nice to you," Alec said, brandishing the statuette, "or I would smite them."

"Can you never be serious?" asked Shinyun. She strode toward the makeshift altar, then suddenly tripped and sprawled onto the ground. There was a silence during which nobody laughed. Magnus and Alec stood identically bug-eyed. After a long moment Shinyun snapped from the ground, "Well, someone look and see what I tripped over, at least."

As she sat up and brushed the dust from her clothes, Magnus walked over and knelt down. Set in the earth floor before the altar was a tiny stone statue of a goat. Magnus knelt down and murmured into the statue's ear the password Johnny Rook had given him. *"Asmodeus."*

"What?" Alec said.

Magnus had deliberately spoken more softly than even a Shadowhunter could hear. He avoided Alec's eyes.

The sound of grinding stone echoed throughout the room, drowning out whatever moment had been brewing between the two of them. The stone cube on the altar unfolded like a flower. It lifted from the altar and floated to the wall behind, where it embedded itself into the stone there. The platform the cube had been resting on crumbled into powder. Red-gold light appeared around the rosette that the stone cube had become, tracing the outline of a door.

The glowing outline solidified into an intricately detailed gold-plated door with a large oval mirror in the center.

Magnus walked up to the new door and studied it. He looked at his reflection in the mirror and then back at the rickety wooden door up front. "This is more what I was expecting," he said, and reached for the handle.

Both Alec and Shinyun were there in a flash, trying to prevent Magnus from entering first. Alec and Magnus's essential desire to avoid conflict meant that Shinyun won, nudging the two of them out of the way and pushing the door open. It swung open easily, revealing a long corridor with a low ceiling. A rush of stale air blew past them. A row of torches along the wall sparked and lit one by one down the line.

The corridor curved around several bends, making what was no more than a five-minute walk seem endless. Magnus had no sense at this point where they were in relation to the palazzo or even the city of Venice. *If it were me, and it might have been,* he thought, *I would just plonk the whole thing in the middle of the lagoon somewhere.* Ahead of him, Shinyun gasped as the passageway opened into what Magnus desperately hoped was the last secret chamber to find. Just the thought of the walk back made him want to lie down and take a nap.

He and Alec followed Shinyun into the chamber, and he understood why Shinyun had gasped. The space was huge, its decor the result of a church and a nightclub having gotten together for a wild night.

There were two sections of golden pews along each side of the room, and tiles flashing like jewels lined the walls beside them. At the far end of the room was a large painting of a handsome man with a long, bony face and sharp features. He would have almost passed for human if it were not for his jagged teeth. The only decoration he wore was a crown of barbed wire.

In front of the painting was a stone altar—a much more impressive one—in the center of a giant pentagram. Small grooves were carved into the stone slab, leading downward out from the four corners of the altar to the points of the star below. The entire space was mottled over with dark red stains whose shade varied, but were all of a piece.

"See?" said Shinyun triumphantly. "Blood on the walls. That's how you know it's the real one."

Alec pointed to the left, puzzlement flashing on his face. "Why is there a fully stocked bar next to the sacrificial altar?"

Magnus gave up. "This is definitely my cult, isn't it?" He paused. "I hope the altar was a later addition."

"Maybe not," said Alec. "There might be another warlock who would have wanted a wet bar next to their blood altar."

"Well, if there is, he should introduce himself," said Magnus. "I think we would get along."

In their haste to leave, the cult had left the place a mess. Half the pews were overturned, litter covered much of the floor, and a pile of mostly burnt debris cluttered a sunken fire pit.

At one point, the fire must have jumped the pit and gotten out of hand, because a few of the pews around it were charred. Magnus walked behind the bar counter. Plenty of liquor, no ice or fruit or garnish, though. He poured himself three fingers of the bitterest *amaro* he could find and sipped it angrily, pacing the room.

Memories were powerful forms of magic. Everything in the universe had them, even events, places, and things. That was how ghosts from particularly tragic moments were born, why houses became haunted. Magnus was willing to bet that a demon-worshipping sanctuary involved in sacrificial rituals would have manifested its fair share of powerful memories from which they could glean clues.

Making a slow circle around the perimeter of the sanctuary, he began to chant. His hands were outstretched as he moved, and a glittering trail of white mist leaked from his fingertips.

The mist lingered and shifted in the air like lazy ocean waves, and then it condensed, taking shape into human bodies in motion. These were some of the strongest memories that had imprinted upon this place.

But something was blocking Magnus's casting. The cult had prepared for this. Magnus reached out and pushed against the strong ward blanketing the entire area. A few memories did coalesce into something tangible, but they remained faint and unclear, dissipating after only a few seconds.

Of these, only three were vivid enough to materialize into something discernible. One was a stained glass window that was no longer here, portraying someone who looked awfully like Magnus being fanned with palm leaves. One was of two figures kneeling in prayer, an adult and a child, both smiling. One was of a woman standing over the altar, holding a long kris knife. Then there were faces, too many faces twisted in agony. He saw mundanes, and even a couple of warlocks, but mainly he saw faeries. Faerie blood, the blood that could be used to call up Greater Demons.

By the time Magnus gave up, he was gasping and wet with sweat. Breathing hard, he waved off the thick haze that had clung to the air around him. After the mist in the room cleared, he noticed Shinyun leaning with her arms crossed against one of the columns. She had been studying his work with great interest.

"Anything useful?" she asked.

Magnus leaned back against the wall and shook his head. "Someone set up a spell to block me from finding anything at all. Someone very powerful."

"Do you notice anything strange about that wall?" Shinyun said, nodding toward the portrait of the man with jagged teeth. Magnus had been trying to avoid the portrait's eyes, as if his father Asmodeus could watch him through them.

Even if he had started a cult, surely he would never have involved Asmodeus. Surely there was never a time he had been that mad or reckless.

"I do," said Alec suddenly, and Magnus started.

"The portrait is hung on a bare stone wall, by itself. That's a big wall, why not use it for anything else?"

Alec strode forward, walked underneath the picture frame, and pulled the bottom outward. He lifted the giant portrait off the wall and put it on the ground against one of the columns. He returned to the now-naked stone wall and banged a knuckle against it.

Shinyun walked next to him and placed a hand on the wall. Orange waves flowed from her hands and over the stone, and the stone shimmered like water to form an alcove tiled in the same glittering stone as the other walls. Set in the alcove was a large book, bound in calfskin dyed deep crimson, with gilt letters set deep into the cover.

The gold letters formed the words THE RED SCROLLS OF MAGIC.

Shinyun drew the book out and sat down on the stone to read. The book looked huge in her slim hands. As she began to turn the pages, the yellowed vellum crackled beneath her fingertips. Alec began to read over her shoulder.

Magnus did not want to, but he made himself take the steps past the altar, to where Shinyun and Alec stood reading the book.

Awe and dread both dissipated somewhat as Magnus read some of the holy tenets laid down by the Red Scrolls.

"Only the Great Poison, he who is handsome and wise and charming and handsome, can lead the faithful to Edom. So cater to the Great Poison with food and drink and baths and the occasional massage."

"They wrote 'handsome' twice," murmured Alec.

"Why is it called the Red Scrolls," said Shinyun, "when it is a book? And not a scroll?"

"It's definitely not *plural* scrolls," said Alec.

"I'm sure whoever this handsome, handsome cult founder is," said Magnus, his chest constricting, "he had his reasons."

Shinyun read on. "The prince wishes only the best for his children. Thus, to honor his name, there must be a hearth crowded with only the finest of liquors and cigars and bonbons. Tithes of treasure and gifts showered upon the Great Poison symbolize the love between the faithful, so keep the spirits flowing and the gold growing, and always remember the sacred rules.

"Life is a stage, so exit in style.

"Only the faithful who make a truly great drink shall be favored.

"Offend not the Great Poison with cruel deeds or poor fashion.

"Seek the children of demons. Love them as you love your lord. Do not let the children be alone.

"In times of trouble, remember: all roads lead to Rome."

Alec looked at Magnus, and Magnus could not entirely understand Alec's small smile. "I think you wrote this."

Magnus winced. It did sound like him. Like his worst self, frivolous and thoughtless, contemptuous and superior. He did not remember writing it. But he almost certainly had. He was, almost certainly, the Great Poison. He was, almost certainly, responsible for the Crimson Hand.

"It's silly," Shinyun remarked with disgust.

"Magnus, aren't you relieved this is a joke?" Alec said, and Magnus realized his smile had been relief. "Why would anyone think you needed to have your memories of this taken away? It isn't serious."

He almost wanted to snap at Alec, though he knew it was himself he was angry at. *Don't you see what this means?* The Crimson Hand might have started out as a joke, but now it was deadly serious. People were dead because of Magnus's joke.

Magnus was responsible for more than just the cult's existence. Shinyun was crouched on the stone before him, her wrecked life a living testament to what he had done. Magnus had told his followers to find the children of demons. He had commanded that warlock children be brought into his cult. Whatever evil the cult had done, whatever Shinyun had suffered, it was Magnus's doing.

Soon enough Alec would realize that too. Magnus cleared his throat, and tried to make his voice light as air.

"Well, the good news is," he said, ignoring Alec's question, "'all roads lead to Rome.' So at least we know where to go next."

MORNING WOULD BREAK OVER VENICE SOON, ILLUMINATING water and sky. The city was coming to life already. Magnus could see the storefronts opening and smell baked bread and sausages as well as brine in the air.

Morning and its transformations were not here yet. The dawn was a line of pearl above the indigo waters. The buildings and bridges were deep lavender and silver by its faint, brightening light. Magnus, Alec, Shinyun, and Malcolm, whom they had found curled up asleep on the remains of the front steps of the palazzo and brought with them, had climbed into a vacant gondola. Magnus waved the gondola in the direction of their hotel, his magic sending bright blue sparks scattering on the surface of the water.

Magnus's party clothes were dust gray and crumpled, which was how he felt. They'd all walked quietly back through the endless corridors and doors and stairs until they had found the stars going out as the sky began to brighten over the canals. They had barely spoken, and Magnus was still avoiding Alec's gaze. Alec was visibly exhausted. He'd abandoned his tattered jacket somewhere in the ruins of the palazzo, and he was in his shirtsleeves, face marked with dust and dirt. He'd been running and fighting and searching for the better portion of the night, trying to fix Magnus's mistakes, diving for and shielding people with his own body as warlock magic shattered the place where they stood.

He lay at the bottom of the boat now, his back leaning against Magnus's chest. Magnus could feel Alec's whole body limp with weariness.

"I'm sorry you had a terrible time at the awful party," Magnus whispered low in Alec's ear.

"I didn't have a terrible time," Alec whispered back, his voice scratchy with tiredness and worry. "I was with you."

Magnus felt Alec's head loll back against his chest.

"Sad the party broke up so soon," Malcolm commented.

"It's almost time for breakfast, Malcolm. Also, the building fell down. Anyone fancy breakfast?"

"Most important meal of the day," Alec murmured, somewhat more than half-asleep.

There was no answer from anyone, even Malcolm, who was clearly brooding on his wrongs. "I can't believe Barnabas Hale," Malcolm said. "He's so rude. I'm glad he's flouncing off to another city. Florence, was it? Or maybe . . ."

"Rome," said Shinyun grimly.

"Oh yes," Malcolm said brightly. "Maybe Rome."

There was a terrible silence. It was broken when Malcolm started to sing a song, soft and off-key, about a lost love by the sea. It didn't matter—Magnus's thoughts were far away.

Barnabas Hale was going to Rome.

All the Crimson Hand's roads led to Rome.

The Crimson Hand and its leader, who had been laying the blame for the cult's current activities on Magnus, were almost certainly in Rome.

Magnus had known Barnabas Hale a long time and had never liked him. His appearance in Venice had been an unpleasant surprise. But it was a big jump from *that guy is annoying* to *that guy is slaughtering faeries and summoning Greater Demons and tried to kill me with a Raum brood mother.*

Still, Barnabas was a warlock with plenty of power. He had said he owned the palazzo, so he had wealth as well. He was someone to follow up on, in any event.

"We need sleep," Shinyun said eventually, "and then we should get down to Rome as soon as possible."

"The sooner we get there, the sooner Alec and I can continue our vacation," said Magnus.

His bright tone did not sound convincing, even to himself. Tomorrow, he told himself, he would do better. He would stop feeling so crushed under the weight of the past and his fear of the future, and enjoy the present as he usually did.

"I'm sure you and Alec will enjoy that," said Shinyun.

It was hard to tell, given her expressionless face, but Magnus thought that might be a peace offering. He smiled at her, as best he could.

"He's very devoted," Shinyun continued, gazing at Alec. His eyes were closed, but his arm was curved protectively around Magnus, even in sleep. "Doesn't he ever quit?"

She reached out a hand to touch Magnus's, but Magnus felt the muscles in Alec's body go tense the moment before the Shadowhunter's hand shot out to grab her wrist.

"I don't," said Alec.

Shinyun went still, then withdrew her hand. Alec's head sagged instantly back against Magnus's chest and he slipped into whatever twilight state between conscious and unconscious he currently occupied.

The gondola drifted under the Bridge of Sighs, a pale crown in the dim sky above them. Prisoners in the old days had seen their city for the last time from this bridge, before they were led to their execution.

Magnus noticed Malcolm watching them, his face white as marble. Malcolm had loved a Shadowhunter. It had not ended well. Magnus had spoken to him about it once, about getting over love and living on, about finding love again. Malcolm had shaken his head. He had said, *I do not ever want another love.*

Magnus had thought he was being foolish.

Perhaps all love sailed too close to madness. The deeper the love, the more dangerous.

The boat slid on across dark waters. When Magnus looked behind him, he saw the last sparks of his magic sinking and vanishing into the depths. The sparks winked, bright blue and brilliant white, the gentle ripples of the canal becoming by turns rich purple, pale pearl, and inky black under the not-yet-morning sky. The water was suffused with a final luminescence before his blue sparks drowned. Magnus slid his fingers gently through Alec's wild, soft hair, and felt Alec's head turn toward him a little in half sleep. He heard Malcolm singing and remembered again his words from long ago.

I do not ever want another love.

CHAPTER SEVENTEEN

Bitter Secrets

"WHEN IN ROME, ALEXANDER," SAID MAGNUS, "ONE drives a Maserati."

They had to get to Rome as fast as possible, and they couldn't use a Portal, so Magnus said he was selecting the next best option. Shinyun was reading the Red Scrolls of Magic and ignoring them both, which was fine with Alec.

"An excellent choice," said the attendant at the luxury car rental lot. "Gotta love a classic 3500 GT Spyder."

Alec leaned into Magnus. "The car is also a spider?"

Magnus shrugged, flashing Alec an irresistibly bright smile. "No idea. I just picked it because it was Italian and red."

Twenty minutes later the three were cruising down the A13 toward Bologna with the top down and the wind whistling in their ears. Shinyun was in the back, lying down with her boots propped up against the window and reading aloud from the Red Scrolls at intervals. Alec was in the passenger seat, struggling to navigate with only the help of an accordion-folded paper map in a language he didn't understand.

Magnus, who was driving, said, "Been a while since I drove a stick shift. No jokes, please."

They were in Florence in time for an early dinner. Magnus had made reservations at a restaurant so tiny Alec was pretty sure it was just the chef's living room. It was the best pasta he had ever eaten.

After dinner, Magnus said, "We can't just drive frantically all the time. We'll crash. Let's try to hit another spot on our old itinerary. We're not far from the Boboli Gardens."

"Sure," said Alec.

Shinyun walked after them, the Red Scrolls tucked under her arm, even though nobody had asked her along.

Magnus narrated where they were going as they walked along the Arno, crossed the Ponte Vecchio, and moved in a zigzag to make detours at assorted street vendors. Magnus bought a scarf, a pair of sunglasses, a *zeppola*, and a cloak that made him look like the Phantom of the Opera.

They reached the Boboli Gardens Amphitheater and circled the statues lining the perimeter, working their way inward to the obelisk at the center.

"It's been a while since we took a picture for the people back home," said Alec.

Magnus linked elbows with him and dragged him past the Neptune Fountain and the Statue of Abundance, until he found a statue featuring a large naked guy on top of a giant tortoise. He declared this the perfect spot for a picture. He tipped back his Panama hat and struck a regal pose on one side of the statue, which he explained to Alec was called Morgante. Alec leaned on the other side, hands in his pockets, as Shinyun snapped several shots for them with Alec's phone.

"Thanks," said Alec. "I'll send these and tell Isabelle we're having a great time."

"Will you?" Magnus asked.

Alec blinked. "Sure. I mean, I miss Isabelle and Jace, and Mom and Dad."

Magnus appeared to be waiting for something else. Alec thought it over.

"I miss Clary, too," he said. "A bit."

"She's my little biscuit. Who wouldn't?" said Magnus, but he still seemed rather tense.

"I really don't know Simon all that well," Alec offered.

Alec didn't know a lot of people. There was his family, Jace included, and Jace's new girlfriend, and the vampire Jace was sneaking in as a package deal. He knew some other Shadowhunters. Aline Penhallow was Alec's age and great with daggers, but Aline lived in Idris, so he wouldn't be hanging out with her even if he was in New York.

It took Alec a few minutes as they prowled around the gardens to realize that Magnus might be worrying about what he might say to his family, his friends, almost all of whom were, of course, fellow Shadowhunters. None of whom would be as inclined to give Magnus the benefit of the doubt as Alec would.

Alec was worried about Magnus, the way he was trying just a little too hard to have a good time. Alec liked it when Magnus was actually having a good time, but he hated it when Magnus was pretending, and he could easily tell the difference by now. Alec wanted to say something, but Shinyun was here, he didn't know what to say, and right then his phone rang in his pocket.

It was Isabelle.

"I was just thinking about you," said Alec.

"And I was thinking about you," said Isabelle cheerfully. "Enjoying yourself on vacation, or have you lapsed into work? Can you not help yourself?"

"We're in the Boboli Gardens," said Alec, which was entirely true. "How's everyone in New York?" he added quickly. "Clary dragging Jace into any more trouble? Jace dragging Clary into any more trouble?"

"That's the cornerstone of their relationship, but no, Jace is hanging out with Simon," Isabelle reported. "He says they're playing video games."

"Do you think Simon invited Jace to hang out with him?" Alec asked skeptically.

"Bro," said Isabelle, "I do not."

"Has Jace ever played a video game before? I've never played a video game."

"I'm sure he'll get the hang of it," said Isabelle. "Simon's explained them to me and they do not sound difficult."

"How are things going with you and Simon?"

"He's taken a number and remains in the long line of men desperate for my attention," Isabelle said firmly. "How are things between you and Magnus?"

"Well, I wondered if you could help me with that."

"Yes!" Isabelle exclaimed with horrifying delight. "You are right to come to me with this. I am so much more subtle and skilled in the arts of seduction than Jace. Okay, here's my first suggestion. You're going to need a grapefruit—"

"Stop!" said Alec. He hurriedly strode away from Magnus and Shinyun and hid behind a high hedge. They watched him go with bemusement. "Please don't finish that sentence. I meant, there's still that small cult problem I asked you about. I'd really like to get it worked out, so that Magnus can be happier. On our vacation."

And so demons could stop trying to kill Magnus, and Magnus would be free from dark rumors and the darker threat posed by the Clave. That too would make Magnus happier, Alec was sure.

"Right," Isabelle said. "Actually, that's why I called. I sent a carefully worded message to Aline Penhallow, but she's not in Idris right now and she can't help. So I haven't been able to turn up much, but I did some digging around in the Institute archives. We don't have a big section on cults. There aren't that many in New York. Probably because of real estate prices. In any case, I did turn up a copy of an original manuscript that might help you. I took photos of some pages. I'll e-mail them to you."

"Thanks, Izzy," said Alec.

Isabelle hesitated. "There was a frontispiece with a drawing of someone who looked awfully familiar."

"Was there?" said Alec.

"Alec!"

"Do you tell me all your secrets, Izzy?"

Isabelle paused. "No," she said in a softer voice. "But I'll tell you one now. Of all the men standing in line for my attention, Simon may be my favorite."

Alec looked across hedgerows, glowing green in the cool Italian evening, and white marble statues to Magnus, who was striking poses in imitation of the statues. Shinyun could not smile, but Alec thought she must want to. Nobody could help liking Magnus.

"All right," Alec said. "Of all the men standing in line for my attention, Magnus is definitely my favorite."

Isabelle squealed in outrage. Alec grinned.

"I'm so glad to hear you sound like this," Isabelle said in a sudden rush. "And I won't pry. I just want you to know that any secrets you have, I keep. You can trust me."

Alec remembered the old days and the old fears, the way Isabelle had occasionally tried to start conversations about boys and let Alec shut them down. He had always snapped at her, terrified to speak and have someone hear, but sometimes at night when he thought about the possibility of being disowned by his parents, rejected by the Clave, hated by Jace and Max, his only comfort was that his sister knew, and she still loved him.

Alec closed his eyes and told her, "I always have."

He had to tell Magnus, then, that he'd mentioned the Crimson Hand to Isabelle.

"I'm sorry," he said as soon as he did. "I'm used to telling her everything."

"You don't need to apologize," said Magnus instantly, but there was misery on his face again, misery he was trying to hide but that Alec could see perfectly well. "*I* need to—look, tell your sister anything you like. Tell anyone anything you want."

"Wow," said Shinyun. "That's extremely rash, Magnus. There is trust and then there is just foolishness. Do you want to be thrown in prison by the Clave?"

"No, I don't," Magnus snapped.

Alec wanted to tell Shinyun to shut up, but he knew Magnus wanted him to be kind to her. So he didn't tell Shinyun to shut up.

Instead he said, "When we get to Rome, I was thinking I should go to the Rome Institute."

"So Magnus can get thrown in prison—" Shinyun began, this time angrily.

"No!" said Alec. "I was going to get more weapons. And carefully and discreetly ask if there's any word of demon-summoning activities that might lead us to the Crimson Hand. All we know is that we're going to Rome. It's a big city. But I was thinking, it'd be better if—if I went on my own. They won't be suspicious of me."

Shinyun opened her mouth.

"Do it," said Magnus.

"You're out of your mind," said Shinyun.

"I trust him," said Magnus. "More than you. More than anybody."

Alec worried that Magnus's trust was misplaced when they found an Internet café near the Boboli Gardens and printed out what Isabelle had sent him. Which turned out to be a scan of the first few pages of the Red Scrolls of Magic.

"Not to be overdramatic," said Magnus, "but—aaaargh. Aaaargh. Why! I cannot believe we broke into a secret sanctum in a creepy dungeon to find something your sister would e-mail us the next day."

Alec looked at the page on the glorious history of the Crimson Hand, in which the Great Poison commanded his followers to paint white stripes on horses and make the wooden mouse the national animal of Morocco.

"It is ironic," he admitted.

"It's not," said Shinyun. "That's not what irony—"

Magnus gave her a look of fury and she stopped.

Alec shrugged. "No harm having another copy. Shinyun's reading the book. Now I can read it too."

It had to be easier reading than the map. As they walked back toward the car, Magnus glanced at Alec and tossed his keys from hand to hand.

"We'll go faster if two of us are sharing driving duties," Alec offered hopefully.

"Ever driven stick before?"

Alec hesitated. "Can't be harder than shooting a bow and arrow while riding a horse at a full gallop."

"It's definitely not," said Magnus. "Besides, you have superhuman reflexes. What's the worst that could happen?"

He threw Alec the keys and slid into the passenger's seat with a smile. Alec grinned and jogged over to the driver's seat.

Magnus suggested some practice loops in the parking lot.

"You have to lift your left foot as you're applying gas with the right foot," he said. Alec looked at him.

"Oh no," he said dryly. "I have to move both feet at the same time. How can I possibly handle such demands of my agility." He turned back, applied the gas, and was rewarded with a high-pitched screech, like a banshee in a trap. Magnus smiled but did not say anything.

Soon enough, of course, Alec was maneuvering competently around the lot.

"Ready to take the show on the road?" Magnus asked.

Alec only answered with a smile as he peeled out. A whoop of delight and surprise escaped from his throat as the Maserati fishtailed on the narrow street. They turned onto a straightaway and Alec punched the acceleration.

"We're going very fast," said Shinyun. "Why are we going so fast?"

The low friendly growl of the little red convertible filled the air. Alec glanced over to see Magnus put on his sunglasses and rest his elbow on the door as he leaned over the side and smiled at the rush of the wind across his face.

Alec was glad to be able to give Magnus a break. Also, he hadn't realized this kind of wild, dramatic driving was a thing available to him. When he thought of cars he thought of Manhattan: far too many vehicles, not nearly enough road, chugging slowly and unhappily through the veins of the city. There, being on foot was liberation. Here in the Tuscan countryside, though, this car was its own kind of liberation, a thrilling kind. He looked over at his unbearably handsome boyfriend, hair blown back and eyes closed behind his shades. Sometimes, his life was okay. He willfully ignored the grumpy warlock ride-along in the backseat.

For the next hour, they followed the Apennines through the heart of Tuscany. To their left were sunset-soaked golden fields spanning to the horizon, and to their right were rows of stone villas on hilltops overlooking a green vineyard sea. Cypress trees whispered in the wind.

It was black night by the time they reached what Magnus said was called the Chianti mountain range. Alec didn't look. He felt pretty confident handling the Maserati by now, but managing a stick shift along the many sharp turns while driving near the edge of a cliff in the dark was an entirely separate and existentially threatening experience.

What made the situation even more harrowing was that the headlights only bought them a few dozen feet of visibility, so all they could see were a narrow stretch of road in front, the sheer face of the mountain, and the cliff edge that led to the open sky. Only one of those options was any good.

Alec managed to downshift correctly on the first few turns, but sweat stung his eyes.

"Are you all right?" Magnus asked.

"I'm great," Alec said quickly.

He fought demons for a living. This was driving, a thing even mundanes did without any unusual talents or sense-enhancing runes. All he had to do was focus.

He was holding on to the steering wheel too tight, and he jerked the stick every time he had to shift around a hard turn.

Alec mistimed a particularly difficult bend that sent the car veering out of control. He tried to punch the accelerator and even out but ended up hitting the brake, sending them spinning down a steep decline.

The vista before them was not a welcome sight. It meant they were going right off a cliff.

Alec threw an arm up to shield Magnus, and Magnus grabbed his arm. Alec had felt this strange connected feeling once before, on a ship in troubled waters: Magnus reaching out for him, needing his strength. He turned his hand under Magnus's hand and linked their fingers, feeling nothing but the warm strong impulse to reach back.

The car had just skidded off the road and dipped over the side when it came to a sudden stop, the two spinning front wheels touching nothing but air and soft blue magic. It hovered for a moment and then righted itself and rolled back onto the narrow dirt path next to the road.

"I told you we were going too fast," said Shinyun mildly from the backseat.

Alec held on fast to Magnus's hand, his own clasped against Magnus's chest. A warlock's heart beat differently from a human's. Magnus's heartbeat was a reassurance in the dark. Alec already knew it well.

"It's just a tiny little cliff," said Magnus. "Nothing we can't handle."

Alec and Magnus got out of the car. Magnus threw his arms out wide as if he was going to embrace the night sky. Alec walked to the cliff's edge and looked over, whistling at the long, sheer drop down to the ravine. He looked off to the side at a small dirt trail leading to a clearing jutting out from the cliff. He beckoned to Magnus. "It's pretty dangerous driving at night. Maybe we should stay here."

Magnus looked around. "Just . . . here?"

"Camping could be fun," said Alec. "We can toast marshmallows. You'd need to summon supplies from somewhere, of course."

Shinyun had climbed out of the car and was coming over to join them. "Let me guess," she said to Magnus in flat tones. "Darling, your idea of camping is when the hotel doesn't have a minibar."

Magnus blinked at her.

"I beat you to that joke," Shinyun informed him.

Magnus lifted his eyes to the night sky. Alec could see the silver curve of a crescent moon reflected in the gold of his eyes. It matched the sudden curve of Magnus's smile.

"All right," said Magnus. "Let's have fun."

ALEC PUT DOWN HIS COPY OF THE RED SCROLLS OF MAGIC to behold the campsite Magnus had conjured. He'd assumed Magnus would conjure up accommodations that would be spacious enough to sleep two comfortably and tall enough for them to stand without hunching over. At least that was what Shinyun had done when she had summoned her own tent, at her insistence.

What Magnus had erected was not so much a tent as a pavilion, complete with curtains and scalloped edging. The spacious living quarters had two bedrooms, a bathroom, a common area, and a sitting room. Alec made a loop around the massive goatskin structure and discovered the kitchen was set up in the back next to a covered deck area complete with a dining set. An ancient Roman-legion Aquila standard was staked next to the front door as a final touch, in tribute to what Magnus said was his "When in Rome" theme.

Magnus opened the back flap and strolled out, looking satisfied. "What do you think?"

"It's cool," said Alec. "But I can't help wondering . . . where did you get this much goatskin?"

Magnus shrugged. "All you need to know is, I believe in magic, not cruelty."

There was the sound of suction, and then a monstrous structure appeared out of thin air, blowing a ring of dust outward in every direction. Where Shinyun's tent had been now stood a two-story treehouse that blotted out a third of the sky. Shinyun walked out of her upgraded living arrangements and glanced in Magnus's direction.

They had engaged in an increasingly less subtle game of one-upmanship ever since they had tried on clothing at Le Mercerie, supporting Alec's theory that perhaps all warlocks tested each other's power, in a magic version of sibling rivalry. Magnus was clearly playing. Alec suspected that Shinyun took the game a little more seriously, but he was loyally of the opinion that Magnus was the superior warlock.

"Love the turrets," Magnus called over cheerfully. It was hard to defeat Magnus with excess, Alec thought. He would just admire it. "Fancy a midnight snack?"

They congregated at the fire pit on the other end of camp, just a few feet away from the cliff's edge. Magnus had originally built it, and Shinyun had improved on it, so it was like a pyre for a Viking funeral. The gigantic blaze looked as if they were trying to send a signal up to Valhalla.

Below the partially covered moon, a flotilla of clouds drifted in front of Mount Corno, the tallest in the Apennine Range. A swarm of fireflies danced just above their heads, and nature had come alive all around them, with crickets chirping and owls hooting to a steady rhythm while the low, wary whistle of the wind floated up from the valley below. Somewhere in the distance, a pack of wolves joined the night symphony with a chorus of howls.

"They sound lonely," said Shinyun.

"No," said Alec. "They're together. They're hunting."

"You're the expert on that," Shinyun observed. "I was alone once, and hunted."

"You were also in a cult once," Alec pointed out, then bit his lip.

An edge appeared in Shinyun's voice. "Tell me, Shadowhunter, where are the Nephilim when Downworlders are in trouble?"

"Shielding us," said Magnus. "You saw Alec in Venice."

"He was there because he's with you," Shinyun snapped. "If he hadn't been with you, he wouldn't have been there. They stalk us, and hurt us, and leave us. When was it decided that a warlock child is worth less than the children of the Angel?"

Alec did not know what to say. She threw up her hands and stood up.

"I apologize," she said. "I am on edge with our destination so close at hand. I will retire for the evening. I have to rest. We reach Rome tomorrow. Who knows what will await us there?"

Shinyun gave them a curt nod and then walked off to her giant tent, leaving Magnus and Alec alone by the fire.

"I suspect Shinyun may be a 'no' on the rousing fireside sing-along I was planning," said Magnus.

He reached over and ran his fingertips in a light, absentminded caress along Alec's neck. Alec leaned into his touch. When Magnus's hand dropped, Alec wanted to follow it.

"Don't worry about her," Magnus added. "Many warlocks have tragic childhoods. We come into a world already made dark by demons. It's hard not to give in to the anger."

"You don't," said Alec.

Magnus's voice was bleak. "I have."

"Shinyun didn't have to join a cult," said Alec.

"I didn't have to found a cult," Magnus pointed out.

Alec said, "That's different."

"Sure. It's much worse." Magnus tossed a twig into the fire and watched as it withered and blackened, and then curled into ash. Alec watched him.

Magnus Bane was always brightly burning, whimsical and effervescent, ethereal and carefree. He was the High Warlock of Brooklyn, who wore blazing colors and shiny glitter around his eyes. He was the sort of person who threw birthday parties for his cat and loved whomever he wanted loudly and proudly.

Only there was dark waiting behind the brightness. Alec had to learn that side of Magnus too, or he would never really know him.

"I think I understand about Shinyun," Alec said slowly. "I wondered why you were insisting on bringing her with us. I even thought maybe you didn't want to be alone with me."

"Alec, I—"

Alec held out a hand. "But then I realized. You feel like she's your responsibility, don't you? If the Crimson Hand hurt her, then you feel like you have to help her. To make it right."

Magnus nodded slightly. "She is my dark mirror, Alexander," he said. "She is in some ways what I could have been, had I not been lucky enough to have experienced love and caring—my mother's, and then Ragnor and the Silent Brothers. I could have been so desperate I too would have joined something like the Crimson Hand."

"You don't talk much about the past," Alec said slowly. "You didn't even tell me you were close to that warlock who died. Ragnor Fell. You were, weren't you?"

"I was," said Magnus. "He was the first friend I ever had."

Alec looked down at his hands. Jace had been the first friend he'd ever had, but Magnus knew that. Magnus knew everything about him. He was an open book. He tried to crush down the feeling of hurt. "So—why not tell me?"

The sparks from the campfire flew upward, brief stars flaring against the black night, then winked out.

Alec wondered if loving a mortal was like that to Magnus, bright but brief. Maybe this was all just a short, insignificant episode in a long, long story. He wasn't just an open book, he thought. He was a short one. A slim volume compared to the chronicles of Magnus's long life.

"Because nobody ever really wants to know," said Magnus. "Usually I get no further than mentioning I killed my stepfather, and people decide that's enough. You've already seen too much. Last night you saw the Red Scrolls of Magic, all the stupid, careless things I said, hidden behind a bloodstained altar. Can you blame me if I wonder, every time, whether this is the time I scare you away?"

"Shadowhunters don't scare easily," Alec said. "I know you feel guilty about Shinyun being taken in by the cult, but you meant it for the best. That's what I thought when I read the Red Scrolls. You didn't say to recruit the kids, to use them. You said not to let them be alone. You were alone, and you didn't want other warlock children to suffer like you did. I came on this trip to get to know you better, and I am."

"I'm sure you've learned more than you wanted to," said Magnus quietly.

"I learned you see snarling animals in cages, and you try to pet them. Your friend died, and you didn't even tell me you knew him, but you tried to comfort a vampire about it. You're always trying to help people. Me and my friends, so many times, and Raphael Santiago of all people, and now Shinyun and other warlock kids, and probably loads of people I don't know about yet, but I know this much. I looked at the Red Scrolls of Magic and saw you trying to help children. That part sounded like you."

Magnus laughed, an uneven sound.

"Was that what you meant? I thought you meant—something else." He closed his eyes. "I don't want this not to work because of me," he confessed. "I don't want to shatter what we have by telling you something that will drive you away. How much truth do you really want, Alexander?"

"I want all of it," said Alec.

Magnus turned his eyes, brighter than firelight, on Alec, and held out his hand. Alec took his hand firmly, drew in his breath, and braced himself. His heart thundered in his chest and his stomach twisted. He waited.

"Um," he said. "Aren't you going to do some magic that shows me your past?"

"Oh, heavens no," said Magnus. "That whole business was traumatic enough to live through once. I was just going to talk about it. I wanted to hold your hand."

"Oh," said Alec. "Well . . . good."

Magnus slid in close. Alec could feel the heat radiating off his skin. The warlock bowed his head as he gathered his thoughts. He made a few false starts at speaking, and each time he gripped Alec's hand tighter.

"I'd like to think my mother loved me," said Magnus. "All I remember is that she was so sad. I always felt as if I had to learn some trick to figure out how to do better. I thought I could prove myself, and she would be happy, and I'd be good enough. I never learned the trick. She hanged herself in the barn. My stepfather burned the barn to the ground and built a shrine to her in the ashes. He didn't know exactly what I was. *I* didn't know exactly what I was, but he knew I was not his. He knew I was not human. One day when the air was hot as soup, I was sleeping and woke to hear him calling me."

Magnus smiled as if his heart was broken. "He used my old name, the one my mother gave me. There is nobody left alive who knows that name now."

Alec held Magnus's hand even tighter, as if he could rescue him, centuries too late.

"You don't have to say anything more," he whispered. "Not if you don't want to."

"I want to," said Magnus, but his voice wavered as he continued. "My stepfather hit me a few times, then hauled me by the neck to the burnt ruins of the barn. There was still a blackened rope hanging from a rafter. I could hear the water of the creek running. My stepfather grabbed me by the nape of my neck and pushed my head into the water. Just before he did, he spoke to me, and he sounded gentler than I'd ever heard him sound before. He said, 'This is to purify you. Trust me.'"

Alec's breath caught. He found he could not stop holding it, as if he could save it for the child Magnus had been.

"I don't remember what happened after that. One minute I was drowning." There was a pause. Magnus held his hands up. His voice was devoid of emotion. "The next, I burned my stepfather alive."

The campfire erupted into a column of flame, roiling in a funnel that shot halfway up to heaven. Alec threw an arm in front of Magnus to shield him from the scorching blast.

The pillar of flame died away almost at once. Magnus did not even seem to notice the giant column of fire he had created. Alec wondered if Shinyun had woken up, but if she had, there was no sign. Maybe she slept with earplugs in.

"I ran away," Magnus continued. "I was in hiding, until I crossed paths with the Silent Brothers. They taught me how to control my magic. I was always fonder of Shadowhunters than most warlocks, because your Silent Brothers saved me from myself. I still thought I was a demon's child and could never be anything more. I'd never met another warlock, but Ragnor Fell had ties to a Shadowhunter family. The Silent Brothers arranged for him to come and teach me. I was the first pupil he ever had. Later he tried to teach Shadowhunter children about magic, and not to fear us. He said all his pupils were terrible, but I was the worst. He complained constantly. Nothing ever made him happy. I loved him very much." Magnus's mouth twisted as he stared intently into the flames. "A little while later I met my second friend, Catarina Loss. Some mundanes were trying to burn her at the stake. I intervened."

"I *knew* I was going to find out about you saving more people," said Alec.

Magnus gave a soft, surprised huff of laughter. Alec caught Magnus's upraised hands in his own, warming them and holding them steady, drawing Magnus closer to him. Magnus did not resist, and Alec enveloped him in a tight embrace. He locked his arms around Magnus's slim body, felt their chests rising and falling against each other, and held him fast. Magnus let his head drop onto Alec's shoulder.

"You saved yourself," Alec said into Magnus's ear. "You saved yourself, and then you saved so many people. You couldn't have saved anyone if you hadn't saved yourself. I would never have found you."

Alec had been right about the darkness waiting in Magnus, and the pain waiting with it. All that darkness, and all that pain, and Magnus was somehow still a blazing riot of life and color, a source of joy for everyone around him. He was the reason Alec looked into a mirror now and saw a complete person who did not have to hide.

They stayed locked together, the fire beside them dying. All was quiet. Alec held on.

"Don't worry so much. It's just a tiny little cult," he said eventually. "Nothing we can't handle."

He felt Magnus's mouth curve, pressed against Alec's cheek, as Magnus smiled.

PART III
City of War

† † †

When Rome falls, the world shall fall.
—Lord Byron

CHAPTER EIGHTEEN

The Treasures That Prevail

THERE WAS NO OTHER CITY LIKE ROME, MAGNUS thought as the domes of the basilicas first appeared on the horizon. Of course, he could say the same about many cities. That was one of the advantages of living forever. There were always new wonders of the world.

There was nothing like Tokyo, with its duality of culture and technology. There was nothing like Bangkok, with its metropolis that spanned as far as the eye could see. There was nothing like Chicago jazz and deep-dish pizza.

And there was nothing as uniquely spectacular as Rome, the golden Eternal City.

Magnus and Alec had fallen asleep next to the fire under the open sky. They awoke to birds chirping and the predawn light heralding the new day. It was honestly one of the best mornings Magnus had ever had.

His only regret was that they hadn't gotten to use the pavilion he'd conjured. In fact, he didn't think Alec had even set foot inside the tent. It was a pity. Magnus was very proud of his work. But there was always next time.

He felt refreshed and his mission was clear: wrap up this cult business, return to romantic vacation. The Crimson Hand were in Rome; Magnus would find them and whomever was leading them, and he would have many stern words and painful spells for that cult-stealing, vacation-ruining, Greater Demon–summoning lunatic. He was fairly confident about his ability to face down almost any other warlock in the world. (Even Barnabas. Especially Barnabas.) Even if the cult was deranged enough to be in communication with Asmodeus, Magnus was pretty sure they hadn't actually raised him yet. He just thought there was no way, if his father walked the earth, that he wouldn't have already made himself known to Magnus.

Maybe this could all be over soon.

Magnus folded and banished all of the camping supplies to whence they had come, Shinyun did the same, and they climbed into the Maserati.

"Don't bother with the map," he told Alec airily. "All roads lead to Rome."

Alec grinned at him. "The map definitely doesn't agree."

It was only about two hours, and soon enough they were struggling their way through the streets of Rome, where the low wide lines of the Maserati were less of a stylish grace note and more of a target for the fleets of scooters and tiny Fiats swarming them from all sides. Rome had some of the worst traffic patterns Magnus knew, and Magnus had seen some bad traffic patterns in his day. They checked into a suite at the Palazzo Manfredi, a boutique hotel across the street from the Roman Colosseum, where without any actual discussion, they unanimously agreed to sleep in comfortable beds with fancy sheets in climate-controlled, beautiful hotel rooms until the evening. Even Shinyun seemed bone weary, heading for the room adjacent to theirs with hardly a word.

Alec whistled when they walked into their suite. He dumped his luggage to the side, leaned his bow against the wall, and sprawled full length on the soft red velvet of the luxuriously wide sofa.

Magnus cast a few protective spells to ward them as they slept, then joined Alec on the sofa, climbing over one arm and crawling on top of the Shadowhunter like Chairman Meow would have if they were home. He draped himself across Alec's body, tucked his face into the curve of Alec's neck, and inhaled the scent of him. Alec's arm went around Magnus's back, stroking a shoulder blade. Magnus dropped a kiss on the underside of Alec's jaw and rubbed his cheek lightly against the rough scrape of Alec's two-day stubble. He felt Alec draw in a shuddering breath.

"You smell amazing," Alec whispered. "Why—why do you always smell amazing?"

"Um," Magnus mumbled, delighted but fighting sleep. "It's sandalwood, I think."

"It's great," Alec whispered. "Come and hold me. I want you next to me."

Magnus glanced up at him. Alec's eyes were closed and he was breathing deeply.

Come and hold me. I want you next to me. Maybe it was easier for Alec to say things like that when he was half asleep. It hadn't occurred to Magnus that Alec might feel self-conscious, saying things like that. He'd thought Alec didn't want to say them.

Magnus did as requested and curled his body around Alec's. Their legs tangled together. Magnus traced a forefinger across Alec's cheek, down to his mouth. Alec's lashes were long, thick, and dark, curving to touch the tops of his cheekbones. His lips were full and soft, his hair a tumble of rough black silk. He looked vulnerable in a way that was hard to square, sometimes, with the cold-eyed, arrow-slinging warrior he became in battle.

He thought about waking Alec up and suggesting they go into the bedroom. He could kiss that full, soft mouth, mess up that silky hair even further. He brushed his lips over Alec's cheek, closing his eyes . . .

He opened them to late-afternoon sun shining through a floor-to-ceiling window and cursed his own exhaustion. Who knew how many hours had passed, and Alec was no longer on the couch with him.

He found Alec on the balcony with a spread on the table of charcuterie, cheeses, breads, and fruits. Alec lifted a champagne flute toward him.

"Alexander Lightwood," said Magnus in admiration. "Well played."

Alec swirled the glass, his silly grin the only crack in his debonair attitude. "Prosecco?"

The balcony was like a cup of warm sunlight. They sat there and Magnus sent messages to everyone he could think of, asking if anyone had seen Barnabas Hale around. He also ate maybe a pound and a half of cured meat. Taking an early light dinner with Alec, even though they had to hurry, felt almost domestic.

He should move in with me, he thought. *No, no, too soon, maybe when it's been a year.*

Magnus was in the shower when he heard Alec's raised voice in the living room. He hastily snatched a vast, cloudlike towel and swathed it around his hips, hurrying into the suite's drawing room in case Alec was being attacked by another demon.

Alec and Shinyun, seated on opposite ends of the couch, both froze. Shinyun quickly looked away; Alec stared. Magnus realized he had burst into the middle of the living room wearing only a towel, his wet hair dripping onto his bare torso.

Awkward.

Magnus waved, snapped his fingers, and was instantly wearing a burgundy T-shirt with a plunging V-neck, a jaunty silk scarf, and a pair of skinny jeans. He padded barefoot over to Alec's side and pressed a light kiss against Alec's burning cheek. Only then did he turn to acknowledge Shinyun. "Good afternoon. Prosecco?"

"I'm leaving," said Shinyun.

"Like, forever?" said Alec hopefully.

"Most people don't find the sight of me half-nude that alarming," said Magnus. "Several heads of state have deemed it 'a privilege.'"

Alec rolled his eyes. He seemed more than a little tense. Maybe he should book them some massages, Magnus thought.

"I have some contacts in Rome who won't want to talk to a Shadowhunter," Shinyun said. "Also, I've been trapped in a car with you for the better part of two days. I need a break. No offense."

"None taken," said Alec. "Off you go."

"Do you want coffee?" asked Magnus, feeling a little bad.

"I can't stay," said Shinyun.

"She can't stay," said Alec. "You heard her. She has to go."

Shinyun gave Magnus what he recognized as a sarcastic imitation of his own wave of greeting and left.

Magnus turned his head toward Alec, and into a kiss.

Alec had moved as only a Shadowhunter could move, swift and silent. He was in front of Magnus now, pulling off his own shirt, then sliding his hands up Magnus's arms, kissing him, deep and desperate, and oh, he'd gotten really good at this in a short amount of time. He broke the kiss only to unknot Magnus's scarf and pull Magnus's T-shirt up and over his head. He threw the shirt in the direction of the window. Magnus dropped kisses on Alec's face, on his hands, urging him along in every way he could. It was like being in the center of a wonderful whirlwind. Alec's hands skimmed up the muscles of Magnus's back, along his sides, over his shoulders, in restless, avid motion. Magnus staggered back, needing something to keep him upright. His back hit the wall.

"Sorry!" Alec said, looking suddenly worried. "I—everything's all right, Magnus?"

Alec hovered, eyes wild, and Magnus reached out, lacing his fingers through Alec's hair and tugging him back into the embrace.

"It is all right, yes," he murmured. "I love it. I love you. Come here."

Alec flung himself back into the embrace, kissing and sucking at Magnus's lower lip, the intoxication of bare skin against bare skin making them both dizzy. Magnus slid his palm down Alec's stomach, the ridges of muscle hard and clear under his hand. Alec made a low, desperate sound against Magnus's mouth as Magnus started to undo his jeans. "Magnus, yes," he whispered. "Please, yes."

Magnus realized his hand was shaking even as the zipper came down and Alec's head went back. His eyes were closed as they had been the night before, his beautiful lashes fluttering, this time in pleasure. His lips parted.

He whispered, "Wait."

Magnus pulled back instantly, his heart pounding. He held up both hands and then put them behind his back.

"Of course," he said. "We can wait as long as you want."

Alec reached to have Magnus back, as if by instinct. Then his hands fell by his side, and he clenched them into fists. His eyes traveled over Magnus, before he wrenched his gaze away. Magnus looked at the severe lines of his face and thought of the relentlessness of angels.

"I want this," said Alec, his voice despairing. "I want you more than I've ever wanted anything in my life. But—we're in this together. You're worried about the cult, and I don't want to just be grabbing some time when Shinyun isn't around, when you're unhappy."

Magnus didn't think he'd ever been more touched by a speech someone had made while zipping up their pants.

"I want to get this resolved," Alec said, yanking on his shirt. "I should go."

Magnus picked up his T-shirt from where it lay in a heap beside the window. He tugged the shirt on and stared out at the flowing curves and lines of the Colosseum, where men had fought long years before even he was born.

"I wish you could stay," he said softly. "But you're right. At least kiss me good-bye, though."

Alec had an odd expression on his face, almost as if someone had hurt him, but not quite. The blue eyes Magnus so loved were almost black.

He crossed the floor in one bound and pressed Magnus up against the window, pushing up Magnus's shirt so Magnus's back was against the sun-warmed glass. He kissed him, slow and lesuirely this time, tasting of regret. Sounding drunk, Alec murmured, "Yes—yes—no! No, I need to go to the Rome Institute."

He backed away from Magnus and picked up his bow, twisting it between his hands, as if he had to be holding something.

"If there are any unusual cult or demonic activities going on, the Institute will know. We have to use every means at our disposal. We can't take the time. We've already slept all day—who knows how much further the cult could have gotten in those hours. . . . I have to go."

Magnus wanted to be annoyed at Alec for his balking; the problem was that the urgency Alec was describing was a real, true fact. "Whatever you think is best," he said.

"Right," said Alec. "Right. I'm going. You stay. Be safe. Don't let anyone else into the suite. Don't go anywhere without me. Promise me."

Magnus had walked infernal realms in hallucinations caused by demon poisons, been homeless and hungry in streets that were now ruins, been desperate enough to set water ablaze, been extremely drunk in the desert. He did not think doom was coming for him in an upscale hotel in Rome.

But he loved Alec for worrying.

"We can pick up where we left off," Magnus said, leaning back against the windowsill. "You know, when you get back."

He smiled a slow and wicked smile. Alec made a hopeless, senseless gesture, to himself, then toward Magnus. His hand eventually calmed to stillness. He started to speak, visibly reconsidered talking, shook his head, strode toward the door, and stalked out of the room.

One second later the door banged open and Alec came back inside.

"Or maybe I should stay."

Magnus opened his mouth, but Alec had already shut his eyes, let his head fall against the back of the door with a thump, and answered himself.

"No. I'm going to go. I'm going. Bye."

He waved at Magnus. Magnus snapped his fingers. Keys landed, glittering, in the hollow of his hand, and he threw them at Alec. Alec caught them reflexively. Magnus winked.

"Take the Maserati," he said. "And hurry back."

CHAPTER NINETEEN

Bound in Heaven

ALEC TOOK THE CORNERS OF THE TANGLED STREETS OF Rome too fast. He was going to miss the Maserati. He already missed Magnus.

He kept thinking of how Magnus had looked when he'd come out of the bathroom, skin warm from the shower, towel swathed around his narrow hips, strong muscles and flat stomach sparkling with water drops. His dark hair had been barely dry, sunlight falling on him, golden and soft. Alec often liked Magnus best this way, silky hair free of gel or spikes. It wasn't that he didn't like Magnus's clothes, but Magnus wore them like armor, a layer of protection between him and a world that didn't always meet someone like him with open arms.

He couldn't think about anything else that had happened in that room. He'd already turned the car to go back to the hotel three times. The last time, he'd reversed in a narrow lane and scraped up one side of the Maserati.

He wished Magnus could've come with him to the Institute. Alec was surprised to find himself restless and uneasy without Magnus in his direct line of sight. They'd been together all the time since they left New York, and Alec had gotten used to it. He wasn't worried about another demon attack, or at least not that worried. He knew the hotel room was warded with Magnus's magic, and Magnus had promised to stay in the hotel room.

It was strange. He missed New York; he missed Jace and Isabelle, and Mom and Dad, and even Clary. But he missed Magnus most of all, and he had only been apart from Magnus for thirty minutes.

He wondered what Magnus would think, when they got home, about Alec moving in.

Like all Institutes, the Rome Institute was accessible only to Nephilim; like many of them, this one was glamoured to appear as an old church, fallen into disuse. Because Rome was one of the most densely populated cities in Europe, there was extra magic layered on the glamour so that not only would the Institute look to be in poor condition, most mundanes would neglect to notice it at all, and forget about it a moment later, if they did.

This was a pity, because the Rome Institute was one of the more beautiful in the world. It resembled many of the other basilicas in the city, with domed tops, tall arches, and marble columns, but as if viewed in one of those funny mirrors that elongated the reflection. The Institute had a narrow base sandwiched between two squat buildings. Once it rose past its neighbors, it blossomed and fanned out into several domes and towers, like a candelabra or a tree. The resulting profile was both distinctly Roman and pleasantly organic.

Alec found a parking spot nearby, but he felt a strong temptation to stay in the car and read the Red Scrolls of Magic for a while longer. He'd already noticed a few differences between the copy they'd found in Venice and the pages Isabelle had sent. Instead he made his way to the Institute door. Looking up at the imposing edifice, he dreaded all the strangers inside it, even though they were fellow

Shadowhunters. He wanted his *parabatai*. He would have given a lot for a familiar face.

"Hey, Alec!" a voice behind him called. "Alec Lightwood!"

Alec turned and scanned the line of stores on the other side of the street. He found his familiar face at a small round table in front of a café.

"Aline!" he called in surprised recognition. "What are you doing here?"

Aline Penhallow was looking at him over her coffee cup. Her black hair fluttered at her jawline, she was wearing her aviator sunglasses, and she was beaming. She looked a lot better than the last time Alec had seen her. He and his family had been staying at the Penhallows' manor the night the wards fell in Alicante. The night Max had died.

"Had to get away from things for a bit. They're rebuilding in Idris, but it's still a mess. My mom's in the thick of it."

"That's right, she's the new Consul. Congratulations!"

Alec couldn't even imagine how Jia Penhallow must feel, being chosen by all the Nephilim to be closest to the Angel and charged with carrying out their mandate. He'd always liked Aline's mother, a calm, clever warrior from Beijing. She could do so much good now. Being the leader of the Shadowhunters meant being able to make changes, and Alec was becoming more and more aware the world needed changing. He crossed the street and jumped the rope encircling the café tables.

"Thanks. How about you?" Aline asked. "What are you doing here? And where did you get your incredibly sweet ride?"

"Long story," said Alec.

"How's everyone back in New York?" asked Aline. "Doing all right?"

The last time they'd seen each other had been not long after Max's funeral.

"Yeah," Alec said quietly. "We're all right. How about you?"

"Can't complain," said Aline. "Is Jace with you?"

"Uh, no," said Alec.

He wondered if Aline was asking for a specific reason. Aline and Jace had kissed in Alicante, before the war. Alec tried to think of what Isabelle usually said to girls about Jace.

"The thing is," he added, "Jace is a beautiful antelope, who has to be free to run across the plains."

"What?" said Aline.

Maybe Alec had gotten that wrong. "Jace is home with his, uh, his new girlfriend. You remember Clary." Alec hoped Aline was not too heartbroken.

"Oh right, the short redhead," she said. Aline was tiny herself, but refused to ever admit it. "You know, Jace was so sad before the war, I thought he must have a forbidden love. I just didn't think it was Clary, for obvious reasons. I thought it was that vampire."

Alec coughed. Aline offered him a sip of her latte.

"No," he said when he got his voice back. "Jace is not dating Simon. Jace is straight. Simon is straight."

"I totally saw scars on Jace's neck," Aline said. "He let that vampire bite him. He brought him to Alicante. I thought: classic Jace. Never makes a mess when a total catastrophe will do. Wait, did you think I wanted a ride on that disaster train?"

"Yes?" said Alec.

As a loyal *parabatai*, he was starting to find Aline's tone a little insulting.

"I mean, Jace is empirically very cute, and I have always liked blonds, and I do like Jace," she said. "He's been great to me. Very understanding, but I hope he's very happy with his—whatever. Or that vampire. Or whomever."

"He's called Simon," said Alec.

"Right. Of course," said Aline. She fiddled with her cup for a moment, not looking at Alec, then added, "I saw you and your Downworlder. You know. In the Accords Hall."

There was silence, awkwardness hanging like the haze in the air. Alec remembered kissing Magnus, under the eyes of the Angel and everyone he loved, and also hundreds of complete strangers. His hands had been shaking. He'd been so scared to do it, but more scared that he would lose Magnus, that one of them might die without Magnus ever knowing how Alec felt about him.

He couldn't read Aline's face. He'd always gotten along with Aline, who was quieter than Isabelle and Jace. He'd always felt they understood each other. Perhaps Aline could not understand him now.

"That must have been terrifying," she said at last.

"It was," Alec said reluctantly.

"Now that you've done it, are you happy?" Aline asked tentatively.

Alec did not know if she was simply curious, or if, like his dad, she thought that Alec's life would be better if he kept hiding.

"It's hard sometimes," said Alec. "But I'm very happy."

A tiny, uncertain smile flickered across Aline's face.

"I'm glad you're happy," she said eventually. "Are you still together? Or is it all, oh, now he knows you like him back, he doesn't like you as much? Maybe it was all about the lure of what he couldn't have? Do you ever worry about that?"

"Not before right this moment," Alec snapped.

Aline shrugged. "Sorry. I think maybe I'm just not very romantic. I've never understood why people get so worked up about relationships."

Alec used to feel the same. He remembered the first time Magnus kissed him, and every cell of his body thrilled to a new song. He remembered the sensation of the pieces of the world finally fitting together in a way that made sense.

"Well," said Alec, "we're still together. We're on vacation. It's great." He shot Aline a challenging glare, then thought of Magnus and added, more softly, "He's great."

"So why are you at the Rome Institute when you're meant to be on vacation?" Aline asked.

Alec hesitated. "Can I trust you?" he asked. "Can I really trust you? I mean it. I trust you with my life, but can I trust you with more than my life?"

"That got serious fast," said Aline with a grin, which faded as she took in Alec's grim expression. She bit her lip. "Your fight is my fight," she said. "You can trust me."

Alec gazed at her for a long moment. Then he explained as much as he could: that there was a cult called the Crimson Hand, that he'd gone to a warlock's party in search of information, that the faerie girl he'd seen making out with a vampire girl there had turned out to be a Shadowhunter called Helen Blackthorn, that the Shadowhunters at the Rome Institute might have been alerted to be suspicious of Alec.

"I need to find out if there's been any sign of cult activity in Rome," he said, "but I can't tell anyone else in the Institute what I'm looking for."

Aline absorbed this. He could see the questions in her eyes, but she pressed her lips together.

"Okay," she said at last. "Let's go check out the logged demonic activity in the last few weeks. I'll just say that my friend, a hero of the war, has dropped by to visit me. I think some more visitors are due. With any luck, everyone will be too busy to ask any questions."

Alec gave her a grateful look. Aline was kind.

"If your warlock is doing something evil, we're going to have to cut off his head," Aline added.

Aline was kind, but perhaps not very tactful.

"He's not," said Alec. "If I'm a hero of the war, so is he."

He saw Aline process this. She nodded, finished her coffee, and paid her bill. Alec took her hand as they stepped over the ropes of the café together.

They passed through the giant golden double entry doors of the Rome Institute and proceeded into the atrium. Alec whistled. This was one of the larger Institutes in the world. Alec had heard it described as "ornate," but this turned out to be a significant understatement. It was an assault on the eyes, far too much to take in at once. There were beautiful and intricate designs and artworks everywhere he looked: the half-dozen statues on the left wall, the lifelike carvings on the right, the mesmerizing gold-and-silver-tiled dome several stories above them. Words were inscribed across the ceiling in Latin: *I will give you the keys of the kingdom of heaven; whatever you bind on earth will be bound in heaven, and whatever you loose on earth will be loosed in heaven.*

"They modeled it after St. Peter's Basilica," noted Aline as she led them through the vestibule and down the side arcade.

Aline already knew her way around. She led him around the side passages, avoiding the more heavily trafficked main corridors. They went up a gilded spiral staircase, past at least ten more statues and a few dozen frescoes, before reaching a glass door.

"We have to go through the training room to get to the records room," said Aline. "I hope there won't be anyone inside, but if there is, we'll brazen it out."

"Okay," said Alec.

Aline hit the glass door with her fist and cheerfully called out, "Hero of the war, coming through!"

"Who?" yelled a dozen voices at once.

Someone else shouted, "Is it Jace Herondale?"

"By the Angel, please let it be Jace Herondale!" said another voice.

Alec and Aline walked into a room as bright as a greenhouse, marble gleaming on the floor between practice mats, and more than a dozen Shadowhunters all in their gear. There were targets set up on the wall farthest from them, with arrows in the outer rings. Clearly, the Italian Shadowhunters needed to practice more, but Alec did not see why it had to be right then.

A girl at the front of the group sagged in disappointment. "Oh, it's not Jace Herondale. It's just some guy."

Alec gave it two minutes before they processed their disappointment and started asking questions. There were too many of these people. He could not give them any answers.

He took a deep breath and drew his bow. He told himself not to worry about all the people, or about the cult, or about Magnus. He'd taught himself focus over many long nights practicing his archery, once he understood that Jace and Isabelle were always going to fling themselves into danger, and he would have to cover them. He could not do that with voices in his head warning him that he would fail, that his father would never be proud of him the way the Clave was of Jace, that he wasn't good enough.

He fired five arrows into the five targets. Each one was a bull's-eye. He put his bow away.

"I'm not Jace Herondale," he said. "But I've learned to keep up."

There was a hush. Alec took the opportunity to walk to the other end of the room and recover his arrows. While he was at it, he took every arrow he found in the targets. He had a feeling he might need them.

"Practice more, guys," Aline suggested. "We're going to the records room now."

"Great," said a voice from the back of the group. "Because I'd like to talk to Alexander Lightwood in private."

Helen Blackthorn stepped away from the crowd and stood, her arms crossed, staring Alec down.

Aline froze. Alec's first impulse was to run and jump out the window. Then he remembered how high above the ground they were.

Helen herded him into the records room, which jutted out from the side of the Institute so there were windows on all sides, and only one door. Aline followed them. She had gone entirely quiet and was being no help. Leon Verlac came too, giving Alec a little wave.

Helen stood in front of the only exit and said, "So, Alec. First you refuse to come to Rome to answer questions, then you hightail it out of Venice from the scene of a murder and head for Rome under your own steam."

"Don't forget all the property damage," Alec said.

Helen did not look amused, though Aline smiled a little. "What do you know about the Crimson Hand?" Helen demanded. "Where is Magnus Bane? What happened in Venice?"

Helen was clearly about to level several more questions when Aline waved a hand in between them. "Excuse me."

"What!" Helen seemed to notice her for the first time. Their eyes met.

"Hey," said Aline.

There was a momentary pause.

"Hi," said Helen.

More silence followed.

"Um, sorry," said Alec. "I was too busy getting interrogated to make proper introductions. Helen Blackthorn, Aline Penhallow. Aline, this is Helen."

"And I'm Leon," said Leon. Aline did not even glance at him.

Helen kept staring at Aline. Alec wondered if his friendship with Aline would bring suspicion on her as well.

"Right," Helen said at last. "Anyway, back to the questions."

"I have a question too," said Aline, and swallowed. "Who do you think you are, Helen Blackthorn, and why are you talking to my friend, a Shadowhunter and a recent hero of the war for Alicante, as if he's a common criminal?"

"Because he's being incredibly suspicious!" Helen snapped back.

"Alec is very honorable," Aline said loyally. "He would never do anything suspicious."

"He's traveling with Magnus Bane, who is rumored to be the head of a cult responsible for the slaughter of many faeries and mundanes," said Helen. "Our only lead was a former cult member called Mori Shu, and Mori Shu was found dead at a party that Magnus Bane and Alec were attending. Also at that party, the whole house fell down."

"That does sound suspicious, when you put it like that," Aline admitted.

Helen nodded.

"Nevertheless, there's an explanation for everything," said Aline.

"What is it?" Helen asked.

"Well, I don't know," said Aline. "But I'm sure there is one."

Helen and Aline were glaring at each other. Helen, who was taller than Aline, looked down her nose at her. Aline's eyes narrowed.

"Clearly, neither of you like me much," said Helen. "I don't care about that. What I care about is solving a murder and destroying a demonic cult, and for some reason, you are both standing in my way."

"If Alec was doing something wrong," Leon put in, "why would he save our lives in Paris?"

Aline darted a glance at Alec. "You saved their lives in Paris?" she said out of the corner of her mouth. Alec nodded. "Great job," said Aline, and turned back to Helen. "Exactly. A fine point made by what's-his-name."

"Leon," said Leon.

Aline paid no attention. She was entirely focused on Helen. "So your position is, Alec saved your life, is a war hero, but is also supporting an evil murderous cult?"

"I don't think he's evil," said Helen. "I think he's been seduced and taken in by the evil leader of a demonic cult."

"Oh," said Aline.

Her eyes had fallen away from Helen's at the word "seduced."

"Magnus has nothing to do with that cult," Alec argued.

"While we were in Venice, I heard that Magnus Bane *founded* the cult," said Helen. "Can you explain that?"

Alec was silent. Helen's hard blue-green gaze softened.

"I'm sorry," she said. "I understand you trust Magnus Bane. I get it, I do. I trust Malcolm Fade and many others. I have no reason to distrust Downworlders, as you might well understand. But you have to see this looks bad."

"Magnus didn't do anything," Alec said stubbornly.

"Really?" asked Helen. "And where is he, while you storm the Rome Institute on his behalf?"

"He's back at the hotel," said Alec. "He's waiting for me."

"Really?" Helen said. "Are you sure?"

"I'm sure."

Alec pulled out his phone. He called the hotel and asked to be put through to his room. He stood and waited as the phone rang, and rang, and nobody answered.

"Maybe he's gone out for a sandwich!" suggested Leon.

Alec called Magnus's cell phone, and waited again. There was still no answer. This time his stomach took a small, cold tumble. Was Magnus all right?

"This is very awkward," said Aline.

Helen was looking sorry for Alec. He glared at her.

"Look," she said. "We have something. We know about a meeting point near Rome that the Crimson Hand used. Why don't we go there together. And then we'll see what we see."

It was clear she thought they would find Magnus there, evilly leading an evil cult.

"Fine," said Alec, putting his phone away. "I want to find the Crimson Hand more than you do. I have to clear Magnus of these allegations. I'll allow you to help me with my investigation."

"Your investigation?" Helen repeated. "This is my investigation. And I thought you were on vacation."

"He can be both investigating and on vacation," Aline said defensively. She and Helen both started talking over each other in low, intense voices, beginning their second argument in the three minutes since they'd met. Alec really hoped he hadn't gotten Aline into trouble.

He looked away from the argument and met Leon's eyes. "I don't think you have anything to do with this cult business," Leon told him.

"Oh," Alec said. "Thanks, Leon."

"I hope Helen's zeal won't get in the way of you and me growing closer."

"Huh," said Alec.

Leon appeared to take this as encouragement. Alec did not see why he would. Leon came closer. Alec edged back toward Aline.

"Helen and I have a lot in common," Leon said.

"Good for you."

"One of the things we have in common," Leon ventured, "is that we are both interested in a variety of company. If you follow me."

"I don't," said Alec.

Leon glanced around, then said rapidly, "I mean, we're both bisexual. Interested in men and women."

"Oh," said Alec. "I don't know a lot about that, but again, good for you."

Alec knew Magnus was the same way. He had begun to learn that there was a whole world he had been entirely cut off from, words like "bisexual" and "pansexual" he'd never really known. It made him grimly sad to think now of his younger self, how desperately lonely he'd been, how he'd been sure he was the only one who'd ever had the feelings he did.

In the dark small corners of his soul, Alec worried sometimes. Why would Magnus choose him if he could choose a girl, a woman, an easier life? He thought of how terrified he'd been once of how he would be judged.

But then, if Magnus wanted an easier life, surely he wouldn't have chosen a Shadowhunter at all?

"When this is over, I could come to New York," Leon suggested. "You could show me a good time."

He winked.

"Please tell me you're getting the implications this time," Leon added.

"I am," said Alec.

"Fantastic!" Leon told him. "We'd have to keep it quiet, but I think we could have fun. You have so much going for you, Alec. You can do better than some Downworlder with a shady past. Hey, do you have any time tonight?"

Leon was handsome, Alec guessed. If Leon had come to New York when Alec was angry and miserable and thought nothing was ever going to happen for him, Alec might have taken him up on his offer.

"No," he said. He turned away, then looked over his shoulder. "I want to be clear," he added. "No, I have plans for tonight that don't include you. No, I'm not interested in fun on the quiet. And no. I can't do better than Magnus. There isn't better than Magnus."

Leon raised his eyebrows as Alec's voice rose. Aline and Helen took notice and looked up from their quiet, intense argument.

"Leon, are you making a pass?" demanded Helen Blackthorn. "Why do you always do this? Stop hitting on people, Leon!"

"But life is short, and I am handsome and French," Leon muttered.

"Okay. We're going to this Crimson Hand meeting place. You're out, Aline's in," said Helen. "Don't seduce anyone until we get back." She turned to Alec. "Let's go get some weapons and do this. Try to keep up." She strode away, and Aline moved to walk alongside Alec, a few steps behind.

"So, have you known Helen Blackthorn long?" she asked gruffly, and coughed. "You said she was kissing a vampire girl at that party? Didn't you say that?"

Alec had a vision of Helen, pale arms around the vampire girl in the moonlight. He shouldn't have mentioned it to Aline. It was Helen's business, and it would be his fault if Aline thought of Helen differently now.

He hardly knew Helen, but he felt a hot rush of protectiveness. It was as if he'd heard someone whispering about him, when he was younger and even more scared.

"I haven't known Helen long," he answered.

"I guess Jace told you about that time we kissed," Aline continued irrelevantly. "Like, why we kissed. He was helping me figure something out."

Alec looked at Aline sadly. Aline had always seemed very levelheaded about boys, but Jace was the exception to many rules.

"My *parabatai* doesn't kiss and tell," he said, in a gentler tone.

"Oh," Aline returned, her voice flat.

Alec had spent so long with a desperate, impossible crush on Jace. He had thought it was a secret: now he knew everyone had always known, especially Jace. Jace had never minded. He had understood Alec needed to have a crush on someone who was safe. On a boy who if Alec said, "I like you," to him, would not have punched Alec in the face or dragged him in front of the Clave. People could be horrendously, violently awful about anyone who was different.

That crush was a memory now. It had seemed part of his overall love for Jace once, the love that made them *parabatai*, but now it seemed more like the passing touch of light on metal. The gleam was gone, but the gold of friendship remained, pure and true.

There were worse people to have a crush on than Jace Herondale. He would never be cruel to Aline about it. But he loved Clary—in a way that had stunned Alec, who had never imagined Jace in love like that—and that wasn't going to change.

"Be nice to Helen Blackthorn," Alec said urgently. "You don't have to like her, but don't treat her differently from any other Shadowhunter."

Aline blinked. "I wasn't planning on it. Of course she's . . . a colleague. I will treat her in a professional fashion. That was my plan for how to treat her. With a calm professionalism."

"Good," said Alec.

"Do you have her phone number?" Aline asked. "In case we get separated, or something?"

"I don't," said Alec.

In the weapons room, Helen came toward them, her arms full of seraph blades, her fair hair curling around her ears. Aline made a sighing sound.

"We were going to check out demonic activity," said Alec to Aline, "in the records room. We never did that."

Aline began taking seraph blades out of Helen's arms and stowing them on her person. "Wouldn't you rather take action than look up records? If this is a dead end, we can always look at the records later."

Through the wide windows set over Rome, Alec could see the sun begin its descent. The city was still gold, but the very tops of the buildings were now crowned with red. "That makes sense," he said. He took a couple of seraph blades for himself.

Helen grinned an eager grin. "Let's go hunting."

CHAPTER TWENTY

Aqua Morte

MAGNUS WAS ALONE FOR TEN MINUTES, DURING WHICH he lolled around and thought of Alec. Then there came a knock on the door.

Magnus brightened. "Come in!"

He was severely disappointed. It was not Alec, deciding he should stay after all. It was Shinyun.

"I've been in touch with a contact," she said without preamble. "I'm meeting her at a Downworlder bathhouse soon. . . ." She stopped and looked around with a surprised air. "Where's Alec?"

"He's gone to find out whatever he can at the Rome Institute." Magnus decided no further explanation was necessary.

"Ah, yes. Well, if you're bored here alone, you could always come with me to my appointment in the Roman baths," said Shinyun. "My contact won't talk in front of you, but if she has information and you're nearby, we could act on it immediately. Your presence in a place like that wouldn't be questioned. Alec's would be."

Magnus considered her offer. On the one hand, he'd told Alec he would stay here. On the other, acting on information immediately might get them closer to being done with this whole sorry business. Magnus took a moment to imagine resolving the cult situation on his own, being able to go to Alec and tell him that it was all over, that Alec could relax.

"I do love the Roman baths," Magnus said. "Why not?"

They walked toward the Aqua Morte bathhouse, in the historic center of Rome, along the golden waters of the Tiber. Magnus had forgotten how much more gold Rome was than any other city, like treasure brought home from a conquest.

"Go back to where you came from," muttered a man in Italian, glancing from Magnus's Indonesian to Shinyun's Korean face. He moved to shove past them, but Shinyun held up a hand. The man froze.

"I've always wondered what that saying is about," Magnus said casually. "I wasn't born in Italy, but many people are who don't fit your idea of what people born here look like. Is it that you think their parents weren't from here, or their grandparents? Why do people say it? Is the idea that everyone should go back to the very first place their ancestors came from?"

Shinyun stepped up to the man, who remained fixed in place, his eyeballs twitching.

"Wouldn't that mean," Magnus asked, "that ultimately, we all have to go back to the water?"

Shinyun flicked a finger, and the man was flung with a brief squeak into the Tiber. Magnus made sure he fell without injury and drifted him to the riverside. The man climbed out and sat down on the bank with a squelch. Magnus hoped he would think about his choices.

"I was only going to make him *think* I would drop him in the water," Magnus clarified. "I understand the impulse, but just making him afraid of us . . ." He trailed off and sighed. "Fear isn't a very efficient motivator."

"Fear is all some people understand," Shinyun said.

They were standing close together. Magnus could feel the tension running through Shinyun's body. He took her hand and gave it a brief, friendly squeeze before he dropped it. He felt a faint pressure of her fingers in return, as if she'd wanted to squeeze back.

I did this to her, he thought, as he always did, the five small words that circled in his mind repeatedly when he was around Shinyun.

"I prefer to believe that people can understand a lot, when offered the opportunity," said Magnus. "I like your enthusiasm, but let's not drown anyone."

"Spoilsport," said Shinyun, but her tone was friendly.

They parted ways once they reached the bathhouse, Shinyun to find her contact and Magnus to find a bath.

The Aqua Morte was a vampire-run bathhouse, which seemed a peculiar marriage to Magnus. It was four giant heated mineral baths, each the size of an Olympic swimming pool, and several smaller rooms filled with single tubs. Magnus paid for time in one of these smaller rooms and went to change.

The vampire clan who ran this establishment were a contrary lot. They had also used the bathhouse as a controlled feeding zone for centuries, until the Nephilim put a stop to it.

Magnus considered that so far this was not such a demanding assignment. He went into his assigned room, let the towel slide down from his waist, and stepped into the sunken tub. Steam drifted up from the near-scalding water. It was just barely tolerable, the way Magnus liked it. He sank into the tub until only his head was above water, letting his body acclimate to the burn, feeling the waves of pain and pleasure shoot up and down his body. He perched his arms over the sides and leaned back. The ancient Romans had known how to live.

He had a few bruises and scrapes left over from the night on the train, and the night the mansion collapsed on them. By now they were faint, and ached only if he moved in a particular way. He could have healed himself anytime, but chose to let time heal the wounds. Not because he enjoyed the pain; far from it. When he had first learned to heal himself, he'd spent copious amounts of time and magic doing away with every single little hurt. Over the centuries, though, he'd learned that these minor injuries were part of life. Suffering through them made him appreciate being whole and well.

Right now was a perfect example. Magnus could feel each individual ache and cut throb in the hot bathwater and dissipate with the steam. He closed his eyes and relaxed.

Magnus had paid for a private room, but after a time he felt a presence hovering nearby. Before he could say anything, someone rudely invaded his tub, disturbing the flat surface and sending ripples of mineral water sloshing over the side.

Several sharp words came to mind and he opened his eyes, ready to deliver them. Instead he was surprised to see Shinyun sitting on the edge of the tub, wrapped in a towel. She was leaning against the wall beside her, resting her face on an elbow.

"Oh," he said. "Hello."

"I hope you don't mind the intrusion."

"I do, actually, but it's all right."

Magnus passed a hand over the water's surface and a towel materialized around his waist. He didn't think Shinyun was making a pass, and he didn't personally have a problem with nudity, but it was an odd situation.

Shinyun carefully moved Magnus's phone, which he had set on the side of the tub, out of the way as she reached for a hand towel. She wiped her face, which she did not actually need to do. She was clearly buying herself time.

"Did you get anything?" Magnus asked. "From your contact, I mean."

"I did," said Shinyun slowly. "But first I have a confession to make. I overheard your conversation the other night, about how you killed your stepfather."

Magnus had been speaking in a low voice. "So you eavesdropped. *Magically* eavesdropped," he added.

"I was curious," said Shinyun with a shrug, as if this excused her. "And you're famous, and you work closely with the Nephilim. I thought you had no problems, that you lived a life of careless luxury. I didn't think you were like me."

She bowed her head. In this moment, there was an earnestness to her that Magnus hadn't seen before. She seemed more vulnerable, more open, and it had nothing to do with the fact that they were both sitting mostly naked in a hot tub.

She looked up at him. "Do you need a drink?"

He didn't, particularly, but he sensed she might want one. "Sure."

A silver platter appeared a few seconds later with a bottle of Barbera d'Asti and a couple of large balloon glasses. Shinyun poured for each of them and floated Magnus's glass over to him. They touched glasses.

She was struggling with her words. "I know your story now. It is only fair you know mine. I was lying to you before."

"Yes," Magnus said. "I thought you might be."

Shinyun drained her glass in one gulp and set it aside.

"When my demon mark manifested, my betrothed did not love me despite everything. My family rejected me—the whole village rejected me—and so did he. Men came with shovels and torches and cries for my life, and the person I'd always thought was my father handed me over to the mob. My beloved was the one who placed me in the wooden box to be buried alive."

Shinyun slid down in the tub until she was nearly horizontal, and only her face, still as a death mask, broke the water's plane. She looked up at the marble ceiling. "I can still hear the dirt falling on the coffin, like the heavy drumming of rain on rooftops during a typhoon." She curled her fingers beneath the surface of the water. "I clawed until my hands were raw."

Magnus could hear the scratching sounds of fingernails on wood as Shinyun wove magic around her tale. He could feel the walls closing in on him and the shortness of breath in his lungs. He took a gulp of wine to soothe his throat and set the glass aside.

"'Seek the children of demons. Love them as you love your lord. Do not let the children be alone.' They dug me up. Together, we slaughtered every soul in my village. We killed them all. I did worse later, at the Crimson Hand's behest. They told me to trust them. I was so grateful. I wanted to belong."

"I'm sorry," Magnus whispered. *Shinyun is me. She is my dark mirror.*

"I know," Shinyun said. "The Crimson Hand always spoke of you, their lord who would return. They said we should make you proud, when the time came. I used to long for you to come back. I wanted you to be my family."

"I would have been," said Magnus. "But I didn't remember the cult. I didn't know anything about you. If I'd known, I would have come."

"I believe you," said Shinyun. "I trust you. My whole life, I was taught to trust you."

Magnus picked his glass up. "I promise I will do whatever it takes to help you, and to put an end to this."

"Thank you," she said simply.

They settled back into the tub. "I met with my informant," Shinyun said, her voice returning to its usual businesslike demeanor. "She suggested a meeting place in Rome where the Crimson Hand are meant to assemble. She said their leader had been seen there recently."

"Did she say if it was Barnabas Hale?"

"She didn't know his name," said Shinyun. "This is all second-hand. Nobody from the cult will talk. Not after what happened to Mori Shu."

"We should tell Alec," said Magnus.

"We can send him a text message," Shinyun said, "but not from within the baths; there's no reception here. I didn't want to tell him before I told you and . . . you and I were able to have a word in private."

Magnus was briefly annoyed, but it seemed petty to quibble when Shinyun had just told him about being buried alive.

"No time like the present," he said. He stood and waved a hand, and his wet towel transformed itself into jeans and a dark blue shirt scattered with yellow stars. He retrieved his phone and frowned at it; the screen seemed to be frozen.

Shinyun cast her own spell, and her towel began to snake all over her body, drying her off. When it was finished, it dropped to the floor. She was already dressed underneath, wearing the same black armored business suit she'd worn in Venice. She patted her waist and thigh, checking for two knives that disappeared as quickly as she pulled them out.

Satisfied, she motioned to the door. "After you."

Magnus turned his phone off, rebooting it. What a time for it to break down. Still, there were plenty of ways to get a message to Alec. Soon they would be together again; soon they would find and stop the leader of the Crimson Hand. Soon they could be done with all this.

CHAPTER TWENTY-ONE

Fire in the Crimson Hand

MAGNUS WAS LATE.

Before they had gotten a block away from the Rome Institute, Alec received a curt message from Shinyun telling him that Magnus's phone wasn't working. She had gotten a tip from one of her local contacts, and she and Magnus were headed to a specific location in a forest somewhat outside the city.

She didn't explain why Magnus was with her or where they had been. When Alec shared the information with Helen and Aline, they all agreed it made sense to meet up with Magnus and Shinyun at this rendezvous—it was more current information than what Mori Shu had given Helen, and even if it turned out to be a dead end, at least they'd all be in one place.

As time ticked by, Alec wondered whether Shinyun and Magnus had somehow gotten lost, or he'd misunderstood the direction. He'd been sure they would arrive by now, or that he would have heard from Magnus if there was a problem.

He felt thrown off-balance by having heard from Shinyun on Magnus's behalf. He checked the time again and looked to see the sun lost behind the trees. Evening was rushing upon them like an enemy, and there was only so much witchlight could do in a thick forest. He eyed the line of trees; he couldn't see farther than a few feet.

The forest felt haunted. Giant gnarled branches huddled close together, some intertwining like lovers, making it difficult to stray far past the narrow dirt path. Blossoming canopies masked the sky. Shadows of leaves danced with the wind.

"Can't cultists get a room?" Aline grumbled. "Like, in town?"

It had rained earlier, so the ground was a wet, slippery slush, making traversing the terrain difficult and messy. Aline in particular was struggling, having worn shoes more suited to sitting at a café than tracking evildoers.

"Here, try this." Helen took out a knife and sliced two long pieces of bark off the nearest tree. She got down on one knee in front of Aline and cupped her heel. Aline froze in place as Helen gently raised Aline's leg and tied the bark to the bottom of her foot. She repeated the operation on the other foot. "There, now you'll have better traction."

Aline's eyes were very wide. Alec noted disapprovingly that she did not even say thank you.

Helen took the lead, and Alec lengthened his stride to keep up with her. His sneakers were sliding in the mud too, but nobody had offered him bark shoes. Helen's footstep was lighter than his or Aline's. She did not move exactly like a faerie. Alec had seen them walk without crushing a blade of grass. Yet she wasn't sliding in the mud like they were either. Under the movements of a warrior was the shadow of faerie grace.

"The bark shoes aren't a faerie trick, if that's what you two are thinking," Helen snapped at Alec as he drew level with her. "I learned it from Shadowhunters in Brazil."

Alec blinked. "Why would we be thinking that? Look, I'm sorry if Aline is being weird. It's my fault. I told her about what happened on the night of the party in Venice—I mean, how I first saw you with the Downworlder girl."

Helen snorted. "Don't you mean the *other* Downworlder girl?"

"No," said Alec. "You're a Shadowhunter. I'm really sorry. I was worried about Magnus, and I'm bad at lying. There was a time I would have hated if anyone told a stranger about me."

"Don't worry about it," said Helen. "It's not a secret that I like girls as well as boys. Too bad if it bothers Aline." She sneaked a look at Aline over her shoulder, then shrugged. "Pity. That girl is hot like hellfire."

Alec ducked his head and smiled. He was a bit surprised, but it was nice to talk with Helen about this, to see how calm and fearless she was.

"Probably," he said. "I wouldn't know." He added shyly, "I think my boyfriend's pretty hot, though."

"Sure, I saw him," said Helen. "I see why you lost your head. I just don't trust him."

"Because he's a Downworlder?" Alec's voice was hard.

"Because I have to be more objective when assessing Downworlders than anyone else does," said Helen.

Alec looked over at her, the curve of her ears and the faint luminous sheen to her skin beneath her Shadowhunter runes. Against the backdrop of a forest, Helen looked even more like a faerie.

"You sure you're being objective?"

"I think Magnus Bane founded this cult," said Helen. "Which makes him the obvious suspect for their leader. From everything people say, this leader is a powerful warlock. There are maybe a dozen warlocks in the world who fit the bill. How many of them were at the party?"

"Malcolm Fade," said Alec.

Helen snapped, "It wasn't Malcolm!"

"It wasn't the warlock you trust," said Alec. "I see. How about Barnabas Hale?"

Helen came to a halt, right there in the sliding mud and gathering dark.

"He was there?" she asked. "He wasn't on the guest list."

"He crashed the party," said Alec. "So hard the mansion fell down."

"I knew Malcolm fought with another warlock," Helen murmured. "I was so busy trying to get people out, I didn't see the fight. I figured it must have been Magnus Bane."

So there was another reason Helen was so down on Magnus. She'd wanted to protect Malcolm, her own local High Warlock.

"It wasn't Magnus," said Alec. "He got in the middle to stop the fight. He tried to get people out. Just like you did."

Helen took a moment to absorb this. Alec was glad to see she didn't know everything, and even more glad she seemed to be willing to consider taking this new idea to heart. Maybe, with Helen and Aline to help him, they could inquire discreetly about Barnabas among the Shadowhunters.

"I don't know any of those warlocks," Aline announced. "But I think this might be the meeting place."

She pointed at a small clearing a few steps away from the path.

It did not take a Shadowhunter to tell that the area was being used for occult activity. The burned-in pentagram in the dirt at their feet was a dead giveaway, but there was more. There was a makeshift altar with two fire pits on either side and several slashes on the trees nearby that were reminiscent of claw marks. There was also a deep circular indentation pressed into the dirt. Helen walked to the edge of the clearing and checked in the bushes. She pulled out a beer keg and rolled it across the grass.

"Whoa," said Aline. "The evil cultists like to party?"

"Partying hard is one of their sacred rules," said Alec. Helen gave him a puzzled look and he explained, "The Red Scrolls of Magic. It's their sacred text. I'll, uh, loan you my copy."

He passed the phone, with the pictures Isabelle had sent, over to Aline, who then passed it to Helen without Alec's permission.

Helen frowned. "The last commandment is not to let children be alone," she said. "That sounds . . . strangely nice. For a cult."

"It is nice, isn't it?" Alec asked blandly.

Everything about Magnus was strange, but nice. Alec did not say this, since Helen would take it as a confession.

"Mori Shu was murdered by vampires," Helen Blackthorn said sharply. "Neither Malcolm nor Barnabas Hale nor Hypatia Vex, the only other warlocks in the vicinity I know of with anything like enough power, have any particular affiliation with vampires. Whereas Magnus Bane is well known to have strong ties, and even romantic entanglements, with some of the worst vampires of the New York clan—several of whom were at the party where Mori Shu and I were supposed to meet up. The party where Mori Shu was killed, before he could tell anyone what he knew."

Alec scoffed silently at the idea of Magnus having romantic entanglements with vampires, especially criminal ones. He had seemed to regard Lily and Elliott and the others as amusing children.

Although it was true he knew very little about Magnus's love life. Magnus had opened up a great deal about his past on this trip, but not that part.

He pushed the thought away. "Raphael and Lily didn't murder anyone at that party."

"Who are they?" Helen demanded. "Are they vampires?"

"Raphael Santiago is definitely a vampire," said Aline, when Alec hesitated.

"Close with them too, are you?"

"No," said Alec.

Helen and Aline were surveying him with identical expressions of worry. Alec did not need them to tell him how bad this all looked. It looked bad.

Magnus was still nowhere in sight. The forest was a maze, and the light was dying. He swept his gaze across the trees. It wouldn't be long before they were veiled in darkness. Night was when demons came out, and when Shadowhunters did their work. Alec would not have minded the dark, except that he wanted Magnus to find them.

Something else nagged at him, a worry under an ocean of worries. It was like taking a blow across the face and feeling, under the wash of pain, the consciousness of a loose tooth.

"Helen," said Alec. "What did you say the last commandment in the Red Scrolls of Magic was?"

"To look after the children," Helen answered, sounding puzzled.

"Excuse me," said Alec.

He retrieved his phone and walked across the pentagram to the other side of the clearing. He had already tried calling Magnus, multiple times. He intended to try someone else.

The phone rang twice and was picked up.

"Hello?" Alec said. "Raphael?"

"They're not close," Helen muttered. "Except he calls him to chat."

"I know," said Aline. "Alec seems so guilty. I swear he's not, but everything he's doing looks really bad."

"Lose this number," Raphael's voice snapped on the other end of the line.

Alec looked around the shadowy clearing at Helen and Aline, who were both shaking their heads sadly in his direction. He was apparently not impressing anybody tonight.

"I know you're not crazy about Shadowhunters," Alec said. "But you did say I could call."

There was a pause.

"That's just how I answer all phone calls," Raphael claimed. "What do you want?"

"I thought this was about what *you* wanted. I thought you wanted to help," said Alec. "You said you'd look into the Crimson Hand. I wondered if you'd learned anything. Specifically about Mori Shu."

The remains of both fires near the pentagram were still warm, and the candles had last been used only a few hours ago. He knelt next to one of the lines of the pentagram and sniffed the residue: blackened earth with charcoal and salt, but no blood.

"No," said Raphael.

"Right," said Alec. "Thanks anyway."

"Wait!" Raphael snapped. "Hang on a minute."

There was another pause. It went on for a very long time. Alec heard the sound of footsteps on stone, and from far away, the silvery but somehow unpleasant sound of a woman's voice.

"Raphael?" said Alec. "Some of us are not immortal. So we can't stay on the phone forever."

Raphael growled in frustration, which was a significantly more alarming sound coming from a vampire. Alec held the phone slightly away from his ear and drew it back when he heard Raphael forming actual words.

"There is one thing," said Raphael, and hesitated again.

"Yes?"

The silence between Raphael's words was so empty. Raphael was not breathing in them. Vampires didn't have to.

"You're not going to believe me. This is pointless."

"Try me," said Alec.

"Mori Shu wasn't killed by a vampire."

"Why didn't you say anything?"

"Who was I going to tell?" Raphael snarled. "Just trot up to a Nephilim and say, oh please, sir, the vampires were framed. Yes, a body was found, and yes, it was missing blood, but not anything like enough blood, and yes, there were marks on the neck, but they were marks made by the point of a sword and not fangs, and oh no, Mr. Nephilim, please put the seraph blade away? No Nephilim would believe me."

"I believe you," Alec said. "Were they made with a three-sided sword? Like a *samgakdo*?"

There was a pause. "Yes," Raphael said. "They were."

Alec's stomach tightened. "Thanks, Raphael, you've been a lot of help."

"Have I?" Raphael's voice was suddenly even more wary. "How?"

"I'll tell Magnus."

"Don't you dare," said Raphael. "Don't call me anymore. I have no interest in helping you ever again. Don't tell anyone about me helping you this time."

"Gotta go."

"Stop," Raphael commanded. "Do not hang up."

Alec hung up.

Raphael immediately tried to call him back. Alec turned his phone off.

"What's happening?" Aline asked. "Why do you look like that?"

"Helen," said Alec. "You mentioned Hypatia Vex as a possible suspect. So Mori Shu never specifically said the leader of the Hand was a man?"

Helen blinked. "He didn't say anything that would indicate either way."

"People at the Paris Shadow Market spoke as if it was a man," Alec said in a low voice. "Because the rumor was that it was Magnus. Even if someone didn't believe it was Magnus, they said 'he' without thinking. And Magnus and I were so busy defending him, we didn't think."

The informant on the Crimson Hand, murdered at the party in Venice. Marked with the point of a three-sided blade.

In times of trouble, remember: all roads lead to Rome.

The line was missing from the version of the Red Scrolls of Magic Isabelle had sent him. The one in the Chamber had been altered to add an extra rule, pointing them toward Rome.

And Shinyun Jung, a warlock who was clearly a well-trained warrior, whose movements were usually quick and graceful, had tripped, and made sure they found the altered book. Leading them here.

"We have to go," said Alec. "Now."

Just as he turned back in the direction they had come, the woods around them came alive. A sharp wind rustled the branches and tumbled the leaves. The air around them warmed, the temperature spiking alarmingly. It had been a cool, breezy night a few seconds ago, but now they were in sweltering heat.

Five pillars of fire rose at the edge of the clearing around them, each several stories tall and as thick as a tree trunk. Branches and rocks snapped, flames licked the vegetation and consumed it, and the air became thick and nearly impossible to breathe. The pillars crackled and ejected large embers into the sky, hundreds of fireflies swirling in the air.

All three Shadowhunters took out steles and rapidly drew some Marks for defense: Accuracy. Stamina. Strength. And, maybe most important, Fireproof.

Putting away her stele, Aline whispered, *"Jophiel,"* and her angel-infused daggers appeared in her hands. Alec took out his bow, and a glowing white light illuminated Helen's hand as she drew her seraph blade and named an angel as well. Alec couldn't hear the name over the roar of the flames.

"At the risk of sounding redundant," said Helen. "Oh no. This is a trap."

They gathered, standing back to back to back, in the middle of the clearing. In light of what they were facing, it seemed very inadequate.

"This was stupid, coming here with only three of us," said Alec. "The Crimson Hand knew exactly where we would be, and when."

"How?" Aline demanded.

Alec nocked an arrow on his bowstring. "Because their leader—she told us to be here."

CHAPTER TWENTY-TWO

The Great Poison

THE ANCIENT VILLA TOWERED BEFORE MAGNUS, ITS broken towers like jagged teeth rising into the sky.

"Subtle, these cultists are not," Magnus commented. He checked his watch. "Alec should be here by now."

Shinyun was standing beside him. He could feel the tension running through her entire body.

"Maybe they're questioning him at the Rome Institute," she said. "You know the Nephilim will not look favorably on anything he has been doing. He could be in a lot of trouble. And if we wait for him any longer, we'll lose our chance to capture the Crimson Hand."

According to Shinyun's informant, senior members of the Crimson Hand were meeting with a group of potential disciples. Their leader might even be present.

Alec would want Magnus to wait for him. Magnus wanted to wait for Alec. But Shinyun was right. Alec could be trapped, answering difficult questions at the Rome Institute, and it would be all Magnus's fault.

The best thing Magnus could do would be to capture the leader and put an end to the Crimson Hand. Surely the Nephilim would be appeased, and Alec cleared of any suspicion.

Shinyun said, "This could be our only opportunity."

Magnus took a deep breath and decided his hesitation was absurd.

This was nothing he could not handle on his own. He had always done just fine by himself before.

"Lead the way," he told Shinyun.

They entered the villa through what had evidently once been a stable and searched their way through a series of rooms. The building had long since been ransacked. Broken cabinets, torn tapestries, shattered glass littered the floors. Nature had already begun the slow process of consuming the villa. Weeds and vines infiltrated the cracks in the walls and windows. The strong scent of stagnant water lingered in the air. Everything was damp. The dank smell was making Magnus light-headed. He was finding it a little difficult to breathe.

"Evil can be excused, sometimes. Squalor, though, never," Magnus murmured.

Shinyun murmured back, "Will you stop making jokes?"

"Unlikely," said Magnus.

They entered a long room with a low ceiling and broken shelves. In another life, it had probably served as a pantry. Now rotting wood, cracked stone, and overgrown vines spiderwebbed the walls. A pool of water rested where the ground had sunk in. Shinyun held up a finger and froze. Magnus listened. There it was, a noise at last; the faint sound of chanting.

Shinyun pointed to the other end of the room and crept across, giving the dirty pool of water a wide berth. Just as she was about to leave the room, a metal portcullis, apparently in much better repair than the rest of the place, slammed down in the doorway in front of her.

Magnus moved toward the doorway behind them, from where they had entered, but it was too late. There was the sound of rolling metal and another gate crashed down before he could reach it. Magnus grasped the gate and pulled. It wouldn't budge. They were trapped.

Shinyun tried the first gate again. Magnus crossed the room and joined her. It was no use; it was far too heavy. He stepped back and mustered his magic, meaning to shatter the iron gate to dust. His hand glowed dark blue, and a streak of energy left his fingertips, but it died before it reached the gate.

He felt unexpectedly weak, as if he had just performed a huge spell instead of something very standard. He blinked away the dimness in his vision.

"Something wrong?" Shinyun asked.

Magnus waved his hand carelessly. "Nothing at all."

Shinyun grabbed a large rock from the ground and began to hammer at the rustiest parts of the gate. Magnus retreated to the center of the room.

"What are you doing?" Shinyun asked.

A green funnel rose up around him, whipping his coat and making his hair stand sideways. He called up every drop of magic he could to help the funnel gain steam, right up to the point that the spell began to fracture. With a final cry, Magnus channeled everything he had into this howling tornado and focused it on the doorway from which they had entered. The iron screeched and groaned, and then the gate tore free of the stone and flew down the hallway. It disappeared into the darkness before clanging into stone off in the distance.

Magnus fell to one knee, gasping. There was something very wrong with his magic.

"How could you do that?" Shinyun asked softly. "How did you get to be so strong? Surely now you have no power left."

Magnus forced himself to stand and began to stagger toward the blasted-open exit.

"I'm leaving."

Just as he was about to pass Shinyun, she threw an arm out and grabbed him by the front of the shirt. "I don't think so."

Magnus studied her still face in the shadowed light. His heartbeat rang in his own ears, signaling danger far too late.

"I see that my beautiful trusting nature has been imposed on," he said. "Again."

Shinyun spun, using Magnus's own weight as momentum to throw him, sending him tumbling halfway across the room. He tried to get back on his feet but was thrown back by a kick to the chest. He fell again, slamming into the remaining gate. Then he heard the sound of metal on metal and the grind of the portcullis lifting upward, and he felt several pairs of strong hands closing on his arms. He was almost unable to see.

I was exposed to a potion that made me lose control of my shape-shifting abilities, Tessa had told him. Magnus should have remembered.

"You put poison in my drink at the Aqua Morte," he said, struggling to form the words. "You distracted me with a sob story. Was it all a lie?"

Shinyun knelt down beside him on the wet stone. He could only make out the outlines of her face, like a mask hanging in the dark.

"No," she whispered. "I had to make you feel sorry enough for me. I had to tell you the truth. That's one more thing I can never forgive you for."

MAGNUS WASN'T THAT SURPRISED TO WAKE UP IN PRISON.

A trickle from the ceiling had found its way to his forehead, bouncing drops off it every few seconds, which reminded him of how the Silent Brothers used to discipline him to get him to stop talking during his studies.

Some of the water dribbled into his mouth and he spat it out. He hoped it was only water. Whatever it was tasted foul. He blinked, trying to acclimate to his surroundings. He was enclosed by a curved windowless wall with an iron gate leading out to more darkness, and a hole on the far side that was either an old escape route or a latrine. Judging by the smell in the air, Magnus thought maybe it had been both.

"It's official," he declared to no one in particular. "This is the worst vacation ever."

He looked up. There wasn't much moonlight, but what there was created a faint glow through a circular grate. This place looked like the bottom of a cistern, maybe, or a well, not that it made any difference. A hole, a cell, the bottom of a well. It was still prison. His hands were chained to the wall over his head, and he was sitting on a bed of hay that looked like it had already passed through the horse. The floor beneath him was cut stone, so he was probably still on the grounds of the villa somewhere. Magnus swallowed. His face and neck hurt. A lot. He could really use a drink.

He hoped Alec truly was stuck at the Rome Institute. That he hadn't gone where Shinyun had told him to go, which, he now realized, was clearly not this place. At the Institute, Alec would be safe.

A silhouette appeared on the other side of the gate. Metal clanged and a hinge squealed as the gate swung open.

"Don't worry," said Shinyun. "The poison won't kill you."

"'Because I will,'" intoned Magnus. Shinyun blinked at him. "That was where you were going with that, wasn't it?" he asked. He closed his eyes. He had the worst headache.

"I measured the poison very carefully," said Shinyun. "Just enough to put you out and obliterate your magic. I want you on your feet when you fulfill your ever so glorious destiny."

That didn't sound good. When Magnus opened his eyes, she was standing in front of him. She was dressed all in snowy white, with silver embroidery at her collar and cuffs.

"My glorious destiny?" Magnus asked. "It's always a glorious destiny. Have you noticed that? Nobody ever references the mediocre destinies."

Shinyun said, "No. Mine is the destiny that will be glorious. You do not deserve glory. You started this cult as a joke. You had people pull pranks and heal the sick. You made a mockery of the name of Asmodeus."

"Mockery is the best use I've found for his name," Magnus murmured.

Shinyun's voice was furious. "We should both have been loyal to Asmodeus. He favored you so greatly. You are not worthy of him."

"He's not worthy of me," Magnus remarked.

Shinyun shouted over him. "I'm tired of your endless mockery and disrespect. We owe Asmodeus life. I will never be like you. I will never betray my father!"

"Your *father*?" echoed Magnus.

Shinyun paid him no attention.

"I had been buried alive for five days when the Crimson Hand rescued me. They told me Asmodeus had sent them to rescue his daughter. My father's people saved me, because my father is always watching me. My mortal family betrayed me, and I slaughtered them. Asmodeus is the only one who loves me, and all I have to love. I have transformed the Crimson Hand from a mockery to a reality, and it is time to destroy the last insult. It is time to remove you, Great Poison. I will kill you for insulting Asmodeus. I will sacrifice your immortal life to him, and let him loose upon this world, and sit by his side for all eternity as his beloved daughter."

"Yeah, about that," said Magnus. "If you had the power of a Prince of Hell, I would have noticed."

"If any warlock alive had the power of a Prince of Hell, they would already rule this world," Shinyun told him impatiently. "All warlocks are Asmodeus's children, if they prove themselves worthy. That's what the Crimson Hand taught me."

"So you've . . . *adopted* Asmodeus?" Magnus said. "Or he's adopted you?"

He looked at her. He was not thrilled about being in prison. He was even less thrilled by the prospect of his inglorious destiny.

But he still couldn't hate her. He still understood why she was the way she was, the forces that had shaped her and where the shadow of his own hands fell across her past.

"Don't look at me like that! I don't want your pity." Shinyun stepped forward and closed her hands about his throat. Magnus gagged and choked—warlocks were immortal, but not invulnerable. He would die if deprived of oxygen. "You were never worthy," she whispered, as he strained for breath. "My people should never have followed you. My father should never have honored you. Your place belongs to me."

After a moment, Shinyun must have realized that she was choking the life out of her so-called father's sacrifice. She let him go.

Magnus sagged back in his chains, gasping, as air rushed into his lungs.

"Why?" He choked. "All this time you were helping us, you were just leading us into this trap. Why didn't you just grab me in Paris or on the train, or at any other opportunity you had? Why go through this charade?"

"*Alec.*" Shinyun said his name as if it was poison. "Every time I was close to seizing you, he got in the way. I had you cornered in the Paris Shadow Market until he arrived at the alley. We actually had you in our grasp on the train until he began cutting down all my demons like chaff. Alec took out the pack of Raum demons and most of the Ravener swarm. All that was left was my maimed brood mother. I couldn't trust her to finish the job, and I couldn't risk losing track of you. I decided I had to stay as close to you as possible."

Shinyun's laugh was different from any laugh Magnus had heard from her before. It was cruel, hollow, and bitter.

"I've become very skilled at pretending, over the centuries, in the service of my father. My face is a gift given to me, that I might serve Asmodeus better. People cannot see what I truly feel. They project onto a mask what they wish for, and never think that I am real beneath the mask. I give them what they want to see and tell them what they want to hear. But that Shadowhunter didn't want anything from me, and the only thing that worked on you was making you feel sorry for me. I hated doing that so much, I hated you so much, and I still couldn't stop him watching you, protecting you, always at the ready. I realized that the only way I could take you down was if I got you away from Alexander Lightwood first."

Magnus thought of his regret earlier that day that Alec had felt driven to go to the Rome Institute. Now he was only grateful. Alec would be safe there, and Magnus could face anything, if Alec was safe.

Shinyun snapped her fingers, and several men entered Magnus's cell. They were all dressed in white, with severe faces.

"Take him to the Pit, Bernard," said Shinyun.

"Don't take me to the Pit, Bernard," suggested Magnus. "I hate the word 'pit.' It sounds ominous, and grubby. Also, hello, evil cult member Bernard!"

Evil cult member Bernard gave Magnus a peeved look. He was stick thin with dark hair slicked back in a way that accentuated his pointy chin and tuft of a beard, and an air of wannabe authority. He snapped the iron manacles off Magnus's hands with unnecessary force. Magnus slid down to the ground with the chains no longer supporting him. Even Bernard posed a significant threat to Magnus right now. He forced himself to stand upright, but it was all he could do. He felt sick, and dizzy, and utterly bereft of magic.

Shinyun had taken no chances with her poison. She clearly wanted Magnus to have no chance in the Pit.

"One last thing," said Shinyun, and she sounded like she was smiling.

She stepped close to Magnus.

"I led you to a place where you could not receive calls. I rendered your phone unusable. And I contacted Alec myself on your behalf." She smiled. "I set a trap for each of you. Alec Lightwood should be dead shortly."

Magnus could face anything, if Alec was safe.

It was a dark explosion in Magnus's mind, a howling scream of agony and rage. A rage that he rarely if ever allowed himself to feel. A rage that came from his father. He lunged for Shinyun. Bernard and the other cult members grabbed his arms, holding him back as he struggled. Blue sparks, faint and pale, appeared at his fingertips.

Shinyun patted Magnus's face, the gesture almost hard enough to be a slap.

"I do hope you said a proper farewell to your child of the Angel, Magnus Bane," she murmured. "I can't imagine you two are going to the same afterlife."

CHAPTER TWENTY-THREE

Helen Blackthorn's Blood

THE PILLARS OF FIRE CLIMBED TALL, EACH RISING ABOVE the tree line. The heat was intensifying, clawing at Alec's skin as though it could tear his runes away. He considered his dwindling options. The pillars were spaced about fifty feet apart in a rough circle. If they were quick, they could charge between two and escape. But just as Alec moved to dive through an opening, the pillars on either side bent to block him, reshaping themselves in an instant, and then returning to their original height when he backed off.

Alec had seen a Shadowhunter jump flames this high once before, but he was not Jace, and he couldn't do it.

"Oh, by the Angel," said Helen.

Alec assumed she was just bemoaning their situation, but when he glanced at her he saw her eyes were closed. Her hair streamed in her face, a silver mirror that almost reflected the firelight.

She said, "I'm so sorry. This is all my fault."

"How could this possibly be your fault?" Aline asked.

"Mori Shu sent me a message asking for protection because he was being hunted by the leader of the Crimson Hand," said Helen

in a rush. "He came to Paris to find me. He picked me, specifically, because my mother was a faerie. He thought I would be more
worried about the faerie deaths and more sympathetic to Downworlders. I should have taken Mori Shu into protective custody. I
should have told the Paris Institute everything, but instead I tried
to deal with it on my own. I wanted to find the leader of the Crimson Hand and prove I was a great Shadowhunter, and nothing like
a Downworlder at all."

Aline pressed a hand to her mouth as she watched Helen. There
were tears sliding down Helen's face, under her long curling eyelashes. Alec kept his eyes moving, checking on the pillars of flame,
which seemed content to simply trap them here until, probably,
something worse showed up.

"But from the start, I kept messing up," Helen went on. "I was
meant to meet with Mori in Paris, but instead the Crimson Hand
caught up with him and sent demons to kill us. Mori Shu fled. Leon
was following me around, and we both would've been killed by the
demons if Alec hadn't intervened. I still didn't ask anybody for help.
Maybe Mori Shu would still be alive if I had. I didn't go to the head
of the Paris Institute, or the head of the Rome Institute once Mori
Shu pointed me there. Now we're caught in a trap, waiting to die,
all because I didn't want to tell anybody that a warlock had chosen
me. I didn't want the Clave to think of me as any more of a Downworlder than they already do."

Aline and Alec exchanged a glance. Just because Valentine's cru-
sade for Shadowhunter purity had been defeated didn't mean the
bigotry he represented had ended. There were people who would
always believe Helen was tainted by her Downworlder blood.

"There's nothing wrong with Downworlders," said Alec.

"Tell the Clave that," Helen said.

Aline said, unexpectedly loudly, "The Clave is wrong." Helen
looked up at her, and Aline swallowed. "I know how they think,"

she continued. "I didn't shake a Downworlder's hand once, and then he became one of the"—Aline darted another glance at Alec—"one of the Downworlder heroes of the war. I was wrong. The way they think is wrong."

"It has to change," Alec said. "It *will* change."

"Will it change in time for my brothers and sisters?" Helen demanded. "I don't think so. I'm the oldest of seven. My brother Mark has the same faerie mother as I do. The others have a Shadowhunter mother. My father had only just married a Shadowhunter woman when Mark and I were sent to their home. That Shadowhunter woman could have scorned us. She loved us instead. She was so good to me when I was small. She always treated me exactly like her own. I want my family to be proud of me. My brother Julian is so smart. He could be Consul one day, like your mother is now. I can't stand in the way of what he could accomplish—what they all could accomplish."

As though they weren't in imminent danger of their lives, Aline went over to Helen and took one of her hands.

"You're on the Council, right?" she asked. "And you're only eighteen. You're already making them proud. You're a great Shadowhunter."

Helen opened her eyes and gazed at Aline. Her fingers curled around Aline's. Hope glowed in Helen's face, then flickered and failed.

"I'm not a great Shadowhunter," she said. "But I want to be. If I'm great, if the Clave is impressed with me, then I belong. I'm so afraid they will decide I don't."

"I understand," said Aline.

Alec did too. He and Aline and Helen all exchanged a look, united against the same lonely fear.

"I'm sorry," Helen whispered, her voice floating to him soft as smoke.

"There's nothing to be sorry for," said Alec.

"I'm sorry I didn't tell anyone what we were doing or where we were going, and now we're going to die," said Helen.

"Well," said Alec, scanning the treetops, "when you put it that way it does sound bad." He spotted a section of a wall of fire that was sputtering slightly where it ran over a swampy portion of ground. The flames there were a little lower than the other barrier walls.

"Just in case we do die," Aline said, "I know we just met, Helen, but—"

"We're not going to die," Alec broke in. "Helen, how high can you jump?"

Helen blinked and came back to herself. She set her shoulders and studied the flames. "I can't jump that high."

"You don't have to," said Alec. "Look." He charged at the space between two of the pillars and, as before, the flames bent to block him.

"So?" said Aline.

"So," said Alec, "I do that again, and then one of you jumps the flames while they're lowered to block me."

Helen surveyed the flames. "That's still going to be a hard jump." Her face hardened with resolve. "I'll do it."

"I can do it," said Aline.

Helen put her hand on Aline's shoulder. "But I got us into this, and I'm going to get us out."

"You'll only have a second or two," said Alec, backing up to make the run. "You'll have to be right behind me."

"I will be," Helen said.

An instant before Alec started toward the wall, Aline yelled, "Wait! What if there's worse on the other side of the flames?"

"That," said Helen, brandishing yet another seraph blade, "is why I am heavily armed. *Sachiel.*" A white, familiar light appeared, the glow of *adamas* a reassuring rebuke to the red, demonic flames around them.

Alec smiled to himself. He was beginning to like Helen. Then he started to run.

He dove for the ground, and felt the heat of the flames as they lowered to block him from escape. He stayed down, rolling, and he heard Aline give a cheer. He sprang up and brushed the dirt off of himself.

There was a small silence.

"Helen?" Aline called uncertainly.

"Demons! Fire demons! They're demons!" Helen yelled back breathlessly. "The . . . pillars . . . are . . . demons! I'm fighting one of them now!"

Alec only now noticed that one of the flame pillars that had bent to stop him hadn't returned to its original position. Instead, he realized, he was looking at the back of a huge humanoid form made of flame, on the other side of which, presumably, was Helen.

He and Aline looked at each other. Alec, uncertainly, drew his bow and fired an arrow directly into the center of the next pillar.

The pillar erupted into motion, splitting and shaping itself into a humanoid figure that Alec recognized as a Cherufe demon. The demon roared, flames like a hundred awful tongues in its gaping maw, and charged at Alec, fiery claws extended. It moved with the speed of a wildfire blaze, closing the distance in the blink of an eye.

Alec twisted away from the claws, trying to roll in the direction of the gap between his demon and Helen's, just managing to avoid being disemboweled and flambéed. The world rattled as he hit the ground hard and skidded several feet. Only the sting of a falling ember on his cheek snapped him back to consciousness.

He could only watch, dazed, as a streak of fire hurtled at him through the dark. The demon was coming back for another round.

Then Aline was there, slashing so quickly with her daggers that her arms were a blur. The angel blades had the effect of water on the demon fire, turning it into steam wherever they passed through it. One slash across its lower torso, one up the middle, and one to lop off its flaming arms, and the Cherufe demon disintegrated into a puddle of magma, ichor, and steam. Aline stood outlined by orange sparks.

She tucked one dagger under her arm and offered Alec her free hand. Helen, singed but unhurt, joined them, appearing through the fading flames of the first demon as it fell into cinders. Together they turned to the other Cherufes, which had all now taken their usual humanoid shape.

Alec dropped to one knee, and three arrows streaked in the air in rapid succession, striking one Cherufe demon in the chest, its wounds spouting jets of flame. It roared and turned toward him, leaving a trail of fire in its wake. He loosed two more arrows, ducked and spun out of the monster's path, and finished it off with one more arrow in the eye. The demon collapsed like a burning house.

Helen and Aline stood back-to-back in the dark of the forest clearing, the glitter of infernal sparks and the glow from angelic blades surrounding them. Helen finished off another demon with a spin move that separated its torso from its lower half. Alec carefully made his way around the melee, keeping himself at a distance, until he had a clear angle. One arrow took off a Cherufe demon's arm, then several more caused it to tip over even as it tried to charge Aline. One downward stab of a dagger ended it.

Helen wore down the last demon with a series of quick slashes, puncturing its magma skin until it was shooting small jets of flame from all sides. Aline joined in, ducking a flaming fist and dashing past the demon to sink her blade into its back.

As soon as the last of the Cherufe demons fell, the fire was gone, leaving black scars on the earth and gray smoke drifting into the sky. There were still a few branches burning and pockets of ground smoldering, but there, too, the fire seemed to be slowly dying.

"Helen," said Aline, panting, "are you all right?"

"I am," Helen answered. "Are you all right?"

"I'm fine," said Alec. "Not that anyone asked."

He stowed his bow and winced as he moved, but decided he could bear the pain. There was no time to celebrate their victory—he had to figure out where Magnus was, right away.

Helen clucked her tongue. "You are not fine."

Alec was startled to recognize the expression on her face, half exasperation and half concern, which he knew he wore constantly whenever Jace or Isabelle was reckless. She really was an oldest sister.

Helen sat him down and pulled up his shirt, grimacing when she saw the red blistered wound. She took out her stele, pressed it over the injury, and began to draw an *iratze*. The outlines of her strokes glimmered gold and sank into his skin. Alec sucked in air through his clenched teeth as ripples of cold strummed his nerves. When the rune's effects had subsided, there was only a raised red patch of skin left on his chest.

"I was slightly distracted by the walls of flame and our impending deaths," said Aline. "But, Alec, did you say that the leader of the Crimson Hand told us to be here?"

He nodded. "There was a warlock who traveled with us named Shinyun Jung. She said she was a reformed Crimson Hand cultist and was trying to put an end to them—but I think she's the leader we've been searching for. We need to find Magnus. He's in danger."

"Wait," said Helen. "So you're saying that your boyfriend isn't the leader of the Crimson Hand, but you have another travel companion who is? Like, do you always insist on traveling with cultists?"

Alec glanced at Aline for support, but she only spread her hands, as if to indicate that she felt Helen was making a fair point.

"No, I always insist on traveling with cult *leaders*," said Alec. He put his hand in the back pocket of his jeans and drew out the silk scarf he'd untied from Magnus's throat this morning. He remembered that Magnus had kissed his wrist as he loosened the knot.

Alec clenched the silk material in his fist and drew a tracking rune on the back of his hand. It took a moment for the rune to take effect, and then he saw rows of figures all in white, and unclimbable walls. To his shock, he felt fear. He couldn't imagine Magnus being afraid of anything.

Perhaps the fear he felt was his own.

He also felt a pull, his heart now a compass leading him in a specific direction. Back to Rome. No, not the city, but south of it.

"I found him," Alec said. "We have to go."

"I hate to mention this, but we did just escape a death trap," said Aline. "How do we know we wouldn't be walking right into another?"

Helen put her hand on Alec's wrist and held tightly.

"We can't go," she said. "I've already made too many mistakes, going off on my own, and someone died as a result. We got lucky here. We need reinforcements. We need to go back to the Rome Institute and explain everything."

"My priority is Magnus," said Alec.

He knew Helen was only trying to do the right thing. Alec remembered his own deep frustration when his *parabatai* had started to chase a girl around on all kinds of lunatic death-defying missions. It felt very different now that he was the one in Jace's shoes.

"Alec," said Helen. "I know you don't want to get Magnus in trouble—"

"I'll go without you if I have to," said Alec.

He couldn't go to the Rome Institute. For one thing, he didn't want to answer a lot of uncomfortable questions—if they were suspicious enough, they might send for the Mortal Sword, to force him to tell the truth. For another thing, he didn't have time for any of that; he felt very certain that Magnus was in danger already. He needed to keep Magnus's secret, and he needed to hurry.

He wished Aline and Helen would come with him, but he didn't even know how to ask. He couldn't demand that kind of faith from them. He had done nothing to deserve it.

"Of course you want to protect him," said Helen. "If he's not guilty, I want to protect him. We're Shadowhunters. But the best way to protect him, and defeat the Crimson Hand, is to use every resource at our disposal."

"No," Alec said. "You don't understand. Think of your family, Helen. You would die for them, I know. I would die for my family— for Isabelle, for Jace." He exhaled. "And for Magnus. I would die for him, too. It would be a privilege to die for him."

He shook off Helen's hold on his wrist and started off in the direction the tracking rune guided him. Aline darted into his path.

"Aline," Alec said with vehemence. "I will not risk Magnus's life. I will not report to the Institute, I will not wait for reinforcements. I am going to get Magnus. Get out of my way."

"I'm not in your way," said Aline. "I'm coming with you."

"What?" Helen cried.

Aline's reply sounded anything but confident, but it was firm. "I trust Alec. I'm with him."

Alec did not know what to say. Fortunately, there was no time to talk about emotions. He nodded at Aline and they surged together out of the clearing and toward the forest path.

"Wait," said Helen.

Aline turned back toward her. Alec barely glanced over his shoulder.

Helen's eyes were shut. "'Go to Europe, Helen,' they said. 'Can't be a homebody forever, Helen. Get out of L.A., soak up some culture. Maybe date somebody.' Nobody said, 'A cult and its demons will chase you around Europe, and then a lunatic Lightwood will lead you to your doom.' This is the worst travel year anybody has ever had."

"Well, I guess I'll see you sometime," said Aline, looking stricken.

"I'm leaving," said Alec.

Helen sighed and made a gesture of despair with her seraph blade.

"All right, lunatic Lightwood. Lead the way. Let's go get your man."

CHAPTER TWENTY-FOUR

Cursed Daughter

THE PIT TURNED OUT TO BE AN EXISTING PART OF THE villa, not a new addition by the cult: a circular stone amphitheater sunk into the ground. Stone terraces led down to a grassy circular lawn at its center, on which an elevated stage of rough wooden planks had been constructed. Two sets of stone stairs, opposite each other, allowed for passage from level ground to the terraces or down to the lawn, and along each terrace wooden benches had been set up. The stage was plain except for several awkwardly planted moonflowers in wildly crisscrossing rows. Most of them must have been crushed by the wooden stage. Cultists had no appreciation for the gardener's hard work, Magnus thought.

The rows upon rows of benches were filled with cultists. Every seat was taken, and there were more people crowding behind them. Magnus supposed if he had to be a show, at least it was standing room only.

The cultists sat silent and still in their seats. They were dressed alike, in hideous fedoras and casual white business suits, with white shirts and white ties. The cult's cleaning bills must have been astronomical.

The two men half-escorting, half-dragging Magnus brought him down the stairs, then threw him roughly onto the lawn next to the stage. Magnus picked himself up from his hands and knees, waved at the crowd, and bowed with a flourish.

He did not want to die in this banal pit, surrounded by the pallid ghosts of past mistakes, but if he had to die, he planned to die with style. He would not let any of these people see him crawl.

Shinyun stepped onto the lawn, her clothes starry white in the night's gloom, and pointed in Magnus's direction. Bernard, who'd followed behind, lifted a sword to Magnus's throat.

"Robe him in white," said Shinyun, "so the mark of the crimson hand will show upon him."

Magnus crossed his arms and raised his voice and his eyebrows. "You can poison me and throw me in a dungeon. You can beat me and even sacrifice me to a Greater Demon. But I draw the line at wearing a white suit for an evening event."

Bernard jabbed the blade toward Magnus's throat. Magnus stared down at the curved sword in contempt. He put a finger on the sharp tip and flicked it to the side. "You're not going to stab me. I'm the main attraction. Unless you guys plan to sacrifice Shinyun to Asmodeus?"

Shinyun's eyes were twin hollows of hate. Bernard gave a nervous little jump and took a hasty step back.

Several cultists held Magnus still as Shinyun leaped toward him, delivering a spinning wheel kick to his chest and another to his stomach, doubling him over. As he struggled to keep his feet and not be sick, they forced him into a white robe.

Bernard shoved him upright, gripping him by the arms. Magnus gazed out at the implacable crowd through pain-hazed eyes.

"Behold, the Great Poison!" Shinyun shouted. "Our founder. The prophet who brought us together and then led us astray."

"It's just an honor to be nominated," Magnus gasped.

He surveyed his surroundings closely, though he had little hope for escape. He noticed a number of Raum demons guarding the tunnel entrances like ushers. Overhead, several large flying creatures swooped by. It was too dark to see what they were, but they were definitely demons of some sort, unless dinosaurs had returned.

"There is no hope for escape," said Shinyun.

"Who was looking for escape?" asked Magnus. "Allow me to compliment you on the high production values of your demonic ritual. I trust there's a full-service bar?"

"Quiet, Great Poison," said the cultist on his left, who had a tight, not particularly friendly grip on his shoulder.

"I'm just suggesting," Magnus said. "Maybe we can settle this in a civilized manner, by which I mean in a conversation over drinks."

Bernard hit him in the face. Magnus tasted blood as Shinyun's eyes gleamed with pleasure.

"Guess not," Magnus said. "Gladiatorial demonic death ritual it is, then."

Shinyun's voice became magically enhanced, thundering over his, booming across the entire amphitheater.

"The Great Poison is a failed prophet of false teachings! Before you, my brothers and sisters, I shall strike him down and assume my place as your rightful leader, and then I will offer this unworthy fool as a sacrifice to my father. Asmodeus will rise in glory. The daughter of Asmodeus will lead you!"

The crowd stirred from their eerie silence. The cultists began to chant. "Cursed Daughter. Cursed Daughter."

Magnus was dragged onto their little stage. Through the haze of pain and disorientation, he noticed that the cultists were careful not to trample the lines of moonflowers that circled and ran underneath the wooden platform.

Bernard had just completed salting a pentagram into the center of the stage. Rough hands grabbed Magnus by the elbow and threw him into the pentagram. Magnus got himself up into a sitting position, legs crossed under him, and tried to look casual. Bernard began to struggle through the incantation that would seal the pentagram.

After a little while, Magnus yawned loudly. "Need any help?"

Bernard's face flushed. "Be quiet, Great Poison. I know what I'm doing."

"If you did, you wouldn't be here. Trust me."

This was going to be an insultingly weak and fragile pentagram. If Magnus had his magic, he could've dispelled it with a breath.

Bernard finished his spell and scurried backward as showers of sparks flew up from each point of the pentagram. Magnus waved his arms around to keep the embers away, and after a moment, a few of the cultists realized that the fire could be a problem given the wooden stage, and began waving their arms and their hats at the sparks to disperse them.

The ritual was beginning in earnest.

Shinyun held out her hand, and one of the cultists put her *samgakdo* in it. She strode forward, the blade pointed at Magnus's throat. She jerked her hand, nicking him just below the Adam's apple, a shallow cut and a twinge of pain. Magnus looked down and saw crimson dripping onto his white robes.

"Do you have any club soda?" he said to Shinyun. "These stains are going to set unless we get to them quickly."

"You will be blotted out," said Shinyun. "You will be forgotten. First, you will know what you have lost. Time to remember, Great Poison."

Shinyun began her own incantation. The crowd resumed chanting "Cursed Daughter," more quietly than before. Black clouds gathered above the amphitheater, and lightning cracked around the villa, once, twice, three times. The clouds began to swirl in a dizzying circle overhead, forming a vortex that, Magnus guessed, was the beginning of the link between this world and the other.

A voice in Magnus's head, dreadful as a door opening onto pitch dark, said, *Yes, time to remember. Time to remember everything.*

A harsh, unpleasant white light appeared at the center of the swirling clouds, and the tip of a funnel began to materialize. Streaks of smoke or insects or black static swarmed the white light. The tip of the funnel began to descend from the sky, directly toward Magnus, who waited helplessly for the storm to reach him. He closed his eyes.

He did not want to die like this, by the hand of a raging wounded warlock, in front of misguided and badly dressed fools, with all the stupid mistakes of his past coming to swallow the possibility of his future. If he did die, he did not want regret to be the last thing he felt.

So he thought about Alec.

Alec, with his heartbreaking contradictions, shy and brave, relentless and tender. Alec's midnight-blue eyes, and the look on his face when they had their first kiss. And their last. Magnus had not thought today's kiss would be their last. But nobody ever did know, when the last kiss came.

Magnus saw all his dearest friends. All his lost mortals, and all those who would live on. His mother, who he could never make laugh; Etta of the beautiful voice that had kept him dancing; his first Shadowhunter friend, Will. Ragnor, always the teacher, who had gone on before. Catarina, her healing hands and endless grace. Tessa of the steadfast heart and great courage. Raphael, who would sneer at this sentiment. His Clary, the first and last child Magnus had ever watched grow up, and the warrior woman he knew she would become.

And then Alec again.

Alec running up the steps of Magnus's brownstone in Brooklyn to ask him out. Alec holding on to him in cold water, offering Magnus all his own strength. The stunning surprise of Alec's warm mouth, his sure, strong hands, in the hall of his angelic ancestors. Alec shielding Downworlders at the palazzo in Venice, coming for Magnus through a cloud of demons, trying to shield Magnus through every land and at every turn. Alec choosing Magnus over the Clave every time, without hesitation. Alec turning against the Laws he had always lived by to protect Magnus and keep his secrets.

Magnus had never thought he would need protecting. He had thought it would make him weak. He had been wrong.

Dread died away. Shaking, hardly able to move, with darkness bearing down upon him, Magnus felt only gratitude for his life.

He wasn't ready for death, but if it came today, he would face it with his head held high and Alexander Lightwood's name on his lips.

The pain hit, shattering and abrupt. Magnus screamed.

CHAPTER TWENTY-FIVE

Chains of Magic

ALEC TOOK THE MASERATI AND FOLLOWED WHERE THE
tracking rune led, up a winding road that spiraled around a mountain. Helen and Aline yelled at him to drive slower. He did not,
taking the curves at breakneck speed. Helen smacked his shoulder,
and then stared.

"By the Angel," she said. "A tornado."

It did look like a tornado. A crazy-looking tornado, black spi-
rals of cloud with a harsh white glow at its center, whirling in the
sky directly above a crumbling villa perched atop the mountain. It
illuminated the night sky with a sickly gleam. They stopped the car
halfway up the mountain and stared at it.

"You think this is the place?" Aline said dryly.

"I'm so glad we didn't get any silly reinforcements," muttered
Helen.

The churning funnel's menace was punctuated by periodic lightning bolts splitting the sky. When they did, thunder shook the air
and the ground below them, unnatural in its closeness.

"I have to get Magnus out of there," said Alec. He gunned the

Maserati's engine, sending it hurtling up the road. Helen and Aline gripped each other for dear life as the car whipped back and forth up the hairpin turns.

At the end of the road were massive iron gates through which they could see the villa's main building. On either side of the gates, high stone ramparts extended in great curves around and then behind the building, circumscribing the grounds.

One gate was open, but two cult members were guarding the entrance, both wearing white suits and hats that might as well have glowed in the dark.

Alec left the car behind the road's last curve, where it couldn't be spotted from the gates. They climbed out of the car and crept to twenty feet away, without either guard noticing. On cue, Aline stepped out of their cover and waved. As they'd guessed, the cultists' leader had made sure that a glamour wouldn't work on the Crimson Hand, but they planned to use being visible to their advantage. In the split second the cultists looked her way, Alec pegged the guard on the left with a well-thrown rock, striking the man between the eyes and knocking him out. When the other guard turned to see what had happened to his friend, Helen charged, her body a blur as she sped across the road and tackled him to the ground. One elbow later, he was out too.

They quickly trussed the cultists up and stowed them behind a row of bushes before continuing onto the villa grounds. The front driveway was packed with cars, parked haphazardly.

Alec counted two more cultists manning the front doors and a handful milling around the driveway, but there was surprisingly little other activity. "Where did they all go?" he wondered.

"Wherever the tracking rune leads, probably," said Helen.

Alec led them around the side of the villa, hugging the outer ramparts, until they reached the back of the main house. The ramparts continued back, but dense, overgrown gardens gone to seed blocked their ability to see farther into the grounds. He checked the tracking rune once more and pointed at the gardens. "Through there."

"Great news," said Aline. "That place looks like a safety hazard."

Helen nodded. "Straight to the death tornado it is."

Once the three of them were in the gardens, they were invisible from view from the house. They had to hack their way through thorny vines and tightly packed branches, but the wind howled and thrashed so loudly that Alec was sure no one could hear them. They crept down the length of the estate, moving from cover to cover, until the garden gave way to a clearing. The clearing ended in the ruins of a high stone wall.

Aline sucked in her breath.

A massive, bipedal lizard with a row of serrated teeth across its forehead was marching back and forth in front of the wall. It had a second, lower mouth as well, full of dripping tusks. Its whipping tail was edged with razors.

Alec squinted. "Rahab demon." He had fought several of those just a few months ago.

Aline shuddered and shut her eyes. "I hate Rahab demons," she said passionately. "I fought one in the war and I *hate* them."

"Maybe it hasn't seen us?" suggested Helen.

"It's smelled us," Aline said grimly.

Alec noticed that Aline's fingers were trembling and her knuckles were white on the hilt of her blade. Helen reached out a hand and placed it on Aline's. Aline smiled at her gratefully, her grip relaxing.

Helen spoke softly. "Maybe the wind will carry away our scent."

The lizard-like demon raised its snout, licked the air with its tongue, and looked their way.

Alec grimly drew his bow. "Well, our luck so far is holding." Without further preamble, he punched an arrow into the demon's chest, making it stagger. Before the arrow had even struck its mark,

Helen was on the move, covering the distance to the Rahab in a heartbeat. A slash to its leg just above the knee caused it to bellow in pain, and then Helen danced nimbly out of the way as it swiped at her with its massive claws. Quicker than seemed possible, its long tail swept the ground, cutting Helen's feet out from under her.

Aline had closed the distance herself and now leaped and buried her daggers in the demon's back. The demon emitted a high-pitched, nearly inaudible whine. Aline yanked one of her daggers out and jammed the blade into its neck. The demon reared and lashed at her with a whiplike tongue. Aline ducked under the tongue and held on for dear life, slicing at the demon with a viciousness Alec had never seen from her before, leaving the demon bleeding from a hundred wounds. She finally dove off, somersaulting onto the soft grass and back to her feet. This gave Alec the clear shot he needed. He took quick aim and buried one more arrow in its exposed neck. With a great crash it fell to the ground and vanished, leaving a sick scent in the air and lashings of ichor on the trampled grass along the stone wall.

Aline went over to Helen and offered her a hand. Helen hesitated for a moment, then clasped Aline's hand and let Aline help her to her feet.

"Thanks for the assist," said Helen.

Alec put his bow away and left the underbrush at the edge of the garden, joining them at the wall. "You two make a pretty good team."

Helen looked pleased. "We do," she agreed.

"You helped too," Aline added loyally. Alec raised an eyebrow at her.

Alec retrieved his arrows from the ground where the demon had vanished. He led them to the lowest part of the ruined stone wall, still well above their heads, but easily scalable by trained Shadowhunters.

On the other side of the wall was a ramshackle building, smaller than the main house. In front of it were six cultists, armed to the teeth and glowing like white neon in their pale suits.

"The tracking rune says through there," Alec said quietly, pointing to the doors of the ramshackle building ahead.

"Right through the cultists," said Helen wearily. "Of course."

"It's all right," Aline said, putting her hand to her weapons belt. "I'm in a stabby mood."

"Okay," Alec said. "If we spread out—"

He broke off as the scream tore the night in half. It was a long scream, of pain and horror, wrenching and deep, cutting into his soul. The voice was unmistakable.

He let out a cry of dismay of his own before he realized what he was doing.

"*Alec,*" Helen said in his ear, gripping his sleeve with her small hand. "Stay calm. We'll get to him together."

Magnus's cry ended, but Alec had already forgotten all his strategy, all his plans. He charged forward, wielding his bow like a staff.

The cultists turned in surprise, but he was already on them. He jabbed the nearest in the abdomen as he passed, then spun and twirled his bow overhead, striking the second in the face. The third cultist threw a punch that Alec caught with his free hand. Alec turned his wrist and twisted the man's body at a severe angle, then slammed him into the ground.

Fighting mundanes was too easy.

Helen and Aline jogged up to him, each holding a blade. Catching sight of two more angry Shadowhunters joining the one who had decimated their associates, the remaining three cultists dropped their weapons and fled.

"That's right!" Aline called after them. "And stop worshipping demons!"

"You all right, Alec?" said Helen.

Alec breathed hard. "Working out some aggression."

"It's the Shadowhunter way," agreed Aline.

"I won't be all right until we get to Magnus," said Alec.

Helen nodded. "Then let's go."

Stepping over the cultists, they cut through the crumbling building, empty save for dust and spiders, and burst out the other side into—

An amphitheater.

It was ancient-looking, sunk into the earth, terraced with stone. Along the tiers an audience of Crimson Hand members, all dressed in the same white outfits, watched the action. A long flight of stone steps led down to a large wooden platform placed on the grass, acting as a stage. Alec's eyes found Magnus immediately: on his knees, with his head hung low, in the center of a pentagram of salt. Shinyun stood over him, a sword in her hand. The maelstrom they'd seen from a distance was up close now, descending like a funnel directly toward Magnus, swirling with ash and light. The whole stage seemed about to be swept into the maelstrom, or burned wholly away.

Alec ran straight for it.

CHAPTER TWENTY-SIX

Old Sins

THE EARTH SHOOK, THE AIR PULSED, AND MAGNUS FELT A thousand needles puncture him from all sides. A force took hold of his mind and twisted it, squeezing it and kneading it like dough into an entirely different shape. He screamed.

Pain washed the world white. When Magnus blinked away the dazzle, he saw a small room with plaster ceilings and heard a familiar voice calling his name.

"Magnus."

The owner of that voice was dead.

Magnus turned slowly and saw Ragnor Fell, sitting across the scarred wooden table from Magnus himself—a second Magnus. A younger, less-incapacitated-by-excruciating-pain Magnus. They were both holding large tin mugs, both in extreme disarray, and both very drunk. Ragnor's white hair was snarled around his horns, like clouds that had been caught in a jet propeller. Ragnor's green cheeks were flushed dark emerald.

He looked absurd. It was good to see him again.

Magnus realized he was trapped inside his own memory, forced to witness.

He approached Ragnor, and Ragnor reached a hand across the table. Magnus wanted to be the one his friend was reaching for. Hope was all it took; he felt his past and present selves reach toward one another, coalescing into a single body. Magnus was once again the man he had been, about to come face-to-face with the things he had done.

Ragnor said gently, "I'm worried about you."

Magnus waved his mug with studied carelessness. Most of the contents sloshed on the table. "I'm having fun."

"Are you really?" asked Ragnor.

The ghosts of old pain burned in him, alive and fierce for a moment. His first love, the one who had stayed, had died of old age in his arms. There had been too many attempts to find love since. He had lost too many friends already, and was too young to yet know how to deal with the loss.

And there was one other thing.

"If I'm not having fun now," Magnus replied, "I just have to try harder."

"Ever since you found out who your father was, you haven't been the same."

"Of course not!" said Magnus. "I've been inspired to create a cult in his honor. A cult to do all the most ridiculous things I can think of. It'll either fail spectacularly, or it will be the greatest prank in history. There's no downside."

This was not the way they had spoken, hundreds of years ago, but the memories had bent and changed over the years and both he and Ragnor spoke in the words and idioms of the present day. Memory was a funny thing.

"That was meant to be a joke," said Ragnor.

Magnus pulled out his fat money pouch and upended it. Hundreds of hacksilver spilled onto the table. All the thieves in the tavern went silent.

Magnus's whole life was a joke. He'd spent so long trying to prove his stepfather wrong, and now it turned out his father was a Prince of Hell.

He raised his arms over his head. "Let's have a round for everyone!"

The room erupted with cheers. When Magnus turned back to Ragnor, he saw that even Ragnor was laughing, shaking his head and drinking deep from a fresh mug.

"Oh well," said Ragnor. "I have been able to dissuade you from your terrible ideas, by which I mean literally all your ideas, exactly none of the time."

If Magnus could make everyone else laugh, surely he would feel like laughing himself. If he was enough fun to be around, he would never be on his own, and if he pretended he was all right, surely that would become the truth.

"All right," Ragnor continued. "Let's say you did start a joke cult. How would you go about it?"

Magnus grinned. "Oh, I have a plan. A fantastic plan." He flicked his fingers, causing electricity to spark and jump to the scattered coins on the table. "Here's what I'm going to do . . ."

The colorful wooden walls of the inn, decorated with weapons, shields, and animal heads, melted away. Ragnor, along with everyone else in the inn, turned to dust. Magnus was left looking forlornly at the empty space where his oldest friend had been.

Then he was in a different room on a different stage, in a different land, asking a crowd if they had ever felt lonely, if they had ever wanted to belong to something bigger than them. He was drinking red wine from a chalice, and as he waved a hand across the room, he saw everyone else's mugs fill with ale. Magnus called upon the name of Asmodeus, and the whole roomful of people laughed with wonder and delight.

The ceiling dissolved into open sky, the chandeliers into hundreds of blinking stars. The wooden floors layered with plush rugs turned into green grassy fields marked off by rows of manicured bushes, a fountain on one side. Magnus raised his hand and noted the champagne flute half-filled with bubbly gold.

"Great Poison!" his followers chanted. "Great Poison!"

Magnus made an intricate gesture, and then a table appeared filled with drinking glasses stacked in the shape of a pyramid. White wine flowed from the very top, filling each glass as it cascaded downward, creating a beautiful waterfall. A huge cheer erupted, sweeping the crowd, and the sound almost swept Magnus's heart along with it.

He toasted to their recent successful raid on a corrupt count's treasure, and their distribution of the treasure to hospitals. His cultists were scrubbing city streets, feeding the poor, painting foxes blue.

All in the name of Asmodeus.

The cult was a joke. Life was a joke, and the fact that his life would never end was its bad punch line.

Magnus walked to the giant pyre burning in the center of the gala. The crowd, who were on the edge of their seats, all linked hands and fell to their knees when the larger-than-life shape of Asmodeus appeared high above them. Magnus had spent most of the week working on this illusion and was particularly proud of the result.

He expected the crowd to cheer again, but they were silent. The only sound was the crackle of flames.

"Isn't this a special occasion," said the giant, shimmering white Asmodeus to his faithful worshippers. "A bunch of fools being led by the great fool, setting a puppet of me above them in a foolish parody of worship."

The gala grounds were as still as the dead after a battle. All the followers were silent on their knees.

Oh. No.

"Hello, son," said Asmodeus.

The bright, dizzy whirl of motion Magnus was in jerked abruptly to a halt. He had mocked the name of Asmodeus, mocked the idea of worship. He'd wanted his actions to blaze across the sky, to fling defiance at both his fathers.

Magnus had done all this because he knew that no matter whom he called, nobody was coming.

Only somebody had come. His father had come to crush him.

Magnus found himself frozen, unable to move even a finger. He could only watch as Asmodeus stepped out from the pyre and approached him, unhurried.

"Many have worshipped me," said Asmodeus, "but seldom has my name been cried so loud by so many. It attracted my attention, and then I saw who their leader was. Trying to reach out to me, my child?"

Magnus tried to speak, but his jaw was clenched closed by some unknown magic. Only a thin moan slipped out from between his clenched teeth.

He met Asmodeus's eyes and shook his head, very firmly. He might not be able to speak, but he wanted to make his total rejection clear.

The living flames that were Asmodeus's eyes went dark for a moment.

"Thank you for collecting these followers for me," he hissed at last. "Be sure I will put them to good use."

Sweat poured down Magnus's face. Once again he fought to speak, and once more he failed.

Asmodeus flashed his rows of sharp teeth.

"As for you, like any erring child, your insolence must be punished. Nor will you remember what you have done, or learn aught from it, for the memory of the righteous is a blessing, but the name of the wicked will rot."

The words were from the Bible; demons quoted Holy Scripture often, especially those with pretensions to royalty.

No, Magnus almost begged. *Let me remember,* but Asmodeus had palmed Magnus's forehead with his bony, clawlike hand. The world washed blindingly white, and then blindingly dark.

Magnus came back to himself, in the present day, kneeling before the members of his own cult, the memories his father had taken from him restored.

He was on his knees. Shinyun was standing over him, leaning down so her face was very close to his.

"You see?" she demanded. "You see what you have done? You see what you could have had?"

The first emotion Magnus felt was relief. In the back of his mind, he had always worried about what he was truly capable of. He knew what he was: a demon's child, the son of Hell's royalty, always afraid of his own capabilities. He'd been so afraid he might have set up this cult with evil intentions, used them for horrific purposes, perhaps erased his own memories so he would never have to face what he had done.

But no. He had been a fool, but he had not been evil.

"I do see," Magnus replied softly.

The second feeling that came to him was shame.

He struggled to his feet. He turned and beheld the crowd, this horde of mundanes that he had accidentally brought together and turned into cultists with an ill-conceived joke, this band of dupes who were probably only searching for something greater than themselves, for some assurance their lives had meaning, that they were not alone in the world. Magnus remembered feeling so much pain that he forgot other people mattered. He'd made a joke of their lives. He was ashamed of it, and he wouldn't want Alec to know the person who had done it.

He'd been trying to be someone different for a very long time.

And, he realized, he didn't feel that savage driving pain he'd felt in that long-ago time drinking with Ragnor anymore. Especially not since he met Alec.

Magnus raised his head and spoke in a clear voice. "I'm sorry." He was met with stunned silence. "A long time ago, I thought it would be fun to start a cult. Get a group of mundanes together to pull some pranks and play some games. I tried to make life less serious than it is. The joke went wrong. Centuries later, all of you are paying the price for my folly. For that, I am truly sorry."

"What are you doing?" Shinyun demanded behind him.

"It's not too late," Magnus shouted. "You can all turn away from this, from demons who are not gods and the folly of immortals. Go live your lives."

"Shut up!" Shinyun shouted over him. "These are your worshippers! My worshippers! Their lives are ours to do with as we choose! My father is right. You are the greatest of fools, the prince of fools, and you will speak folly until someone cuts your throat. I will do it myself. I will do it for my father."

She stepped out in front of Magnus and faced the crowd.

"Now is the time of destiny. Now is the time when you, my brothers and sisters, will be elevated above all others, above even the angels, answerable to none save the greatest of demons and warlocks. You will sit at the base of my father's throne!"

She paused and waited expectantly, as if for a cheer of agreement. It didn't come. At the top of the stone stairs to the rear of the amphitheater, Magnus saw chaos breaking out. Cultists converged at the top of the steps and then were violently pushed back, several of them tumbling down the seats and stairs.

Shinyun faltered. She motioned for the guards near the stage.

The disturbance was spreading and growing louder. Magnus couldn't see what was happening—it looked like a knot of fighting, with cultists being tossed down the stairs and onto one another with abandon. The more well-armed guards near the stage were having trouble pushing through the crowd to get up to the disturbance.

Magnus felt a flicker of hope. Perhaps some of the cultists had thought better of their stupid, dangerous plan. Perhaps they would fall on each other—cultists often did—and forget about him, and about Asmodeus. Perhaps—

"Apparently," said Shinyun, a blaze of orange fire gathering in her fist, "I have to do everything myself."

She walked to the edge of the stage. But just as she reached the perimeter, she struck an invisible barrier and was thrown violently off her feet. The circle of salt and the moonflowers began to glow with pale fire.

Magnus stiffened with realization: the moonflowers lining the edge of the stage weren't merely decorative. His eyes followed the crisscrossing lines of flowers that ran underneath the platform. Together they formed a giant pentagram. A much larger, and stronger, pentagram. But who had made this one? Not Shinyun—she seemed shocked to find she was trapped within it.

Shinyun picked herself up and stared at the moonflowers. She tried to leave again, only to be repelled even more forcibly the second time. She groaned and staggered to her feet.

Bernard was standing just outside the pentagram, watching them with a certain anticipation.

Shinyun hissed at him, "What is the meaning of this?"

Bernard gave her a small, mocking bow. "My sincerest apologies, Cursed Daughter. The thing is, though we realize you belong to our more militant and murderous fringe, this cult has always been about hedonistic pleasure rather than strict dedication to evil. The Crimson Hand have agreed that we do not want to obey your joyless rules or live under your rather too-stern leadership."

"My, my," said Magnus mildly.

"Do you disagree, Great Poison?" asked Bernard.

"By no means," Magnus said. "Let the good times roll."

Shinyun was staring at Bernard, and then at the faces of the cultists sitting in rows around her. These people were not here to watch their prophet, Magnus realized. They were gathered here for a spectacle of blood and betrayal.

"But I am one of you," Shinyun said forcefully. "I belong with you. I am your leader."

Bernard glanced at Magnus. "With all due respect to the Great Poison, we know how easily a leader can be replaced."

"What have you done?" Shinyun asked.

Bernard said, "You are not the only one who can communicate with Asmodeus. You are not the only one who can summon demons to serve you."

"Oh," said Magnus. "Oh no."

Bernard continued, with gathering triumph, "He comes when we call!"

Magnus closed his eyes. "Evil always does."

Outside the pentagram there were cultists screaming, demons roaring, and black shapes against the sky. Inside the pentagram, the loudest sound was Shinyun's ragged breathing.

"We don't want any warlock to rule us," said Bernard. "We want ultimate power, and to host the ultimate parties. So you are *both* imprisoned in this pentagram and we intend to sacrifice you *both* to Asmodeus. No offense, Great Poison. This isn't personal. In fact, you're something of a style icon of mine."

"Whatever Asmodeus has promised you, he's lying," said Magnus, but Bernard sneered.

Once a Greater Demon was summoned, he would corrupt whomever was in reach. Asmodeus offered temptation none could resist and played games crueler than mortals could dream. No wonder Bernard had looked startled when Magnus had joked about sacrificing Shinyun.

Shinyun had never been the enemy. Shinyun had never been the true leader of the Crimson Hand. From the moment Magnus had lost control, all those years ago, it had been Asmodeus. It had always only been Asmodeus.

Bernard turned away, trusting the pentagram to keep his quarry trapped. Shinyun raced around the pentagram as if she were on fire. She tried to cast spells to break free, but it was useless. She screamed at the cultists to break the barrier, but they all watched her with the same perfect impassiveness.

At last she wheeled on Magnus and screamed, "Do something!"

"Don't worry, Shinyun. I know a spell that can break out of all but the most powerful pentagrams." Magnus waved his hands around for a second, then stopped and shrugged. "Oh yes, I forgot. I could have broken us out, but I lost my powers because someone poisoned me."

"I hate you," Shinyun whispered.

"I might add, Cursed Daughter is a terrible nickname," said Magnus.

"Are you really one to talk?" Shinyun demanded. "Great Poison?"

"That's fair," said Magnus. "It was a pun on my name. Magnus Bane? I admit to a weakness for puns—"

Shinyun gasped. A flying demon crashed to earth, landing with a horrible scream among the panicking cultists. The crowds parted and Alec Lightwood emerged, already halfway down the amphitheater steps.

Magnus felt stricken. Unexpected pain could hit in the same way, catching you off guard and rattling your whole universe, but what Magnus felt was not pain.

It was a great explosion of overwhelming emotion: fear for Alec, and love and relief, and a painful desperate joy. *Alec, my Alexander. You came for me.*

Cultists threw themselves at Alec, and he tossed them aside. For every one he knocked away, three took their place. They were hampering Alec's progress, but they could not stop him, and neither could any demons of the earth or the air. He was not alone, either: there was a pale-haired girl at his left, and a black-haired girl at his right. Both wielded blades, keeping the throng away from Alec as he fired arrows at another demon, then swept a cultist off his feet with the base of the bow.

Magnus drank in the sight of him: the strong shoulders, wild black hair, and blue eyes. Magnus had always loved this particular shade of blue, the shade of the last instant when the evening was still full of light.

Magnus walked to the shimmering edge of the pentagram. There was something bright rising in him, along with love and hope. He could feel his power coming back, just out of reach.

He stretched out a hand toward Alec, and his fingers were able to breach the shimmering lines of magic, passing through the magic haze as if the magic were water. When he tried to step through to Alec, though, he slammed to a stop as if the magic were a stone wall.

Being able to put his fingertips outside the edge of the pentagram was not going to be very useful.

"None of this matters!" Shinyun's voice behind Magnus was a roar. "My father is coming! He will strike you down, the faithless who should have been most faithful, the false prophet, the disgusting Nephilim. All of you! He will place me at his side, where I belong."

Magnus whirled, his happiness abruptly replaced by sick dread.

All the color was draining from the stone around them. From the top tiers and moving downward, the stone bleached to white until it seemed to spread to the air, forming a column of white static that joined the funnel of cloud and smoke that marked the site of the ritual. A blizzard of tiny black specks flitted within the column. Wisps of smoke danced inside the light. Buzzing filled the air, a torrent of sinister whispers from another world.

A voice in his head said, *I told you, it is time to remember everything.*

It had not been his own fear speaking, but his father.

"He is coming!" Shinyun shouted.

"Why?" Magnus shouted at her. "No one's done any sacrificing yet!"

I come because my followers wish it, said the voice. *The way is open enough for me.*

There was a terrible thickness in the air, the feeling of a dank breath that froze the veins. It was a ripple of agitation that made Magnus want to run somewhere, anywhere, to get away, but his body would not let him move. Some animal instinct deep inside him knew there was nowhere to run that would be safe.

The approach of a Greater Demon, empowered by the adoration of so many worshippers, filled every sense, destroyed every other feeling, until only horror remained.

Above the pentagram, the static was resolving into a shape.

CHAPTER TWENTY-SEVEN

Forged in Fire

ALEC UNDERSTOOD THAT THEY WERE BADLY OUTNUM-
bered. Every soul sitting in the amphitheater—and there were
many—had turned to face them. Quite a few had already risen to
their feet and were reaching for weapons—clubs and staffs mostly,
though he saw several blades flash in the light.

"Wow, there are a lot of cultists," Aline muttered. "They must
have carpooled."

Helen's quick smile dimmed when two cultists grabbed her arm.
Aline elbowed one in the throat and Helen head-butted the other
in the chest. A fool charged at Alec and was summarily punched in
the face. He lost sight of Magnus, faced with a wall of clawing hands
and kicking feet.

The only way to Magnus was through them.

"Ladies," said Alec. "Shall we?"

"Gladly," Helen murmured sweetly, and kicked a man in the
kneecap.

Alec dodged a badly thrown punch and returned it with a well-
thrown one. In the pauses between brawling, Alec shot his bow at
demonic shapes wheeling in the sky.

He could keep this up all day. He only knew how to move in one direction. Toward the stage. Toward Magnus. Nothing mattered until he reached Magnus.

He could see Magnus in gaps between the crowd: he was standing onstage as though he'd been addressing the assembly. Shinyun was next to him, shouting and waving her arms, thankfully not participating yet in the battle. Magnus turned halfway; there was blood on Magnus's throat and his shirt, and a dark bruise on his face.

Alec's heart wrenched. Then Magnus caught his eye: there was one of those brief moments of battle stillness, like the eye of a hurricane, where time felt stretched thin. Magnus seemed so close, as if Alec could reach out and touch him, gentle his bruises, stand between him and the crowd.

He remembered running to Magnus's Brooklyn brownstone one day. They had just started dating. There had been so much going on then, in the world and inside Alec. The war was beginning, and Alec could not work out the mess of rage and confusion and longing in his own heart.

He'd known Magnus only a couple of weeks. It did not make any sense that he was seizing this chance to see him, when his family thought he was training, when his lies could be discovered at any moment. He was so afraid, all the time, and he felt so alone in his fear.

Alec already had a key—Magnus had explained it was easier for him, and he had enough wards on the apartment to know if anyone other than Alec entered with that key. Alec had run in, heart beating too fast. He'd seen Magnus in the center of his loft, absorbed and intent on his work. He was wearing an orange silk shirt and flipping through three spell books at once, turning pages with two ringed hands and a flurry of blue sparks. There was a pit of dread in Alec's stomach, at the thought of what his father would think if he knew Alec was here.

Then Magnus had looked up from his spell books, seen him, and smiled. And Alec's heart had stopped its frantic pounding, like a prisoner desperate to escape. Alec thought he could be all right just standing in that doorway, watching Magnus smiling to see him, for the rest of his life.

Magnus smiled the same way now, despite the horror unfolding around them, the corners of his golden eyes crinkling. It was such a sweet, surprised smile, as if Magnus was startled enough—and happy enough—to see Alec that he had forgotten everything else.

Alec almost felt like he could smile back.

Then Helen shouted, *"Shinigami demons!"*

The Crimson Hand was not messing around. Of all flying demons, Shinigami were among the worst. With their leering, sharklike jaws and vast, untidy black wings, Shinigami demons took pleasure in ripping people's faces off and crunching their bones into powder.

A shadow fell on Alec. He looked up into a grinning maw, crowded with teeth, and loosed an arrow.

The first Shinigami narrowly avoided the arrow and dove straight for the Shadowhunters. Several more of the large creatures followed close behind. A second arrow knocked the closest Shinigami out of the air, sending it careening into the seats. And then the rest of the demons were upon them.

The closest one landed on the steps with a heavy thud. Aline darted in and slashed it with her seraph blades, carving deep gouges into its chest. It roared and swept her away with its wing, knocking her off her feet.

The Shinigami reared up, towering above her. Its wings repelled starlight, outlining a jagged black hole against the night. Another of the Shinigami demons crash-landed among the cultists, sending them scurrying for cover.

"Eremiel!" Helen's yell rose above the din as she danced among

the large figures, the white slashes of her seraph blade lighting up the night.

Alec jumped to the side and avoided a swooping demon, its talons nearly raking his shoulder. He skidded on his back and pierced its wing with another arrow, sending it crashing to the ground. He checked the others. "Aline, look out!"

Aline was back up, darting between two Shinigami, cutting them up with her seraph blades. Another demon was diving toward her.

Helen tackled Aline to safety at the very last second. The demon missed them and went past, then turned for a second charge. It bared its fangs, each as long as a human hand. Helen rose to her feet, clutching her hurt shoulder. She dropped to her knees as the monster leaped, jamming her seraph blade upward, slicing the demon from its navel to its neck.

"By the Angel!" Aline shouted. "That was amazing."

Helen beamed, but not for long. No sooner had she finished the kill than another demon landed in front of her and swung a taloned wing at her face. This time Aline was there and sliced the wing at the joint, completely severing it. Helen followed with a spinning slash that lopped off its head.

Alec turned his attention to another diving Shinigami and managed to avoid getting cut in half by a sharp wing. He tracked its trajectory as it passed and shot it in the back. The demon crashed at the base of the amphitheater.

"Alec!" Aline shouted. "The stage!"

Alec whirled just as a massive column of light descended from the whirling vortex and struck a massive glowing pentagram of flowers that surrounded the stage. The entire amphitheater was illuminated.

Magnus was a silhouette, bathed in scorching brilliant light. Alec could only just make out his eyes. They were fixed on Alec. Magnus's mouth moved, as if he wanted to say something.

Then Magnus and Shinyun disappeared. The scorching dazzle of the light filled the moonflower pentagram, erasing everything inside.

Alec's heart lurched. He ran for the stage, only to be cut off by a cultist looming up in his path. He cut him down with a blow and looked into the startled face of the next man. He spoke quietly, but loud enough for all of them to hear.

"If you value your life," Alec said, "run now."

The nearest cultists scattered. It cleared a space for Alec to cut a path to the pentagram. His head buzzing with panic, he flung himself toward it—and slammed into an invisible barrier as hard as a granite wall.

There was a skinny man with a tuft of a beard standing in front of the cultists beside the pentagram, as if he was their leader. Alec had never seen him before.

"Where is Magnus?" Alec demanded.

"Who are you?" asked the bearded man.

"We are Shadowhunters," said Helen, striding to flank Alec. Aline slid into position at his other side. "And you are all in a lot of trouble. What's going on here? Who are *you*?"

"I am Bernard, the leader of this cult."

Someone behind the cult leader said, "We agreed to betraying the Great Poison and the Cursed Daughter. Nobody agreed to you leading us, Bernard."

Bernard went purple above his white robes.

"Who's the Great Poison?" Aline inquired.

"Our founder, Magnus Bane," answered Bernard.

Helen sucked in her breath.

"However, we broke away from his teachings of caring for the children and pranking the rich many years ago," Bernard asserted. "Since his departure we have had a much more wickedness-based agenda. A few of us do murders. Lately, a lot of murders. Mostly we're evil but laid-back about it."

"So Magnus is innocent! Kind of," Aline said. Helen looked disconcerted.

Alec didn't care about any of it. He shoved past Bernard, took a deep ragged breath, and drew a seraph blade from his belt.

"Raguel." It burst into angelic light.

Using a seraph blade on a mundane was a horrible thing. His father had told him no true Shadowhunter would dream of doing it.

Before anyone could move to stop him, Alec swung the tip of the glowing seraph blade so close to Bernard's throat that the collar of his white shirt began to blacken and smoke.

"Where is Magnus?" Alec demanded. "I will not ask again."

Bernard's eyes went white. His lips parted, and a voice that was clearly not his issued from his throat. It rumbled and crackled like a bonfire.

A demon's voice. The voice of a Prince of Hell.

"The Great Poison? Why, he's right here."

Bernard waved jerkily to the pentagram awash in awful light. In its fiery heart, the palest of shadows began to resolve. Alec was able, more and more clearly every moment, to make out shapes.

"Find him," said the demon within Bernard. "If you can."

The scene inside the pentagram clarified. Alec's mouth went dry with horror.

He could see Magnus. He could see more than one Magnus.

"One of these pairs of fighters is the real Magnus Bane and the real Shinyun Jung. Consider it a test, little Shadowhunter. If you recognize him, you can save him."

Alec had his bow and blade in his hands, every muscle straining. He was ready to fight, frantic to rescue Magnus, and he was locked in place with terror.

A hundred Magnus Banes were fighting for their lives against a hundred Shinyun Jungs. All were identical. A hundred Magnus Banes in white robes stabbed another hundred Shinyuns, and any one of them could have been the real Magnus. The one on the ground, awaiting the killing blow, might have been the real Magnus, desperately needing Alec's help. Or the one winning the fight could be the true Magnus, only for Alec to kill him by trying to help him.

"An ingenious bit of magic, if I do say so," the demon said, through Bernard. "Clever, but at the same time, very cruel, for it does offer you hope. All you need to do is recognize the true Magnus Bane. Isn't that always the way it is in fairy tales? The prince can tell his true love even when she is transformed, a swan among other swans, a pebble on a beach of sand." Bernard chuckled. "If only the world were a fairy tale, Nephilim."

CHAPTER TWENTY-EIGHT

The Prince of Fools

THERE WAS QUIET TERROR INSIDE THE PENTAGRAM, AND chaos without. Then there was light. The light seemed to switch off the rest of the world. Everything outside the pentagram, including Alec, was gone. There was only his father.

A man in a white suit floated in the darkness of the funnel, looking down at Magnus and Shinyun. He wore a crown of barbed wire on his head and matching dull-silver cuff links. He descended to the ground gracefully, like water sliding downstream over a bed of pebbles.

Asmodeus wore just a hint of a smirk, showing off his jagged, hungry teeth. He looked at Shinyun, and then at Magnus. "You've brought me a gift."

"Father?" said Shinyun. She sounded almost like a child.

Magnus swallowed down terror and hate and carelessly flicked a lock of hair off his forehead. "Hi, Dad."

Asmodeus's eyes, and his hungry half-smile, were fixed on Magnus.

Magnus saw the exact moment the truth hit Shinyun. One second she was completely still; the next, her body shook as if she had just been electrocuted.

She turned slowly to look at Magnus. "No," she moaned, her voice barely a whisper. "*You* can't be his son. Not his real son. No."

Magnus grimaced. "Unfortunately, yes."

"I did tell you, my dear, that this was going to be a family gathering." Asmodeus's smile grew as he soaked in her pain. He licked his lips as if relishing the taste. "It's just not yours."

Asmodeus had been playing with her, fooling her as easily as Magnus had tricked the cultists of the Crimson Hand long ago.

Shinyun kept looking at one of them, then the other, and looking away as if the sight burned her eyes. Magnus wondered if she could see the resemblance. She was breathing hard, and erratically. At last her eyes fixed on Magnus.

"You get everything," Shinyun whispered. "You've taken everything from me."

"What a good idea," said Asmodeus. "Why don't you do that, son? Take back the cult you made. Take the place she dreamed of. At my right hand."

Shinyun screamed, "No!"

Her burning eyes filled. Her tears fell, even as she pounced. Magnus dodged the swing of her sword, stumbling under her onslaught. She swung again and Magnus hit the ground, rolling to avoid the blow. There was dust in his eyes. He could see no way he could escape steel and death for long.

No third blow came. Magnus looked up, then scrambled cautiously to his feet.

Shinyun was frozen mid-lunge, as if she were about to fall over. Magnus looked into her eyes. They were frantic, darting side to side. Her body was as frozen now as her face had always been. Only her eyes were alive.

Magnus looked at Asmodeus, who spread out his hands with a flourish Magnus recognized. He had made the same gesture many times himself, when performing a feat of magic.

"Now, this I don't understand," Magnus said. "You've had your fun. You performed your signature move, made your offer, caused as much pain and fury as you possibly could. Why stop her? Why not let this play out? Not that I'm keen to be turned into a shish kebab by an enraged cultist, but I don't get your angle."

"I want to talk to my son," said Asmodeus. "It has been almost two centuries since we last spoke, Magnus. You don't write, you don't call, you don't make sacrifices on my altar. It wounds your fond parent."

He moved, grinning like a skull, to give Magnus a fatherly pat on the shoulder. Magnus threw up an arm to shove him back.

His arm went straight through Asmodeus. "You're not actually here."

Asmodeus's grotesque grin grew impossibly wider. "Not yet. Not until I take away someone's immortality and use it as my anchor to this world."

"My immortality," said Magnus.

Asmodeus waved a hand at Shinyun. "Oh, no. Hers will do."

His hand was smooth and pale, the fingers ending in claws. Magnus saw Shinyun's eyes, the only moving part of her, fill with fresh, humiliated tears.

"So I am to be spared," said Magnus. "How splendid for me. May I ask why? I presume it is not overflowing paternal affection. You can't feel that."

A plush high-backed chair appeared and Asmodeus sat down in it. He looked Magnus over.

"The angels have children," Asmodeus told Magnus, his voice a horrific parody of a father telling a child a bedtime story. "They are said to be the greatest blessings this world has—the Nephilim, destroyers of demons. And we Princes of Hell have our children too. Many of our children burn into ash and void, unable to bear what they are, but there are those who survive. They are meant for thrones of iron. The tales say they are made to be the greatest curses of the world."

Magnus could scarcely breathe. It felt as if the air was burning away.

"I have had many children in this world," Asmodeus said. "Almost all have disappointed me. A few have proved useful, for a little while, but they were hardly worth the trouble. Their powers were extinguished, or their minds broke after a century. Two at the most. The children of Greater Demons can be very powerful, but they are seldom stable. I waited a long time for a true child to be a curse upon this world, and eventually I gave up. My children have been unable to thrive in this world or any other, weak lights begging to be put out, not worthy of me. But you. You're strong. You fight. You sought me out with a scream that could have torn a world apart. You speak, and the blood of angels listens. You have cut doorways through the worlds. You have performed feats you did not realize were impossible, and continued merrymaking on your way. I've been watching you a long time now. Demons can feel pride. We are rather good at it. My son, I am proud of you."

A hollow space in the center of Magnus's chest hurt. Long ago, it would have meant something to him to hear that.

"How touching," he said at last. "What do you want? I really don't think it's a hug."

"I want you," said Asmodeus. "You are my most powerful child, and therefore my favorite. I want your power in my service. After all I've done for you, I want your loyalty."

Magnus started to laugh. Asmodeus opened his mouth to speak again, but Magnus held up a hand to silence him.

"That's a good one," he said, wiping away tears. "When have you ever done anything for me?"

In one breath, Asmodeus moved from sitting in the chair to standing next to Magnus. His whisper in Magnus's ear was like the hissing of a furnace.

"What did I say?" Asmodeus asked his son. "Time to remember everything."

He pressed his clawed hand to Magnus's face.

Magnus's eyes blurred, and his mind recoiled at the intrusion as the world changed in a blink. One moment he was standing on the stage in the center of the pentagram, the next he could feel the sting of the burning sun prickling his skin. Sweat began to bead at his brow. He took a step backward and felt sand crunch under his shoes. He smelled the scent of the ocean and heard the sounds of waves crashing against the shore.

Magnus knew exactly where and when he was now, and it filled him with dread. He was on the sandy beach at the edge of a jungle. It was lifetimes ago. From the very start of his first lifetime, in the first and last place he had ever called home.

Magnus became suddenly, keenly aware of how small he was. His shirt hung loosely from his narrow shoulders, his thin limbs lost beneath the material. His body had been adult and unchanging for centuries. He had forgotten how it felt to be weak and frail, to be so terrifyingly vulnerable.

Clear in the hot air, he heard a man's low, gravelly voice. "Come here, my boy."

The language was an old Malay dialect, one that had fallen into disuse centuries ago. Magnus hadn't heard or spoken it since he was a child.

His stepfather walked out of the jungle and struck the trembling boy who would be Magnus, sending him sprawling into the sand.

Magnus shook under his father's blows. All the memories he had of his stepfather he'd worked so hard to forget flooded back, one with every pang of pain. He could taste the sand in his mouth and feel the damp clothes sticking to his body. He could feel all the terror of those days, and all the rage. He balled his hands into fists, desperate to do something, anything.

He could feel his stepfather's rough fingers wrap around his bicep and pull him to his feet. He was dragged, through the sand and into the trees, to the mouth of the old barn.

This was the past, his past. Magnus knew exactly what would happen next, and the fear he felt now was worse than the first time.

The barn where his mother had hanged herself was a charred tomb. There were gaping holes in the roof, one of the walls had collapsed under the pressure of encroaching tree limbs, and weeds seethed from between the floorboards.

In the dark there still hung a cut rope. A narrow creek ran across one corner of the ground in the barn, shadowed by the remains of the roof. There was a low table bearing a cup of incense sticks, and two offering bowls and a rough sketch on stone of a woman. Magnus looked at the picture and remembered his mother's sorrowful eyes.

Magnus as a child looked up at his stepfather and saw him weeping. Magnus could feel the boy's shame for hating him, the boy's desire to love him.

The adult, watching part of Magnus knew what came next.

His stepfather put his arm around the boy's shoulder and led him to the creek. The boy felt the stiffness of his stepfather's fingers, as if the man were willing himself to keep from shaking.

Then Magnus felt rough hands close around his neck as the man grabbed the boy and pushed him into the water. Cold swallowed him, and it became impossible to breathe. His lungs spasmed desperately as he choked in gulps of water. The boy, fists pounding the water, struggled but could not escape his stepfather's grip.

Then there was a twist in the air, like the snap of twigs when something moved in the jungle. There was the first stirring of magic. The boy was somehow able to twist away from his stepfather's strong grasp.

Magnus coughed and choked, clawing long, wet hair out of his eyes, and gasped out painfully, "I'm sorry. I will be good. I try to be good."

"This is the only way for you to be good," his stepfather shouted.

Magnus screamed.

His stepfather's hands closed around his neck once more, his grip unyielding, his breath panting in Magnus's ears. There was an awful gentleness in the finality of his voice.

"This will make you pure," whispered the only father he had ever known. "Trust me."

He plunged the boy's head back underwater, this time so deep it smashed into the stony bed of the creek. Magnus felt the numbing pain, felt his knees weaken as the boy began to lose consciousness and sink toward death.

Magnus was drowning, but at the same time he was terribly distant, watching a small boy die. As he watched, he saw a shadow move over the water.

A whisper flooded the boy's head, colder than the water in his lungs.

"Here are the words that will free you. Speak them and trade his life for yours. Only one of you can survive this. Take hold of your power or die."

In that moment it was an easy decision.

Calm swept over the boy, and the spell flowed out of his mouth into the water. His hands, flailing in panic, stilled and then made a series of complex gestures. He could not breathe, but he could do this magic.

Magnus had never been able to work out how he had done the spell that killed his father.

Now he knew.

The boy burst into a column of blue flame, so hot it brought the water in the creek to a boil. The fire crawled hungrily up his step-father's arms and consumed him.

His stepfather's screams echoed through the dark barn where his mother had died.

Magnus found himself standing across from the boy and saw his younger self looking back at him. His shirt was charred black, and smoke was still drifting off his body. For a moment, he thought the child could see him. Then he realized the boy was staring at the charred remains of his stepfather.

"I never wanted any of this to happen," Magnus whispered, to all his old shadows and ghosts, to his mother and his stepfather and the lost, wounded child he had been.

"But you did," said Asmodeus. "You wanted to live."

His father was standing beside the boy Magnus had been, looking at Magnus across the smoke.

"Go now," he murmured to the boy Magnus. "You did well. Go and make yourself worthy. I may come back to claim you one day."

Magnus blinked away the smoke and found himself in the center of the stage of the amphitheater under a dark sky.

The ground felt unsteady beneath his feet, but that was because he was shaking. Only a few seconds had passed. Shinyun was still frozen, her eyes fixed on him with a desperate intensity. Outside the pentagram, the blank blackness was starting to fade into gray. Magnus could nearly make out the outlines of people, watching him.

Asmodeus was standing beside him, hand curved around Magnus's shoulder in what almost felt like an embrace.

"You see now," he said. "I saved you. You chose me. You are my favorite child, because I forged you in that fire. I have come back for you as I said I would. Across all the worlds, there is nobody who will accept you and understand you. There is only me. All you could ever be is mine."

A knife appeared in Magnus's hand, its cold weight heavy. His father's voice was low and crackling with hellfire.

"Take the blade, draw Shinyun's blood. Sacrifice her, so I can cross the world to you. I have seen all your struggles and been proud of all your rebellions," said Asmodeus. "My kind has always responded to a rebel. Every pain you have suffered has had a purpose, has made you strong, has led you to this moment. You have made me so proud, my child, my eldest curse. Nothing pleases me more than to lift my worthy son up to a high place, and lay all the kingdoms of the world before him."

Magnus could almost feel his father's hand on his shoulder. The faint heat of Asmodeus's other hand was on Magnus's wrist, as if Asmodeus would guide the blade straight into Shinyun's heart.

As he had led Magnus to kill his stepfather, so long ago. Magnus had made a choice, back then. Maybe it had been the right choice.

"You see . . . ," Magnus said, "the thing is . . . I don't want the world. The world's a mess. I can't even keep my apartment organized. I'm still cleaning glitter out of the lampshades after my cat's birthday party, and that was months ago."

Despite the heat and pressure of Asmodeus's hand, Magnus lowered the knife. He was grown now, worlds and lives away from that terrified child. He did not need to be told what to choose. He could choose for himself.

Asmodeus began to laugh. The world shook. "Is this about that boy?"

Magnus had thought he could not feel more afraid, until he realized he had unwittingly called Asmodeus's attention to Alec.

"My love life is none of your business, Father," Magnus said with as much dignity as he could. He knew Asmodeus could feel how deathly afraid he was. Magnus simply would not give him the satisfaction of admitting it.

"I find it very amusing that you have tangled up one of the Nephilim in your net," said Asmodeus. "Nothing is more fun than a challenge, and what else is it, to corrupt the purest of the pure? The Nephilim burn with such righteous fury. I see the temptation to cast a shadow over all that light. Even the Nephilim are amenable to lures, the sins of the flesh, and all the raging delights of jealousy, lust, and despair. Sometimes especially the Nephilim. The higher they are, the more completely shattered when they fall. I applaud you, my son."

"That's not how it is," Magnus said. "I love him."

"Do you?" Asmodeus asked. "Or is that just something you tell yourself, so you can do what you want, the way you did when you burned your stepfather alive? Demons cannot love. You said that yourself. Everything you are is half mine. Surely that means you inherited only half a heart."

Magnus turned his face away. Long ago the Silent Brothers had told him warlocks had souls. He had always chosen to believe it.

"Everything I am," said Magnus, "is all mine."

"And does he love you?" asked Asmodeus, and laughed again.

His voice was a mimicry of Catarina's, calling back her voice asking the same question, telling Magnus that there was no love that he could hold sacred and safe away from Asmodeus.

"He could never love something like you," Asmodeus pursued. "Alight with magic from Hell, and burning everything you touch. He may want you now, but you never told him about me, did you?" Asmodeus smiled. "Which was wise of you. If he did know, I'd have to kill him. Can't have one of the Nephilim knowing about my eldest curse."

"He doesn't know," Magnus said through his teeth. "And stop calling me that."

"You knew telling him might endanger your warlock friends," said Asmodeus, and Magnus knew, with some despair, that Asmodeus was flipping through his memories like a card deck. "But you were glad for the excuse, weren't you? You feared if Alexander Lightwood knew about your kinship to me, he would turn away in disgust. You know he still will. He will come to hate and resent you

for your immortality as he withers away. He was born to righteousness, and you were born to night everlasting. Your corruption will
eat away at him. He will not be able to bear you long, being what
you are. It will destroy him, or he will destroy you."

Asmodeus's voice was no longer fire and smoke. It was drops of
cold water into an ocean of despair. It was nothing Magnus had not
told himself.

He looked down at the knife. The emblem on the handle and
guard, an insect with spread wings, marked its master. He looked
over at Shinyun, whose eyes were glued to the point of the blade.
Sweat poured down her face even as she was frozen in place.

"You understand. You have always known it would not last."
Asmodeus's breath stirred Magnus's hair. "Nothing will ever last for
you, except me. Without me, you will be truly alone."

Magnus bowed his head. He remembered stumbling through
scorching-hot sand, filled with despair and smelling smoke from the
ashes of his whole life. There had been a time when he had been
so desperate, he did not know what his answer to Asmodeus would
have been.

He knew now.

Magnus turned and walked away from his father, and threw the
knife down in the dirt.

"I'm not alone. But even if I was, my answer would be the same.
I understand what faith is," said Magnus. "I know who I am, and I
know who I love. My answer to you is no."

Asmodeus shrugged. "So be it. Remember, when you die, that
I tried to give you this chance. I wanted you, but I am more than
happy to adopt."

Asmodeus lazily waved a hand, and Shinyun fell to the ground,
gasping. Her hand was still closed tight upon the sword hilt. Magnus did not know how much she had seen, or absorbed.

Shinyun, finally able to move, climbed to her feet. She looked up at Asmodeus, then at Magnus, and then back at the blade.

"Shinyun, my daughter," said Asmodeus. "You have been chosen. Embrace your glorious destiny."

Her unreadable face was tipped up to his. She walked toward him, his most faithful worshipper.

"All right," said Shinyun, and drove her sword into Asmodeus's side.

Asmodeus's bright form blurred until he was only a shimmer in the air, then resolved into shape farther away, a shining image above them both.

"Treachery amuses me," he said. "I forgive you. I understand your rage. I know your pain. This is all you are. I know how deep your loneliness has always been. Seize this opportunity. End Magnus's life, and you will have all that you wished for: a father, legions of demons at your command, and a world to rule."

Shinyun's head turned toward Magnus. Her shoulders slumped, then bunched, muscles gathering with new resolve. She hurled herself at him, sword in hand, and knocked him to the ground.

Her tears fell hot on Magnus's face. She hit him with her free hand, again and again. She hefted the sword. Then she hesitated.

"Don't," Magnus choked out, through a mouthful of blood.

"I have to!" Shinyun raged. "I need him. I'm nothing without him."

Magnus said, "You can be something more than this."

Shinyun shook her head. There was nothing in her eyes but despair. Magnus scrabbled in the dirt for the knife he'd thrown away, touched the hilt with his fingertips, then drew in a deep breath and sighed. He let the knife go.

Shinyun lifted the blade in both hands, held it above Magnus's heart, and brought it down.

CHAPTER TWENTY-NINE

The Fool's Knight

ALEC LOOKED DESPERATELY AT THE VISION WITHIN THE pentagram. He stared at every Shinyun, and every one looked the same. He searched the face of every Magnus, and they were all Magnus. Magnus swinging a blade, Magnus gasping on his knees, Magnus with his hands held high, Magnus with Shinyun on his chest, her sword held high for a killing blow.

"Joke's on you, Shadowhunter," said Bernard, speaking with his own voice now.

There was a ripple of laughter from the members of the Crimson Hand around him. Helen swung toward them, seraph blade shining in her hand—and tears shining on her cheeks. *She's crying for me,* Alec thought with distant surprise. *For me.*

"Shut *up,*" she hissed. Their laughter died.

"I just think it's really funny," said Bernard. "He came here thinking he was a hero. Determined to bring down the enemy! But he can't even find the enemy. He doesn't know which one she is."

Alec strung his bow, held it steady, and took aim.

"I don't have to," he said. "I know which one *he* is."

Through the shining light of the pentagram, he let his arrow fly.

CHAPTER THIRTY

The Aftermath of Glory

MAGNUS WAITED FOR A BLOW THAT NEVER CAME. WITH A sudden scream, Shinyun jerked back, an arrow embedded in her arm.

A *familiar* arrow.

"*Alec!*" With a cry, Magnus wrenched himself free. He rolled across the dirt, scrambled up on one knee. Another arrow passed over his head and toward Shinyun; he dove for the shadowy form he could dimly perceive through the shimmer of the pentagram and thrust his hand through the magical barrier, into the light.

Being able to put his fingertips outside the edge of the pentagram had turned out to be useful, after all.

Magnus felt a hand seize his. Alec's hand, clasping his as Alec had twice before, in cold water, on the edge of a cliff, and now in a pentagram with the Greater Demon who was Magnus's greatest fear. *Take my strength,* Alec had told him once, and Magnus, who had always had to be strong enough on his own, had been amazed. Power flowed into Magnus as, once again, Alec gave him his strength. Magic returned, warm and bright, terrifying and transformative.

Energy sang through his veins. The eerie light of the pentagram began to change. Magnus released Alec's hand and turned to face his father.

"No," Asmodeus called out, as though by his command he could reverse what Magnus had done. "Magnus, wait—"

Power exploded from Magnus, love and magic and angelic power all fused together, and the barriers of the pentagram shattered. The world around them returned, a chaos of fallen cultists and demons.

But Asmodeus could not. Even as his projection into the mortal world faded away into shadow, the Greater Demon Asmodeus, ruler of Edom and Prince of Hell, raised his arm, and a deep blackness began to expand from the pentagram's center, drawing in the light.

The blanket of swirling clouds overhead cracked, and the vortex pulsed and wavered. It began to lose its form, and blinding-white and midnight-black light burst from the fissures in the sky. The earth buckled beneath their feet, and a black pit opened at the former pentagram's center, its hungry mouth sucking everything toward its abyss. Magnus began to slide as the wooden platform crumbled beneath his feet like earth.

Magnus fell to his knees. The pull grew in intensity, tearing at every cell in his body. His nerves screamed, and he found himself clutching at the warped boards of the stage like a lifeline.

Next to him, Shinyun was doing the same. She cried out as the force of the whirlwind lifted her feet off the ground.

"Magnus! Grab my hand."

Magnus could hear Alec's voice through the falling barriers and hiss of dying light. He lifted his head, searching for him.

The ground beneath Magnus was crumbling away. Shinyun grabbed for him and screamed, her fingers clawed in his blood-stained jacket, as they both began to tumble into darkness—

They came to a jerking stop, dangling in midair. Alec's hand had closed around Magnus's wrist. Somehow he had lunged across the destroyed pentagram and the shattered stage: he was stretched out, half his body dangling over the edge of the abyss. He tried to pull Magnus up but the weight of Magnus and Shinyun was too great. He slid forward, gripping the edge of the abyss with one desperate hand.

Fear clutched at Magnus. Shinyun was still holding on to them. They might all fall together.

"Let *go*," he shouted at Alec. *"Let me fall."*

Alec's eyes went wide. His fingers held Magnus's wrist even tighter.

There was a swirl of movement behind Alec. The two Shadow-hunter girls who had fought beside Alec appeared at the edge of the abyss. One reached down and grabbed hold of Alec, hauling him up. The other grabbed for Magnus. The abyss howled in despair as Magnus and Shinyun tore free of its pull and tumbled, along with Alec, onto the charred ground.

Then it vanished.

In the strange silence that followed, the two girls ran to seize hold of Shinyun and tie her wrists behind her; Shinyun made no move to resist. Magnus rolled to a sitting position, gasping, and realized he was still gripping Alec's hand. He was still holding Alec—or more precisely, Alec was still holding him.

Alec was filthy, covered in dirt, with blood on his face and a wild look in his blue eyes. Magnus was vaguely aware that people were still running around in the distance somewhere and that Shinyun was being led away. But he could see only Alec. Alec, who had come here to save him.

"Alexander," Magnus whispered. "I told you not to hold on."

Suddenly Alec's arms were around him, crushingly hard. Magnus swallowed a breath that wanted to be a sob and buried his face in the curve of Alec's neck and shoulder. Magnus's hands ran up Alec's back and shoulders, touched the softness of the back of his neck, his dark hair, feeding on the reassurance that he was alive and well and real.

Alec pulled him even closer. Into Magnus's ear he whispered, "I would *never* let you go."

THEY HAD EXACTLY THREE SECONDS TO BASK IN THE relief of reunion. The fallout from a failed ritual of this magnitude was spectacular on many levels.

The ritual's last gasp was a sudden, violent expulsion of magical energy, a thunderous crack followed by an explosion that blew a mushroom cloud of smoke and dust into the air. Magnus wrapped his arms around Alec, casting a hasty spell to protect them both from flying wreckage.

When the explosion had finally ended, Magnus warily lowered his magical shields. He was still sitting with his arms and legs wrapped around Alec, who was blinking and glancing around.

"Stop telling me to let you go," said Alec. "I will never listen. I want to be with you. I never wanted anything more in my life. If you fall, I want to fall with you."

"Stay with me," Magnus said, taking Alec's face in his hands. The fires burning around them, reflected in Alec's eyes, became stars. "I love being with you. I love everything about you, Alexander."

Magnus drew Alec into a kiss and felt Alec soften against him, his tightly knotted muscles relaxing. Alec tasted like heat and dirt and blood and heaven. Magnus felt the butterfly-soft brush of Alec's lashes against his own cheek as Alec's eyes fell shut again.

"Guys!" said a woman's voice. "I'm happy for your reunion, but there's still cultists all over this place. Let's go."

Magnus looked up at the dark-haired woman, one of the Shadowhunter girls who had helped Alec. Jia Penhallow's daughter, he realized. Then he looked around at the devastation surrounding them on all sides.

The air was still alive with magic, and part of the villa had caught fire, but the danger seemed to have passed. Most of the Crimson Hand cult members had fled; the rest were in the process of fleeing or were on the ground, wounded. A few of the more fanatical and stupid ones were trying to rally the rest to take control of the situation.

"You're totally right," said Magnus to the Penhallow girl. "This is not the time for love. This is the time for leaving immediately."

He and Alec scrambled to their feet and made their way beside Aline to the front of the villa. The area seemed to be free of demons and cultists, at least for now. Helen was already there, and had bound Shinyun's wrists to a broken marble pillar.

Shinyun was silent, her head bowed. Magnus did not know whether she was physically hurt or only despondent. The two Shadowhunter women were deep in a whispered conversation: he studied them both, suddenly recognizing the golden-haired one from Council sessions. "You're Helen Blackthorn. From the Los Angeles Institute, right?"

Looking startled, Helen nodded.

Magnus turned to the smaller woman. "And you must be Jia's daughter. Irene?"

"Aline," blurted Aline, her eyes wide. "I didn't think you knew my name. I mean, you were close enough. I saw you and Alec from a distance at the Gard. I'm a big fan."

"Always a pleasure to meet a fan," said Magnus. "You're the image of your mother."

He and Jia occasionally made cutting remarks about various Clave members to each other in Mandarin. She was a nice lady.

Alec nodded to Aline and Helen. "I couldn't have gotten to you without them."

"Thank you both," said Magnus, "for coming to rescue me."

The golden-haired girl with the fey ears and the Blackthorn eyes twitched.

"I didn't come to rescue you," Helen confessed. "I was planning on bringing you in for questioning. I mean . . . before. Not now, obviously."

"Well," said Magnus. "That worked out pretty well for me. Thanks anyway."

"There's about a zero percent chance the Shadowhunters at the Rome Institute aren't going to notice a gladiatorial ring going supernova in the hills," said Aline. She leaned against a crumbling marble wall and looked cheerfully up at Helen. "Congratulations, Blackthorn. You get to call for reinforcements at last."

Helen did not smile back at Aline. She scribbled a fire-message and sent it on its way, her face very pale.

"What are we going to tell the other Shadowhunters?" Aline asked. "I still have no idea what happened in the pentagram."

Magnus began to talk his way through an abbreviated version of the night's events, leaving out only the detail of Asmodeus being his father. He knew he should tell them, and yet his father's words echoed in his head. *If he did know, I'd have to kill him. Can't have one of the Nephilim knowing about my eldest curse.*

Asmodeus was gone, but he wasn't dead. Magnus hated obeying his father, but he would not do anything that meant he might lose Alec. Not now.

Shinyun's bowed head lifted as Magnus spoke, and he saw her eyes narrow in her still face as she realized what he was leaving out.

She could tear Magnus's last facade apart, he knew. She could tell these Nephilim the whole truth right now. Magnus bit his lip, tasting blood and fear.

Shinyun said nothing. She did not even open her mouth. Her eyes seemed to be fixed on the distance, as if the real Shinyun were far away.

"Shinyun did try to stop the Greater Demon, in the end," Magnus said, almost against his will.

"And then she tried to kill you," pointed out Alec.

"She didn't have a choice," said Magnus.

"She had the same choice as you."

"She's lost," said Magnus. "She's desperate. I was once all those things too."

Alec's tone was grave. "Magnus, we can ask the Clave to show leniency to her. But that's all we can do, after everything she's done. You know it is."

Magnus remembered his father's voice talking about the children of the Angel, born to righteousness. Maybe he only wished for mercy for Shinyun because he was so flawed himself. Maybe it was because she was keeping his secret, for now.

"Yes," said Magnus. "I know."

"Why are we even having this discussion?" Helen raised her voice, and as she did so, her voice cracked. "The whole Rome Institute is on its way by now! We all know that the Clave will have her executed."

It was the first thing Helen had said in some time, and her voice shook. Aline studied her with some concern. Magnus did not know Helen well, but he was entirely certain it was not Shinyun's fate that had upset Helen so badly.

"What's wrong?" said Aline.

"I was trying so hard to do the right thing, but I got it all wrong. If it hadn't been for you and Alec, I wouldn't have come, and innocents would have died," Helen replied in a curt voice. "That isn't the kind of Shadowhunter I want to be."

"Helen, you made a mistake," Alec said. "The Clave tells us not to trust Downworlders. Despite the Accords, despite everything, we all get indoctrinated, and we—" He broke off, looking up at the clear, cold stars. "I used to follow the rules because I thought it would keep everyone I cared about safe," he said. "But I've started to realize that 'everyone I care about' is a bigger group and a different group than the Clave was built to accept."

"So what are you suggesting we do?" Helen whispered.

"We change the Clave," said Alec. "From inside. We make new Laws. Better ones."

"Institute Heads can suggest new Laws," said Aline. "Your mother—"

"I want to do this myself," said Alec. "And I want more than to be head of an Institute. I've realized—I don't need to change. And neither do you, Helen, or you, Aline. It's the world that needs to change, and we're going to be the ones to change it."

"The Shadowhunters are here," Shinyun croaked unexpectedly. They looked at her. "Look."

She was right. The Shadowhunters of the Rome Institute had arrived. They spilled through the gates, gaping around at the burning villa, the charred ground, and the cultists—some lying wounded on the ground, some ranging around—in their white suits.

The moment the cultists caught sight of the Shadowhunters, they began to run. The Shadowhunters gave chase. Bone-weary and exhausted, Magnus slumped against the wall of the villa and observed the shenanigans.

He couldn't help noticing that Shinyun was watching them too. She had shrunk back against the pillar, but was still silent.

The Clave would kill her. The Spiral Labyrinth would not be inclined to treat her more kindly than the Nephilim. There wouldn't be a lot of sympathy for a warlock who had murdered innocents and nearly summoned a Greater Demon prince into the world. Magnus could understand all that, and yet he was sorry.

Alec squeezed his hand.

A dark-haired Shadowhunter stalked toward their small group and began jabbering at Helen in Italian. Magnus gathered that she was Chiara Malatesta, head of the Rome Institute, and that she was both confused and annoyed.

Eventually Magnus broke into the conversation. "Helen is very brave," he said. "She knew she could not delay if the ritual were to be stopped. I owe my life to her and to Aline Penhallow."

"Hey," said Alec, but he was smiling. Magnus kissed his cheek. Chiara Malatesta raised her eyebrows, then shrugged. Italians had a philosophical view of love.

"Warlock," she said, in perfect English. "I recall you from some Council meetings, I believe. Quite a few of the cultists are wounded. Can you help us heal them?"

Magnus sighed and rolled up the sleeves of his abominable, hopelessly ruined white robe.

"This is partly my mess," he said. "Time to clean it up."

Helen and Aline agreed to join Signora Malatesta and the others as they swept the grounds for stray cultists and demonic activity. Alec remained to watch Shinyun—and, Magnus hoped, rest a little.

Dust hung thick in the air, turning the fiery explosions in the sky into hazy brightness as Magnus walked across shards of stone. Every time he found a wounded cult member, he thought of how Alec had come for him, and healed them as if he were Catarina.

Eventually he saw more Shadowhunters emerging from the smoke and fire. He tried to think of Alec and not of what would happen to Shinyun.

"Oh, hello," said a Shadowhunter boy, coming to an abrupt stop beside him. "Magnus Bane? I've never gotten a good look at you, not up close."

Magnus snorted. "I've looked better." He gave some thought to his current state, bruised and battered and wearing a blood-stained, ill-fitting jacket. "*Much* better."

"Wow," said the boy. "Will my heart be able to take it? I'm pretty close with Alec, by the way. We were talking about making plans for later. You'd be very welcome to join us. We could do any-thing you like." He winked. "Anything."

"Hmm," said Magnus. "And who are you?"

"Leon Verlac," said the boy.

"Well, Leon Verlac," Magnus drawled. "Keep dreaming."

CHAPTER THIRTY-ONE

The Quality of Mercy

LEANING AGAINST A PILLAR OF CRACKED STONE, ALEC watched his friends. Helen and Aline were spreading out across the villa grounds, securing the cultists they came across. Their weapons were out, ready to deal with lingering demons, but the force of Asmodeus's exit seemed to have dispelled them entirely. Not that there wasn't plenty to handle—cultists half-buried under rubble, small fires to smother, Rome Shadowhunters to direct to relevant locations.

Magnus was healing the cultists who had been eager to watch him get sacrificed. He went from person to person calmly, as Catarina had done at the party. Alec could always find him by the flowering of blue sparks at his fingertips. As far as Alec was concerned, Magnus's actions weren't just kind, they were practically saintly.

He turned to look at Shinyun. *My dark mirror,* Magnus had said, but as far as Alec was concerned, they had nothing in common. She was still tied to the marble pillar, still staring out into the darkness. With a start, Alec realized tears were streaming silently down her face.

"Hoping to gloat?" she said bitterly when she saw Alec watching her. "I was a fool. I thought Asmodeus was my father. I thought the Crimson Hand was my family. I was wrong. I was always alone, and I'm going to die alone. Satisfied?"

Alec shook his head. "I was just wondering what you would be like if you found someone who didn't betray you."

"Are you suggesting I should date Magnus?" Shinyun sneered.

Even she, who had imprisoned Magnus and dragged him to an ugly public death, saw who Magnus was. Anyone could see. Uneasiness stirred in Alec at the reminder that surely a vast number of people wanted to be with Magnus. He didn't want to think about it. Maybe he would never have to think about it.

"You tried to stab him," said Alec. "So obviously not."

Shinyun only scoffed. Alec tried not to think of her blade, hurtling down toward Magnus's heart.

"I'm sorry I tried to kill him," Shinyun muttered, her eyes on the dirt. "Tell him that."

Alec remembered Magnus, in the moment when the barriers of the pentagram had fallen. Magnus had turned, and the elements seemed to turn with him. His hand was uplifted, magic wrapping around his smooth brown skin, magic lucent white against his corona of black hair, fire and wind in the light of his brilliant eyes. He was incandescent with power, impossibly beautiful, and dangerous.

And he had hurt none of the people who had hurt him.

Magnus had trusted Shinyun, and she'd betrayed him, but he would keep trusting people, Alec knew. Alec had trusted Aline and Helen and even the New York vampires, and it had worked out. Maybe it was the only thing that worked, taking the risk of trust.

He didn't want Shinyun to get away with this. It was only right that she be punished for her crimes, but Alec knew that if the Clave got hold of her, her punishment would be death.

So be it, he told himself. *The Law is hard, but it is the Law.*

His father had always told him to be careful, not to make mistakes, not to strike out on his own, to obey the spirit and the letter of the Law. He thought of Helen and how she was trying to be the perfect Shadowhunter for her family. Alec, uneasily aware that he was different, that he was sure to disappoint his father, had always tried to follow the rules.

Magnus could have struck Shinyun down when he broke the pentagram, or at any moment since then. Instead he clearly and desperately wanted to spare her. When he had a choice, the Magnus he knew always chose to be kind.

Alec leaned down and cut Shinyun's cords with the edge of his seraph blade, its angelic power carving even through the magical binding.

"What are you doing?" Shinyun breathed.

Alec was hardly sure himself.

"Go," he said roughly. When all Shinyun did was sit and stare, Alec repeated himself. "Go. Or do you want to stay and throw yourself on the mercy of the Clave?"

Shinyun scrambled to her feet, wiping her tears with the back of her hand. Her eyes flashed with a bitter hurt. "You think you know Magnus Bane. But you have no idea of the depth and darkness of the secrets he is keeping from you. There is so much he hasn't told you."

"I don't want to know," Alec said.

Her smile was twisted. "One day you will."

Alec turned on her with sudden fury. Shinyun gulped and ran, as fast as she could, into the smoke.

The Rome Shadowhunters were already on the villa grounds. She might be caught, but Alec had given her the best chance he could. Nobody could blame Magnus, or Aline, or Helen. Alec had done this himself.

He looked out at the swirling dust, and the lights turning the sky deep purple and brilliant red. One day he would follow the rules again. When the rules were changed.

He started when two figures emerged from the smoke, tense and ready to answer a barrage of questions from Italian Shadowhunters, but it was only Aline and Helen. Magnus was following after them, some distance behind. Aline was in front, and her mouth fell open as she saw Alec standing alone by the ruins, discarded ropes at his feet.

"By the Angel," Aline breathed. "Shinyun got away?"

"Well," Alec said, "she's gone."

Aline closed her mouth. She looked like she had bitten into a lemon.

"She's gone?" Helen repeated. "What are we going to tell the other Shadowhunters? 'We had a dangerous fugitive in custody and we let her slip through our fingers, guys, sorry!'"

When she put it like that, it didn't sound great.

There was shouting nearby already. Alec could see the shapes of figures in gear, marching cultists away. Magnus joined their small knot around the sliced ropes. Alec's heart gave a sharp little twist at the sight of his face, half joy and half painful concern. Magnus's white robe was smeared in ash and blood. He was hurt, and he looked so tired.

"Shinyun's gone?" he asked, and shut his eyes for a moment. "I'm almost glad."

Magnus being almost glad made Alec's rash decision seem worthwhile.

"Listen, everyone," said Magnus carefully. "You three deserve a lot of praise and gratitude for the work you did today. You triple-handedly tore through a mundane demon-worshipping cult and leveled a villa in the Italian countryside and prevented a Prince of Hell from encroaching on this world. I am sure there will be accolades and pats on the back for each of you at the Institute."

Dread rose in Alec, a shadow of the same cold fear he had felt when he saw Magnus in the arena, at the prospect that Magnus might throw his life away before Alec could get to him.

"And?" Alec asked warily.

"And the Clave will not have the same reaction to me. I was the one in the pentagram tonight, and I was the focus of this little soiree. I am the one the Shadowhunters will be questioning. I don't want any of you to get into any trouble because you came for me. I think you should all use the glory of a big mission, successfully accomplished, to cover any awkwardness this situation might create for you. You stumbled upon this mysterious scenario. You don't know anything more. Tell them to ask me."

Alec exchanged a look with Aline, then another with Helen.

"We stopped the Crimson Hand," Alec said. "That's what's important, right?"

Aline nodded. "An evil cult tried to summon Asmodeus. The three of us tracked them down and put an end to their ritual before they could summon him."

"We also shut down their headquarters," added Helen. "And we saved the man they were planning to sacrifice in their ritual. That's the truth. That's all that needs to be in the report."

"That's not lying to the Clave," Aline said hastily. "Which I would never do, because Mom would strip my Marks and worse, tell me how disappointed she was in me. Really, we are just trying to clarify the issue to the Clave, and not bother them with irrelevant details. You don't have anything to do with the Crimson Hand, Magnus, other than being their victim. Who cares about ancient history?"

"I'll explain that I should have come to the Paris Institute when a warlock approached me for help, instead of trying to do this all on my own," Helen continued.

"If my name isn't getting dragged through the mud," said

Magnus, "certainly yours shouldn't be. You had a lead, and you followed the lead with praiseworthy dedication. Who cares why a warlock approached you, whether it was because of your faerie heritage or any other reason? As the result shows, he chose well."

"He could not have made a better choice," said Aline. "You brought down the Crimson Hand. You did everything you could. No other Shadowhunter could have done better."

Helen looked at Aline. Faint pink stole into her cheeks. Alec was startled to see a feeling he recognized on Helen's face, something he often felt around Magnus: uncertain delight at Magnus's high opinion of him, twined with the creeping doubt that Magnus would realize he did not deserve it.

Alec suspected he had missed some crucial details about his companions while he was worrying about Magnus.

"The problem, of course," said Magnus, "is that with Shinyun gone, the Clave will be looking for *someone* to pin the leadership of the Crimson Hand on."

Alec felt a lurch of panic. "Not you," he said. "It can't be you."

Magnus gave him a look of surprising sweetness. "Not me, love," he said. "We'll think of something."

He fell silent as a group of Italian Shadowhunters who were scouting the grounds approached. Helen exchanged a few words with their leader as the rest of the Shadowhunters rushed past.

The four began making their way back to the villa's entrance. Alec caught Helen's eye.

"I'm sorry if I almost messed anything up."

"What did I say to you, Alec Lightwood?" said Helen. "Disasters follow wherever you go. Buildings collapse. Fugitives escape. I'm getting used to it." She stole a glance at Aline, who blushed fiery red. "I think I'm getting to like it."

Aline cleared her throat. "I know this place. It's nothing special. Just a little café on the Tiber. Maybe we can hang out there sometime.

I mean, whenever you have time. If you like." She glanced around. "That invitation was for Helen, by the way. Not you and Magnus."

"I get it," said Alec, who finally did.

"I'm on my travel year," Helen said slowly. "I'm supposed to be at the Prague Institute next week."

"Oh." Aline sounded crushed.

Helen seemed to be working something out in her head. "But after this big mission, I could use a rest. I can probably arrange to stick around the Rome Institute for a while longer."

"Really?" Aline whispered.

Helen stopped and looked at her squarely. Alec and Magnus tried to pretend they were somewhere else. "If you mean it like I think you mean it," said Helen. "If you mean a real date. With me."

"Yes," said Aline, clearly abandoning any idea of playing it cool. "Yes, yes, *yes*, a real date. You are the most beautiful person I've ever seen, Helen Blackthorn. And you fight like poetry. When you talked about your family, you made me want to cry. So let's get coffee, or dinner, or we could go on a weekend trip to Florence. Wait, no, or I could say something more suave and sophisticated than that. I'll read some romantic books and learn to phrase things better. I'm so sorry."

She looked mortified.

"Why are you sorry?" Helen asked. "I liked that."

"Yeah?" asked Aline. "Do you want to get breakfast?"

"Well, no," said Helen.

Aline looked dismayed. "I messed it up. When did I mess it up?"

"I just meant," Helen said hastily, "let's get lunch instead. That way, we can get back to the Institute first and clean up. I have ichor between my fingers."

"Oh." Aline paused. "All right. Fantastic! I mean, okay."

She began to outline elaborate plans for lunch. Alec did not know how she was going to pull together a jazz combo in three hours, but he was happy that she looked so happy—her eyes shining, her cheeks flushed with excitement. Helen must have thought she looked more than just happy, because when Aline paused for breath, Helen leaned over and kissed her.

It was a quick brush of lips against lips, a gentle kiss. Aline smiled into it, then cupped Helen's elbow and drew her in close. The sunlight just beginning to glow at the horizon caught the Penhallow ring on Aline's finger and made it shine as she brushed Helen's hair away from her face, kissing her over and over.

Alec said, in a low voice, "I hope this works out for them."

Magnus said, "I thought they were already together. Cute couple. Ladies, I hate to interrupt, but Leon Verlac is headed this way."

Helen and Aline broke apart, both smiling. There was an unusually surly expression on Leon's normally bright face as he hove into view. He was shoving Bernard ahead of him.

Bernard's hands were tied, and he was protesting furiously. "You can't do this to me! This is all Magnus Bane's fault!"

"Like we're going to believe a word you say," Leon sneered.

"I am the leader of the Crimson Hand, its dark and charismatic overlord, the power behind the throne but also the one meant to be sitting in the throne. I refuse to be treated like a common criminal!"

Leon Verlac glanced over his shoulder at Helen and Aline, and then at Alec and Magnus. Alec stared back at him blankly.

"Yeah, well," said Leon, and gave the dark and charismatic overlord of the Crimson Hand another push. "We're all having a tough day."

Aline gave Magnus and Alec a grin of slow-blossoming delight. "I guess that's the 'leader of the Crimson Hand' issue sorted."

"Who'd ever have thought I'd be glad to see Leon?" Helen wondered.

"I think we should make a pact," said Alec. "We all four keep what we know about the Crimson Hand a secret. In fact, I'd prefer if we didn't mention any of this to anyone in New York. Not ever."

"Wise," Aline remarked. She was still pink about the cheeks, her hand in Helen's. "If Jace and Isabelle find out we had all this fun without them, they'll kill us."

Helen nodded. "The four of us never met here. This never happened. Look forward to meeting you sometime, Alec. For the first time."

If Alec's dad heard anything about the cult and Magnus's past, he would make the same assumptions Helen had, only worse. Alec didn't want that to happen. He still believed that if his dad got to know Magnus, he would end up seeing what Helen and Shinyun had learned to see, what Alec had seen almost from the very first.

Of course, his dad might be pleased to hear that Alec had been a big help on a mission in Rome. The leader of the Crimson Hand had been captured, and they had put an end to the cult and the terrible ritual. It really was possible that the Rome Institute was going to commend all three of them on a job well done.

But compared to Magnus, the approval of his father—of anyone in the Clave—didn't matter at all. Alec knew who he was. He knew what he had done and what he had fought for, and he knew what he would fight for in the future.

And he knew exactly who he loved.

The dust was settling, and the rays of the sun were growing ever stronger, brilliant white lines of light that washed the new day clean. The makeshift amphitheater, the stone seats of the audience, and the villa that had been the Crimson Hand's last stronghold were all in ruins under what looked like it would be a clear autumn day.

Alec surprised himself by laughing out loud.

He held out his hand and found Magnus's waiting for him.

EPILOGUE
City I Call Home

† † †

New York is the most beautiful city in the world?
It is not far from it. . . .
Here is our poetry, for we have
pulled down the stars to our will.
—Ezra Pound

"SO THAT'S THE WHOLE STORY OF OUR HUNT FOR THE Crimson Hand," said Magnus, making a dramatic gesture with his teacup. Liquid sloshed over the rim of the cup and splashed through the illusion of Tessa.

Tessa's solemn gray eyes lit with her smile. She always had an appearance of gravity, and yet she smiled often. Magnus grinned back. He had snatched a moment before he and Alec were due to go, while the Shadowhunters were still busying themselves with official reports about the business with the Crimson Hand.

Magnus had his own report to give, and it was good to see Tessa's face, even if it was only a Projection.

"That's quite a story," Tessa observed.

"Will you be telling the Spiral Labyrinth?" asked Magnus.

"I will tell the Spiral Labyrinth something," said Tessa. "Something not even remotely resembling the story you just told me. But you know, a lot of narratives depend on interpretation."

"You're the audience," said Magnus. "I'll leave it to you."

"Are you happy?" asked Tessa.

"Yes, I am happy to no longer be falsely accused of leading a cult bent on global destruction," said Magnus. "I am also happy that a lunatic warlock is not sending demons to chase me across Europe. It's all very gratifying."

"I'm sure," said Tessa gently, "but are you happy?"

Magnus had known her a long time. He let his defenses drop a little, enough to answer with a simple, "Yes."

Tessa smiled, without an ounce of hesitation or grudging. "I'm glad."

Magnus was the one who hesitated. "Can I ask you something? You loved a Shadowhunter."

"Do you think I stopped?"

"When you loved a Shadowhunter, were you ever afraid?"

"I was always afraid," said Tessa. "It's natural to be afraid of losing the most precious thing in the world. But don't be too afraid, Magnus. I know warlocks and Shadowhunters are very different, and there is a divide between your worlds that can be hard to cross. But as someone once said to me, the right man will not care. You can build a bridge over the divide and find each other. You can build something much greater than either of you could ever have built on your own."

There was a silence after she spoke, as they both thought of the ages they had seen pass already, and the ages to come. The sunlight was still bright through the window outside Magnus's Rome hotel room, but it would not last.

Magnus said reluctantly, "But we do lose love, in the end. We both know that."

"No," said Tessa. "Love changes you. Love changes the world. You cannot lose that love, no matter how long you live, I think. Trust love. Trust him."

Magnus wanted to, but he could not forget Asmodeus telling him he was a curse upon the world. He remembered begging Shinyun with his eyes not to tell Alec who Magnus's father was. He did not want to lie to Tessa. He did not know how to promise he would do what she advised.

"What if I lost him by telling the truth?"

"What if you lost him by hiding it?"

Magnus shook his head. "Take care, Tessa," he told her, instead of telling her he would follow her advice.

Tessa did not push him. "And you, my friend. I wish you both the very best."

The illusion of Tessa faded, her soft mass of brown hair dissipating like a cloud in the air. After a moment, Magnus got up and went to get changed, to meet Alec at the Rome Institute and at long last continue their vacation.

A PORTAL OPENED AND SPLIT THE AIR AT THE BOTTOM of the front steps of the Institute. Magnus stood at the top of those steps. He had already hugged everyone, including two Italian Shadowhunters who'd seemed very startled to be hugged and had to introduce themselves while in his embrace, but enthusiastically hugged him back. Their names were Manuela and Rossella. Magnus thought they seemed nice.

Alec did not hug anyone except for Aline, but his arms went around her tight. Magnus looked at the back of Alec's head, bent toward Aline's, and exchanged a glance and a grin with Helen.

"I hope the next stop on your holiday is fabulous," said Helen.

"It will be. I hope the next place you hit on your travel year is great."

"The thing is," said Helen, "I'm feeling a little tired of traveling. I'm happy where I am."

Aline strode over to Helen's side.

"Traveling?" she repeated. "I was thinking, if you wanted company when you go to the Prague Institute, I could come along. I'm not doing anything, except fighting the forces of evil. But we could do that together."

Helen smiled. "I think we can work something out."

Alec dodged Leon Verlac's attempt at a hug and left Leon giving a double-cheek kiss to the air. He came to rejoin Magnus at the top of the stairs.

"Are you ready to get back to our vacation?" asked Magnus, holding out a hand.

"I cannot wait," said Alec, taking it.

Together, with their luggage following close behind, the two stepped into the Portal. They left the Rome Institute behind and came out into the living room of Magnus's Brooklyn loft.

Magnus lifted a hand, pivoting slowly. All the curtains swung apart, all the windows snapped open. Sunlight flooded across the floorboards and the colorful rugs knotted with scarlet and yellow and blue, gleaming on calfskin-and-gilt spell books and the new coffeemaker Magnus had bought because Alec disapproved of him stealing coffee by summoning it from local bodegas.

Chairman Meow approached Magnus with tilted-head furrowed hesitation before slinking in between his legs in a few figure eights. The cat then leaped onto Magnus's body like a mountain climber, bounding into his hands and scaling up his arm to perch on his shoulder. He purred near Magnus's ear, licked his cheek with his sandpaper tongue, and jumped off without even a look back, having completed his necessary greeting.

"I love you, too, Chairman Meow," Magnus called after him.

Alec reached for the sky with his hands and stretched, swaying his body side to side before collapsing into the love seat. He kicked off his shoes and sank into the cushions. "It is so good to be back in New York. Home. I need a vacation from that vacation."

He reached out a hand to Magnus, and Magnus crawled onto the love seat beside him, and felt Alec's fingers thread through his hair.

"No must-see tourist destinations. No elaborate dinner dates requiring flying machines, and definitely no cults and murderous warlocks," he whispered in Alec's ear. "Just home."

"It's good to be back," said Alec. "I missed the view from this window."

"Yes," said Magnus wonderingly. There had been so many windows, and so many cities. He had never thought to miss a view before.

"And I missed Izzy."

Magnus thought of Alec's fierce sister, whom Alec protected before his own life. "Yes."

"And Jace."

"Eh," said Magnus.

He smiled against Alec's cheek, knowing Alec could feel his smile even if he could not see it. He had never missed a view before, but it was nice to miss this one. It was strange, to look out on brownstones and blue sky, the swoop of the Brooklyn Bridge and the glittering towers of Manhattan, and think of returning, think of a place filled with family and friends.

"I don't think anyone expects us back yet," said Alec.

"We don't have to explain to them why we're home early," said Magnus. "I never explain. Takes less time and adds to my air of mystique."

"No, I meant . . ." Alec swallowed. "I miss them, but I could stand to have a little more time alone with you. We don't have to tell them we're back at all."

Magnus brightened. "I can always Portal us back on vacation, if we feel like it. We can still make the opera, like you wanted. In a while."

"I can say my phone broke," said Alec. "I can say I dropped it in the Tiber."

Magnus grinned mischievously. "I have a better idea."

He jumped off the sofa and strolled to the back of his loft. He cast a spell and made two wide sweeping gestures with his arms to push all the furniture to the side.

He spun to face Alec, suddenly wearing a very bright and very green pair of lederhosen. "I believe the next stop on our trip was supposed to be Berlin."

For the next hour, they made up for weeks' worth of trips, posing in front of backgrounds conjured up by Magnus on the wall of the loft. The first was of them dancing at a disco in Berlin. They moved the party next to the front of the Prado Museum in Spain. Alec gave some crackers to a small group of pigeons that Magnus had summoned in from the roof.

"I could summon a bull, too," Magnus proposed. "For verisimilitude."

"No bull," said Alec.

Their last shot was in New Delhi, among the brightly colored throngs in front of the Jama Masjid for Eid-al-Fitr. Magnus conjured silver bowls of gulab jamun, rasmalai, kheer, and a few other favorites, and they took turns feeding the sweets to one another, mugging for the camera.

Alec reached out to pull Magnus in for a kiss, then hesitated, his fingers sticky with sugar. Magnus gestured, and a glittering ripple of magic followed his hand, cleaning up the desserts, the backdrop, and the syrup from their hands. He leaned in, fingers curled under the line of Alec's jaw, and kissed him.

"Now that we've got the vacationing part of our vacation out of the way," said Magnus, "we can enjoy ourselves."

He leaned against a bookcase crowded with ancient spell books and took Alec's hand. "That would be great," Alec told him shyly.

"In retrospect," said Magnus, "an extravagant holiday may have been slightly excessive for something as new as . . . this." He gestured to indicate the two of them.

Alec began to grin. "I kept worrying I would mess things up."

"How could you possibly mess things up?"

Alec shrugged. "Could I keep up with you? Would I be interesting enough?"

Magnus started laughing. "I wanted to show you the world, show you the grand and romantic adventure that life can be. That's why I planned that balloon-ride dinner over Paris. Do you know how long that took to figure out? Just keeping the table and chairs upright with the crosswinds was hours of magic you never saw. And I still crashed."

Alec laughed with him.

"I might have gone a little overboard," Magnus admitted. "But I wanted to lay all the grandeur and dazzle of Europe at your feet. I wanted you to have fun."

When he looked at Alec again, Alec was frowning.

"I did have fun," he said. "But I didn't need any of that. They were just places. You don't have to set any scene to convince me. I don't need Paris, or Venice, or Rome. I just want you."

There was a pause. The afternoon sun was streaming through the open windows, making the dust in the apartment twinkle and casting a warm glow on their linked hands. Magnus could hear the sound of Brooklyn traffic, yellow cabs honking and jostling.

"I've been meaning to ask," said Magnus. "When Shinyun and I were fighting in the pentagram in Rome, you shot her. You told me that you could see dozens of illusions of me fighting dozens of her. How did you know which one was really her?"

"I didn't," said Alec. "I knew which one was you."

"Oh. Was one version of me more handsome than the others?" Magnus said, charmed. "More debonair? Possessed of a certain je ne sais quoi?"

"I don't know about that," said Alec. "You reached for a knife. You had it in your grasp, and then you let it go."

Magnus deflated.

"You knew it was me because I'm worse at fighting than she is?" Magnus asked. "Well, that's terrible news. I imagine 'pathetic in combat' is on the top ten list of Shadowhunter turnoffs."

"No," said Alec.

"Number eleven, just below 'doesn't actually look good in black'?"

Alec shook his head again. "Before we were together," he said, "I was angry a lot, and I hurt people because I was in pain. Being kind when you're in pain—it's hard. Most people struggle to do it at the best of times. The demon who cast that spell couldn't imagine it. But among all those identical figures, there was one person who hesitated to hurt somebody, even at the moment of utmost horror. That had to be you."

"Oh," said Magnus.

He took Alec's face in his hand and kissed him again. He had kissed Alec so many times before, and he could never get used to the way Alec responded to him, the way he responded to Alec. Every time, it felt new. Magnus never wanted to get used to it.

"We're alone," Alec murmured against his mouth. "The loft is warded. No demons can interrupt us."

"The doors are locked," Magnus said. "And I have the best locks money and magic can buy. Not even an Open rune works on my doors."

"Great news," said Alec.

Magnus barely understood him. The movement of Alec's lips against his own sent all reasonable thoughts flying out of his head.

Magnus flicked his fingers at the bed behind his back and sent the gold-and-scarlet duvet flying to the other side of the room, fluttering like a rogue sail. "Can we . . . ?"

Alec's eyes lit with desire. *"Yes."*

They tumbled onto the mattress, twining together against the silk sheets. Magnus slid his hands under Alec's T-shirt, feeling hot smooth skin under worn cotton and the flutter of muscles in Alec's bare stomach. His own desire was a flame low down in his belly, spreading through his chest, constricting his throat. *Alexander. My beautiful Alexander. Do you know how much I want you?*

But a shadow voice whispered in the back of Magnus's head, murmuring that he could not tell Alec the truth about his father, his life. Magnus wanted to lay every truth of his existence at his beloved's feet, but this one would only endanger Alec. It would have to be held back.

"Wait, wait, wait," Magnus gasped.

"Why?" Alec asked, mouth kiss-swollen and eyes dazed with desire.

Why indeed. Good question. Magnus shut his eyes and found light still brimming behind them, the lines of Alec's body fitting warm and sweet and perfect against his. He was drowning in light.

Magnus pushed Alec back, though he could not bear to push him away far. Alec ended up a handspan away from him, across an expanse of crimson silk.

"I just don't want you to do anything you might regret," said Magnus. "We can wait for as long as you want. If you need to wait until—until you're sure how you feel—"

"What?" Alec sounded bewildered, and a little irritated.

When Magnus pictured beautiful and sensual moments with his beloved Alec, or moments in which he himself was self-sacrificing and noble, he had not envisioned his beloved Alec looking so annoyed.

"I kissed you in the Hall of Accords, in front of the Angel and everyone I know," said Alec. "Couldn't you tell what that meant?"

Magnus remembered facing Alec at the start of a war, thinking he had lost him forever and realizing he had not. He had known certainty for only a single glorious moment, ringing through the Great Hall and his whole body like a bell. But such moments could not be kept. Magnus had let shadows of doubt about himself, about his past, about Alec's future, insinuate themselves and dislodge that certainty from his grasp.

Alec was watching him intently. "You started a demonic cult centuries ago, and I didn't ask any questions. I followed you all around Europe. I slaughtered a whole pack of demons on the Orient Express for you. I went to a palazzo full of murderers and people who wanted to make small talk and dance, for you. I lied to the Rome Institute for you, and I would have lied to the Clave."

Put together, it was a lot. "I'm sorry you had to do all of that," Magnus murmured.

"I don't want you to be sorry!" said Alec. "I'm not sorry. I wanted to do it. I wanted all of it, with you. The only thing that bothered me was when you were in trouble without me. I want us to be in trouble together. I want us to be together, no matter what. That's all I want."

Magnus waited in the silence. After a moment, Alec said quietly, "I've never loved anybody like this before. Maybe I'm not saying it right, but it's what I feel."

I've never loved anybody like this before.

Magnus's heart seemed to break open, spilling love and desire through his veins. "Alec," Magnus whispered. "You said everything perfectly."

"Then is anything wrong?" Alec knelt up on the bed, his hair deliciously mussed, his cheeks flushed.

"It's your first time," Magnus said. "I want it to be perfect for you."

To Magnus's surprise, Alec grinned. "Magnus," he said, "I've been waiting for this for *so long*. If we don't do this literally right now, I will jump out the window."

Magnus started to laugh. It was odd to laugh and feel desire at the same time; he wasn't sure he'd had that with anyone but Alec.

He reached out across the space between them and pulled Alec toward him.

Alec gave a sharp gasp as their bodies collided, and very quickly neither of them were laughing anymore. Alec's breath came short as Magnus drew off his shirt. His touch was hungry, exploring. He found the collar of Magnus's shirt and ripped it open, pushing it off Magnus's shoulders. His hands smoothed down Magnus's bare arms. He pressed kisses to Magnus's throat, his bare chest, his flat navel-less stomach. Magnus wound his fingers into Alec's wild dark hair and wondered if anyone had ever been this lucky.

"Lie back," Magnus whispered at last. "Lie back, Alexander."

Alec stretched out on the bed, his beautiful body bare from the waist up. His eyes fixed on Magnus, he reached back, grabbing the headboard of the bed, the muscles in his arms standing out. The sunlight from the window fell on Alec, bathing his body in a faint luminescence. Magnus sighed, wishing for magic that could stop time, that would let him stay in this moment indefinitely.

"Oh, my love," Magnus murmured. "I am so glad to be home."

Alec smiled, and Magnus bent his own body over Alec's. They moved and curved and fitted together, chest against chest, hips against hips. Alec's breath stuttered and caught as Magnus's tongue found its way into his open mouth, and Magnus's hands rid Alec of the rest of his clothes, and they were skin to skin, breath against breath, heartbeat against heartbeat. Magnus trailed his rings down the line of Alec's throat, up to his lips; Alec licked and sucked at Magnus's fingers, the stones of his rings, and Magnus gave a shiver of shocked longing as Alec bit gently at his palm. Everywhere they kissed and everywhere they touched felt like alchemy, the transformation of the commonplace to gold. They progressed together, starting slow and moving to sharp urgency.

When movement had stilled and gasps had turned to soft whispers, they lay holding each other in the fading light of the sun, Alec curved in against Magnus's side, his head on the warlock's chest. Magnus touched Alec's soft hair and looked up in wonder at the shadows above the bed. It felt like the first time anything like this had happened in the world, felt like the start of something shining and impossibly new.

Magnus had always had a wanderer's heart. Over the centuries, he had adventured in so many different places, always looking for something that would fulfill his restless hunger. He never realized how all the pieces could fall together, how home could be somewhere and someone.

He belonged with Alec. His wandering heart could rest.

THE PORTAL OPENED JUST OUTSIDE THE WORN *hongsalmun* near the top of the hill. The red paint that had once brightened the wooden gate had peeled away a century ago, and choking vines had crawled up its poles and bars.

Shinyun stepped out of the Portal and breathed in the crisp mountain air. She surveyed her domain and its impassable wards. Only a fox had trespassed here, long ago, starving and searching for food. It had found none, and only its skeleton remained.

She followed the winding trail of broken stones and undergrowth as it snaked up the hill. Her family's old home in Korea was known to the locals as a cursed, haunted place. Shinyun supposed, in a way, that it was. She was the ghost of her family, the last one. She had been abandoned here and she could never truly leave.

As she walked into her home she waved the house alive. A fire burst in the fireplace. Her two Nue demons, red eyes and razor teeth shining in their monkey faces, started from the hearth and came toward her with their snake tails waving in the air.

The two demons followed close behind their mistress as they walked down the main hallway to the back of the house. They reached a dead end, and then the wall flickered and disappeared. Shinyun and her demons passed through, and the wall became whole again behind them as they descended the hidden staircase.

At the back of the cellar, there stood a rusty metal cage reinforced by powerful wards. Shinyun's demons were not pets. They were guardians. They kept intruders out. They also kept things in.

She slid the bolts free and walked into the cage. The demons hissed at the pile in the corner, and the filthy, green-skinned warlock raised his head. His face was almost obscured by a snarled mass of hair that had once been white as snow, but was now gray with grime.

"Oh, you're alive," he said. "That's too bad."

He leaned back against the pile of hay and sacking as if it were silk.

"I'm thrilled to see you don't look well," he added. "Magnus Bane proved a more formidable opponent than you imagined? Who could have guessed? Wait, I told you that you had no chance against him. Repeatedly."

Shinyun aimed a vicious kick at his midsection. She kept kicking, until she was rewarded with a groan.

"Maybe things didn't work out as I hoped," she panted. "You'll be as sorry for it as I am. I have another plan, a plan for all the eldest curses, and you are going to help me."

"I doubt that," he said. "I'm not the helpful type."

Shinyun hit him. She kicked him until he curled up around the pain, and she turned her face aside so he would not see her tears.

"You have no choice. Nobody is coming to save you," she said, cold and sure. "You're all on your own, Ragnor Fell. Everybody thinks you're dead."

Acknowledgments

ALEC LIGHTWOOD FIRST TOOK SHAPE IN MY MIND IN 2004, a boy in frangible old sweaters with holes in the cuffs, with angry blue eyes and a vulnerable soul. Magnus exploded into my heart not long after, all outsized personality and carefully guarded emotions. And I knew they were perfect for each other: the Shadowhunter and the Downworlder, the warlock and the archer boy.

When I was a teen, LGBTQ+ representation in young adult lit was something found largely on the pages of "problem novels"— when it was found at all. My gay, lesbian, and bisexual friends searched in vain for representations of themselves in the kind of books they *liked* to read: swashbuckling fantasy adventures. When I set about to write the Shadowhunter books, including Alec and Magnus was something I did because I loved their characters and thought they belonged in a swashbuckling fantasy adventure: the pushback from schools, from book fairs, from stores that didn't want to carry the books because of them, the marking out by media watchdog sites who noted the presence of gay characters as "sexual content" though they had not yet even kissed shocked and sobered me, just as the groundswell of support from LGBTQ+ readers made me more determined to tell their story.

There were challenges. I tried to maintain a balance in which Magnus and Alec were always present in the books, always human and relatable, always heroes, without pushing past what was considered "acceptable content" and resulting in a situation that would keep the books off the shelves of bookstores and libraries, so the kids who most needed to read about characters like Alec and Magnus would still be able to find them. But I itched to do more.

The writing and publication of *The Bane Chronicles* in 2014 was a shot across the bow: a book unapologetically about Magnus, his life and loves of both genders and his eventual commitment to Alec. It did modestly well—well enough for me to feel like the time had come to do something I had always wanted, and tell a swashbuckling romantic fantasy story in which Magnus and Alec were the protagonists. I had already left a gap for that story to take place— the "vacation" Magnus and Alec take during *City of Fallen Angels*, during which their relationship clearly deepened in seriousness. We knew they'd rollicked across Europe—but what *happened exactly?* This book aims to tell that story.

So thank you to my friends and family who supported me during the writing process, to my publisher for taking a chance, to my editor and agent, and to my cowriter, Wesley Chu. And thanks above all to Alec and Magnus and to those who've loved and supported them over the years. In 2015, a Texan librarian took one of my cowriters aside at a convention and told her that *The Bane Chronicles* was the only LGBTQ+-led book she was allowed to have in her library. All others were ruled out as "inappropriate," but as kids who were Shadowhunters fans persistently asked their parents for the book, she was told she could make an exception.

Thank you above all to the kids who asked, and to that librarian and all other librarians, teachers, and booksellers who get the right books into the right hands. And let us hope for a world in which someday everyone knows that LGBTQ+-led books are not only "appropriate" but necessary.

—C. C.

THE RED SCROLLS OF MAGIC WAS WRITTEN DURING A TIME of significant transition. Before I was asked to cowrite Magnus and Alec's story, I thought my heart was full living in Chicago with my wife, Paula, and our Airedale terrier, Eva. Then we welcomed our son, Hunter, to the world and moved cross-country to Los Angeles, and like the Grinch who stole Christmas's, my heart grew three sizes and burst out of my chest. These past few years during the time I worked on this book have been the most fulfilling and challenging in my life, both personally as well as professionally, and I feel that my growing capacity to love and what I feel for my family, my new home, and this project shows on these pages.

I am grateful to my beautiful wife, Paula, for showing me what unconditional love and support looks like, and for offering eternal patience as I spent the thousands of hours on the keyboard. I am also grateful to my parents and in-laws for helping take care of Hunter, which gave me the time and space to dedicate my thoughts to Magnus and Alec. Thanks also to my agent, Russ Galen, for believing in me enough to trust me with this project, and to the teams at Simon & Schuster for making everything else happen.

The love and dedication of the Shadowhunter fans never ceases to amaze and inspire me. Thank you. We're all in this together. Burn strong. Burn vividly.

A very special thank-you to Cassie for allowing me to help tell

ACKNOWLEDGMENTS

Magnus's story. This has been one of the most rewarding experiences of my life, and I am truly honored and blessed to be a part of something as special as the Shadowhunter universe.

Lastly I have to acknowledge Magnus and Alec. Your love is an inspiration and a beacon to so many. May your first days until your last days shine equally bright.

—W. C.